# The DELICATE VOWS Duet

The Delicate Vows Duet: by L.A. FERRO Published by Pine Hollow Publishing

Copyright © 2025 by L.A. FERRO

All rights reserved.

No portion of this book may be reproduced in any form without written permission from the publisher or author, except as permitted by U.S. copyright law. Additionally, no part of this book may be used or reproduced in any manner for the purpose of training artificial intelligence technologies or systems. For permissions contact: L.A.Ferro@hotmail.com

This is a work of fiction. Names, characters, businesses, places, events, locales, and incidents are either the products of the author's imagination or used in a fictitious manner. Any resemblance to actual persons, living or dead, or actual events is purely coincidental.

Cover by K.B. Barrett Designs

Proofreading & Editing: Lawrence Editing

Published by Pine Hollow Publishing

Cataloging-in-Publication data is on file with the Library of Congress.

❦ Created with Vellum

# Prologue

## TWO MONTHS EARLIER

### GIANNA

"Hello, miss, my name is Officer James Harlow. Are your parents home?"

I had never put an ounce of thought into what I'd say to a police officer. I was a good kid, always coloring inside the lines and keeping a low profile. The last thing I cared about was being seen, but with his imposing silhouette blocking the sun, I was suddenly center stage. A quick flick of my eyes revealed a small throng of people behind him.

"No, my parents are at work," I answered cautiously, considering I had no idea why this cop was on my porch. I tried not to let my nerves show as the crowd sneered at me.

"I'm going to need you to do two things, miss. First, call your parents and let them know they are being evicted. Once they've been informed, you'll need to let us in the house so we can start moving you out."

My heart sinks, and my face heats from embarrassment over my current predicament. Already, some neighbors have started looking out their windows at all the commotion. Their prying eyes watch my every move, mocking me. For a split second, I consider refusing his demands until I see the paperwork he's holding, which is no doubt legal documentation backing up his claim. Ultimately, I know I'm on the losing end of a battle that's not mine to fight. This is my parents' fuckup, not mine. I'm just the lucky one who gets to deal with the fallout. With a shaky hand, I retrieve my cell phone from my back pocket and dial my mother.

"What couldn't wait until your shift started?" she answers on the third ring. Thirty more minutes, and I wouldn't have been home. What would have happened then if no one had been here?

I lick my lips and pray this doesn't somehow become my fault before saying, "There's a cop at the door... He says he's here to evict us."

I wait for her to yell and for the outrage to come through the phone, but it never does. Instead, she releases an exasperated breath of annoyance before she says, "You know I can't leave. I'll risk losing my job. Pack what you can into your car and take it to your cousin's house. I'll see if I can grab some boxes from the back office on my way home." There's a pause before she adds, "I'll let work know you can't make it in today... I gotta go." She cuts the call.

I don't know why I thought she'd be surprised. That was negligent thinking on my part. People don't just lose their house overnight. She and my father must have been missing payments for months. I stare blankly at my phone, stupefied at this hell I'm currently enduring alone a few weeks shy of my eighteenth birthday.

"Miss." The officer breaks through my haze, his tone softer than before. "I'm not supposed to do this. I should ask you to get in your car and vacate the premises immediately, but I'll give you ten minutes. I suggest you use that time to grab anything you don't want broken or lost."

I nod my understanding, too stunned to speak. Officer Harlow sees me for the upset minor I clearly am. Unfortunately, I soon discovered he would be the only one who sympathized with my misfortune.

After loading what special items I could into my car, I

watched who I considered looters pilfer through my belongings and comment on my life. I couldn't help but feel like my family had indeed hit rock bottom. My only solace came from knowing that at least my nine-year-old brother, Elio, was at school while all this was happening. The entire experience was jarring in more ways than one. I can't imagine his pre-adolescent brain trying to make sense of something so traumatic.

The people uprooting my life felt it was their job to inform me of every piece of drug paraphernalia they found as if I wasn't already very much aware of my parents' addiction. Today, my shame was their delight. They didn't see my struggles or everyday fear about my physiological needs being met, or if they did, they didn't care. There was no remorse or trepidation for the fact that they were putting a high school girl and a little boy on the street.

On the outside, it appeared my family had their lives together, but we were utterly broken under the surface. Their cruelty only solidified what I already felt inside. I was alone, trapped, and powerless. Everything happens for a reason; reasons cause change, and today, their joy in my hardship would be mine.

# ONE
## Gianna

"Gigi, have you seen any of my Nintendo games? I found a couple of cases, but the games weren't in them," Elio questions, walking into my room unannounced.

I stare up at him from my seated position on the floor, where I've been going through a box of things thrown together in haste with no rhyme or reason, considering I had zero time to pack anything. It's been two months since we lost our house, and while my parents haven't tried to keep that truth hidden, I know Elio doesn't comprehend the extent of the word eviction and what it entails. He doesn't understand our belongings were lying in the front yard while people stuffed their pockets with his games to pawn later.

"You can check the box in my closet. I haven't opened it yet."

That's a lie. I didn't go through the box, but I did open it to sneak his favorite game inside. I bought it yesterday and unwrapped it to make it look like it was haphazardly thrown in the box instead of stolen.

"Yes! RBI Baseball is my favorite. At least I still have one game. If you find any more, bring them to my room."

His excitement is contagious, and I can't help but smile.

"Yeah, Lo, I'll bring them over if I find any more. Is dinner ready?"

He shrugs. "I think Mom made Hamburger Helper, or that's what it smelled like when I went to grab a glass of Kool-Aid."

"Make sure you eat something."

"Yeah, yeah. I will after I play for a while. You don't have to worry about me, Gigi."

I'll always worry about Lo. Someone has to. We've been in beautiful St. Albans for over a week now. I'd like to say we ended up here because my parents searched for hours to improve our living situation, working around the clock to ensure our family was brought back together, but nope, that was me. We ended up in St. Albans because I searched high and low and wouldn't settle for another subpar house too close to the wrong side of town. My parents hadn't even thought to look in St. Albans, deciding it was too expensive to live here and we couldn't afford it.

However, I was determined to rise above, and that's when I found Gerry. She was a kind older woman with many rentals on her hands, and the second she saw Elio, she couldn't turn us down. One of her properties neighbored a park, and she thought it would be the perfect home for Elio to grow up. Her kindness gave me hope and strengthened my belief that I don't have to be a product of my environment. I am the master of my destiny. All I must do is plant the seeds and start living it.

This house could be a home. I'm trying to remain optimistic that this move is exactly what we needed and at the right time to be the change my parents are ready for. But I've learned over the years that I can't rely on my parents to be what I need. That's why, as soon as I can save enough money to get out, I will. I don't think my parents would ever give me custody of Elio, but I plan to stay close enough for him to be with me regardless. After all, they won't miss him while they're high.

Thus far, it appears that getting evicted might have been one of the best things that has happened to our family. After years of living paycheck to paycheck, borrowing beyond their needs to feed their addictions, and losing everything, they are finally cleaning up their act. For once in my eighteen years, I think we might be getting the fresh start we all deserve.

So here I am, going through the few items I have left of the life I'm trying to leave behind. It turns out that having your items pilfered and broken is a gift in disguise. You're forced to start anew and let go of things that may not bring you joy. The walls in my new room are bare, and that makes me happy. They represent a clean slate. Everything I have from here on out will have purpose and meaning. Now I can focus on what's essential: school and my new job. Everything is about to fall into place. I can feel it in my bones, and Monday is just the beginning. On Monday, I start my new full-time job at Reds. Luckily, it won't be my actual first day, only my first day as a full-time employee. My last semester of high school, I only had to attend morning classes, which left my afternoons open to pick up a part-time job. That's been one of the only good things my mother has done for me. She helped me get my foot in the door with the part-time job, and I worked my ass off to land this full-time summer position.

My mom has worked at Reds for the past ten years. While she is an addict, she managed to hold down a job. Go figure. She's still a functioning alcoholic, and that may never change, but at least she and my dad appear to have kicked the blow habit. Now if I could convince them to drop weed, maybe we could genuinely be your average middle-class household living the American dream, complete with the white picket fence.

It's Friday night, which I typically spend hanging out with my longtime friend Bryce and the guys, but not tonight, and I'd be lying if I said I wasn't a little sad about it. They came to my rescue the day my family lost their house. Bryce rounded up the guys, and they showed up in their trucks and helped me pick up the pieces of my life that were thrown out on the lawn.

"It's just one Friday... One weekend," I say as I expel a breath of resolve.

I need to stay home this weekend and prepare for the upcoming week. When I began working at Reds part-time, I started making real money. Part-time work there paid more than any restaurant job ever did. I can't wait to see what my full-time pay looks like. The money I make this summer will help me pay for community college in the fall. I need this job, which is why I want to pick out my outfits and finish unpacking the few boxes I have left. I need to focus, which means decluttering my space and getting organized so my mind isn't busy worrying about the small stuff. Sometimes I wish I could be carefree and undisciplined so I don't miss out on the moment, but that's not who I am. Thus far, my circumstances in life haven't afforded me that luxury. But for now, tomorrow looks promising. We live in a lovely house, and my parents are clean. However, that doesn't mean I'll stop planning for the minute it all falls apart. That's why I'm home now, prepping for Monday. This is my time. It's time to change my life for the better.

## TWO

## *August*

"August, you have to try this new beer I picked up. It's the summer brew O'Fallon just released. You can taste all the orange peel, coriander, and star anise notes. I love a good Belgian ale," Grant says as he barges in with Ethan hot on his heels, pre-party bottles in hand.

Classes ended this week. Ethan and I are officially done with school. On the other hand, Grant is a sports med major with a few years left. However, for a few weeks, he's on break, too, and we're celebrating. Grant sets the six-pack on the kitchen island before popping the top on two beers and thrusting one into my hand.

"Thanks, G! But I'm going to need you to pull back on that nerd energy tonight if you're expecting to party with the opposite sex," I rag as I take a pull off the beer he shoved into my hand.

Taken aback by the comment, he furrows his brows before saying, "What's that supposed to mean, bro?"

My eyes shoot up at his balk. "Oh, I don't know. You're over here spitting lines about notes of coriander. I know you're a med major, and details are key, but not when we're trying to get fucked up."

"Damn, you're right. My head is not in the game. So where

should we start out tonight?" He shakes his head at his oversight and takes a drink.

Ethan is spitting out his demands before we can get a word out. "We'll be hitting up Crushed first. I told a few girls from class that we'd be making the rounds tonight, and they mentioned going to Crushed at 9:00 p.m. for live music. There's a brunette with big blue eyes that I won't be mad about running into."

Ethan always has some girl lined up, with his dad being a big-shot mogul. Out of the two of us, he's the only one excited to take over his family's business. He'll be at the helm of Grand Media. While I have zero interest in being glued to my phone trying to keep up with the ever-changing social media plane, it's got to be more exciting than the manufacturing card I've been dealt.

My family business makes store-brand health and beauty products for the masses. We distribute to every major retailer across the United States, and while that's a huge accomplishment, it's not what I want for myself. My life and what I'd do with it were mapped out the minute I was born. The only son to take over the business and keep the Branson name present and profitable. I'm so tired of doing what I'm expected to do. Growing up, I played the sports my parents chose for me and joined every club they insisted would develop my character, i.e., maintain our social status. Hell, even the girl I'm dating was selected for me. It's why graduating has been bittersweet. I achieved something, but school afforded me freedoms I'll soon no longer have once again. On Monday, I'll be forced into my next role: taking over Reds. Two more days of freedom are all I have.

"What happened to that girl Andrea you were seeing? Won't she be a little pissed you're out prowling the town picking up numbers?" I ask as Ethan spots the bottle of Macallan I had out before they arrived.

"I never said we were going steady. Besides, I wouldn't be surprised if she has a few guys lined up herself. Girls these days always have a backup plan, and if I know her, she has someone else as well. Otherwise, she'd be blowing up my phone tonight."

I shrug off his comment because his words don't surprise me. By the sound of it, Andrea is already yesterday's news. "Well then, I guess you and G are on the market tonight, so we better do some serious pre-gaming if you guys plan on picking up any girls."

Grant lets out a deep laugh before saying, "Well, as long as you keep your pussy-whipped ass away from our game, we should have a couple of girls lined up to come back here by eleven!"

*Did he seriously just call me pussy-whipped?*

"Okay…Grant, you act like I sit at home wallowing because Carson decided to go away for school. In fact, it's just the opposite. I party with you assholes every weekend. Just because I'm not bringing girls home doesn't mean I'm pussy-whipped. I'm pretty sure last weekend I had more girls on the dance floor than both of you combined, so fuck off!"

My girlfriend, Carson, decided to go to the East Coast for her last semester of college and isn't done with finals for another two weeks. Things between us have changed. We've never been your typical couple, but something is up with her. Growing up in a fake world, I've learned that not everything is what it seems. She's up to something, and I'm sticking around because I'm intrigued. If you don't want to be in a relationship anymore, why not end it? I've had my suspicions that she's seeing someone else for a while, but honestly, she's the one thing I haven't minded being forced into. The girl knows how to have a good time.

"Come on, August, that pretty face deserves a little sucky-sucky action from time to time, and we all know you're not getting it from Carson. Is it even cheating if you guys are on a break? She did say that you guys were taking this time 'to reconnect with your inner selves.'" Grant gestures with finger quotes. "Maybe your inner self needs to grind on some chick at the bar tonight and get your dick wet."

As tempting as that sounds, every time the opportunity presents itself, I can't bring myself to do it and trust me, there are many nights I wish I could. Part of me wants to move on from Carson, but I also haven't had a good enough reason to abandon ship. She'll be home in two short weeks. If I broke now, it would feel like holding out all this time was for nothing. Plus, I've never been the cheating type.

"You know how I feel about Carson and our so-called break, so just drop it. She'll be home soon, and we'll see where we stand then."

I walk around the island to grab my wallet off the counter just as a text comes through.

> Augustus: August, I can't tell you how proud I am that you'll be starting at Reds on Monday. You'll finally be stepping into the shoes you were destined to fill.

*Did he think I needed the reminder? What am I even supposed to say to that?* So many times over the years, I have come close to telling him I want nothing to do with Reds. However, every time I think I'm ready for the conversation, I back out. It feels like an obligation that there's no way around. Instead, I stay the course.

> August: Thanks, Dad. I'm sure training will be enlightening.

I can't help the sarcasm laced in my reply. He never catches on to it anyway. I suppose no harm, no foul, but God, how I wish he would catch on sometimes. While he wants me to take over the company, he thinks I need to do it from the bottom up. Of course I won't be a janitor or anything, but he believes sitting through training will give me a sense of perspective. I get it. Working in various departments should deepen my understanding of how the business operates, and it would make me more approachable. Employees would see me as someone who understands their struggles rather than just a figurehead who was put into a position because of his name. The problem is I don't care. I stopped caring years ago when it became clear what I wanted didn't matter.

> Augustus: That's the spirit, son. Let's plan on lunch on Friday.

Great! Another mind-numbing lunch talking about a future I never wanted. Time to get drunk.

* * *

"Ethan, over here."

We all turn toward the voice and find a cute brunette with a pixie cut wearing a short blue dress. This must be the girl Ethan was telling us about.

Ethan flashes his megawatt smile and makes a beeline toward her. "Megan, I was hoping I'd run into you tonight."

Megan just so happens to have two friends with her as well. A coincidence? I think not. If I had my guess, more words were exchanged than Ethan was letting on earlier.

He pulls her into a big bear hug and says, "Why are you guys waiting in line? Come with me. I'll get you in."

"We all got here later than expected. We planned to get here an hour before the band started, but that didn't exactly happen."

To her credit, she did seem sincere, like she hadn't planned on Ethan's celebrity to get her into the bar tonight. That earns her points in my book. In our world, the girls we meet are always trying to be a part of our lives for what we can give them: money, status, or celebrity. That's another reason I'm not anxious to cut the cord with Carson. Carson's family isn't poor by any means. We both went to the same prestigious private high school and knowing she's not with me for my trust fund is a significant factor in our relationship.

Megan's red-headed friend breaks me out of my train of thought. "You must be August. My name is Ivy."

I turn to her with what I'm sure is a quizzical expression. If I want to talk to a girl, I will. I hate when women come on to me.

"You spaced out during introductions, so I figured I'd save you from the group's ridicule for being completely oblivious."

She is gorgeous, I'll give her that. Maybe I would be interested under different circumstances, but that's not tonight. As we follow the others to the entrance, I shrug before responding, "Thanks. I'm easily distracted... I was trying to remember if I locked the door before we left." A lie, of course, but if she catches it, she doesn't let on.

Crushed is your typical small cocktail bar. It serves tapas, which are constantly changing as they only serve what they can grow organically out back. It's a millennial hot spot. Overall, the place is not very big. The bar juts out from the back wall, cutting directly down the entire restaurant with its high-top tables lining the perimeter. I was wondering where they were planning to put a live band, and now that we're inside, I can see that they've opened the passageway to the organic garden, so the band must be outside. Before heading that way, the group follows Ethan and Megan toward the bar for a quick drink.

I'm just sidling up along Ethan's right when a hand gently squeezes my bicep. Before turning toward the movement, hot breath fans my ear, followed by Ivy's request. "I'd love a cosmopolitan."

"How forward of you, asking me to buy you a drink." I give her a teasing smile, but inwardly, I can't help but cringe at her eagerness to get cozy with me. It screams desperate and easy. Don't get me wrong, I'm not against buying a woman a drink, but I also don't care to lead someone on. I have no interest in hooking up with her tonight. Before leaving, she gives me a coy smile and saunters out back with Megan and the other girl whose name I haven't yet caught. Ethan takes that moment to drill Grant and me about the girls.

"Isn't Megan fucking hot? I knew she mentioned she'd be out with her friends. From the looks of it, Ivy and Kelsey aren't too bad, either. You guys are lucky to know me."

Grant slaps him on the back. "Sure, man, you did well this time, but the real story is the way August is checking out Ivy. Maybe you just needed to find the right girl to take your mind off Carson, and I think maybe you just met her."

"Don't get me wrong. She's something to look at, but looks aren't everything." These guys clearly can't tell when I'm interested in a girl. If anything, I'm attempting to be obliging, but I'm not interested.

Ethan snorts. "Okay, bro, whatever you say, but she's someone to have fun with tonight. So what do you say we clear the cobwebs and get you some action?"

The bartender places our drinks in front of us, saving me from a reply, and we head out back to find the girls. We step outside, and I notice the bar has transformed the dormant side of the garden into a stage for the band. Gold lights run up the trunks of the trees surrounding the space, and overhead lanterns are hung to create a fancy ambiance. It would be romantic if I were here with the right person. We make our way to the front, where the girls are sitting at a high-top café table. The band has already started playing what sounds like smooth jazz ballads. While I'm not against smooth jazz, this isn't the scene I was looking for tonight, but I'm trying to go with the flow and not be a wet blanket.

If I must be subjected to this whimsicality for the remainder of the evening, I'll need to head back to the bar for a shot or two. I discreetly excuse myself and make my exit. As it turns out, heading back inside was more than a great idea. When I step up to order my shot, I run into Mike, another one of our college buddies.

"Hey, Mike, who are you here with tonight?"

When he turns around, I don't miss the mischievous grin on his face.

"August! Man, it's good to see you. I haven't seen you since our marketing final two weeks ago. I'm here with Big Al, but tonight's vibe is not it. So we're closing our tab and heading down to Smokey's."

"Why do I feel you're up to something tonight?"

Mike is known for starting a party, especially since he usually brings party favors in the form of uppers.

"Maybe I am, but you sure as shit aren't going to catch me wasting my goods here. Come with us."

"I'm here with Ethan and G tonight, but Smokey's sounds more appealing. Let me close out my tab."

After, I follow Mike and Big Al out the front door, not bothering to say bye to the others. I don't need their glares and disapproval. We came out to have fun tonight, not woo some chicks listening to smooth jazz. The way I see it, Ethan organized a lame meet-up, one he knew I wasn't into, so I give zero fucks about ghosting him.

## THREE
## Gianna

"Perfect. Early, just as intended."

It's 6:45 a.m. I still have fifteen minutes before training starts. This is why I picked out my outfit ahead of time. It saved me the stress I would have endured this morning trying to find something professionally acceptable in my wardrobe. I've never had money to spend on clothes, but I think I've managed the task by selecting a pair of black Dickies and pairing it with a white button-down and gray cardigan. My shoes, on the other hand—a pair of red flats—may not fit the bill. The entire week will be spent in training, so my attire doesn't need to fit my role just yet, which will be more laid back considering the type of work I'll be doing. For training, I tried my best to aim for business casual. I flip down the mirror on my visor and swipe on some fresh lip gloss before deciding this is as good as it will get and head inside.

The front of Reds looks like any typical office complex, with blacked-out windows lining the exterior of the red brick building. A person would be none the wiser that a complete manufacturing operation is attached to the back of the complex. As you walk into the main lobby, the receptionist, Anette, who's been there for decades, greets you. She has a thick Southern drawl and emanates warmth should she deem you worthy. You don't want to cross her. I've heard she can be treacherous should you get on her bad side. While I feel I'm on her good side, I never let my guard down. From a young age, I learned people will tell you what they think you want to hear regardless of its merit, and depending on how old you are, they're not concerned with the integrity of their words. People are only faithful to their word if they believe you have something to offer them in return.

"Good morning, Ms. Anette. How are you doing this morning?" She's not someone on whom good manners are lost. On the contrary, she expects to be greeted and takes it personally should you try to engage without a proper hello first.

"Good morning, Gianna. Are you finally here to stay with us the entire day? I know you were hoping to be brought on full-time, and since you're here bright and early, I'm assuming that means you're here for training."

Shifting my weight from foot to foot and twisting my fingers tightly around my phone, full of nervous energy, I say, "Yes, it would appear they like me more than I thought. Of course I'm only here for the summer for now, but hopefully, they'll see my dedication and ability to get tasks done promptly as an asset and keep me forever."

Then, with a smirk and a faint chuckle, she retorts, "That's just the attitude you need, my dear, to survive in the shark tank. Good luck. I'll buzz you back."

Making my way down the hall to the front conference room where training will be held for the week feels surreal. I, Gianna Moretti, worked my butt off, and now I have a real job and an incredible opportunity to show for it. As expected, I'm the first person to make it in. Phyllis is in the back of the conference room, sorting out materials. Phyllis is an older woman, probably in her sixties, with short gray hair and a squatty body, and she dresses like my grandma. I've only met her one other time, and she seems to be as lovely as any grandma would be. If you work in HR, that's an excellent trait to have.

"Good morning, Phyllis. I know I'm early, but I figured I could get a good seat."

"No worries, Gianna, you're not that early, and I'm sure it will be an interesting week given who our new hires are. So you may as well get in early to clear your head before the drama begins."

Before I can question her more on whom she's referring to or why they'd hire someone they thought would cause issues, other new hires begin to file in. I take a seat up front. It's closest to the door and brings me comfort for some reason. I don't like to feel as though I'm trapped.

Nearing seven o'clock, I look around at the people in my group, sizing them up. There are five guys and me. Typically, the tables in this room are arranged in one big rectangle so that people can collaborate face-to-face, but the rectangle has been broken up into rows of two tables each. Every table faces the entry door, and the projector is set up for viewing on the wall beside it.

No one has sat by me, and that's fine. Of course I'm the youngest person in the class. The closest person to my age is most likely thirty. Phyllis makes her way to the front of the room, preparing for introductions.

"Good morning. I'm glad to see you're all on time and settling in. My name is Phyllis, and I am the HR Training Manager. Today, we will take a few minutes to go around the room and introduce ourselves. Then we will dive into corporate policies and procedures as well as workplace violence and harassment—" She's cut off as a man walks through the door, looking somewhat disheveled. He doesn't acknowledge Phyllis and walks straight to the back of the room to take his seat. A thought occurs to me then. Maybe this is the person Phyllis was referring to this morning that would cause drama. It would be all too serendipitous that this guy walks in when she mentions workplace violence and harassment. Talk about omens. Phyllis tries to appear unaffected by the interruption and clears her throat to pick up where she left off, not even addressing the newcomer. "As I said, we will discuss violence in the workplace and sexual harassment, and then we will break for lunch. The schedule is somewhat lax, so we have time for questions and discussions should the need for clarification arise."

As she continues her spiel, my mind is anywhere but on her words. I can't help but feel distracted. No less than two minutes ago, I was perfectly content, relaxed, and ready to kick some training ass, but now it feels like a heavy fog has settled in the room, and the air is thick with tension. Not only is it hard to breathe, but the hairs on the back of my neck are starting to prick up as if I'm being watched. *How can one person change the dynamic of an entire group with just their presence alone?*

## FOUR
## *August*

I have the worst hangover known to man, and now I must sit in training like I'm not the fucking guy who'll be taking over the company. Seriously, this is not only a misuse of resources, it's degrading. If my dad wants me to show interest in this place, this is not the way to do it. Sitting through boring-ass corporate policies that don't even apply to me is a complete waste.

When my dad was brought into the company at a young age, he took the bull by the horns and worked in every department. He was over-the-moon excited to start working with his father and carry on the family legacy, going above and beyond to make sure he knew all the ins and outs. Now that I'm starting, he expects the same from me, which is why I'm sitting in training rather than just starting at the top. What he doesn't seem to get is that I'm a smart person. I don't need to do someone else's job to understand it. But I'm still stuck in hell for a week.

I'm determined to find a way to get out of this. Maybe I'll just not show up for the remainder of the week. I'm sure Phyllis doesn't have enough balls to tell my dad in person that I decided training week was unnecessary.

The only issue with skipping out is that training was moved to the executive conference room this week. It just so happens to be in the same hallway as good ole Dad's office and right outside the Sales team's offices where my uncle Eduard sits.

If my dad happens to be in the office this week, my presence will be missed. I could bet my inheritance on it that he'll make a special appearance just for my benefit alone. While today is the first day of the end of my life, it's the beginning for my dad. He couldn't be happier, and isn't that just perfect?

The weekend was spent on a bender. If not for that, today wouldn't be half as bad. After I left Ethan and Grant at Crushed, I was fucked up for the remainder of the weekend. But, my God, did Mike and I get ripped. I can't remember the last time I had that much fun.

Don't get me wrong, Ethan and Grant are entertaining, but it's on a different level. Mike is a straight-up walking party. There's never a dull moment. Once we got to Smokey's and popped a few addies, it was all over from there.

We had a group of girls with us all night and took the party back to Mike's lake house. The girls were fucking hot as sin. They definitely were not the type of girls I grew up with in East Lake.

Sure, the girls where I'm from are attractive, but they're conservative attractive. Of course they have fake tits, fake asses, fake lips, you name it, but they keep that shit covered with tight-fitting clothes that don't show too much skin. On the other hand, the girls this weekend were straight-up stripper hot and dressed like it.

I'm not going to lie and say I didn't let one grind up on my cock for a lap dance. I can't tell you how much I was tempted to take things to the next step. The relentless throb between my legs was begging for release. You'd think I'm a saint from the amount of restraint I've shown in Carson's absence, but I'm far from it. I have my reasons beyond Carson for my choices, but the more I try to justify those, the more I want to let it all go. But once I let her go, the next girl will be the one. Not someone my parents pick out for me, but one I can be my authentic self with.

I didn't get back to my place until Sunday. We literally partied from Friday through Sunday. I got home that afternoon and fell asleep immediately, but I haven't had enough coffee or non-alcoholic liquids to feel human.

That's when I spot a coffee pot off to the side in the training room next to an array of pastries. Those must be for trainees, which apparently, I am. Scooting my chair back, I inwardly cringe at the screech it makes as it drags along the floor from my abrupt movement. I'm fully committed to my task now, so I head over to the refreshment table.

As I'm pouring my coffee, the room goes silent, and I realize all eyes must be on me. There's no good way not to look like an ass for getting up in the middle of Phyllis's talking. So I play the cocky, arrogant, entitled prick card that is expected of me.

"Sorry, Phyllis, I noticed this subpar display of breakfast pastries and coffee, and since I wasn't sure when you'd take a break from boring the class, I thought I'd help myself. I'm sure I am not the only one who survives on coffee in the morning, yet no one has one."

My complete disdain for the situation is not lost in my tone, and judging by the shock on Phyllis's face, she couldn't believe I just spoke to her like that. Well, good. I want people to fear me. This isn't little league where everyone gets a trophy. You either make the cut, or you don't, and these assholes need to learn that on day one.

Deciding to take pity on Phyllis and her loss for words, I motion with my arm for the others to grab a coffee and return to my seat.

Phyllis finally recovers by clearing her throat and patting down her blouse.

"Yes, well, August, you couldn't be more right. I'm sorry I got swept away in the excitement of corporate policy. But as you know, I can't get enough of the employee handbook."

Her voice is thick with sarcasm as her eyes sear into me with a heat that would burn me alive if it were tangible. I shrug casually and tap my fingers on the desk absentmindedly as if the entire interaction was nothing but a mere inconvenience.

The break in her lecture gives me time to scan over the other new hires. Five guys and one girl, all of them older, apart from the girl, who's probably in her early twenties like me. I can't really tell because, out of everyone in the class, she's the only one who decided to stay seated and not take advantage of the break to grab a coffee, and her back is to me.

Her stature, clothing, and overall choice to sit in the front of the class like a good little new hire give her away. It screams I'm young and green. This is probably her first job out of college, and she wants to make a good impression. Well, joke's on her. Sitting in the front of the class to review the employee handbook isn't going to win you any accolades. But, to her credit, her seat choice earned me my attention, as now I'll spend the remainder of this stupid training week trying to crack Miss Goody Two-shoes.

*** 

We're finally granted a bathroom break. I think Phyllis is starting to pick up on my not-so-subtle cues as to when I've had enough. If she doesn't want another verbal assault to occur, she better fall in line. I've never thought much about the type of boss I'd be, but I'm starting to think ruling by browbeating isn't so bad.

I haven't been paying any attention to all the crap she's spewing, but I'm sure it's necessary information for the rest of these peons I've been forced to endure hell with.

Making my way to the bathroom, I catch a glimpse of the blonde from my class walking toward the Sample Room, which piques my interest. However, taking a leak currently takes higher priority than following Miss Goody Two-shoes.

Once I've relieved my bladder, my phone pings with a text message from Carson.

> Carson: Hey, I just thought I'd let you know that my return home will be delayed another week.

My blood boils. Not only has she refused to answer my phone calls or respond to my texts, but now she ends her silence, only to let me know she isn't coming home as initially planned. I'm starting to think this relationship has a sooner expiration date than later. As much as I want to hold out to see how things play out, this shit is getting old.

Rounding the corner, I head down the hallway toward the training room and run smack dab into a very pretty blonde. My blonde. I catch her by the elbows to keep her from falling backward, and instantly tendrils of heat flare in my veins and head straight to my groin.

Before I have time to analyze my body's reaction to her touch, my eyes lock on her big green ones staring straight into the depths of my soul with a look of pure disdain. The woman couldn't be any more incensed than she is right now, all because I ran into her.

Noting her obvious discomfort, I reluctantly let her go. However, now that she's standing in front of me, I notice she's not at all the mousy girl I pegged her for while staring at the back of her head for the past two hours. No, she is drop-dead gorgeous, and I can tell by how she carries herself that she's entirely blind to that fact.

"Sorry, I wasn't paying attention. I was hoping to steal a peek at the show samples before class started back up, and I guess I got a little too excited."

*Show samples? What the fuck is she talking about? Who even cares?*

"Well, if you're okay, I'll just be on my way. Again, sorry."

Before I can even respond, I'm watching her perfectly plump ass walk away. *What the hell was that? Girls never render me speechless, and why the hell did she look so mad when she ran into me?*

This training just got a whole lot more interesting. I need to know this girl. I need to know everything about her. I've just found my newest obsession.

\* \* \*

Surprise, surprise, I'm the first one back to the conference room. Hell, I'm even shocked. But running into my mystery woman gave me a whole new take on this week. Maybe it's the hangover talking, and by tomorrow I'll be over whatever the hell feelings I stumbled upon by running into her in the hallway, or perhaps I won't.

Everyone starts filing back into the class when she walks over to the snack table and grabs a granola bar. I can't help but take the time to admire her perfect body. The temptress has an athlete's body like she played sports in college. She has lean, muscular legs that make me think she was a dancer, a toned stomach, and fit arms. While her breasts aren't huge, they're perfect. I'm so tired of fake tits, and seeing them on the smaller side assures me they're real, which is ideal.

Before returning to her seat, she tosses her long dark-blond hair over her shoulder and quickly glances in my direction. As fast as our eyes connect, they disengage as if she was disturbed by the fact that I happened to catch her looking my way. We'll have to fix that because her ignoring me won't do. I get what I want, and right now, I want her.

Just as Phyllis begins to make her way up to the front, I clear my throat.

"Phyllis, I believe you mentioned introductions at the start of class, but we never got around to it. Maybe now is a good time. I sure wouldn't mind a break in the monotony."

"That's a great idea. I completely forgot. Would you mind doing us the honor of starting?"

I should have seen that coming. *Damn it.*

"Well, I wouldn't want to be rude. I insist, ladies first."

Stealing a glance at my mystery woman, I notice her cheeks flush and her spine straightens. Well, now isn't that something? A moment ago, she was all too confident in the hallway, and now she seems so much less assured of herself. Serves her right. She should know her place.

"Gianna, dear, you don't mind going first?"

So my mystery woman not only has a name but a beautiful

name. From where I sit, I can see her twisting her hands together nervously on her lap before she brings them up and lays them flat on the desk to respond.

"No problem, Phyllis. My name is Gianna Moretti. I've been working here part-time for the past few months in the afternoons, but I was recently brought on full-time to work in the Sample Room for the summer. I'm excited to join the team and start my next chapter."

When she finishes, her eyes quickly catch mine one last time. It was so fast that I would have missed it if I had blinked. I think I make her uncomfortable, which is perfect. I don't want her to see me coming.

"Thanks, Gianna. We are excited to have you with us full-time. Ryan, would you like to go next?"

Phyllis goes around the entire room and ends with me. I suppose since I opted out of going first, she decided I would go last. Little did she know, I have no reservations about going last. After all, don't people always save the best for last?

"Well, it was nice to meet all of you formally, and I'm hopeful that you all will be value added to Reds. My name is August Barron Branson IV. I'll be working in the Marketing department as the head of new business ventures in branding."

Once I dropped my name, I think everyone in the room stopped breathing, including Phyllis, and she knew who I was all along. I'm not a name dropper in general, and it's not like my family is world-renowned or anything, but when I'm here, people obviously know the Branson name. Wanting to ensure everyone takes a breath, I try to make light of the moment.

"Don't worry, guys. I don't have the power to fire you." *Not yet anyway.*

That earned me a few half-smiles and some nervous chuckles, but hey, at least everyone took a breath. My girl has yet to look my way again, but she will. I'll make sure of that. I found a treasure in Gianna, and I plan to make her mine.

# FIVE
## Gianna

Oh my God! Am I really in training with August Barron Branson IV? That explains Phyllis's cryptic statement earlier about how this class would be entertaining. Not that I expected a heads-up or anything, but it would have been greatly appreciated. I wouldn't have been so rude when I ran into him in the hallway.

Before I knew who he was, I thought he was some punk not taking his new job or training seriously. I still believe that he's a jerk. However, he's the next owner, so maybe I shouldn't be so quick to judge.

Maybe he's just having a bad day and he's not as big of a douche as he's making himself out to be, or perhaps he's simply a proud narcissist. Regardless, who talks to Phyllis that way? She's like a lovely old grandma, and I'd never speak to my grandmother that way. Now that I'm thinking about it, he deserves the cold shoulder I gave him. Why should I show him respect if he can't respect his elders or the people who keep this company running? He did say he doesn't have the power to fire us, so I think I'm in the clear.

I need to make sure I stay off his radar. That shouldn't be terribly difficult if I face forward in class and watch where I walk in the hallways. Technically, I'm only the summer help, so I don't need to get on anyone's bad side, especially not the owner's son. I just wish I weren't so affected by him. That would make ignoring him a lot easier.

When he walked into the class, I swore he took all the air in the room with him. Hell, before I even ran into him in the hallway, I felt his eyes on me. It's like I have this innate draw to him that's left me on edge and unable to calm down. I only wish I could figure out where all these feelings are coming from.

As I sit here watching some training video on workplace safety, my mind is a million miles away. All I can think about is the instant electricity that ran through my body when he grabbed my arms in the hallway. Scents of cedarwood and leather quickly enveloped my senses, but I could also smell hints of alcohol. Usually, that would be a turn-off, but his devilish good looks easily compensate for the questionable scent.

Don't even get me started on the man's eyes. He has the most velvety smooth shade of caramel eyes I've ever seen. Taking a step back from him was by far the most challenging step I've ever taken, and that's just ridiculous.

It was the strangest thing being that close to him. As if some magnetic energy was pulling us together, and the longer I stood next to him, the more I was lost to it. I had to truly focus on the fact that I had never met this man, and we in no way had any relationship to warrant the butterflies swarming in my stomach or the fast-paced beating of my heart.

My brain was indeed the only functioning part of my person since my traitorous body saw no reason to flee. I've never felt that type of pull to anyone in my life. Sure, I've dated, and I have Mason, but never have I been so enticed, so drawn in. No, this is bad, so bad, seeing as how we'll be coworkers, and in the long run, he'll be my boss.

While I've been mentally checked out of training, I'm almost positive that we covered how workplace romances are forbidden. This could be a total disaster if I don't watch myself. I need this job. It's imperative that I keep it. So much is riding on my ability to make good money this summer to pay for college and get my own place. That settles it. I can't let some little crush, if you could even call it that, stand in my way. In fact, I'll alleviate some of this built-up tension tonight.

Quickly glancing behind me over my left shoulder, opposite from where August is sitting, I see that Phyllis is distracted, so I take a moment to pull out my phone and text Mason.

> Gianna: Hey, are you busy tonight?

> Mason: You know I'm never too busy for you, babe.

> Gianna: What time do you get off work?

> Mason: I'm off at 4. Didn't you start your new job today? I can pick you up. We can get something to eat.

I forgot Mason works in the area. He started helping his dad with his IT company a few months ago. Mason was a year ahead of me in school and is on the fast track to finishing his degree early. He started taking college classes while in high school. Seriously, he is one of the most brilliant guys I know. I'd rather not leave my car and have to come back, but if he's already out this way, I'll let him pick me up now instead of driving to my house later.

> Gianna: Yes, I started today. See you at 4 unless things change.

> Mason: Nope, you're stuck with me tonight. No take backs!

Mason and I met through my best friend, Vivian. Vivian was the first friend I made when my family moved to Arrowhead from California. We've been friends since we were six years old. When we were ten, her family moved a town away, which meant I only got to see Vivian on weekends when our parents would carpool us to see each other. That's how I met Mason.

Mason was Vivian's new neighbor. The first time I met him, I thought he was cute, but the more we hung out, the more I was drawn to him. When everyone started having boyfriends in middle school, I would claim him as my boyfriend. He didn't go to my school, so he was none the wiser about the label I had put on our relationship from a young age. Eventually, I fessed up, and he said he had done the same thing with my name a time or two.

We have never discussed what we were or if we were technically anything outside of that confession. But as we got older, my feelings grew, and one night at a party, I got ballsy and decided to kiss him, and what do you know? He liked it. I think he knew for a while that I had been crushing on him, but we had been friends for so long that I think he had reservations about changing our dynamic. *What if things didn't work out? Would we still be friends?*

I'm not going to lie and say that didn't cross my mind as well, but you can spin the what-if card however you like to fit your narrative. What if we didn't work out was one way to look at it. Or what if we were the most incredible love story ever to exist is another way. Either way, we became each other's first for many other things after that first kiss. Well, PG things anyway. As much as I like Mason, I'm not in love with him. I think I could be if I thought he'd want that. While I'm comfortable with him and have given him many of my firsts, I've never really been ready to go further. I've wanted to, believe me. Mason is very attractive in a hot geek kind of way. He has blond hair, alluring blue eyes framed by what I call his "Clark Kent" glasses, and a slender, muscular physique.

I've never asked him about other girls, nor has he asked me about other guys. He could potentially be saving himself, but I highly suspect that's not the case. Most people my age are not virgins, but for me, it's a choice. Or maybe that's just the lie I tell myself so I don't have to deal with the feelings that come after being with someone intimately. Lord knows I have enough emotional baggage as it is without adding that complication. At the end of the day, Mace has always been my safe place, and if he's content with how things are, so am I.

\* \* \*

Lunchtime has finally rolled around, and Phyllis has dismissed the class. We are only given thirty minutes for lunch during training. Once we're in our positions, we can take an hour. I make sure I'm the first one out the door, which isn't too difficult, seeing as how I'm sitting next to it. I'm also making it my mission to avoid accidental run-ins with August.

I power walk to my car at a pace that could almost be considered a slow jog. To any onlooker, I probably look ridiculous, but I don't care. I need to get away. I need to breathe, clear my head, recenter myself, and that cannot happen if I'm in the vicinity of August. Climbing into my car, I quickly throw my purse in the passenger's seat, buckle myself in, and head out.

We don't have very long, so I head down the street to Grinders. It's a small coffee shop right down the street from Reds. From what I've noticed over the past few months, not many people who work at Reds come here. There's not much down this way in terms of shopping or places to eat. So coffee and a pastry will be perfect. I can't imagine eating a heavy lunch with my stomach in knots over today's events.

Standing in line to order my coffee, I pull my phone out of my purse and lazily scroll through emails. I'm quickly pulled out of the menial task when the hairs on the back of my neck rise and heat envelops my back. I don't even have a chance to turn around before an unmistakable voice asks, "How do you like your coffee?"

I gasp, wholly startled and caught off guard. I mean, why him out of all people to run into at Grinders?

"Um, you really don't have to do that, but thanks for offering."

With a smirk, he responds, "Who said I was offering?"

Oh my God, could that be any more embarrassing? Why

would I assume he wanted to buy me a coffee? On second thought, what a jerk. *Why would he ask me such a question if that wasn't his intent?* Maybe lead with, 'What's good here?'

"I'm sorry, I just assumed..." I clear my throat and try to recover from my faux pas before adding, "I usually have a latte and a pastry, not really one for ordering a big lunch."

God, I sound so lame. *Why am I so nervous around this guy?* It's like my brain forgets how to form sentences. Finally, it's my turn to order, but August places his hand on my lower back and steps around me before I can step up and place my order.

"I'll take two lattes and two cinnamon scones."

I haven't even finished processing that he just took an awkward moment and turned it into an unbelievably sexy gesture. Not to mention his hand on my back has sent warmth straight to my center in ways I've never felt before. He keeps it there as he guides me over to the side to wait for our order, but when he removes it, I can't help but feel unsettled by the loss.

"Thank you for that. As I said before, you didn't need to pay for my lunch." I'm fiddling with my purse strap, trying to compute this entire encounter. For a minute, I think he might actually be decent, but then he opens his mouth.

"No, I didn't buy you lunch, but I'd like to. This is merely coffee, mi Tesoro." He has this mischievous glint in his eyes, like he's up to something. This moment was already perplexing. Now it's just downright embarrassing. Just because I have an Italian name doesn't mean I speak it. Well, if it's his goal to make me feel small and beneath him because he's well-versed and rich, both of which I am not, he's got another thing coming.

"Oh, you must think I speak Italian since I have an Italian name, is that it? Well, joke's on you, I don't."

To that, he smirks. "Actually, I was counting on the fact that you didn't. Glad to know I was right."

*Jerk.*

Our order is called, and he hands me my coffee and scone. We then walk out of the coffee shop in silence. Once outside, he heads to his car, and I go to mine. Before opening my door, I stop and look over my shoulder toward his car, only to find his stormy eyes staring back at me. I quickly break our eye contact and climb into my vehicle. He has the most consuming gaze I've ever felt. I swear, when his eyes are on me, it's like he really sees me, which makes me uneasy. I've worked hard on my mask to hide my insecurities over the years, and I don't like his disarming gaze.

The drive back to Reds has me in complete knots, with a million questions and zero answers. Was it a coincidence that we both went to the same place for lunch, or did he follow me? Does he really want to buy me lunch? Is it possible he knows the effect he has on me? Most importantly, why did I feel such a profound loss almost in my soul when his hand left my back? In the end, seeking answers to any of those questions would spell disaster for me, seeing as how I need this job and can't afford to mess it up.

* * *

The remaining four hours of training were the longest of my life. I felt like I was in a blistering inferno. A ball of nervous energy, I was wound so tight I thought I could snap any moment. Sitting in class, I could feel the heat of his gaze on the back of my neck. It felt as though he was daring me to turn around. I wanted to steal a glance so badly. To see his eyes one more time, to analyze his demeanor, and see if today's exchange was just a product of my overactive imagination. Or was he, in fact, just as affected by me as I am by him? But, again, I knew none of those answers would do me any good.

My phone vibrates in my pocket, and as I peek at my messages, I see that Mason is waiting in the parking lot. That's good because that means at any moment, Phyllis will wrap things up for the day, and I can escape all this sexual tension, if that's even what this is. How do I have sexual tension with someone I don't even know, someone who hasn't been exactly friendly to me?

"All right, class, that's it for today. Tomorrow will be much like today, but we will be taking a tour of the facility, so please feel free to wear jeans and comfortable closed-toed shoes."

I quickly read Phyllis's disposition to make sure she's done speaking before swiftly exiting the class ahead of anyone else. The minute I'm outside the lobby and heading to the parking lot, I can breathe. My skin was so hot for the last few hours that the breeze in the spring air feels exhilarating.

No sooner I start to search for Mason than he's pulling around in his blacked-out Audi. His dad got it for him as a graduation gift when he announced Mason would be joining the family business. It's a hot car, but there's no way Mason could have afforded it on his own, not yet anyway.

Rolling down the window, he catcalls, "Hey, sexy, need a ride?"

I can't help but laugh at his antics. He's always finding ways to make me smile. After getting in, I fasten my seat belt, only to settle in and find August standing by the entrance with Ryan from training. Ryan is saying something to August, but August is too busy openly glaring at me with an annoyed look on his face. He's so fixed on me that he doesn't notice Ryan has walked away. Tucking my hair behind my ear, I slowly and inconspicuously reach to roll the window up. He looks absolutely livid, and for some reason, my stomach twists with what feels like regret. This afternoon, he mentioned buying me lunch, but did that mean he was suggesting a date?

I hold my breath until Mason finally pulls away.

"Where to, babe?"

Releasing a groan, I can't help but push out a frustrated breath. Closing my eyes, I throw my head back against the seat. Suddenly, going out with Mason feels like a bad idea, and I have no clue why. Mason and I have been friends for so many years. So how is it that August can get under my skin with just a look? When I open my eyes, Mason looks at me with concern written all over his face.

"I know something is wrong, and that's okay. I know just what you need."

I don't respond as I continue to stew on the day's events. Usually, I tell Mason everything. I tell him about the men I'm interested in and vice versa, to an extent. We never ask about details. If anything, it's always felt like an overall interest assessment, like do we think this relationship could be serious? Neither one of us has ever really had a serious relationship. A part of me wants to tell him about August, but at the same time, I don't. I think that's because I don't know how I feel about August. But I do know how I should feel, which is nothing.

As we round the corner toward The Loop, I know precisely where he's taking me. Our favorite Mexican restaurant El Tapatio! This place is only our favorite because Mason is friends with the owner's son, who lets us order drinks even though we're underage. It's not like I'm a big drinker, but a good margarita always hits the spot.

Mason parallels on the street out front before we make our way in. The smell of fresh chips and the sound of salsa music immediately put me at ease. It's incredible how the environment alone can alter one's mood.

We take our seats in a private booth toward the back of the restaurant before Mason quickly places our order and then turns his attention to me.

"So are we going to talk about what's bothering you, or will you continue to sulk?"

My eyes bug out. "Pfft, I'm not sulking. Today just sucked the life out of me, but I'm already feeling better now that we're here."

His eyes bore into mine, and I know he's aware I'm avoiding talking about something. I tell him everything. He's known about every crush and all my guy friends, but this feels different for some reason. The waiter brings over our margaritas, coupled with chips and salsa. I take a big gulp of my margarita just as Mason stands up, swings around the booth, and pushes into my side. Now we're sitting next to each other instead of across. Usually, a gesture like this would make me feel giddy inside, but tonight it's uncomfortable, and that's unsettling.

Playfully, he nudges his shoulder into mine while putting his hands firmly on the table, almost like he's trying to deescalate the tension that I'm sure he feels rolling off me in waves. The last thing I want to do is make him feel like he's done something wrong, so I grab his hand and lace my fingers through his. Immediately, he loosens up, knowing I want him there. We both take another sip of our drinks before noticeably relaxing.

We've just started on our second round of drinks when Mason leans in and puts his forehead to mine in a move that takes my breath away. He knows I'm a sucker for those big blue eyes behind his dorky glasses that somehow make him hotter.

"When are you going to let me in, babe?"

My heart skips a beat.

"Why does that sound like a loaded question?"

Rather than answer with words, he takes my lips in what might be one of the most sensual kisses we've ever shared. His tongue explores the seam of my lips before coaxing them apart and slowly dipping inside to taste me. The saltiness of the margarita on his tongue draws me in as he deepens the kiss.

His hand slowly moves up my thigh to my hip bone, where he gently squeezes it before tracing slow, methodical circles on my hip with his thumb, making my stomach coil with desire. I put my hand on his chest, grabbing him by his shirt to pull his body closer to mine. He smiles against my mouth, clearly pleased by my eagerness. Then, breaking our kiss, he starts to trail kisses along my jaw and down my neck while deliciously running his fingers up my back, coaxing a little whimper out of me.

I love when he touches me. When he does, it's like only I exist, and he can't get enough of me. I'm a sucker for him like this, and he knows it. I'm too drunk off the way he's trailing his tongue up my neck to my lobe, where he gently nips me before returning to my mouth, to realize my hand has made its way down his well-defined chest to his belt. Gently, I tug at it while simultaneously dipping my fingers inside to feel his warm, taut abs against my fingertips. He moans into my mouth before breathlessly panting, "Babe."

Right then, the waiter places our plates on the table. I'm

trying to play it cool like we weren't just caught getting incredibly handsy in the middle of a restaurant.

Clearing my throat, I mumble, "Perfect timing."

He sits up and discreetly rearranges himself before stifling a smirk.

"You would think that was perfect timing, wouldn't you?"

I pause before taking a bite of my food to look at him and get a read on his expression. We've never done more than grope each other in private, so I'm confused about where this angry energy is coming from.

"What is that supposed to mean?" I was trying to make light of being caught making out in front of a waiter. But he seems to be perturbed by my comment.

"Never mind, just leave it. I shouldn't have said anything."

Suddenly, I'm feeling uncomfortable, and that's not a feeling I'm used to having around Mason. He gets up and moves back to the other side of the booth, further solidifying my concern that he's upset.

"Look, I'm sorry I've been terrible company. That was not my intent when I texted you this morning. The rest of my day after that was just very perplexing and unsettling. I haven't wanted to discuss it because I'm still digesting it myself."

I look down at my plate, feeling unease settle over me and hoping Mason will just let this go.

"Does it have anything to do with the guy who was staring at you when I picked you up? He had an unmistakable jealous rage in his eyes when you got into my car this afternoon."

My eyes feel like they've now bulged out of my head. Of course he saw the glare August dished out. He wasn't being exactly subtle about hiding his obvious contempt for me. *Wait a minute, did he say jealous?* I drop my fork and put my head in my hands, unsure what to say.

"Gianna, you know I've always been there for you. I'm sorry I've made you uncomfortable, but what I can't wrap my head around is: why now? What's different about today that you feel like you can't talk to me? We've known each other for nine years now, and this vibe from you is new."

I let his words marinate because they genuinely do resonate. As much as I don't want this to be something more than it is, I simply can't avoid it. My connection with Mason has suddenly shifted. He knew it when he kissed me, and while he liked it, he knew I was different. I'm not one for PDA, but I egged him on because it felt good, and I wanted to forget this afternoon.

"Mason—" I start, but he cuts me off.

"Gianna, we've never talked about this, and honestly, I never felt the need until now. But something has changed, and I need to say this."

I feel sick with anxiety over what he might have to say.

"I was content with never putting a title on us because we were young, and honestly, I thought our relationship would be stronger not having a title. We have always been free to go to parties, flirt, date, and see other people, which worked for us. For some reason, we were still us, but you're different today, and I need you to know that I want you. I want you as more than just my friend Gigi."

I swear I've been holding my breath since he started talking, and he must have noticed because he smiles at me. I've wanted to hear those words for so long, and he knows it. But why now? Why today of all days when he's had the past nine years?

"You can stop holding your breath now. I don't want you to say anything. I just want you to think about what I said."

He takes a drink of his margarita with a shrug as if what he said was no big deal. That's what he wants me to think, but I know in my heart it wasn't easy for him to say that. The problem is, I'm not sure where to go from here. If he had said those words yesterday before I met August, the answer would have been clear. But now there's something I can't quite put my finger on, making me hesitate about what I once hoped would be my future.

After taking care of the check, we head out. I don't want the drive back to my car to be awkward, and honestly, it shouldn't be.

It's not even that I don't want what he's asking, so I'll just be truthful.

"Mace, about what you said earlier. I don't want you to think I have no interest in taking things further with you. If I'm honest, it's just somewhat intimidating. You know I've never had a long-term relationship. In fact, you are my long-term relationship. I don't want to ruin what we have. You're my best friend."

Yes, I just used the argument that's always been his against him. I know I'm being a total hypocrite, but his timing is off. I almost feel like he's saying all this just because of how August looked at me. Some guy I don't even know gives me a look of what he considers jealousy, and suddenly, he wants to put a title on our relationship. I've always wanted Mason's affection but not like this. I want to be his first choice because there's no doubt in his mind that I'm worth it, not because he felt like his hand was forced.

Reaching out, I take hold of his hand resting on the center console, and we drive back to my car in silence. Once we pull into Reds and park, he picks up our joined hands and kisses the back of mine before saying, "I'll wait."

We're parked next to my car, and I need to get out, but getting out feels heavy. Releasing his hand, I lean over and kiss his lips softly before I cup his cheek and say, "You're perfect."

He is perfect, always has been. But the utter look of longing in his eyes right now makes my heart scream. His breaths have become erratic, like my actions are bringing him physical pain. I want to tell him *yes*, that I'll try, but I just can't. Something is off. I can feel it. Leaning in, I rest my hand on his chest, over his heart, before placing one last kiss on his mouth.

The way he reciprocates my kiss tells me he's holding back because he's on the verge of breaking. I've never seen him this emotional. With a heavy heart, I pull away and say, "Good night, Mace," before climbing out of the car.

All I can think about on my drive home is how Mason reacted to me tonight and how everything felt so different. I've waited years for him to want me this way because it's how I've wanted him for so long. He truly wanted me to say yes to being more than just friends. It felt like I was breaking his heart tonight by not giving him an answer, and that's hard to wrap my brain around because that has not been our dynamic.

Over the years, I worked hard to bury my feelings for Mason so that I could keep his friendship. While our friendship is different from most, it has worked for us. Maybe subconsciously, I've always held out hope that he'd wake up and want more, but now that it's being offered, I can't help but feel that taking it keeps me from moving forward.

I need to go home, sleep, and put this bizarre day behind me. Tomorrow will be a new day. Tomorrow will bring me clarity. Or at least I hope so.

## SIX
## *August*

Gianna bolted after class yesterday. Not sure how I didn't see that coming, but I was determined to run into her one more time. So I followed her as quickly as possible, only for Ryan to intercept me at the last second, who rambled on about his new role in the Art Department and how we could collaborate. *Couldn't he tell I was in a hurry?*

As I walked out the front doors, I heard Gianna being catcalled, which ignited a fire in my veins. Before I even had time to process my own reaction to that feeling, she was happily getting into the offender's blacked-out Audi. It dawned on me then that she must have hurried to meet him. He must be her boyfriend. Sitting in class today, obsessing over every detail of the back of her profile, it never occurred to me that she might have a boyfriend. *Fuck.*

I have no right to be upset that she has a boyfriend. We've said maybe ten words to each other, and I do kind of have a girlfriend, which, for the first time in years, repulses me.

Carson and I have been together for so long, I never gave much thought to not having her in my life, but now it's like I can't get rid of her soon enough. I've decided to give her the space she requested and then some. She wanted to take a break. Well, now I want a clean break. The guys might have been right after all. All I needed was the right girl to make me leave. I don't even know this girl, but she's already under my skin in ways I never thought possible.

Gianna having a boyfriend only means I'll have to work harder to make her mine. I've never been one to shy away from a challenge, and something tells me she's worth the extra effort. I've known her for less than twenty-four hours, and I can already tell she has more self-respect, grit, and fortitude than most of the people I know combined. Most of the women I meet want nothing more than to catch my eye and keep it, while Gianna wants nothing to do with me, and that type of moxie is badass.

For this reason, I woke up extra early this morning, with a renewed sense of purpose. I may not want to work at Reds, but if Gianna's there, then that's where I'll be.

I put a little extra effort into my appearance today since I have to up my game. Yesterday I went in extremely disheveled, even by my standards. I can admit it was not my best moment, but I thought I'd be in training with a bunch of old hags. Today we were told to dress casually since we'll be touring the production plant.

Personally, I'm not a fan of jeans. I have never felt they do anything but make me look drab. So today I'm dressing in all Ralph Lauren: blue chinos, blue-and-white-striped polo with a heather-green quarter zip, tan belt, and tan boat shoes. My hair is styled but tousled. I fucking look good, and I know it. She's not going to be able to resist me.

Looking good isn't going to be enough to win my girl, though. I'll be getting to work early with the coffee and scone she likes from Grinders. She'll be eating out of my hand by the end of the day. They always do when I lay on the charm. I get what I want, and I want Gianna. She may not see it yet, but I think she wants me as much as I want her.

\*\*\*

Pulling into the parking lot, I notice her burgundy old woman's car is already here. It occurs to me that maybe she never came back for it last night, and that thought has me perturbed. However, before I get any more worked up, I notice the conference room lights are on from where I'm sitting in the parking lot. That's when I remember her saying she's only hired on for the summer, and if I have her pegged correctly, she'll be nothing if not prompt, hoping that it leads to a full-time position. Again, something to admire about her: she goes after what she wants.

Before I reach the conference room door, I hear giggling coming from the room. I don't hear any other voices, so she must be on her phone, which is perfect. I want to catch her when her guard is down and she isn't expecting me. That's how you get a genuine read on someone. When you surprise them, you get their raw emotion, not one they've practiced. I need to see the real her and not what she wants me to see.

Once I round the corner, I notice she's looking down at her phone, sitting in the same spot she did yesterday. She's so beautiful that I take a minute to observe her while she thinks no one is watching. Sitting cross-legged in her chair, laid back and comfortable, she has no idea I'm here. Her hair is pulled over one shoulder. She's wearing dark blue skinny jeans, a long-sleeved black T-shirt, and black biker boots. She looks fucking edible, and my cock notices. I quickly decide to enter the room before my thoughts get too carried away and I can't.

Before she has time to notice, I'm sliding into the chair beside hers, placing a scone and coffee in front of her. She glances up from her phone, eyes wide with shock.

"August." She startles. "Good morning. You're here early."

She nervously fidgets in her seat, tucking her hair behind her ear and putting her phone down. Good, I like that I make her nervous. That means I affect her.

"Yes, well, yesterday was rather out of character for me," I lie as I gesture toward the coffee and scone. "I brought you coffee and a scone. I noticed you didn't touch anything offered here yesterday, and I wanted to rectify the situation."

Her cheeks immediately start to flush as she flashes me a half-smile. "Thank you, that's incredibly thoughtful and not necessary, but truly, thank you."

I can tell she still feels uncomfortable with my proximity, which is strangely arousing. *Why does her discomfort please me?* Maybe because it's an honest response, not rehearsed. It's authentically her.

"Well, if you play your cards right, maybe I'll bring you coffee and scones every day."

Her eyes widen at my words, and knowing I've made her feel more than uncomfortable with my antics, I attempt to put her at ease.

"I'm joking, Gianna. I want to get to know you, is all."

Phyllis walks in carrying a box before I get the chance to say anything more. Gianna jumps out of her seat, takes it from her, and places it on the counter that runs the room's length. Of course the action makes me feel like a complete ass. I should have been the one to do that. I'm not a complete tool. I was raised with manners, but with Gianna around, I lose my ability to think clearly.

"Oh, thank you, dear. I have two more in my office. Do you mind helping me, seeing as you're here early?"

There's no way I'm letting either of them carry more boxes while I sit back and watch. I'm out of my seat before they can make another move.

"Phyllis, please let me. I'll be right back."

She looks at me like I've suddenly grown two heads, and maybe I have because the way I'm acting today is entirely contradictory to how I presented myself yesterday.

Once I've returned, I find Phyllis and Gianna unpacking the boxes and laying safety glasses, hairnets, and earplugs at our respective seats. Setting down the last box, I notice Gianna has started to eat her scone, which pleases me. I have this strong innate desire to take care of her and see that her needs are met.

"Is there anything else you need me to grab, Phyllis?"

She puts her hand to her chest while taking a moment to glance around the room.

"No, I think we got everything. Thanks for helping."

Gianna makes her way back to her seat. I swear, her jeans couldn't be any tighter. They hug her ass perfectly. Not wanting to get an erection in the middle of class, I take a breath, run my fingers through my hair, and head over to start the coffee for Phyllis. It's then I realize Gianna set today's PPE at the desk I sat at yesterday. That makes me stifle a laugh, to which Phyllis asks, "Is everything okay?"

I meet her concerned gaze with a smile.

"Why yes, Phyllis, everything is perfect."

I can tell she has no clue how to read me, and that doesn't bother me in the slightest.

The rest of the class starts to file in. I grab the PPE placed at my seat and make my way to the front of the class to join Gianna at her table. That earns me curious stares from the other trainees, Gianna included. As this isn't a big class and everyone can have their own table, I just made it awkward by sharing one. The problem is, I don't give a fuck.

Giving Gianna a half-smile, I take a sip of my coffee like I don't have a care in the world. No one is going to question my seat change. Gianna slowly lets out a breath and turns to face forward. Then, ever so slightly, she scoots her chair away, effectively putting more space between us.

That's when I lean in and whisper, "I promise I won't bite."

At this proximity, the electricity between us is unmistakable. Her spine straightens as she peers at me over her shoulder with a mix of lust and ire. I can tell she feels it.

Our moment is cut short as Phyllis is suddenly in front of the class, demonstrating how to wear the PPE properly. I'm left trying to figure out how I didn't even hear Phyllis's approach. This girl is a total mind fuck.

Maybe sitting next to her was a bad idea, considering how she seems to consume me. I literally shut down all other brain activity, including being aware of my surroundings. I need to get my shit together. The only redeeming nugget of knowledge I gained from this interaction was that Gianna has the same struggle. She was just as surprised by Phyllis as I was.

* * *

Touring the factory was uneventful. It's not my first time being here. I've been coming here off and on my entire life. The others were thoroughly impressed, and I noted the people who already seemed to know Gianna.

At one point, one of the forklift drivers all but ran her over to share a secret handshake with her, and it took everything I had not to have the guy fired on the spot. I followed her around like a lost puppy all day. It was utterly pathetic. However, the day wasn't a complete waste. I did learn something. Everyone she spoke with called her Gigi, like they had been lifelong friends.

I don't consider myself a jealous man, seeing as how I can have anything I want, but today, I found myself envious of every person she spoke with. I want to know her well enough to call her Gigi, I want her to be excited when she sees me, I want to have secret handshakes, I want everything, and at the moment, I'm reminded of how I have nothing.

Phyllis is wrapping up the tour and letting us know what we can expect upon returning from lunch. I'm on a mission to take my girl to lunch today. I didn't stare at her perfect jean-clad ass and mouthwatering toned legs accented with biker boots all day to not have my moment with her. Exiting the warehouse into the main office, everyone breaks off and goes their separate ways. I watch as Gianna makes her way to the front lobby, leading the group out, and I know I need to make my move.

"Gianna, wait up. I'll walk with you."

Once again, I've caught her off guard, and I can tell she's not thrilled that I called her out. She gives me a once-over and waits, holding the door open with her foot.

"I noticed you already know quite a few people here."

She smiles and nods in agreement. "Well, yeah, that will happen when you've worked somewhere for a few months."

"That's right. I forgot you mentioned working here part-time. Speaking of which, why were you only working part-time anyway?"

She's about to respond, but once we reach her car, we spot a bouquet of flowers on her hood with a note. That's when I remember she has a boyfriend.

Picking up the flowers, she plucks out the note and reads it. I can't help but strain my eyes to see if I can make it out. It says,

*"I'm sorry. I won't pressure you again."*

*What the hell does that mean? Are these from the boyfriend?*

She sighs, opens the car door, and tosses the flowers in the driver's seat.

"From your boyfriend?" I question.

She looks up at me and furrows her brow. "August, if you want to say something, you need to just say it."

My brows shoot up at her forwardness. I usually don't like being called out, but from her, I more than like it. Rocking back on my heels, I put my hands in my pockets and clear my throat to speak. The roles are now reversed, and she has caught me off guard.

I start, "Well—"

Suddenly, a motorcycle pulls into the parking lot, loud as hell, and Gianna breaks out into a massive smile before saying, "That's my ride."

*She can't be serious right now.*

"Gianna, you are not seriously thinking about getting on the back of that thing, are you?"

Cocking her head to the side, she looks at me like I'm crazy. "Well, yes, that's been the plan. Why did you think I was wearing biker boots?"

She goes to step around me as some hooligan pulls up on a Harley behind her car. I grab her wrist and pin her with a glare.

"Gianna, I don't want you getting on that bike."

The electricity running up my arm from touching her has me frozen. I'll fucking lose my mind if she gets on that bike. She glances up from where I've grabbed her wrist with a pensive look in her eyes before pulling out of my grip.

"August, you can't ask me that."

And just like that, she grabs a helmet from the biker boy, hikes her leg over, and gets on. Then, as if that wasn't enough of a blow to my ego, she wraps her arms around his waist, and they drive off.

I'm left staring at her car, dumbfounded, trying to figure out what just happened. I know I affect her. I saw it in her face when I grabbed her wrist. She knew I was upset, and I can tell that it bothered her, but she did it anyway. If she wants to cross me, that's fine. I'll show her exactly what happens when you play with fire.

## SEVEN
### *Gianna*

"Well, what do you think? Isn't it great? I can't believe I finally have a motorcycle. I've wanted one for so long," Bryce says as we pull into Spanky's Frozen Yogurt with the biggest smiles plastered across our faces.

Bryce picked me up for lunch today. He texted me last night before I went to bed and asked if I had riding boots. I didn't, but my friend Ashton had a pair. So this morning, I swung by her place on my way in and picked them up. She's dating one of the guys in the group, and we've become close over the years. I can't believe Bryce bought a bike. That seems so crazy to me. He's been one of my closest friends since the beginning of high school.

I joke that he forced me into our friendship. Bryce would go out of his way to mess with me, whether on the bus or in the hallways. I tried to ignore him for the longest time because I didn't want the attention. Let's be clear; he was never mean to me. If anything, he was overly affectionate, which was off-putting for me. I never wanted to be the center of attention. In fact, it was quite the opposite. I never had the nicest clothes, wasn't fashion-forward, and never really fit in. Heck, in middle school, I was bullied for being weird. So when high school hit and this guy two grades ahead of me started showering me with nonstop attention as if I were the hottest girl in school, my discomfort reached an all-time high. Bryce would come up behind me at my locker, pick me up, slam the locker closed, and run down the hallway with me over his shoulder. Every time, I wished the floor would swallow me whole right then, never to be seen again. Once I got over his antics, we became fast friends.

"I love it. Do you still have your truck? Or is this your new mode of transportation?"

"Of course I still have my truck, Gigi. You'll never believe it. I won thirty grand on a scratch-off ticket and used some of it to buy this baby."

I mean, that's different from what I would have done with thirty grand, but hey, he said only some of it was used for the motorcycle. That could mean he saved the rest.

"Bryce, I can't believe you won that much money. That's amazing! What are you going to do with the rest?"

He looks down and kicks a few pebbles around. "Well, I'm thinking about moving to Florida."

My heart clenches in my chest. He's one of the last people I want to lose right now. "Florida! What the heck is in Florida? Why do you want to leave Missouri? Never mind, don't answer that, but seriously, what's in Florida?" I'm completely shocked. I can't believe he's leaving.

"Well, actually, I'm not going alone. Aiden's coming with me. I'm going to use my remaining winnings to open a board shop." Shrugging, he puts his hands in his pockets like it's no big deal. Aiden going, however, is a double whammy straight to my heart. I guess I'll never get my chance with my secret crush.

"Board shop, like skateboards or surfboards? I don't want to assume skateboards because I never pegged you for a motorcycle guy, yet here you are riding one. Who knows, maybe you have secret surfer ambitions as well."

He throws his head back, laughing. "Well, that's not what I expected you to say, but yes, a skateboard shop." He shoulders me as we walk toward the counter to order our frozen yogurts.

"What were you expecting me to say?" I ask, genuinely curious.

"Honestly, I thought you'd care more about Aiden taking off with me than me leaving."

Wow, that comment stings. We've been friends for so long. The fact that he thinks I'd care more about Aiden makes me feel like a shitty friend. It's easy to like Bryce. He's not hard to look at, either. Your typical skater boy rocking Vans on his feet, Dickies over his tight ass, and the standard black hoodie you'd find at any Hot Topic store. With shaggy brown shoulder-length hair, striking brown eyes, and a lean muscular body, he was many girls' wet dream. For some reason, I've just never seen him like that. At the end of the day, he's the guy from that Vertical Horizon song "Everything You Want." That song is Bryce to a T. He was everything I should've wanted, but the feelings weren't there for me in the end.

"Bryce, me having a crush on Aiden has nothing to do with my feelings toward you, and apparently, my crush is all it will ever be. How can I be heartbroken over a guy I've only spoken to a handful of times? You, on the other hand, are one of my best friends. Just because you're leaving doesn't mean you get to skip out on that title."

We sit on a bench with our yogurts and silently eat for a moment.

"Any chance you'd tag along?"

Now it's my turn to throw my head back laughing. "Yeah, right. With what money? Even if I could afford to go, you know I wouldn't leave Elio."

I've grown increasingly protective of him over the years as my parents struggled with their drug addiction. I started working at age fifteen to buy things I wanted and needed. But for the past three years, I've spent my paychecks on back-to-school shopping, hot lunches, and whatever other necessities we needed. Initially, I'd help my parents make ends meet when they fell short, but I quickly stopped when I realized the funds weren't going toward anything but drugs. There's no way I'd leave my brother now, especially with everything we just went through.

"I knew you'd say that, but I had to ask. You'll come to visit once we get settled, right?"

"Of course I'll come to visit. If you're close enough to the beach, I'll be there so often you'll think I live there."

"Well, then I'll make sure it's beachfront," he says as we toss our trash before getting back on his bike to return to Reds.

* * *

I'm the last one back to class when I return to training. I wasn't late, but nobody likes walking into a room full of people staring at them. Everyone looks up as I enter, except for August. Walking back to my seat, I notice he still shares a table with me. What was once my table now seems to be our table.

He's casually sitting in his chair. It's angled toward mine. With one leg crossed over at the knee, you'd think he's relaxed, but the way his fingers fiercely drum on the table suggests otherwise. If I didn't know better, I'd think he's been sitting there staring at my chair, waiting for me, but I quickly dismiss that thought. We just met yesterday. While there's serious tension between us, I'm not naive enough to think he's sitting here obsessing over me.

I take my seat and blow out an exasperated breath before looking directly at him, trying to get a read on him. His expression doesn't change. It doesn't give away anything. I slowly face forward in my seat and attempt to ignore him and his antics.

The guy runs hot and cold, and I don't need any more drama, not to mention there's no way in hell I can afford to have any type of relationship with August. I honestly don't even want a professional relationship with him. I don't think my psyche can handle it. In fact, I know it can't. I'm barely managing the emotional overload Mason laid on me.

Phyllis starts the class back up, and August doesn't move. He continues glaring at me for what feels like forever. Waves of tension radiate off him as his eyes bore into the side of my head. *What the hell is his problem?*

"Unfortunately, we will have to cut today's training short. We planned to tour the tank farm with one of our chemists. However, there's been a spill. Instead, I will send you all home with some materials to study tonight. There will be a short test in the morning, followed by a Q&A of the material."

Phyllis dismisses us, and the class begins to file out. This time I plan to stay back, hoping that August takes off before me instead of following me as he has the past three dismissals. I mean, seriously, talk about a stalker. Clearly, it could be worse, but still, it's a little creepy.

Making my way to the back of the class, I act like I'm grabbing something while everyone else packs up and leaves. *Perfect.*

I casually glance down the hallway, ensuring the coast is clear before taking my leave. The executive hall is quiet, considering most everyone is still out to lunch. I make it halfway down the hall before being pulled into an office and shoved against the door with a hand over my mouth.

Once I get my bearings and my eyes adjust to the darkness of the office, I realize who my assailant is—August. Narrowing my eyes at him, I attempt to bite his hand. That only makes him smile. *Bastard.*

"Oh, so mi Tesoro likes it rough, does she?"

I'm now fuming. What the hell is he going on about, and why does he keep calling me that?

"I'm going to remove my hand from your mouth, and you're not going to scream. Do you understand?"

I nod while narrowing my eyes at him. He removes his hand from my mouth but keeps me pinned between him and the door. His actions should scare me. A man I don't know pinning me up against a wall in a dark office should send up a million red flags. But one thing I'm learning about myself is that with him, I like that he's arrogant, vain, and pompous. While none of those things are endearing traits, for me they scream confidence, something I've always struggled with. He doesn't mind pushing the limits on socially acceptable behavior because he goes after what he wants, and right now, that's me. The fact that he's giving me any attention makes me feel like maybe I could fit into his world if that's what I wanted.

"Earlier, you told me if I had something to say, just to say it, so here we are."

He's so close to my face that I can barely think straight, and as I take note of his stance, it's more sexual than aggressive. I may be pinned to the door, but his knee is between my thighs, and his hands are gripping my wrists on either side of my head. If I were a smarter girl, I'd fight him. Instead, he's left himself vulnerable in this position, showing me his hand, but whatever game he's playing has my heart beating out of my chest, and I couldn't make myself move even if I wanted to.

"What do you want, August? And what do you keep calling me?"

My voice comes out way too breathy for someone who should be annoyed, and he notices. He gives me the most sinister smile before whispering in my ear.

"For someone who likes playing games, you don't seem like you're trying very hard to win right now." He's right. I'm not because I'm enjoying his proximity way more than I should.

"That's because I'm not playing any games, August."

His breath is hot against my ear and sends tendrils of pleasure straight to my core. I can feel every ridge of his body pressed up against mine. I feel like I'm about to self-combust, but right before I catch on fire, he pulls away completely. As he turns to walk away, he says, "If you weren't playing games, you wouldn't have been so bold as to call me out this afternoon by your car and tell me to say what I mean."

Reaching the desk across the room, he leans against its front, crossing his feet at the ankles while his hands grip either side of it. I do my best to act casual as if our encounter didn't affect me as he desired, but he knows better. He got exactly what he wanted just now; he riled me up, and I fell for the bait, not even trying to push him off me.

"I want to know whose car you got into last night and what guy I need to kill for putting your life in danger on a motorcycle."

You have got to be shitting me.

"Are you serious right now? How is any of that your business?" My voice is way too squeaky, but I'm livid. "You have no right to ask me any of those questions."

"That's where you're wrong, sweetheart. I've just made it my business."

The nerve of this man.

"I want to take you out Friday night, and here's the thing. You're going to say yes because you don't have any other option."

"Are you threatening me?"

This can't be happening. There's a whole movement right now against this type of intimidation tactic. Standing up, he grabs his keys off the desk behind him. And that's when I realize whose office we're in. It's his dad's. Kill me now. Casually, he strolls over to me and grabs my chin between his thumb and forefinger.

"No, sweetheart, I don't make threats. I'm simply calling your bluff. Friday night after work."

And then he walks out.

\* \* \*

My head is a literal mess right now. It's Friday morning, and I guess I'm going out with August tonight after work. After our little encounter in his dad's office on Tuesday, he returned to his own desk for the remainder of the week. There were no more run-ins, no more random coffees. He treated me as if nothing ever happened.

In the meantime, I've been racking my brain. I've been trying to wrap my mind around his innuendos all week. *Does he really want to go on an actual date with me?* He did directly ask me about Bryce and Mason, but then he added that he was calling my bluff. What bluff that is precisely, is beyond me.

I'm so utterly confused and mad. This is the last thing I want, but a part of me is curious. I've never been pursued by a man, and while I wish it weren't August, that's only because of who he is—the CEO's son and the future face of the company. I need this job for financial security so I can support myself and get away from my parents. Getting involved with August is the absolute last thing I need, a risk I can't afford to take.

The problem is, the carefree woman I've always wanted to be would absolutely go after August. The man is delicious. His muscles are beyond toned, they're stacked, stretching his clothes in all the right places. The way his pants hug his ass should be a sin. Women aren't supposed to show too much cleavage or skin because it's distracting and inappropriate in the workplace. Well, his pants should be inappropriate. I mean, my God, the man is drool-worthy.

This is why I don't want to go out with him. I don't know that I am strong enough to resist him, and I know nothing good can come of this. We come from two very different worlds. Getting involved with him could impact both my mom and me. While my mom's overall welfare isn't something I'm overly concerned about, I do need her to keep her job and pay the bills a little bit longer, so carelessly risking her job security for an office fling isn't in the cards.

That hasn't stopped me from fantasizing about the possibility of being with August. What if we did start something and things worked out okay for a while but then ended badly? Would my mom lose her job in the wake of our horrible breakup? It's not just my well-being I have to consider, and that's a sorry state to be in at my age. I should be living it up, making mistake after mistake, but I don't have that luxury. Any other employee could probably risk an office romance with August, and if it ended terribly, so be it, they could go find another job. I, on the other hand, have no degree to just go land another job that pays this well. So tonight, I must resist. I need to make sure he hates our date and never looks my way again.

I've already tried to think of a way to get out of going, but from what little interaction we've shared, I don't think he'd be so easily shelved. If it's not tonight, it will be another time.

Now I need to figure out what to wear. While I'm not aiming to impress him, I also don't want to feel like someone who isn't worthy of being on his arm. No one wants to feel like they don't fit in, especially me, someone who has worked hard to rise above her circumstances.

The man wears nothing but designer clothes, and I'm afraid I'll stick out like a sore thumb next to him. My entire outfit will probably cost as much as his pants. I seriously don't understand what his game is. He can have any girl, so why me?

Eventually, I decide on white skinny jeans, a yellow long-sleeved boho top, and black espadrille wedges. I'm wearing my hair down in loose curls, and I've applied light makeup. Hopefully, he's not planning on taking me somewhere formal.

Making my way into the class, I'm a ball of nerves. I barely slept, and now I'm self-conscious about what he'll think of my outfit. Maybe he's forgotten all about our run-in, and there will be no date. I mean, he's ignored me ever since he asked me out.

Once I enter the conference room, I know that's just wishful thinking as a coffee and a note are sitting at my desk. I put my purse down and take my seat. I'm the first to class, so I quickly read the note.

*I won't be in class today. My dad's in the office. I will be with him all day. I'm looking forward to our date. A*

I have mixed emotions about the note. On the one hand, the coffee and note are super sweet. After all, what girl doesn't like being wooed? But what's unsettling is that he referenced tonight as a date, and nothing good can come from that.

\* \* \*

It's lunchtime, and I feel like the morning has flown by. As I'm making my way out to my car, I notice Mason leaning against my driver's side door, typing away on his phone. My heart immediately sinks. I never said anything to him after he sent me the flowers, and we haven't spoken since his confession. It's not that I haven't wanted to talk to him. I'm just not sure how I feel. I've worked hard to move past my desire to be more than just friends with Mason, and his revelation brings many of my insecurities to the forefront. When you want someone for so long and they don't reciprocate the feeling, it's hard not to feel flawed, and I'm trying to be the best version of me that I can be.

Once I'm at my car, he notices me and puts his phone away. Then, running his hand through his beautiful blond hair, he meekly says, "Hey, babe."

Immediately, I throw my arms around his shoulders and hug him. He hugs me back, and we stay that way for a long minute before he whispers in the crux of my neck, "I'm sorry."

I pull away and look up at him.

"What are you sorry for, Mason? You have nothing to be sorry for."

He takes a deep breath and throws both hands into his hair.

"I have everything to be sorry for! I don't want to lose you. I don't want to lose us, and by confessing my feelings for you the other night, that's exactly what I've done. I've lost you."

My heart is hammering so hard in my chest. I hate that he feels this way, that I've made him feel this way. Grabbing his hand, I pull him into me and lay my head on his chest as I wrap my arms around his waist. Then, for a few short seconds, we just breathe. With my ear placed above his heart, I listen to it race before it finally calms down.

"You didn't lose me, and you won't lose me. I'm not going anywhere."

He takes my head into his hands and kisses my lips ever so gently before putting his forehead to mine and whispering softly, "I think I love you."

Before I can respond, someone is clearing their throat behind us.

"I'm not sure what you think you're doing, but you need to get your hands off my girl."

Oh my God, this can't be happening right now. Mason steps in front of me. "Excuse me? What do you mean, your girl? I'm pretty sure if she was anyone's girl, I'd know about it."

The two are evenly matched in the physique department, so I couldn't say that August would completely annihilate Mason, but I also don't want to see this come to blows. We are in the parking lot at work, for crying out loud.

I step between them, trying to deescalate the situation.

"August, you can't be serious right now. We haven't even been on a date."

He's quick to add, "Yet. We haven't been on a date yet, but I'm pretty sure the plan was to remedy that tonight, and seeing as how you already said yes, that makes you mine."

If my eyes could spit fire, August would be a pile of ashes.

"Is this guy for real, Gianna? You're going on a date with him tonight?"

When I turn to face Mason, his eyes immediately catch mine, and I know he can see my shame and regret. He knows it's true. Immediately, he turns and walks off toward his car. I start to go after him, but August grabs my wrist. As I try to pull away, he says, "Don't make me angrier than I already am."

*Is he fucking serious? He's mad?* I'm about to lose my damn mind.

"You're mad? Do you have any idea what you've just done? I hate you!"

He still doesn't release my arm.

"Right now, I don't care if you hate me as long as his lips aren't on yours."

Then he releases me and turns to walk back into the building. It's too late to run after Mason. He's already pulled out and left. After opening the door to my car, I take a seat. Looking up, I realize my car is parked directly in front of the executive offices. August must have seen our entire exchange. *Damn it.*

## EIGHT

## *August*

I'm fucking seething as I sit in my dad's office, waiting for him to get off a call across the hall, when, what do I look up and see? Gianna, standing outside the windows in the parking lot, hugging the guy from Monday night. *Is she fucking kidding me right now?* We have a date tonight! I never made her answer my questions about who the men I saw her with this week were, but that's because it didn't matter. She's going to be mine.

When I noticed how low the prick had his hands on her back, I was out of my seat and storming to the parking lot. I wasn't going to let whatever the fuck was going on outside play out. By the time I made it outside, he was kissing her. It took all my self-control not to break his nose right there. The only reason it didn't happen was that we were at Reds.

I might be a pigheaded asshole at times, but I'm not going to bring that kind of attention to Reds, not to mention, my dad would be furious.

Whoever this dick is, Gianna clearly has feelings for him. I could see it in how they looked at each other, which made me want to rage. She was going to run after him until I stopped her.

I disagree that this is my fault. She's the one who decided to have a full-on PDA moment in the parking lot for all to see. I'd already made it abundantly clear that she had no option but to go on a date with me tonight. Why she thought it was okay to let another man touch her is beyond me. She's mine. She just doesn't know it yet.

If she thought telling me she hated me would cancel the date, that was wishful thinking. I told her I was calling her bluff. Gianna had a week to cancel, and she didn't. If she genuinely didn't want this date, she would have found a way out.

\* \* \*

It's 4:00 p.m., and I'm waiting in the parking lot by Gianna's car. I'm trying to calm my nerves from earlier. I know things will be less heavy once we can sit down and have a drink. I'm taking her to this little Italian bistro by my place. The ambiance is mellow, it's never crowded, and it's the perfect place to unwind.

Scrolling through emails, my heart rate spikes again when I get a text.

> Carson: Hey, babe, you haven't been texting me. I'll be home on the 20th. See you soon, miss you.

Finally, she noticed I was giving her the space she requested. It only took her a week to care that I hadn't responded to her last text. Carson is a lot of things, but stupid isn't one of them. I hate when she tries to play that card. She's up to something or someone, but now that I'm not sending her a weekly text, she decides to play the girlfriend card. *Miss you*. We haven't said that to each other in months—hell, maybe even years.

Just as I'm starting to get annoyed again, I catch sight of a yellow shirt and look up to see my girl walking my way.

Schooling my expression, I keep it neutral as I check her out from head to toe. I was so caught up in my fury earlier that I didn't take the time to admire her flirty outfit. She looks fantastic, apart from that scowl she's wearing.

Once she makes it to the car, she says one word, "Ready?"

I guess she hasn't realized that I like it when she's feisty.

"I'm always ready for you."

Stepping off the car door and into her, I place my hand on her lower back to guide her toward my car. She instantly pulls away from my touch.

"Stop touching me all the time."

I knew she was headstrong, but the fact that she's not even politely allowing me to extend a common courtesy without a fight makes me chuckle.

"I can't make any promises. My car is the black BMW i8 over there."

I really can't help but touch her. Her body is like a magnet. I'm drawn to her, and I can't help myself when she's close.

When we get to my car, I open her door before walking around to my side. She doesn't even acknowledge my politeness, and I love it. I have her sprung tight, and that's exactly how I want her.

After all the silence I can handle, I ask, "Do you want to tell me about it?"

She shoots me a dirty look that has fuck off stamped all over it, but she surprises me and responds, "He's not my boyfriend if that's what you're thinking."

Not wanting to interrupt her moment of sharing, I stay silent. However, I'm glad to know he isn't her boyfriend.

"He's been one of my closest friends for over nine years, and you show up for all of five seconds and ruin everything."

Rubbing my hand along my chin, I swipe my tongue over my lower lip, all but dying to respond but holding back.

Finally, she fixes her focus on me and says, "What, suddenly you have nothing to say?"

"Sweetheart, I think you ripped his heart out long before I showed up."

Her eyes widen, and she punches my arm. "You're a dick. I did not. You have no idea what you're talking about."

"First of all, there's no way I could ruin nine years with one sentence, and you're angry because you know I'm right. Secondly, if you want me to keep my hands to myself, you need to follow your own rules."

Her cheeks immediately flush, and I can't help but find it adorable.

Pulling into Lombardo's, I park in the back of the lot in case I don't drive home. If she notices my strange choice of parking spot, she doesn't say anything. Once I'm out of the car, I go around to open her side. But before I can get there, she's already climbing out.

"I can open my own door, you know."

Her tone is bitter, and she's still upset about our earlier altercation. What makes me mad is that she's on a date with me thinking about another guy.

"I know you can open your own door. But that doesn't change the fact that I wanted to do it for you."

She rolls her eyes as I gesture toward the restaurant for her to lead the way. Gianna does so without hesitation, for which I'm grateful. Walking inside, Mara, the hostess who happens to be the owner's niece, greets me. I come here often enough that I know everyone.

"Good evening, August. Would you like your usual table?"

"Yes, Mara, that would be perfect. Thank you."

We follow Mara to the back of the restaurant, where a corner booth awaits. It's my favorite because it allows me to take in the entirety of the space and people-watch. While we walk back, I can't help but notice Gianna's perfectly round ass on display in her white skinny jeans. Her long dark-blond hair hangs halfway down her back in soft curls that I ache to run my fingers through and see if it feels as silky as it looks. She is by far one of the sexiest women I've ever laid eyes on.

We make it to the booth where Gianna slides in, making sure to sit specifically on one side and not toward the middle, so I take the other side.

"Should I have Carlo bring you your usual Bordeaux?"

"Yes, Mara, that would be perfect. Thank you."

Mara walks away, and I turn my attention to Gianna, who's

looking around the restaurant in awe. This might be a small Italian restaurant, but it's not your typical run-of-the-mill spot.

The inside is rustic chic. Wooden beams run the length of the ceiling, with Edison bulb chandeliers hanging overhead. The walls are soft black velvet accented with mirrored, circular gas-flame pendant lights that give the place a cozy, speakeasy vibe. A brick wall lined with metal wine racks takes up the entire back of the restaurant. Every time I come here, the day's stress instantly fades away. Tonight is no exception. I decide to break the silence and risk starting a conversation.

"Do you like it?"

I've startled her, and as she brings her gaze to meet mine for a moment, I think she has forgotten that she's mad at me. But then she opens that smart mouth.

"Did you bring me to an Italian restaurant because of my name?"

I purse my lips as the question catches me off guard. But then I realize she would think that, especially after the use of my nickname for her.

"Actually, I hadn't thought about that until just now. This place happens to be one of my favorite spots. I live right up the street, so it's very convenient."

She nods, seemingly appeased by that response, when Carlo appears at the table with our wine.

"Good evening, August. Glad to see you here tonight with such a beautiful Tesoro. It's about time."

Shit, what were the chances of him using the same Italian term of endearment that I used? Now my fun with it has been ruined. I start, "We—" but I'm cut off.

"Carlo, can I ask you what that word means?"

"Si, mi amore, it means treasure."

Her eyes land on mine in question, but I need to send Carlo away.

"Good to see you too, Carlo, and yes, Gianna is exquisite."

He sets down our glasses and proceeds to pour us both a glass of wine.

"Can I bring you any appetizers?"

When I look at Gianna, I find she's watching me as if this entire exchange entertains her. I quirk a smile and place our order.

"Yes, please bring some bruschetta and prosciutto with mozzarella."

Carlo sets the bottle down and bows before walking away. I pick up my glass and take a long sip. I know wine is meant to be savored, but fuck it. Gianna follows my lead, picks up her glass, and takes a drink before gingerly placing the glass back down. If I didn't know better, I'd think she was nervous.

"Do you not like the wine?"

She furrows her brow. "No, it's fine. I just need to make sure I don't drink too much, seeing as how I have to drive home."

I hadn't even thought about that, and I certainly don't want her to worry about driving.

"I can get you an Uber home should you need one. It's not a problem."

She spins the stem of her glass ever so slowly.

"It seems somewhat presumptuous of you to think I'm the kind of girl who takes an Uber home on a first date."

"I'm sorry. I got the impression you ate men's hearts for lunch. I figured a few glasses of wine was child's play."

If she wasn't riled up before, she is now.

"I didn't realize you brought me to dinner to discuss other men. While I don't owe you any explanation, if you must know, both men were just friends."

"You say just friends as if that's supposed to put me at ease. Tell me, Gianna, do you kiss all your friends?"

She leans back in her seat, takes a drink of her wine, and glares at me. That's fine. I can play her game. A few minutes pass, each of us staring at the other until I finally decide I've had enough.

Moistening my lips, I finish my glass, stand up, and slide into her side of our corner booth. She slowly moves toward the center to escape my invading presence.

"What are you doing?"

"Sitting next to my date. What does it look like?"

She clears her throat before taking another sip of wine.

"Exactly what type of date do you think this is, August?"

I can tell I've just made her uncomfortable, but if my instincts are right, my presence isn't as unbearable as she's letting on. My girl gets feisty when she's mad, and right now, she's being too genial for her words to hold any real offense. So I shrug and move close enough that my thigh bumps hers. "The kind where I sit next to my date."

I watch as she rolls her lips and then takes another sip of wine. I'd be lying if I said I didn't want to see us go back to my place, but I also know she's not that type of girl, regardless of the men in her life. I've laid down enough hints about my intent, she's had more than enough chances to reciprocate or flirt back, and she's rejected me at every turn. If she were that type of girl, she would have been in my bed Monday night.

"Can I ask you something personal?"

She raises a brow at my question.

"Does everyone call you Gianna?"

A smile crosses her face, and she visibly relaxes. I can't help but laugh.

"Did you think I was going to ask you something scandalous?"

"Yes, actually. I expected you to ask me something ridiculously personal and make me uncomfortable on purpose. But, to answer your question, no. Most of my friends call me Gigi."

I make her uncomfortable. Good.

"I'd like to say that I'm sorry for making you uncomfortable, but I'm not. It's quite the opposite. I'm inexplicably drawn to you, and I've found that the only way to break down your walls and see the real you is to make you uncomfortable."

Her breathing has slightly picked up, and I can see that the rise and fall of her chest is more pronounced. She quickly looks away before reaching for her wine and finishing it.

"August, look, I'm not sure what your expectation of tonight was, but there's no good outcome with the direction you're going. I can never be your treasure."

Picking up her purse, she starts to move as if to make her way out of the booth. There's no way I'm letting her walk out on our date. I grab her thigh hard before she can escape. She gasps, and her eyes widen in surprise as I pull her toward me.

Leaning in close, my mouth is only a hairsbreadth away from her ear when I say, "Baby, there's no good outcome of you leaving this booth."

Her skin breaks out in goose bumps as I slowly pull my face away from hers. This woman undoes me, and right now, I know I have the same effect on her. She's biting her lip, no doubt to keep that smart mouth in check, and her thigh tenses up under my touch. I bring my thumb to her plump bottom lip to release it from her teeth. If I have to watch her bite her lip all night, I'll fucking lose it. Women pay good money for lips like hers, and all I want to do is nip, lick, and suck on them until she's begging me for more.

"You better not bite that lip unless you want me to punish that mouth."

She gasps, and I don't miss the flash of desire that crosses her expression as she watches my mouth. She wants me to make good on that promise, and I will. However, when I kiss her for the first time, it won't be in this booth in the middle of a restaurant.

My hand doesn't come off her thigh for the remainder of our dinner, which we have in silence. The air between us is pulsating with sexual tension. I know deep down it doesn't bother her that my hand is on her thigh. What bothers her is that I haven't done anything more than rub lazy circles on it with my thumb. I've felt her subtly rub her thighs together, trying to relieve the ache building at her center.

Touching her is like getting a taste of the sweetest drug. It's euphoric, erotic, and barely sates the carnal desires she sparks inside of me. I tried to avoid her lustful gaze as we finished our meal. I already know I won't be sleeping with her tonight, and I don't need any more enticement to push her for more and make her uncomfortable. It's taking all my self-control not to cross the line with her now.

Finishing my glass of wine, I remove my hand from her thigh to stand. The loss of contact is unbearable, and I can see that it has the same effect on her as she looks over at me with a mixture of loss and need in her eyes. I quickly hold my hand out for her to take so we can leave. As much as I don't want this date to end, we can't stay in this booth all night.

When she takes my hand, I place a kiss on hers before I help her out. As we leave the restaurant, my hand makes its way to her lower back, but this time she doesn't ask me to remove it. It seems my touch isn't as unbearable to her now as it was earlier tonight. The walk to my car is cloaked in more silence. The heat radiating from where my palm touches her back at the base of her ass all but brings me to my knees with desire. I want more. I need more. I must have her.

When we reach her side of the car, I know I should do the gentlemanly thing and open her door to let her in, but I can't resist the pull I feel toward her. If I wasn't sure she felt it too, I wouldn't make my next move. Rather than play it safe, I pin her between myself and the car, leaving no mistake of my intent. Her lips part with a gasp, and as I lean into her deliciously soft curves, I run my nose up the side of her neck before she starts to protest.

"August, don't—"

Pressing my finger to her lips, I shush her before she can tell me to stop. A part of her wants me. Of that, I'm sure. She doesn't strike me as a woman who would cower to my advances. Gianna would push me away if she was genuinely not interested.

Pulling her hair over her shoulder, I whisper into her ear, "Don't tell me to stop when we both know that's not what you want."

I let my lips lightly graze her ear before I kiss the soft spot at the base. Her body shudders against mine. She smells like coconuts and summertime, and I'm hooked. I start kissing my way along her jaw until I reach her mouth, where I pause briefly to find her eyes, pleading for consent with my own. When she drops her gaze to my mouth, I know I have it. Taking her lips in mine is like getting a taste of the sweetest drug. You know there's no way one hit will ever be enough.

Her lips are lush and filled with sin, but it's not enough. Coaxing them apart with my tongue, I deepen the kiss, and my tastebuds are immediately overwhelmed with the fruity notes of the wine we've been drinking all night. My hand goes into her thick hair, and it's just as silky as I imagined it would be. I wrap it around my fist and lightly tug her head back to give me better access to her mouth. The faintest whimper escapes her throat, and I swallow it down with my own groan as I press my growing erection into her stomach. My knee is pinned between her thighs, and she ever so slightly rocks her hips against me, seeking relief for her swollen clit. The thought of her pussy hot and wet for me makes me crazy. Right now, this woman wants me, and I can't help but feast on it. I want everything she'll give me.

Slowly, her hands make their way to my waist, where she puts her fingers under the hem of my sweater, seeking skin but finding none. For once, I wish I weren't such a preppy bastard, wearing two shirts. What I wouldn't give to have her soft hands trailing up my bare skin right now.

I'm so incredibly turned on, a bead of pre-cum leaks out of my dick. Fuck, it's like I'm back in high school, trying to get to second base for the first time. I grab her ass hard with my free hand, and she moans into my mouth with appreciation. She's now full-on grinding herself on my leg. I can feel her heat through her jeans, and it's making my cock ache for release.

Breaking our kiss, I bring my lips to her neck and suck hard. Her head rolls back, and her eyes flutter shut as she continues to grind onto my thigh, lost in ecstasy. Placing both hands on her hips, I bring her pussy down hard on my leg. No more being shy, no more hiding. I don't want there to be any mistake about who's making her feel good right now. Her beautiful green eyes meet mine, and I say, "I want that pretty pussy to come on my leg, baby."

Bringing my lips back to her mouth, I bite her plump bottom lip enough to taste the sweet tang of her blood before sucking it into my mouth. Our teeth clash as her kiss gets desperate. We can't get close enough.

Tugging on my undershirt, her hands finally find my bare skin, and she slowly rakes her nails up my back until she reaches my shoulders, where she digs in, and that's when I know she's about to come. I keep one hand on her hip to keep the pace and slowly move my other hand up under her shirt. Her skin is so soft, so warm; fuck, I could come just thinking about it. I gently trail my fingers up her stomach before cupping her breast through her silky bra. I pinch her nipple hard, and it sets her off. Watching her come on my leg is the sexiest thing I've ever seen. Her face is flushed, the hairs framing it are damp from exertion, and her full lips are parted as she pulls air into her lungs.

When she moans out her release, I bring my mouth back to hers, unable to resist the way her sexy moans vibrate through to my soul, bringing me to life. She slows her pace on my leg before reluctantly pulling out of our kiss. Her hands are still on my back under my shirt, but she brings them down to rest on my hips as she lays her head on my chest. We're both trying to calm our erratic breathing as we come out of the throes of ecstasy. Pulling her head away from my chest, she peers up at me, and for a moment, I see contentment. I place a light kiss on her lips.

"You are so incredibly beautiful."

Her eyes search mine as if looking for something before she pulls out of my embrace. I'm not ready to let her go, so I pull her back.

"Come home with me." She puts her hand on my chest to push me back, but I don't budge.

"August, we don't even know each other. I'm not coming home with you tonight."

This time I let her push me back. I stand there, chest heaving from the arousal still pumping through my system, waiting for her to meet my eyes.

"Baby, I think we're more than getting to know each other. The evidence of that is still on my leg."

She blows out a frustrated breath before turning to open her door. Once she's in, I close it and put my hands on the side of the roof to collect myself. If I push too hard, she'll pull away, but I know she feels the same magnetism that I do.

My soul is literally calling to hers. I've never felt this connection with someone in my life, and I'll be damned if I let it slip away.

I get in the car to drive her back to Reds and catch a glimpse of her expression. She looks irritated and hurt, so I grab her hand and kiss her fingertips.

"I'm sorry if asking you to come back to my place sounded presumptuous. I don't want to let you go."

She doesn't respond. Instead, she rolls her lips and faces forward as an unspoken *take me home*.

The ride to Reds is drenched in silence, but all hope is not lost. I never let her hand go after I kissed it earlier, and our fingers remained intertwined the entire drive back. She hasn't pulled away from my touch, and that's how I know part of her wants me. She's fighting it, but I can be patient for now.

Once we get to her car, I release her hand and walk around to open her door. When she gets out, she smirks.

"Really? You're going to keep opening my doors?"

That makes me chuckle. "Yeah, I guess I am. Maybe I like doing things for you." I pull her into me and drape my hands around her waist. "You said you weren't coming over tonight, but what about tomorrow?"

She laughs. "August, you're insatiable." I lower my hands to her ass and grab an ample amount of cheek in each hand before gently squeezing while I nuzzle my nose into the crook of her neck and place a light kiss there.

"That's not true. I just met this woman who walked into my life and consumed every ounce of my being since I laid eyes on her. Now she wants to leave, and when she does, she's taking a piece of me with her. A piece I didn't know she owned."

She sucks in a breath, and I pull my face away from her neck to look into her eyes and see it. She shares the same sentiment. Leaning in, I take her lips in mine before slowly sliding my tongue in to meet hers. Her body molds into me as we share an earth-shattering, passion-filled, binding kiss that I know she can't deny. I am completely enamored by this woman. Her hands make their way into my hair, and I swear every nerve ending in my body lights on fire. Everywhere she touches me sends a delicious trail of heat straight to my groin, and I know I need to pull away before my cock gets carried away again.

"Meet me tomorrow?" It's a desperate plea that leaves my lips.

She drops her hands. "I can't."

Putting some space between us, I lean back against my car with my arms crossed over my chest. Looking back at her, her mask slips back into place. She's shutting me out.

"You can't, or you won't?"

She fidgets with her purse before opening her car door and tossing it in. I'll lose my mind if she gets in that car without responding. That's when she turns around and runs her fingers through her hair. "I can't."

I'm just about to press her for more when she says, "Give me your phone."

I reach into my pocket and hand it over, then watch as she programs her number.

She hands it back. "Please don't ask me to explain."

Without another word, I take my phone back and get into my car. I basically just told her I wanted her, and she turned me down. The thing is, I know she wants me, so why is she saying no?

I'm not going to lie. I've never been rejected. And by a girl like her, nonetheless. It's a blow to my ego. I'm sure I made confessions to her tonight that would rival any fictional man out there, and she still shut me down. Fuck! Why did I say any of that? This isn't me.

# NINE
## Gianna

It's 6:00 a.m. Saturday morning, and while I've never been one to sleep in, I usually stay in bed until at least 7:00 a.m. on weekends. That's not going to happen today. I'm wound up so tight that I'll lose it if I don't get up. After throwing on my leggings, sports bra, and tank top, I grab my running shoes and head for the park. I'm not a runner. If anything, I'm a power walker, but right now, I feel like anything short of running won't suffice. I need to clear my head, and the only way to achieve any bit of mental clarity is through exercise.

Heading out the front door, I make my way down the street. One of the perks of our new house is living next to a hundred-acre park. This will be my first time using the trails, so I brought my phone and mace in case there's anything sketchy. St. Alban's isn't a place where I need to worry about getting mugged, but I grew up in an area where you always watched your back, and that habit doesn't leave you. Plus, I've seen way too many scary movies growing up.

Once I'm at the end of my street, I cross over to the park and notice people are already out jogging on the trails, which puts me at ease. Finally, I'll be able to let out some pent-up frustration instead of being consumed by paranoia that some creeper might pop out from behind a bush and attack me.

Jogging around a public park was not how I saw my Saturday morning going after completing my first full week of work. I had planned on getting online and starting to figure out what classes I might be able to take this fall. My schedule would obviously be limited to what I could afford, not to mention what was offered at night. Until I landed this job, I hadn't even attempted to look into college courses. I knew I wouldn't be able to afford them, but now it's a possibility, and if I somehow turn my summer internship into a year-round gig as planned, I'm hoping I can get work to help pay for some of the costs. I know Phyllis mentioned something about tuition reimbursement for full-time employees during training this week, and I hope to capitalize on that. However, all of that will have to wait until tomorrow because I need to make things right today.

Starting my pace, I go back over my afternoon with Mason. I can't believe he showed up and told me he loved me. There's a difference between telling someone you want to take your relationship to the next level and telling someone you love them. He must be going through something. He knows I want him. There's no question that I've always had a thing for him. But I'm holding back now because I feel like he's not being honest with me. Why, out of nowhere, is he all in? And not even just all in, let's be boyfriend and girlfriend, but confessing his love for me all in. He's never acted like this before.

Sure, I know Mason cares about me. I never felt like he was using me for our hot and heavy make out sessions, but after so many years of wishing he saw me as more than just a friend and not getting that wish fulfilled, I had to find contentment in what we had, and I did. For some reason, taking what he's offering me now almost feels like an obligation. As if I should say yes because it's what I always wanted, and now is my chance. However, if I said yes now, it wouldn't be for the right reasons, and that's unsettling.

There's a reason I never really had a boyfriend, and it's not because I couldn't get one. I honestly never had the emotional capacity to entertain the idea of one. Plus, what guy wants a girl with my baggage? The kind who wants sex, that's the type. Growing up around addicts, you learn how to decipher a person's true intent, and let me tell you, most people are selfish assholes.

At the end of the day, I don't have time for any relationship, boyfriend or not. I need to focus on my goals, but I also know sometimes letting people in can be a good thing. Everyone needs to have a healthy balance in life. It can't be all work and no play. I'm desperate for change, but it needs to be the right change, and with Mason, I'm where I've always been. And while there's security in that, there's also complacency.

Regardless of how I feel about taking our relationship to the next level, I need to fix what happened yesterday. That entire exchange was shitty. I knew the moment Mason pulled out of the parking lot and things were left in tatters between us, I would be finding him today. I just need to figure out what I'm going to say to him.

Until this week, I don't think we ever even had a falling-out. Vivian has always said that we'd end up together like some sort of fated mates, written in the stars, storybook romance. With Mason's confession in the parking lot yesterday, I thought she might be right, until August showed up, and I was reminded of why doubt was ever cast.

While I have no plans to start a relationship with August, I don't want to stay away. I even gave him my number last night. Why would I do that? It's like I'm asking for trouble. Now I'm running my ass off, lungs on fire, because August Barron Branson had to come into my life like a wrecking ball and tear down everything I built up, from my relationships to my own will. I may have sworn him off and said I wouldn't let him in, but by the end of the night, I was humping his leg like some floozy. And that's not even the root of my problem with him.

The problem with August is that I can't fight him off. From the moment I laid eyes on him, we had this instantaneous, undeniable, magnetic connection. When I'm with him, it's like I let go of everything I've held on to because, in those stolen moments with him, I feel like I'm indeed the center of his focus. He doesn't see my past, my baggage, my insecurities, or a girl who needs rescuing, and that's empowering. It reassures me that my past doesn't have to define my future. So now I'm left trying to separate my heart from my head and my past from the future.

* * *

I've just finished showering and dressing and decided to text Vivian to see if she's home. I was able to conjure up a plan while I was running. Mason is currently still living at home, at least for the next month until his condo is ready, which means if Vivian is home, she can run surveillance on him. She only lives two houses down. I know if I call or text Mason, he isn't going to answer.

August was correct in his observation that I ripped his heart out, but in my defense, I wasn't trying to. My phone pings. She's home.

> Gianna: Can you look out the window and see if Mason's car is in the driveway?

> Vivi: Sure. What's going on?

> Gianna: It's a long story, and I promise to tell you everything after I fix things with him.

> Vivi: G! This sounds serious. You better not break his heart.

> Gianna: Why are you jumping to the conclusion that I'm breaking his heart?

> Vivi: Because I've always known you would if you didn't marry him.

OMG! She can't be serious. Marriage? We are eighteen years old, for Christ's sake.

> Gianna: Quit with the dramatics. I'm leaving my house now. Can you make sure he doesn't leave?

> Vivi: Sure, G!

Driving to Mason's, I still have no idea what I'll say or where to begin, but I need to see him in person. That's the only way to salvage what we have, if there's any hope of that.

When I finally make it to his house, I quickly regret my decision to wear light blue skinny jeans and an off-the-shoulder, chunky gray sweater. I'm sweating bullets, I'm so nervous. I should have worn a T-shirt. *Hell.*

Sitting in my car, I'm trying to collect myself before knocking on the door when my phone pings.

> Vivi: Get in there already!

She's right. I can't hide in here all morning. Exiting my car, I start walking up the driveway when Mason suddenly comes out looking hot as hell in his gym attire.

He's wearing gray joggers with a fitted black tee and black ball cap, looking like fucking sex on a stick. As he strides to his car, he doesn't notice me at first, but when he does, he stops momentarily and scowls before shaking his head and continuing to walk to his vehicle.

"Mace, please, I need to talk to you."

He tosses his gym bag in the trunk and continues to the driver's side door. That's when I start running. I open the passenger side door and hop in before he can take off on me.

"Get out of my car, Gianna. I have nothing to say to you."

Okay, so he's really mad. Not that I hadn't expected that, but thinking about it and experiencing it are very different things. My cool as a cucumber, flirtatious, laid-back Mason is gone, and I don't know how to talk to this one. So I reach for his hand before saying, "Mason, please let me explain. I'll tell you everything, but please don't do this to us." I can tell he's grinding his teeth as he looks out his window.

"I don't need you to tell me how the story goes, Gianna. Did you forget I was there? For the first time in our relationship, I told you I wanted to try at there being an us. I don't hear from you and figured it was too much, too soon, only to find out you decided to date another guy."

I'm fighting back the tears now, and I don't want him to think I'm playing the victim here, so I turn and look out my window to avoid his gaze.

"I never put much thought into how our story would end, but I didn't think it would end with you crushing my heart. But I guess you never knew you had it."

I can't help the tear that slips down my cheek. I try to quickly wipe it away before he notices. He's right. I didn't know I held his heart in an intimate way, which makes my already jumbled-up heart more confused.

"Don't cry, Gianna. We're just not meant to be, and I need some time before I can see you again."

Now it's my turn to be mad.

"How can you say that? You haven't even let me speak since I showed up. All you have done is run and shut me out. You have no idea how I feel!" Shoot, I don't even know how I feel.

He hits his steering wheel hard.

"Damn it, Gianna, then spit it out!"

My heart is galloping through my chest, and my mouth is suddenly way too dry, as if the words don't want to come out, but I finally manage to speak.

"My heart always wants you." Because it's true. Whether or not I'm ready to be more with him is beside the point. He means the world to me, and I'm here because I can't stand to be the reason for his pain.

I meet his gaze and a mixture of relief and annoyance flashes through his eyes before he asks, "Is it enough?"

I know what he's asking. Does my heart want him enough to commit to him? That's when I do the only thing that feels right.

Awkwardly, I crawl over the center console and into his lap, where I take his face in my hands. His eyes are pained, and he makes no attempt to touch me, and it fucking hurts.

"I'll give you all that I have."

His nostrils flare, and his breathing becomes more labored as he pulls me into his chest and holds me.

## TEN

## *Mason*

Since Monday, I've been on an emotional rollercoaster. I finally revealed my desire to take my relationship with Gianna to the next level, and she didn't reciprocate that wanting. As a result, I've been angry, bitter, annoyed, pessimistic, and heartbroken. I couldn't tell you when I gave her the power to dismantle my heart, but she ran away with it somewhere along the line. They say your soul is supposed to continue existing after your body is dead, but if I learned anything this past week, it's that there's no me after her.

If I lose her in the end, I have no one to blame but myself. I should have made my move sooner, but I thought we had more time. Gianna just lost her home, her family finally landed on their feet, and now she's started her first real job. So the timing for me to confess my feelings and ask for more didn't feel right.

When I picked her up on Monday and saw how August looked at her, I knew I had to make my move, but now I'm wondering if it's too late. The truth is, I've always seen this day coming, the day another man might turn her eye away from me, but I didn't think it would be him or now.

Last night was yet another sleepless night. All I could do was repeatedly replay our moment in the parking lot as if I enjoyed the torment. This is all my fault. Sitting there blaming myself for the outcome felt better than accepting that she was putting some random guy in front of me. The self-pity eventually morphed into animosity, and I felt compelled to hit something. That's when I decided to pick my pathetic ass up off my bedroom floor and hit the bags at the gym. Then she showed up.

Now I'm sitting in my car with Gianna on my lap, and as I hold her, I swear I can feel her putting pieces of me back together. She's here with me, and it's real. I can leave the hell I put myself in. I've never felt this way around Gigi. I'm so nervous that I might say the wrong thing or push her for more than she's ready to give. Gianna deserves my best. She's the only thing that kept me from breaking all these years, and I took her for granted. She just told me she's willing to give me all she has, but that's a fragile gift, and I want nothing more than to protect it so it never slips away.

My racing heart has finally calmed. But when I pull back to look at Gigi, her eyes are filled with tears.

"Babe, please don't cry. The last thing I ever want to be is the reason for your tears."

Reaching up, she removes my ball cap and runs her fingers through my hair.

"I hurt you, and I'm so, so sorry. You mean so much to me. You are everything to me."

Before I know it, I've pressed my lips to hers ever so gently. When she relaxes against me, I deepen our kiss, sinking my tongue deep into her mouth, committing her taste and feel to memory. I sense she's doing the same to me, slowly rubbing her tongue against mine, exploring this new shared intimacy. Then, running both my hands up her back, I pull her into me, eliminating the distance between us. Heat courses through my body, setting every nerve ending ablaze.

We've been intimate before, but I feel so exposed now that I've revealed my heart. *Why have I never felt this before?* My hands move to her waist, finding the hem of her shirt. I raise it and stroke my fingers over the soft, warm skin of her hips. Her body breaks out in goose bumps as the tiniest whimper escapes her mouth, and I swallow it, letting it consume me.

I've always been able to read her so well, and I can't help but wonder if she can read the apology on my lips. My heart is hammering out every selfish move I've made, every tactless dismissal of her advances, every time I took us for granted. Her hands are laced behind my neck, holding me to her as if she's afraid I might pull away. And that thought hurts worst of all because if she does feel that way, it's only because I gave her reason to.

I don't want to lose her. I can't. All of this is so much more intense, so raw, and I can't get enough. When she loosens her grip on the back of my neck, it feels so much heavier than it should. It's as if she's releasing a piece of me. Sliding her hands down my chest, she pushes back, and I immediately feel the loss of her lips on mine deep within my soul.

"Is your mom home?"

When I look into her soft eyes, I know what she's asking, and fuck me if I don't want to give it to her. Brushing my hands up and down her arms, I attempt to dampen the arousal flaring between us.

"No, she's gone all weekend."

She leans into my neck and gives me a shy smile. "Can we go inside?"

Because I have no willpower when it comes to her anymore, I say, "Whatever you want, babe."

Once I have her inside my room, I know what she's expecting, so I pull back. As much as I want to take what she's offering, I don't want it to be like this. We're both emotionally strung out and weak from the pain we've inflicted on each other. When I take her virginity, I want it to be because it feels right, not because she's trying to make things better or prove a point. I hate to admit it, but I know that, because of him, I'll have to work for her heart, something she has always tried to give me freely.

"Lie with me," I say as I pull her toward my bed.

Her big green eyes search mine, looking for the meaning

behind those words, and I know she understands what I'm asking without speaking the words. Gianna has spent most of her life reading between the lines and having people tell her what they think she wants to hear. I don't want her to think that's what I'm doing right now. Sometimes silence speaks louder than words, and tonight I'll show her my heart by wrapping her in my arms.

Reaching for the hem of my sweatshirt, she pulls it up, and I let her take it off. She puts a hand on my chest and pushes me back on the bed. Once we've lain down side by side, she snuggles in under my arm and wraps her leg around mine. When her head lies across my chest, the smell of coconuts envelops my senses, and it feels like home.

We lie there in silence for a while before she lazily runs her fingers up and down my chest. She knows how much I love it. Her nails gently dragging over my skin initially always give me goose bumps, but it's not long before I settle into a blissful state of relaxation. I can tell she's about to doze off since her movements are slowing. I place a kiss on top of her head before she's too gone to notice. It's another few minutes before her hand has stilled, her breaths have softened, and I follow her into one of the deepest nights of sleep I've had in months.

## ELEVEN
## *August*

It's Friday afternoon, and I'm sitting in a sales meeting to discuss upcoming item launches and possible brand avenues to explore. We ordered lunch, and Maria went up to reception to grab it. Sitting around the conference table making idle chitchat with the team, movement out the front window catches my eye.

Immediately, I notice Gianna's thick dark-blond hair blowing in the wind as she walks to her car. I haven't spoken to her since our date last Friday, and it's fucking maddening.

I was livid when she told me she couldn't see me the next day. At first, it was because I got turned down, but then I realized how obsessed I was acting over someone I'd just met, which doesn't sit well with me. I don't chase women, and I'm not about to start. So this week, I went out of my way to avoid her. I even thought about deleting her number from my phone to eliminate any possibility of texting her. I needed space to clear my head and wrap my brain around everything. She makes me feel things I've never thought possible, and I'm spiraling.

Thoughts be damned. Seeing her now makes everything else inconsequential. Watching her walk out to her car makes me want to claim her right now, especially when I know all these other men are looking at her. She's seriously stunning without even trying. I must remind myself that I'm mad at her and have no plans to chase her. The problem is, I can't deny that she affects me, and I can't just let that go.

"Hey, Maria, isn't that your daughter, Gianna?" John, one of the lead salesmen, calls out.

Maria looks up and out the window before setting the food down on the credenza. She's smiling. "Yes, that's Gianna. This was her first week as a full-time employee."

My head snaps up toward Maria. I had no idea her mom worked here, let alone that her mom was Maria. Maria worked for my grandfather for years before she came to Reds. So she knows my parents well. That must have been why Gianna was hesitant to go out with me. Her mom is close to my family. However, that relationship isn't a deal-breaker. If anything, it's potentially a minor inconvenience if things don't work out.

Apart from her mother's blond hair, Gianna looks nothing like Maria. Maria has dark brown eyes framed by glasses. She's tall, curvy, and has the biggest set of tits I've ever seen. Gianna is the opposite. She has deep green eyes, can't be any taller than five-foot-four, and didn't get her mom's huge tits, but my God, does she have a peach for an ass. My cock twitches just thinking about how plump it was in my hands and how when I squeezed it hard, she fucking loved it.

John spins back around in his chair to face the conference table and starts tapping his pen on his notepad.

"Well, how does she like it so far? Has she decided where she wants to go to school in the fall?"

That snaps me out of my sex-induced fog fast. *What is he talking about? Where does she want to go to school? How has she not started college yet?* I quickly realize I didn't know the answers to these questions because I assumed she was my age and done with college, but now I'm sweating bullets waiting for Maria's response. Maria walks around handing out lunches, and I'm trying hard to refrain from asking her to hurry up and answer the question already.

"I think she plans on starting at a community college this fall to get her prerequisites out of the way before transferring them to a university. She's just happy to be done with high school and feels blessed to have landed this job."

Wait a minute. She's glad to be done with high school? Before John can reply, I bite out, "How old is your daughter, Maria?"

It took everything in me to try to stifle the distress in my tone, but I think Maria caught it anyway. She sits in her chair, pushes her blond hair over her shoulder, and adjusts her big glasses before locking eyes with me.

"She just turned eighteen a month ago."

I snap the pen I was holding in half, and Maria looks at the ink dripping onto the table while John throws a napkin at me.

"August, you're dripping ink all over the table, son. Clean it up."

*Are you kidding me right now?* She's only eighteen? I know any misconceptions about her age are squarely mine. But in my defense, she doesn't carry herself like an eighteen-year-old. If anything, it's quite the opposite. In her, I see a reflection of myself, an old soul of sorts. Hell, that's half of what attracted me to her. Twenty is one thing, but eighteen is another. Fuck, why didn't I ask any questions on our date? I fucking took an eighteen-year-old girl out for dinner and drinks before making her come all over my leg. Oh my God. Why the fuck didn't she tell me how old she was? This was a mistake, and I need to rectify it immediately.

I scowl at John in annoyance before excusing myself from the conference room.

I'm furious at this point. I need to see her right now. As I walk out to my car, I shoot her a text.

> August: Meet me at Grinders now! Coming is not optional.

And to make sure we are clear, I add,

> August: That's a threat!

It's not a threat, but I don't need her playing games right now. How can she only be eighteen? I must clarify that Friday was a mistake that will never happen again.

I'm leaning up against the side of my Mercedes G-Wagon when her old burgundy car pulls into the parking lot. She parks on the opposite side, probably not recognizing the car I'm driving today. My pulse rises as she gets out of her car wearing black skinny jeans, Converse, and a gray Reds sweater. She looks like a fucking snack. Even dressed down, she's sexy as fuck. *Damn it.*

I have to remind myself I can't touch her again. She's too young. While she might not be jailbait, I'd look like I'm taking advantage of her or coercing her, on top of it being taboo in the workplace. Before I knew who she was, I knew it was frowned upon, but now add in who her mom is and her age? *Fuck.*

She spots me and starts to make her way over. I can't read her expression since she's wearing sunglasses, but if her body language is any sign, she's pissed. Once she's in front of me, she lifts her sunglasses off her eyes and puts them in her hair. Her green eyes immediately pierce my soul, and my body physically aches from the words I'm about to say.

"What the hell was so important that I had to drop what I was doing and meet you here or get fired?"

That fucking smart mouth, I swear.

"I'm sorry. Did I pull you away from another hot lunch date?"

Her eyes narrow as if she's trying to read my mood.

"Are you serious right now? You asked me over here to throw insults at me?"

And there it is. A flash of hurt crosses her expression before she straightens her spine.

"Just do us both a favor and leave me alone, August. Lose my number while you're at it!"

Turning to walk toward her car, she thinks I'll let her have the last word, but I'm not done. I grab her wrist and spin her back around to meet my annoyed gaze. The move shocks her, and her eyes widen in surprise as she tries to pull out of my grip. I can't hurt her. Hurting her would hurt me, and that's a glaring truth I'm not ready to acknowledge, so I soften my words.

"Look, I just wanted to say I'm sorry about last week. Friday was a mistake, and it won't happen again."

Her eyes hold mine for a beat, annoyance written all over her face. She rolls her lips together, pulls her sunglasses back down over her eyes, and walks away. This time, I don't stop her.

\* \* \*

It's 9:00 p.m. Saturday night, and I'm headed out to Club Social with Ethan and Grant. Club Social is in the town of Arrowhead, which is a run-down shithole if you ask me, but Grant said his cousin was going there tonight, and it was worth checking out. While it might be in a drab part of town, it has the type of entertainment we're looking for tonight.

Basically, that means hot girls and easy E. I drove tonight as soon as I heard where we were going. Ethan and G wanted to Uber, but I wanted to be able to bounce fast, knowing this place was going to suck.

My foresight is proven appropriate the minute we pull up. I'm convinced we're in the wrong place. We're in the middle of what appears to be a shipping distribution hub by the river.

Grant grabs my shoulder from the back seat. "This is it, bro. Pull around to the other side of the building."

Pulling around, I notice a lot full of cars, so I grab a spot by a light post to avoid getting robbed. This place has shady written all over it.

"Why do I get the feeling this is going to be a terrible night? Where the hell is the front door even at?"

Ethan claps my shoulder as we start walking up toward the only door located on the metal building.

"Auggie baby, you need to chill and get your head right. We're here for a good time. Don't even think about ghosting like you did last time. Shit, if you need to start swooning over Carson again just to get over Gianna, then do it, but stop being so fucking lame!"

I told them about my meeting yesterday, where I found out how Gianna was closely linked to my family through her mom, and the fact that she was only eighteen. They fucking laughed like it was no big deal. Maybe it's not in the scheme of things. The older we both get, the more acceptable the seven-year gap would be, but I don't think that's what pissed me off. If anything, I think I used it as a crutch to push her away because I didn't want to face my own emotions.

"First off, don't fucking call me Auggie. You know I hate that shit. I ghosted you assholes because you tried to set me up on some bullshit date I didn't want, and if that's what I have to look forward to walking through this door tonight, let me know now so I can turn around and leave."

Grant throws his head back, laughing. Ethan caught him off guard that night too, and he got stuck playing wingman with two chicks that night after I ducked out. "That's not the plan tonight, man. I promise."

We get to the door, and you can hear the bass from the music inside before we even open it. The atmosphere when we walk through the doors takes me aback. It's not what I expected from the outside. It's a distribution center turned into a club. The concrete floors have been glazed obsidian, with streaks of silver running through them. Dock doors line the back wall of the building, and in front of them is a bar that runs the length of the warehouse, with giant TVs above playing music videos. The ceiling is painted black, so the big-ass fans and ductwork pop out, giving it an old, renovated warehouse vibe.

They've created two levels. The main level is the dance floor, skirted by pub tables and booths. The upper level that frames the entire space appears to be a VIP section, seeing as how you can't really see what's going on up there. Strobe lights beat with the rhythm of the music, and soft blue backlighting lights the seating areas. Definitely not what I was expecting.

We make our way to the bar, order Manhattans, and before I know it, Grant's cousin Ray has found us.

"You guys made it. I was starting to think you'd puss out and not show your preppy asses."

Grant goes in for a pound hug. "These assholes might be too preppy, but this place is a gem, bro! You've been holding out on me."

Ray laughs. "Come on, get your drinks. We're going upstairs."

We collect our drinks and follow Ray to the VIP area. I was expecting rows of booths. There are some, but there are also private lounge areas.

"Bro! This place is legit. I can't believe it's in Arrowhead."

Grant looks around in awe when Ray replies, "Yeah, well, there are tax incentives here to bring business to the area."

Once we're done gawking at the place, I notice the girls bringing the drinks up here are wearing next to nothing and fucking hot as hell. Ethan catches me looking.

"See, man? I told you we'd have a good time tonight."

I smirk and sip my drink before heading to the rail that overlooks the club. Now that I'm up here, I can see other people standing around looking over the rail. Downstairs, you can't tell there's anyone up here. That must be intentional, considering the outfits the wait staff are wearing. They're basically wearing pasties and underwear. While it's nice to look at, I'm unsure how legal it is.

Ethan is standing next to me, people-watching, when I hear him hiss, "Fuck me, bro. I think my next girlfriend just walked in."

Following his line of sight, I see who he's eye-fucking and go stiff. Gianna just walked in wearing black stilettos, a white miniskirt, and a black crop top tank with a deep V. Her long blond hair is perfectly straight and almost skims the top of her perfect ass. *Fuck.*

How is she even in this place? She's only eighteen. I made up my mind yesterday that I'd let her go. The problem is, when I see her now, none of the reasons I've listed for myself to stay away matter. I want her, and I'll be damned if I let Ethan touch her.

Ethan goes to step around me as if to head her way. Before I realize what I'm doing, I've grabbed him by the collar of his shirt and pinned him up against the wall.

"You won't lay a fucking hand on her. Are we clear?"

His eyes are bugging out in confusion. "Fuck, August, what's your problem? Let go of me, bro."

Realizing I'm making a scene, I release my grip on his shirt. "That's Gianna."

Understanding floods his expression, but he's still pissed.

Grant shows up. "What the hell is going on?"

"Fucking August is losing his mind, that's what's going on. The hottest chick in the club just walked in, and he's claiming her like some fucking deranged lunatic."

Now I'm furious. He knows she's my girl. I just told him who she was. I'm pull my fist back to punch him in the face when Grant drags me back before I make contact.

"August, are you serious right now? You're going to punch Ethan for checking out a girl?"

That's when I spit out, "That's my girl. It's Gianna."

Grant loosens his hold. "You mean Gianna, as in the one you told to fuck off?"

*Are these assholes serious right now?* I turn to walk away, but Grant stops me.

"August, it doesn't even matter." He nods toward the bar downstairs where Gianna is standing. She's ordering a beer, and a guy has her caged in, saying something in her ear that makes her laugh. I fucking see red. Pulling my phone out of my pocket, I shoot her a text.

> August: Lose the guy.

She pulls out her phone and the girl she's with leans in to read it with her.

> Gianna: Who is this?

> August: Don't play with me, Gianna. I'm not in the mood.

> Gianna: You can't tell me what to do.

> August: I beg to differ. My title says differently.

She nods and shakes her head. I can tell I'm getting under her skin. Good. It feels like she's practically crawling under mine.

> Gianna: The last time I checked, we are not at work. Therefore, you can't tell me what to do.

He places his hand on her bare shoulder, and my eye twitches. It's too close to the neck I had my mouth on.

> August: I'm only going to say this once, Gianna. Tell him to take his hands off you, or you won't like what happens next.

She looks around in search of me, slowly scanning the crowded space, her eyes only briefly flicking up to the VIP balcony that can't be seen from below before she gives up.

> Gianna: Fuck off! You said we were done. Now lose my number and leave me alone.

> August: You better tell the guy you're with to take his hands off you.

My blood is now boiling as the guy leans in again to whisper something in her ear. She smiles and puts her phone away as his hand drops to her waist, and they leave the bar area. This is my fault. I pushed her away, and now she's with another guy. Fuck this! I can't even think of why I pushed her away, which means the reasons don't matter. Time to get my girl.

"That girl is fine as hell, man, but seriously, Ethan's pissed.

You could have just said something. You didn't have to make a scene."

I know he's right, but I'm too pissed off to see it that way. Glancing back at Ethan, I see him making his way down the steps. *Damn it.*

Heading downstairs, I lose sight of Ethan. I'm not sure where he went. He may have left, and that's probably a good thing. Then, finally, I spot Gianna, and she's not with the guy she had around her earlier. Instead, she's with her girlfriend, heading out to the dance floor.

The DJ took a break from playing the new trendy shit, and now Fetty Wap's "Again" is playing, and the girls go crazy. The song couldn't be more prophetic of my current situation. Gianna and her friend are dancing to the music, looking sexy as hell, when I see two guys close in.

Her friend appears to know the guy approaching her as she starts grinding on him the minute he steps up. Gianna, on the other hand, seems apprehensive about her partner. He goes to put his hands on her hips, and I bolt.

Making my way through the crowd, I yank the guy back. "We will have a problem if you don't stop touching my girl."

The guy stares at me, mystified, before looking at Gianna in question, which only further infuriates me.

"Don't fucking look at her. Don't so much as breathe in her direction, or I'll break your nose."

Gianna grabs my arm. "August, stop! Just stop. I'll come with you."

The guy breaks eye contact with me to look at Gianna, and before I realize it's happened, I punch him. His head snaps back, and his face is instantly bloody.

Gianna gasps. "August, oh my God! What did you do?"

"I warned him. He still thought it was okay to look at what's mine. I think we're clear now."

She's physically trying to move me off the dance floor and away from this punk with an eyebrow piercing.

"Aiden, I'm so sorry."

Great, of course she knows the sorry fucker.

As she fails to move me, I look the asshole in his eyes. "Aiden, is it? I'll fucking ruin you."

He's breathing heavily like he wants to take a shot at me, adrenaline clearly running through his veins, but he thinks better of it and walks away. Knowing the message has been received, I let Gianna pull me away. I thought she was taking me toward the exit, but instead, she pulls me into a storage room.

"What the hell are you doing here, August?"

She's pissed off, that's for sure, but at this proximity, I can tell she's also aroused. Her face is flushed, her pupils are slightly dilated, and because she isn't wearing a bra, I can see her nipples hardening. She might not like me right now, but she is turned on.

"Are you following me?"

Again, I don't answer her. Adrenaline is coursing through my veins, and I don't want to waste time talking. I'd probably only say something I'd regret later like I did yesterday. In this confined space, all I need to take is one step before our bodies are close enough that I can feel the swell of her breasts touch my chest, and my cock stiffens.

"Answer me," she pants.

Leaning down, I bring my hand to the nape of her neck, pulling her into me before crushing my mouth to hers.

## TWELVE
### *Gianna*

Oh my God, this can't be happening. I came to the club tonight with Ashton and the guys to have one last night out together before Bryce and Aiden take off for Florida on Monday. The next thing I know, August punches Aiden in the face on the dance floor. And now, here I am in a closet, clawing at his back as he shoves his tongue down my throat.

The man kisses like a god. When I'm with him, he completely consumes me. Nothing else matters, and all rationale goes out the window. Every time he looks at me with those hungry eyes like he literally might die if he doesn't touch me, I go weak in the knees. It doesn't matter how much I hate him or how wrong we are for each other. I can't resist him. He brings out the free spirit, uninhibited risk taker I long to be.

His hand grips my ass, and when he does, half of it grabs my bare cheek due to my skirt being so short. He groans into my mouth with pleasure from the feel of my nakedness in his hand. I feel his hard cock against my stomach, and I slowly reach down between us to stroke him over his pants. Breaking our kiss, he pulls back and hisses before removing my hand. I'm immediately embarrassed, and I'm sure my cheeks are flushed, showcasing my humiliation. *Why am I even letting him touch me right now?* As of yesterday, I was a mistake. And apparently, I'm still a mistake he can't stop making. He promptly grabs my chin and tilts it up so that I'm looking at him.

"Don't do that, baby. Don't be embarrassed and don't hide from me. We're just not doing this here." Then, leaning down, he places a kiss on my temple before taking my hand and pulling me out of the closet.

We're heading toward the exit when Bryce spots me and says, "Hey, Gigi, wait up."

I stop and look over my shoulder to see Bryce approaching us with something in his hand. August tightens his grip on my hand while possessively pulling me to his side. Once Bryce has finally made it over to me, he notices my new accessory and frowns.

"Is this the fucker who punched Aiden?"

Bryce isn't a petite guy, but I'm surprised he's taking that tone in front of August because I'm sure August could kick his ass.

Before I can respond, August asks, "Is there a problem?"

Bryce scoffs, "No, man, there's no problem, but I think your girlfriend is looking for you, and you kind of fucked up our plans. So if you don't mind, I'm just going to take Gigi, and we'll be on our way."

I screech out, "Girlfriend," before whipping around and searching his eyes for truth, hoping this is a misunderstanding. August holds my gaze but doesn't give me anything.

Bryce steps forward to take my hand, but August blocks him. "I wouldn't do that if I were you."

However, Bryce doesn't back down. "Why don't you let her decide who she wants to go with? Her lifelong friends or some lying d-bag?"

I'm looking at August, waiting for him to deny Bryce's claim, but he doesn't. Instead, he sets his jaw and glares at me. His breaths are more erratic, like he's struggling to contain his temper. I want to question him, but there's no point. I already know the answer. Before I can even turn around to walk away, some blonde with huge boobs wearing tight white jeans with a red top rushes by me.

"Auggie, I was so worried. I heard some guy got punched, and we couldn't find you."

Throwing her arms around his neck, she stands on her tippy-toes and places a kiss on his mouth. The mouth that was just all over mine. I feel like I can't breathe and I might pass out. Bryce notices my face go pale, and he comes up beside me to let me lean on him.

"Gigi, we need to get you some air. I have your purse. Let's leave."

August doesn't take his eyes off me, but it doesn't matter. He's dead to me.

When we finally make it outside, the cold night air on my heated skin feels like heaven. My mind is reeling. I can't believe, after everything, he has a girlfriend. We never really talked about anything in-depth, but before you actively pursue someone, wouldn't you make sure you were single, especially if there's a chance the two people could meet, like tonight? I mean, what the fuck?

With all the *my girl* talk and extreme possessiveness, I never would have thought he was a cheating bastard. Why am I so upset anyway? I have Mason. Oh my God, Mason! I'm such a bitch. We still haven't technically labeled anything, but he'd be heartbroken.

"Bryce, I'm so sorry I ruined your going away party. I had no idea August would show up here. This isn't even his side of town."

We start walking toward his truck when he asks, "So who is that guy anyway? You've never mentioned him, not that I can blame you. He seems like a prick! Wait, wasn't he standing outside with you when I picked you up on my new bike?"

"I haven't mentioned him because he's no one worth mentioning. Last week, I met him at work, and he has continued to pursue me regardless of my objections. Then tonight, he shows up here and punches Aiden for dancing with me, and all the while, he has a girlfriend."

I'm so mad I'm about to cry, but I won't let that fucker have my tears. This is why I don't let people in. For this very reason, I keep a select group of people close to me. People suck. They'll tell you what you want to hear so they can get what they want, and August wanted to get laid, period. He wasn't interested in me. He was interested in my body, and I was too swept away with the idea of him to recognize what was really happening. Why would a guy like him be interested in an underaged, lower-class, hot mess like me? Oh yeah, that's right, he wouldn't be. At least I found out before things reached a point of no return.

We finally get to Bryce's truck, and I bend down to take my heels off before opening the cab door and climbing in. Bryce climbs in the other side, and I ask, "Where are the others? Should we wait up?"

He shakes his head. "No, they all took off after Aiden had his nose broken. You know it was really shitty of you to leave."

I throw my head back against the truck seat and close my eyes.

"You have no idea what I'm dealing with, Bryce."

How do I tell him not only does August work with me, but he's the owner's son, and he has threatened my job? Or that even after he threatened my job and told me I was a mistake, I still wanted him to kiss me just now. Sensing my inner turmoil, he reaches over and grabs my hand.

"Gigi, is there more you want to tell me? We can figure it out. I'll help you, whatever it is."

Shaking my head, I turn to look out the window. I don't need anyone else involved in my drama. Bryce was a lifesaver when my family and I got evicted, and that was about all the embarrassment and help I could ever accept from him in this lifetime.

Movement from the club catches my eye, and that's when I notice August has exited the building and is now searching the parking lot. He looks around, clearly frustrated, before running his fingers through his hair. Suddenly, his eyes find mine, and he starts making his way toward the truck.

"Bryce, drive!"

He follows my line of sight and then tears out. When I look out the car's side mirror, I see him standing there with his hands in his pockets, watching us drive off.

\* \* \*

It's 10:00 a.m. on Sunday, and I don't want to get out of bed. Last night was the worst night ever. All my friends are upset with me. They believe it's my fault that Aiden got punched. While no one has come out and said that, they don't need to. It was supposed to be our last party night before the guys moved to Florida, and then I went and ruined it. I want to bury my head under my pillow and shut out the world. I'm about to do just that when there's a knock on my door.

"Go away, Mom. I'm not hungry."

"It's me, Mason. Can I come in?"

Last night, I threw on a T-shirt and went straight to bed when I came home. I'm sure I look like hell, and it's nothing Mason hasn't seen before, but now that things are changing between us, I've been getting nervous around him. I'm tired of being the girl he picks up the pieces for and puts back together. That's what he's always done for me. He's always been my security blanket and helped me wash away my pain. I don't want that now. I want to be something he's proud of, that he wants to hold on to because I'm worth keeping. *So why can't I get my shit together?*

"Babe?"

"Yes, Mason, I'm decent. You can come in."

Of course he saunters in wearing tight-fitted light blue jeans and a light gray long-sleeved Henley that shows off his fit physique. I groan loudly, bury my head in my pillow, and throw the covers over my head.

"Babe, what are you doing?" He chuckles.

"Why do you have to come in looking like a J.Crew model?"

The bed dips where he sits as he tries to pull the covers back. I grip them tighter so he can't.

"Seriously, maybe you should just go wait in the living room until I can get dressed and come out looking somewhat human."

He laughs, and the next thing I know, he's straddling me and pulling the covers off. "There she is, my sexy little minx." Then he plants a kiss on my forehead before falling on the pillow next to mine.

"Mason, I don't know what you see in me. You're too good for me."

He frowns and scrunches his eyebrows. I'm about to pull the covers back over my face when he stops me.

"Gianna, what's wrong? Did something happen last night? Why are you acting like this?"

I don't want to have this conversation with him in my bedroom while my parents are in the other room. He deserves the truth and all my attention with no distractions.

"Everything went so wrong."

"Is that why you've been ignoring my texts this morning?"

I quirk an eyebrow at him. While I may be dreading this conversation, I wouldn't flat-out ignore him.

"You haven't texted me."

Reaching my nightstand, I pick up my phone and see it's dead. I hold it up for him to see. "It's dead."

When I reach for my charging cable, I see it has fallen between my nightstand and bed. As I struggle to reach into the small gap, my T-shirt rides up just enough to reveal the lower half of my bare cheeks. I hear Mason groan behind me, and before I can reach back to cover myself, he has gripped my bare ass cheek, and his mouth is next to my ear, sending delicious tendrils of heat straight to my core.

"Get dressed, babe. I can't be in here a minute longer knowing you have no panties on." He squeezes my ass and leaves a kiss on my neck right below my ear that makes my tummy tighten with need.

In the next breath, he's standing by my door. "I'll wait in the living room." Then he's gone.

*I am so fucked.*

\* \* \*

I want to confess every detail of last night to Mason, but at the same time, I don't want to mess up what we have. If the roles were reversed and he was making out with girls who weren't me, I'd want to know. But as much as it might hurt him, I don't want to start this new chapter by keeping things from him. That's just asking for failure.

After jumping out of the shower, I put on some jean shorts, a long-sleeved white T-shirt, and Converse. I quickly applied mascara and lip gloss before grabbing my gray hoodie and heading out.

When I get to the living room, it's empty. Looking around, I spot movement out the front window. Mason is out front playing catch with Elio. I take a minute to admire the view. A calm Sunday in a peaceful neighborhood. These are the kind of days I've prayed for. Now, hopefully, I can keep them. I make my way down the front steps and outside right as Elio calls out, "Heads-up."

Looking up just in time, I catch the football they were tossing around.

"Very funny, Lo! Mason, are you ready to go?" I toss the ball back to Elio before asking, "Where's Mom and Dad?"

"Mom is downstairs doing laundry, and Dad went to get gas for the lawnmower." Wow, my parents sound domestic for once, and yet I can't shake the feeling that the other shoe is about to drop.

I pull Elio in for a hug. "Is everything going okay?"

"Yes, Gigi. I'm okay."

I scrub my hand over the top of his hair before heading toward Mason and calling out over my shoulder, "I'll be home for dinner. Tell Mom to make her spaghetti."

Elio starts walking back to the front door and calls out, "Okay, but if you're not back in time, I can't make any promises that there will be any left for you."

Once I reach Mason, I stand on my tippytoes to kiss his perfectly plump lips. He leans in to give me more access and runs his hands up from my hips to either side of my face before pulling back to look at me. The man's eyes are as blue as the ocean. He's so pretty, the kind of beautiful you can get lost in. He breaks my focus with a smile.

"What are you thinking about?"

I smirk. "You don't need to know everything that goes on inside my head."

He pushes a loose strand of hair behind my ear. "That's debatable."

The next thing I know, he's taking my hand and pulling me toward the car.

"Come on. I have somewhere I want to take you. That's kind of the whole reason I came out here today."

\* \* \*

Finally, we make it to our destination, which happens to be in the middle of nowhere.

"You know, this seems like a good place to hide a body. Maybe I'll stay in the car."

Mason tosses a smile my way. "Now why would I want to murder my favorite person?"

He pops the trunk and climbs out. I get out of the car and meet him around back. In his trunk are a hiking pack and two water bottles, and he hands me one. "Ready?"

I eye him suspiciously before taking it and nodding.

We've been hiking for at least twenty minutes when I say, "I'm not trying to be high-maintenance, but are we almost there? I didn't exactly wear the right shoes for this."

He looks down at my feet and smiles. "Your shoes are fine, princess. The spot is right around the bend up here."

A few more paces, and my mouth drops open before I can protest anymore. "Wow, you can see for miles up here. This is beautiful."

I'm staring in awe out over the Missouri River, framed by trees that are starting to bloom with flowers now that spring is officially in full swing. If I look close enough, I can even see some blue herons along the banks of the river. The valley below is straight out of a painting.

When I look back at Mason, he has laid out a blanket to sit on and motions for me to join him. I do and we sit silently, just taking in the serene view for what feels like forever.

I can't tell you the last time my mind felt so relaxed and I could breathe.

Mason puts his arm around my shoulder and kisses my temple. "I was hiking last week and stumbled upon this spot and thought of you. I knew I wanted to bring you here the moment I found it. Being up here helped me escape the noise, and I wanted to give that to you."

I lay my head on his shoulder and let his words sink in. He wanted to help me escape the noise like he always does. When I think about our relationship over the years, he's always been my sanctuary. Whenever I felt defeated, let down by my parents, or bullied at school, he was there. I mean, Vivian was there as my best friend, but somewhere along the line, Mason was there too, helping calm the storm inside of me. Things between us have always been easy, natural, and comfortable. We always chose each other even back then, and now here we are today, still choosing each other. My stomach growls, and I immediately feel terrible. But I'm nowhere near ready to leave. We just got here.

"I almost forgot. I brought food." Mason reaches into his hiking pack and pulls out salads from Bread Co. I sigh in relief.

"Seriously, stop being so damn perfect! You make the rest of us feel inadequate."

He passes me a salad, and we eat in silence for a few minutes.

"Are you ready to tell me about last night?"

I sigh, setting down my bowl. "Honestly, I don't even know where to start. Let me preface this with I'm sorry, and I need you to listen to the entire story even when it gets hard."

Setting down his salad, he looks at me with a furrowed brow before staring out over the river and setting his jaw. It's like he knows what I'm about to say before I even say it. As if he already knows I'm going to hurt him, which makes me hate myself more than I already do. *Am I really the shittiest kind of predictable?* What sucks is, none of this was in my cards a few weeks ago. My focus was on making money, planning for school, and getting away from my parents. Now my love life is taking center stage, and I'm unsure how to get everything back on course.

No longer wanting to delay the inevitable, I breathe and brace myself for the hate I know is coming my way. In the end, I have no one to blame but myself. I made my bed, and now I must lie in it.

"When we got to the club, Ashton and I made a beeline to the bar, ordering a round of beers for everyone. While we were waiting for the bucket, Bryce came up behind me and said, 'I'm glad you could make it out tonight.' He was standing behind me, speaking in my ear, when my phone vibrated. I pulled my phone out to read the text, and it was from August. It read, 'You better tell the guy you're with to take his hands off you.'" Risking a glance at Mason before continuing, I notice he's rubbing his jaw in annoyance, but I keep going.

"I answered the text, basically telling him to fuck off. I put my phone back in my purse because I had nothing more to say to him after that. Bryce wasn't doing anything inappropriate, and August had no right to tell me who could touch me. When I looked around, I didn't see him, so I thought he could have just been messing with me. Ashton and I decided to head out to the dance floor, where TJ and Aiden came out after a few songs. Aiden went to put his hands on my hips and was immediately pushed back. That's when I realized August was there at the club. The next thing I knew, he was threatening Aiden. August told him not to look at me or even breathe in my direction, or he would break his nose. Aiden glanced at me, and just like that, August broke his nose no faster than he could blink. I couldn't believe what was happening. I tried pulling August off the dance floor in hopes of defusing the situation, but he wouldn't budge. I asked Aiden if he was okay, and that's when August said, 'I warned you not to touch what is mine. Do it again, and I'll ruin you.'"

Mason gets up off the blanket and starts pacing. I look up at him with concern written all over my face. I start to get up to go to him, but he says, "Gianna, stay down and finish the fucking story."

The disgust in his voice and the fury in his eyes have me second-guessing how much of what happened next I should divulge. Then, taking a deep breath, I read his face and decide he needs to know the truth even if it hurts.

"After August was convinced Aiden understood, he let me guide him off the dance floor. I wanted to confront him privately and not make a bigger scene in front of everyone. I wanted him to know that he couldn't treat my friends or me that way. I wanted to tell him I'm not his girl, which he had clarified the day before."

Mason cuts in. "Hold on, what do you mean he clarified you weren't his girl the day before?"

"Oh, I forgot to tell you. It wasn't a big deal. It was a relief. He threatened me, telling me to drop what I was doing on Friday and meet him at Grinders for lunch. When I arrived, he said he was sorry for how he acted last week, that Friday was a mistake, and it wouldn't happen again."

Mason already knew about our date Friday night. He was there for the announcement. What he doesn't know is how the night ended.

"Wait a minute, he threatened you? Gianna, what the hell is going on? Do you think I wouldn't stand up for you?"

Looking down, I shake my head, not wanting to meet his gaze. I don't want him to see the discomfort in my eyes. He'd have my back in a heartbeat. He always has. How do I tell him I don't want his help because whatever this is between August and me is impossibly wrong, but I crave it? Not to mention, I'm done running to Mason with my problems. I don't want to be a burden on him anymore. I want him to like me because I'm strong, assured, independent, and stable, not the guarded, apprehensive, self-loathing, insecure girl I've been.

"Mason, you need to let me finish the story before you decide if you want to be my knight in shining armor."

His blue eyes catch mine briefly, and I see his worry. I quickly look away before starting again, not wanting to see the pain.

"We entered a storage room, and I asked him, 'What the hell are you doing here?' He didn't respond, just stepped in closer to me, and then I demanded, 'Answer me.' But instead of using his words, he used his mouth and kissed me, and I kissed him back. I kissed him back, Mason, and I wanted to so badly at that moment."

Finally, Mason stops pacing and runs his fingers through his hair. He's standing too close to the cliff's edge, and it's making me uncomfortable.

"I'm not going to jump if that's what you're worried about," he scoffs.

I remain seated with my elbows resting on my knees as I stare down at the dirt. I can't bear to look at him. I can't stand to see the disappointment, hurt, or pain in his eyes. I'm selfish, and I don't deserve him. Now I'm only waiting for him to figure that out.

## THIRTEEN
### *Mason*

Standing here looking out over the river in the spot I brought Gigi so we could relax, I'm now anything but. Why do I keep giving this girl the power to break my heart? She just told me she kissed another man last night, not just any man but the same prick who threatened her and called her a mistake. Not to mention, she kissed him back because she wanted to. I'm trying to stay calm and think this through so I don't blow up at Gianna and make things worse, but I also need to decide how much I'm willing to put up with.

Maybe I need to break things off now before we reach a point of no return and end up in neither an intimate relationship nor a friendship. My issue is that I feel like I deserve the pain of this moment. For the years I've known Gigi, she's seen the parts of me I want her to see. Yes, we're both broken in our own ways, but she doesn't know the extent of my cracks.

The fact that she's telling me everything that happened means she cares, even if her actions last night don't show it. She knew what she had to tell me was going to hurt. She prefaced the conversation by saying as much, but that didn't take the sting out.

I hesitate to ask what happened after they kissed because it could go in a very wrong direction, which makes me sick to think about, but I ask anyway.

"What happened next?"

She blows out a resigned breath. "We left the storage room and started heading toward the front when his girlfriend showed up."

Wait a minute, this fucking d-bag has a girlfriend? So this entire time, he's been stalking Gigi and messing shit up between us... He had a girlfriend? Then it dawns on me.

"Wait, did you know he had a girlfriend?"

She shakes her head. "I had no clue. She stormed up to him like I wasn't there, threw her arms around his neck, and kissed him. That's when Bryce showed up looking for me, and we left."

She sighs and lies down on the blanket, throwing an arm over her eyes to shade herself from the sun. I can tell she feels terrible, but a part of me also believes she's upset, not just because she hurt me but because some part of her likes him.

As I stand here staring at her, laid out on the blanket before me, I can't help but think he's using her, and she can't do anything about it. It doesn't change the fact that she wanted him to kiss her, but if I know Gigi, the fact he has a girlfriend probably changed how she feels about him. I'm not going to pretend I can read her mind, so I ask.

"What are you thinking?"

I want to know how she feels now that all the cards are on the table. While we haven't labeled our relationship thus far, it doesn't change that we're attempting to go to the next step. So with that in mind, I return to the blanket and sit beside her.

"I think I'm screwed for so many different reasons, and here I am again with you, being the embodiment of disappointment. Last night I let my friends down. Today, I let you down, and overall, I let myself down. I've been fighting this from the beginning, and so far, he's winning. Right now, though, being here with you is the most upsetting. I'm tired of being the girl who's always coming to you with a problem, always somehow broken. I don't expect you to keep taking my crap. I'm waiting for you to open your eyes and realize you deserve better than me."

I let her words sink in, hating how untrue they are. This is the perfect opportunity to reveal my skeletons, but I don't. Do my secrets matter if I give them up for her? So instead, I say, "You're wrong. I don't think I deserve better. Actually, it's quite the opposite. You're perfect for me. Relationships constantly evolve as we grow into the people we are meant to be, and I want to support you. I've never felt like you were a burden. I want to be your rock. I want to be your strength when you are weak. I care about you deeply, Gigi."

She removes her arm from her face and turns to look at me. "You're crazy." She moves to sit up, and I pull her back down to me.

"Just humor me for a minute. Lie with me."

I know I shouldn't feel happy being here after she confessed that she wanted to kiss another man last night. I should be upset, wound up, and pissed off, but I find it hard to be any of those things when she chooses to be here with me. She decided to tell me the truth, knowing it would hurt, and while it did hurt me, I know it hurt her just as much.

Hesitant to give in to my demands, she finally concedes, and I pull her close so she's hovering above my chest. I place her hand over my heart, and she follows the movement with her eyes before I lift her chin between my forefinger and thumb so she has to give me her big green eyes. When she looks at me, I see the pain in her eyes, the torture it's causing her, knowing how I feel about her and knowing she feels unworthy of that affection.

"Please stop feeling sorry for me. I choose to stay. I choose you, babe."

She lays her head on my chest, and we soak in the silence together on the cliff overlooking the river for hours.

\* \* \*

The sun is setting when I realize we should start heading back to the car before the trail gets too hard to see. When I move to sit up, I notice Gigi has fallen asleep. So gently, I nudge her awake.

"Babe, wake up. You dozed off. We should probably start heading back."

She sits up to stretch, and her dark-blond hair falls down her back. That view against the backdrop of the sunset makes her look like a goddess. I sit up beside her and press a kiss on her shoulder. She gives me a sleepy smile before leaning in to kiss me, and I let her.

I pull her into my lap so that she's straddling my hips. She pulls out of the kiss to look at me, running her fingers through my hair. I place a kiss on her throat and then on her collarbone. Then, pulling me in tight like she can't get close enough, she wraps her legs around me, keeping me locked in her embrace, and there's nowhere in the world I'd rather be. I hold her for a few long moments before I whisper into her neck, "Tell me what you're feeling right now isn't worth fighting for. If you want me to walk away, I will." If she isn't ready for the next step with me, I need to walk away. I'd rather keep her as a friend than lose her.

Her eyes frantically search mine.

"Why would you say that?"

I cup her face with one hand while my other rests on her hip. "Are you saying that you feel the connection between us?"

She rests her forehead on mine. "Mace, I always have. I was only waiting on you."

Her mouth lands on mine, and her kiss consumes me. The hand she already had at the base of my neck locks as her tongue demands entrance to claim mine. There's no denying that I let her own me. I don't care if she breaks my heart. The high of having her now outweighs the pain of picking up the pieces later. When she shifts the weight of her body against mine, I can feel her heat against my groin. I'm already hard, but now I feel like I could spear her through my jeans. The sensation of her pressed against me is incredible. Fuck, I want her so bad.

We've never crossed that line, but it seems like she's been

trying to do just that since she told me she'd give me everything. I don't want her to think that's what I'm in this for, but my God, is she making it hard to be a better man. I break our kiss, and she whimpers.

"Babe, I want to make you feel good. You have no idea how bad I want you, but I need you to know that's not all I want. I want everything."

Her eyes study mine as the meaning behind my words sinks in. Then, before I have time to question her resolve, she grinds her clit against my cock, seeking friction, her eyes never leaving mine. My mouth is hanging open in awe of her. She has never known how incredibly sexy she is. If anything, she's always been timid. That's one of the things I've always loved about her. She's hot without the ego most hot chicks come with.

Paralyzed by this beautiful woman, I barely have time to catch my breath before she pulls her shirt off. Her skin pimples in the cool spring air. The sun is setting, and it's getting chilly. Reaching behind her back, she unclasps her bra and slowly drags the straps down her arms. I've felt her breasts through her shirt and under her bra plenty of times, but this is the first time I've ever seen them fully exposed, and my cock twitches with appreciation.

I take a minute to admire her topless in nothing but jean shorts with her legs wrapped around my waist before I lean down and take her breast in my mouth. Throwing her head back, she lets out the sexiest moan I've ever heard, and a bead of pre-cum drips from my dick. Groaning against her breast, I swirl my tongue around the bud of her pert nipple. She starts to rock against my cock before I take her other nipple in my mouth.

Her hands roam down my body, searching for the hem of my shirt, and when she finds it, she quickly lifts it up, and I break away to let her take it off. She's seen me shirtless plenty of times and explored my abs with her fingers for hours, but both of us being exposed like this together is an intimacy we've never shared. Her eyes roam my body with a renewed appreciation.

She pushes me back to lie down on the blanket beneath her. I can see the hunger in her eyes when she looks down at me, raking in my body sprawled out beneath her. I'm hers for the taking. Leaning down, she gently kisses me. Her hair cascades around our faces like a shade, and for a moment, it's just us, no outside world. Her lips leave mine, and I'm cold from the loss of her heat until she begins to blaze a trail of kisses from my collarbone down my chest.

My breath catches in my lungs, and I remind myself to breathe as I take in the hottest woman I ever laid eyes on kissing her way down my stomach. When she reaches my jeans, she traces the outline of my cock with her tongue, and it takes everything in me not to explode right then.

As she reaches to unbutton my pants, my phone rings loudly. I reach over to silence it, but the name on the screen catches my eye. *Shit.*

"Babe, you're calling me." Her head snaps up, and she abandons my jeans to reach for my phone. She quickly climbs off me like we've been caught in the act and grabs my shirt to cover her exposed breasts. Swiping, she answers the call on speaker.

"Hello."

"Hey, you left your phone at home," her brother, Elio's, voice rings out. "I've been trying to get ahold of you. You need to come home quick. Mom fell down the steps, and Dad's freaking out and says she needs to go to the emergency room."

Gianna looks at me, eyes wide. "Does Mom want to go to the ER?"

Elio sighs. "No, that's the problem. Can you just get here quick and help defuse the situation?"

I gather up her discarded bra and shirt and hand them to her.

"Yeah, we were on our way back anyway. We'll be there in about fifteen minutes."

Fifteen minutes? We still need to hike back down to the car. I guess I'll be speeding all the way back to her house. She hangs up the phone and quickly puts her bra and shirt back on while I pack up the blanket and lunch from earlier. Once we're ready to head back down the hill, she grabs my hand. I turn to look at her, and I see the apology in her eyes before she even says anything.

"Hey, I'm sorry."

Before she can say anything more, I pull her into me and hold her. "You have nothing to be sorry for. We'll have our moment. I'm not going anywhere, babe."

Seemingly satisfied with my response, we head back to the car.

# FOURTEEN

## *Gianna*

Once I got back to the house Sunday night, my phone had a ton of missed texts and calls.

> Bryce: Meet me in the parking lot at 11:20 for lunch on Monday.

> August: It's not what you think. We need to talk.

> Ashton: You've been holding out on me! Need Details!

> Ashton: You finally got your shot with Aiden. You messed it up!

> Bryce: Gigi, call me back. Are you okay?

> Elio: Come home now. Mom fell!

Bryce drove me home Saturday night. We didn't say much to each other after we left the club. There wasn't anything left to say. I wasn't going to continue to apologize for something I didn't do. While I felt terrible for what happened to Aiden, I'm tired of being someone's runner-up. I want to be someone's first choice, and Aiden had years of me pining over him. While it sucks that he got punched, I had no idea August was there waiting to start a fight.

I spent the better half of the weekend feeling like an asshole, and then Ashton made me feel like shit to top it off. I feel like she's a fake friend. Oh, suddenly, she wants details. Why, so she can go back to the guys and tell them what a slut I am? And for her to say, 'Oh, you finally got your chance with Aiden, and you messed it up.' No, trick, I didn't mess shit up. You were there. August came out of nowhere! Not to mention, if she was so concerned about my relationship with Aiden, shouldn't she be saying it's a good thing August showed up since Aiden is leaving for Florida in three days? A good friend would see a guy she's been crushing on for years finally paying her attention as a sign to run for the hills because he will break your heart when he leaves.

I'm so tired of being nice Gigi. The girl who goes along with shit she doesn't always agree with out of fear that if people look too closely, they'll unfairly judge me. So I skirt all drama. But I'm done. I think I used my friends as a crutch for a long time because I found comfort in them when I couldn't find comfort at home. Now that my home life isn't consuming my every waking moment and filling my head with dread, I can see things clearly, and I know I'm being used as well.

I was the spare wheel, the single girl to tag along with Ashton and TJ to parties. After all, who doesn't want single chicks showing up at parties? While I didn't have much, I had a car to get me from point A to point B, and Ashton didn't, so I was her ride. Even Bryce uses me. He's always wanted to be more than just friends, but he knew I didn't want that. So what does he do? He goes and becomes everything I want and need exactly when I need it, hoping he'll wear me down and I'll eventually see him as more.

Anyway, I'm starting to feel like I'm better off alone. I can't be used when I'm alone, and I can't use others. I don't want to hurt anyone, and as much as it kills me to admit it, I know I'm using Mason. I meant it when I told him I'd give him everything I had.

The only problem is I don't know how to fix my heart, and I don't think it was made for love.

There's only one conclusion I can draw from all this: I need to let go of all the chains I've put on myself. I've drawn myself into a box because of how I was raised, but I'm an adult now. I can be who I want to be, and fuck whoever doesn't like it.

Everyone blazes their own trail. I can still have everything I want: the job, the education, the freedom. I need to embrace the pace of my own journey. There's no record of right or wrong here that says I must check X number of boxes by said time. The only way forward is to choose me, and that's precisely what I plan to do.

* * *

It's 11:15 a.m. on Monday morning, and I'm walking to my car to meet Bryce. While I can't escape the prying eyes that hide behind the windows that run the entire length of the Reds building, I've learned to park in the back of the lot. This way, I'm at least not giving everyone a front-row seat every time I sit in my car or meet a friend for lunch.

Spring in Missouri is hard to dress for. The mornings are freezing, and the heat picks up quickly in the afternoons. I wore black slacks with cute tan crisscross espadrille wedges and a white V-neck sweater. I'm sure I tossed a flouncy white poet shirt in the car this morning just in case I got too hot. Sure enough, when I get to my car, I see the white blouse laid out on the back seat. Thank God I had the foresight to bring it, or I'd be melting.

I'm wearing a white camisole underneath, so I decide to pull off my sweater quickly, and as I do, I hear a guy whistle, followed by "looking good." I turn around and notice Bryce walking up. I throw my sweater in his face.

"Ha-ha, very funny. Did you drive the truck? I didn't notice it when I walked out."

Bryce chucks the sweater into my car as I open my rear door to grab my extra shirt.

"No, Chica, I rode my bike. I parked right over there." He motions to the aisle right behind me, and sure enough, there's his bike parked in the shade of the dogwood tree.

I go to put on my new shirt, but he goes in for a hug before I can. It's not meant to be sensual, but he holds me for a beat before releasing me and sitting on the trunk of my car. Pulling my shirt on, I meet him around the back of my car.

"So what's up? Are you here to give me the *I'm a terrible friend* speech?"

He shakes his head and smiles. "You already know I don't think you're a terrible friend. But no, I just came by to say goodbye. I wouldn't say I liked how we left things on Saturday night after everything that transpired. I wanted to see you before I took off."

He shrugs and then hops off the car. I nod and wait to see if he plans to elaborate on anything else because I feel I'm reading this entire discussion wrong. Not to mention, he's the one who called this pow-wow.

"I just want you to know that leaving you will be hard for me. You're actually one of the reasons I'm going."

I let that sink in for a minute. Did he just hit me with a double negative? I'm the reason he's leaving? That's news to me. I pull in a deep breath before looking up to find him watching me, ensuring that he doesn't miss a moment of my reaction to his words. I start, "Bry—"

"Before you say anything, I don't want you to think I came here expecting anything because I don't. I've known from the beginning that you don't see me as anything more than one of your best friends. The problem is I've always wanted more, and I think you know that."

I swallow hard, not sure what to say. *Is he mad at me right now?* He glances over my shoulder and steels his spine before looking back at me. I quickly look back to see what caused the change in his posture, and that's when I see August standing right outside the front doors.

Of course I don't see his ass all morning, and then he decides to show up as I'm in the middle of an important conversation with Bryce.

I turn back to him. "Just ignore him."

To which he replies, "I planned on it." Then, clearing his throat, he continues, "I don't think I can move on from my crush unless I leave. If I stay, I hold onto hope that things between us will change in my favor, but seeing as how it's been four long years, I need to get a grip and extinguish that hope. This is my way of doing that."

He runs a hand through his shaggy brown hair before putting both hands in his pockets. The thing is, I understand all too well about holding onto hope. I've done it for years with Mason, but I never had the luxury of running away. Glancing behind me, I make sure August hasn't moved. He's now leaning against the wall, glaring daggers at me. Screw him. If anyone should be angry, it should be me. I turn my attention back to Bryce.

"Bryce, I've honestly wished I could catch feelings for you because it would have made things much easier. I'm sorry I've caused you pain. It has never been my intent."

He shakes it off. "Gigi, you know you've never caused me pain. Crushing on you was one of my favorite pastimes, but it's time to move on. Of course I still expect you to come to Florida once we get settled."

I shake my head and laugh. "Yeah, I'm sure Aiden would just love that!"

He chuckles. "He's not mad at you, in case you were wondering. He hasn't said much about what happened, just shrugs it off, but he doesn't blame you."

"Well, I guess that's good to know."

He shrugs and then steps forward to pull me into a bear hug, picking me up a spinning me around just like he used to do in the hallways at school. He sets me down just as we notice August walking in our direction. Bryce calls out, "I know, fucker, I'm leaving." Then he kisses me on the head. "I'll call you when I get there." And just like that, he walks to his bike.

I watch Bryce drive off on his motorcycle, and for some

reason, I'm happy. While I'm sad to see my friend go, a weight has been lifted off my shoulders. His leaving means that I have one less person in my life to let down. But he's also one of the last people I had here supporting me. Before I can put more thought into my feelings about Bryce leaving, I'm reminded that I'm not alone. August bursts my moment of reflection.

"We need to talk, and not here in the parking lot."

I turn around and stare at August with a look that I hope shows my annoyance with him.

"August, we have absolutely nothing to talk about. You can go to hell." I practically spit the last part.

He puts his tongue in his cheek before pressing his lips together. "Do you get off at four o'clock today?"

So that's how it's going to be. He's just going to act like I didn't just tell him to fuck off. Of course I'm no longer glaring at him. In typical 'Gianna sees August' fashion, I've thrown all my good sense out the window, and now I'm drinking him in from the bottom up. He's wearing brown wingtips, light khaki pants that stretch slightly across his thick muscular thighs, and a dark green polo button-down rolled up to the elbows that makes his hazel eyes pop. Meeting his gaze, he narrows his eyes at me as if to say, 'Are you seriously checking me out?'

"Gianna, I'm going to need you to act like an adult today. I know the concept is new for you, but I need your words."

I scowl at him. How dare he interrupt my lunch hour once again to hurl insults at me?

"Why even bother, August? I clearly piss you off. I'm sure you know plenty of girls willing to drop their panties for you. Go call one of them."

I turn to open my driver's side door, and he closes it, essentially caging me in from behind. Then he leans down to my ear, his words laced with venom as he says, "The problem is there's not another you, so no, Gianna, I won't be getting another girl." Then he pulls away and heads back toward the office.

*Damn it.*

Once again, I have my chance to confront him and tell him off, and all I manage are weak-ass replies. I stand there, taking his insults as if I don't have a backbone. Why the hell do I keep letting him talk down to me? What's more pathetic is that I crave his attention, good or bad. But even when his words are laced with hate, when he looks at me, his eyes can't lie. He looks at me like his world starts and stops with me, and I'll be damned if I don't feel the same way.

As I head back to the office, I remember I carpooled with my mom today. Unfortunately, that means I can't meet August after work. My heart sinks at the thought. I quickly shoot him a text.

> Gianna: Sorry I can't meet you after work today. Maybe tomorrow.

> August: I don't remember giving you an option.

I swear, the nerve of this guy. I mean, seriously, who does he think he is?

> Gianna: I carpooled with my mom. I'm her ride.

> August: I'll drive you home.

It's just after 4:00 p.m., and I'm running behind, tactfully trying to hurry without causing a scene as I weave through the maze of cubicles after dropping my car keys off at my mom's desk. We had a lot of samples to get mocked up today for the trade show taking place at the end of the month. I'm tasked with locking up the Sample Room today, ensuring that none of the products mysteriously disappear. The sales associates are good at stopping by and looking, only to grab a product they like and leave with it.

Walking down the hallway, I know that if I wanted to, I could get out of going with August tonight, but deep down, that's not what I want. I can't help but wonder if consciously making a bad decision makes it any less wrong. For my sanity, I hope it does. Making my way through the lobby, I can see August standing outside his black Mercedes G-Wagon, talking on the phone. From the looks of it, he doesn't seem too pleased. *Great.*

I decide to give him a minute and check my emails on my phone before heading out. After about five minutes of going down the rabbit hole of social media, I see that August is no longer on the phone, and it's now four thirty. *Shit.*

I quickly grab my purse and head out the door. He immediately sees me and glowers at me. I can tell he's frustrated, but that doesn't stop him from walking around to my side of the car and opening the door anyway. I climb in without saying a word.

Once he gets in the car, he starts it up and backs out. He doesn't even glance my way as if I repulse him that much. I have so many things I want to say. So many questions I want to ask, but I don't because, with him, it's always the same. He immobilizes me. I have no defenses when it comes to him, and I lose my ability to reason. It's very pathetic. I know this.

We finally pull up to what looks like a condominium, and I break the silence to ask, "Where are we?"

He glances at me as if I've just asked the stupidest question on earth. "My place."

Then, getting out, he comes around to open my door. Once my door is open, I say, "As if I didn't realize we were at a residential complex, let me rephrase that question. Why would you bring me to your place? We've been over this."

He rolls his lips together. "Oh, I'm sorry, I didn't realize you were trying to get a minor-in-possession ticket this evening." He climbs out and slams his door.

*Ass.*

I reluctantly exit the car and hold his gaze in a challenge as he comes around.

"So you know my age." It's not a question but more of a statement at this point, but his expression doesn't reveal anything about his feelings on the subject. "I suppose that's a problem for you."

He shrugs. "I thought it was. Turns out it's not."

Closing the door, he puts his hands in his pockets and turns to me like he's waiting for me to make some smart-ass remark. Instead, I make a big gesture with my arms outstretched.

"Well, please don't keep me waiting. Lead the way."

He shakes his head and takes off toward the complex.

The complex is a modern three-story building with a mix of cedar wood and dark gray stained concrete. There are balconies on each level with glass railings and green topiaries in each corner. It has a very millennial vibe, at least on the outside.

When we reach the front door, he holds it open and gestures for me to enter. Once inside, I follow him up three flights of stairs. Of course he'd be on the top floor. I'm surprised this building doesn't have an elevator, but I suppose the steps aren't so bad.

Once we reach his door, he looks at me with a mischievous smirk. "Last chance if you were planning on running." I quirk a brow at him in answer before he shakes his head. Then, opening the door, he gestures for me to walk in.

I don't know what I expected walking up to his condo, but I wasn't expecting it to be so intoxicating. The space is very masculine. It smells like cedar and leather. It smells like him.

The ceilings are vaulted with cedar wood and have recessed, black can lights. The walls are dark gray concrete, just like the complex's exterior, apart from one wall encased in a cedar wood bookcase that pops against the dark contrast of the wall. In the middle of that wall is a gas fireplace flanked by gray stones that run from floor to ceiling. It's an open concept living space, so you walk into the living room, kitchen, and dining all at once.

The kitchen has a considerable light gray waterfall island with dark walnut cabinets underneath. Behind the island is a chef's dream stovetop with one of those fancy pot filler spouts. The place screams money and sophistication, and I'm quickly reminded of how out of my element I am with this man. I'm reminded of how we come from entirely different backgrounds.

Watching him stroll into the kitchen and open the refrigerator pulls me out of my gawking. He turns to me, slowly running his eyes up my body. "What can I get you to drink?"

"I'll have whatever you're having." I decide to walk to the island instead of standing by the front door looking like a no-class fool. He pops the top on an IPA and slides it across the island. Narrowing my gaze, I say, "I thought you had a problem with my underage drinking."

"No, Gianna, no problem with the drinking, just the honesty."

I scoff. "Well, it's not like you ever asked me for my age. In fact, we tend to do a lot of not talking when we're together, which is fine, but don't you dare insinuate that I'm a liar."

I take a long pull off my beer before turning around and noticing the deck off the front of the living room. The building must have sunset sensors because the railings are now lit with a soft amber light. It's breathtaking.

He sets his beer down rather loudly to pull my attention back to him.

That's when I decide to grow a pair and speak my mind.

"While we're on the subject of lying, how about omitting the fact that you have a girlfriend?"

He meets my gaze and furrows his brow while thinning his lips. I can tell I hit the mark with that one. He doesn't like being called out on his shit.

"That's what I wanted to talk to you about. I would not have pursued you if I was in that kind of committed relationship."

Does he think I'm stupid? If you have a title, you have a commitment.

"Well, from what I witnessed, your relationship as boyfriend and girlfriend seemed pretty solid, and I'm not interested in being the other girl, so I'm glad we cleared that up."

He shifts and starts to round the island toward me. That's when I begin to walk around it in the opposite direction. Then, placing both hands on the countertop, he leans in and says,

"Gianna, don't walk away from me." I meet his irritated gaze with one of my own.

"Here's the thing: if you get too close, you and I both know what needs to be said won't get said, and I'm tired of the games. So you stay on your side of the island, or I leave."

That seems to sate him for the moment because he grabs his beer and leans back against the countertop opposite the island, contemplating my words. "Deal... For now."

# FIFTEEN
## August

Finally, I have her right where I want her: in my place. Here there won't be any distractions. There are no waiters interrupting stolen moments, no random friends vying for her attention, or, God forbid, trying to touch her.

I've had it with all these men she keeps around touching her. Every time I turn around, some guy is hugging her, kissing her, or trying to grind on her ass. I'm getting pissed just thinking about it.

I take a pull off my beer before hopping up to sit on the counter. Gianna started pacing the end of the island after requesting I keep my distance. I'm trying to appear casual and non-threatening even though every cell in my body is screaming to get closer to her.

While watching her fidget and nervously straighten my bar stools is undoubtedly entertaining, I'd rather be touching her. When I touch her, words aren't needed because everything is as it should be. She's meant to be mine. I just need to convince her. My movement must have caught her peripheral because she stops pacing, but not before flushing with embarrassment.

"Do I make you that nervous?"

She glares at me, and I throw her a wink. I can tell I'm riling her up. However, she hasn't yet figured out that it's one of my favorite things to do, so I decide to give her a break and get on with our plans to talk.

"The girl you saw at the bar was my girlfriend. She no longer holds that title and hasn't for the past six months really. Saturday was the first time I've seen her since she left six months ago."

I don't mention why Carson was there Saturday night as the details are irrelevant, but I have my suspicions about how she knew where to find me. Seeming somewhat pacified by the information she just learned, she pulls out a stool and sits before looking at me to continue.

"Her name is Carson. We started dating in high school, and we dated throughout college. Six months ago, out of nowhere, she decided she wanted to finish her last semester on the East Coast. In her words, we needed a break, time apart to see if we were meant to be. Basically, she wanted to see other people."

I jump off the counter and throw my empty bottle in the trash before grabbing two more from the fridge. I slide one over to Gianna and then walk through the living area toward the deck. After sliding the door open, I gesture for her to join me outside.

The deck is a lot bigger than it appears from the street. It runs the length of the front and then down the entire side of the condo to the back where you can enter the master bedroom. One of the reasons I fell in love with this place was its outdoor space. It's an older, rehabbed building, so the trees surrounding it are well-established, leaving you to feel like you're sitting amongst the branches. Gianna picks up her second beer and follows me outside.

I keep my distance as promised and watch her take in the treehouse-like atmosphere the fully-grown trees create around the balcony. As she looks around, I can see the tension in her shoulders release, and the wonderment that fills her eyes tells me she loves this space as much as I do. I sit on one of the lounge chairs before continuing my explanation.

"The only reason I didn't follow you out immediately on Saturday is that I was completely shocked to see her there. Not only because I wasn't aware she was back in town, but none of my crew ever goes to that side of town."

Gianna's spine straightens as if that comment has made her uncomfortable.

"Gianna, you're the only one I want, but I wasn't going to be cruel. Carson and I have a history. I owed it to her to tell her in person that we would not be getting back together. She didn't seem very surprised, nor did she seem to care." That stung a little, I'm not going to lie, but only because who wants to feel like they didn't mean anything? "While I have a history with Carson, we weren't your typical couple. We didn't practice monogamy, by her choice. Our relationship was arranged, and I stayed for the wrong reasons. In my world, women marry and become trophy wives who screw the pool boy while their husbands are away on business screwing their interns. Everyone gets fucked, and no one bats an eye. As misogynist as it might sound, that's the reality of my world."

It's honestly depressing. The only successful marriage I've ever seen is the one my parents have. They genuinely seem to be in love and married for all the right reasons, but that hasn't stopped them from meddling in my affairs.

I want my girl to sit by me, and I'm trying hard to respect her space, but I have my limits. She's leaning on the railing, holding her beer in her hands and tearing the label off, deep in thought, while I stare at her perfect ass. All I can think about is coming up behind her, pressing my cock into her ass, placing my lips on that spot behind her ear she likes, and inhaling her intoxicating scent. Fuck, my cock is getting hard. Luckily, she breaks my train of thought.

"While this walk down memory lane has been enlightening and explains some of your chauvinistic tendencies, it's getting late. I think you should take me home. I live at least forty-five minutes away from here."

Is she serious right now? I lay it all out there, and she's ready to leave. I stand up, closing the distance between us in two long strides. I'm in her space before she can blink, close enough to feel her breath on me as she looks into my eyes and says, "We had a deal." She seems utterly disappointed in me, and at this point, I'm getting agitated. I lean in, about to kiss away this madness, when she pushes me back and storms inside. I follow hot on her heels.

"You have no right to try to kiss me. I'm done being your mistake, August. You brought me here to clear the air, and now we can leave the past in the past and move on. So now, you stay out of my way, and I'll stay out of yours."

What the hell is she talking about, mistake? She *would* choose this moment to mince words and conveniently forget I just told her I wanted her. "Let's get one thing crystal clear. I never said you were a mistake. My comment was regarding my actions and the date itself. I had just found out who you were and how old you are. I felt misled. In hindsight, that wasn't your problem."

She huffs. "Well, I'm glad my age no longer bothers you, but I can't change who I am or where I come from. You only see the details you want to see, and that's why you can't see that we don't fit. We are from two completely different worlds, August. You know that wrong side of town you visited on Saturday is where I grew up."

Her breathing is erratic, and I can tell she hates the words she spewed at me. Breaking our eye contact, she makes her way back to the kitchen and disposes of her bottle. This right here, right now, is half of the reason I'm so spellbound by this woman. She knows what she wants, and apparently, it's not my money, influence, or position because I would have already had her in my bed if that were the case. If Gianna lets me in, it will be because she wants me and not what I have to offer, and that's everything for someone like me.

When she goes for her purse, I know her next stop is the door. I quickly change course and cut her off. Throwing my arms around her waist, I pull her into me before she can make it to the door. She yelps, surprised by my actions. I look down at her widened eyes. "I said I want you, and I'm a man who gets what he wants. We both have pasts. Everything else is just semantics."

Her lips part in surprise, and I can't help but cover them with my own. My kiss is gentle at first, testing the waters until she kisses me back. I secure one arm around her waist, keeping her firmly pressed against my front as I trail my other arm up her back, where it gets tangled in her purse straps. I pull her purse from her shoulder and toss it back on the kitchen island. Once it's gone, I bring my hand to the back of her head, running my fingers through her silky hair before tugging it back to deepen our kiss. She whimpers into my mouth before fisting my shirt in her hands, urgently pulling me close, trying to eliminate any space between us.

That hunger is all the sign I needed to bring my hands down to grip her ass and lift her up. Immediately, her legs wrap around me, and her hands loosen their grip on my shirt as she glides them up my chest and around my neck, sending a tantalizing line of heat down my back and straight to my cock.

I walk us over to my oversized couch, where I lay her down. Then, breaking our kiss, I begin trailing my lips along her jaw toward the spot behind her ear I know she likes. It gives her goose bumps, and I smile against her neck when I feel them.

"Do you like it when I kiss you here, baby?"

She doesn't give me her words, only a coy smile and a nod. I know she's shy, but I need to hear her voice to know this is real. That she's here beneath me, letting me touch her intimately, letting me taste her. I need to hear that she's mine.

I kiss her neck before grabbing her jaw and pulling her face to mine, where I catch her gaze. "I need to hear your voice tonight, Gianna."

Her big green eyes close tight like she's embarrassed, but she affably replies, "Okay."

I lower myself down on top of her and occupy the space between her thighs, making sure my cock is firmly placed against her clit. Her eyes immediately fly open when she feels how hard I am. I teasingly pump my cock into her. She bites her bottom lip, clearly enjoying the feel of me pressed against her, before wrapping her legs around my waist to keep me pinned. She likes what

I'm doing, and I fucking love that I'm the one making her feel good.

Her hooded eyes meet mine as she reaches up to run her fingers through my hair before gripping the nape of my neck and crushing her mouth to mine. She tastes like the hops from the beer we were drinking earlier, and for some reason, that's sexy. Maybe it's because most girls don't drink beer, or at least the girls I'm used to. Beer has too many calories for the stuck-up bitches I know. It's yet another reminder of how authentic she is. I can't help but release a moan into her mouth, lost in complete ecstasy.

I reach between us and grab the hem of her shirt, breaking our kiss, only to pull it off and find a black satin camisole underneath. Eager to put my mouth on her beautifully bronzed skin, I start to trail kisses along her collarbone before rasping, "Still too many clothes."

She laughs and tugs at my shirt. I sit back on my haunches and swipe my tongue across my bottom lip before unbuttoning my Oxford shirt. The hunger in her eyes is enough to undo me. Her eyes are the most exquisite color of green I've ever seen. I could stare into them all day, and it wouldn't be long enough.

She reaches down to pull her camisole over her head, and my cock twitches in anticipation when I see her soft skin and perfect curves. My eyes move from her narrow waist up to the swell of her breasts. Her chest is heaving, probably from a mixture of nerves and lust. Immediately, I cup her face in my hands and gently kiss her lips to calm her erratic breathing. I know she's turned on, but I sense she's apprehensive and nervous. It's as if our being topless together is pushing some sort of boundary for her. I lay her back down before settling on top of her. Brushing the hair out of her face, I kiss her forehead.

"You're so beautiful, Gianna. If you want me to stop—"

She cuts me off by putting her finger to my lips. "I want you, August."

Fuck, if those weren't the best four words I ever heard in my life. I close the distance between our mouths, pulling her plump bottom lip into my mouth, where I bite down enough to draw blood and suck hard. I wouldn't say I have a blood kink by any means. I haven't ever bitten another woman hard enough to draw blood, but her blood speaks to me on a deeply personal level that I can't explain.

I bring my hand up to cup her breast through her bra, but she promptly pushes it away. Confused, I watch as she reaches between her breasts and unclasps her bra from the front. Her perfect tits fall out, and pre-cum drips from my dick. Groaning, I put my face into the crook of her neck to calm my raging libido.

She runs her fingers through my hair and caresses my neck. "I'm sorry that was too fast. It's just you said there were too many clothes between us, so I thought—"

I place my palm over her mouth to stop her from talking before pulling back to look at her, dumbfounded. *Why would she think it's too fast?* I'm sitting here trying not to pound her into tomorrow, and she thinks it's moving too fast.

"Baby, you're so fucking perfect. I've never wanted someone so bad in my life. I'm trying to calm my need to rip your pants off, part those creamy thighs, and ram my cock into your swollen pussy in one stroke."

Her chest is heaving while her nipples stand perfectly erect. I know her panties must be soaked, and I can't wait to find out how wet she is for me, but I'm not done with her perfect tits yet.

I take her rosy-pink nipple in my mouth and suck hard before nipping it. She gasps and throws her head back, purring with pleasure. I take her other nipple between my fingers and gently tug, making her hips buck into me, seeking friction I'm more than willing to provide. I grind my cock against her pussy, where I can feel the heat of her arousal through my pants.

I'm done acting like a horny teenager dry-humping my girl, so I kiss my way down her stomach, slowly dragging my hands down her sides, taking in every luscious curve of her body. Once I get to the waistband of her pants, I trail my tongue along her band from one hipbone to the other. Her body shudders beneath my touch as I slowly unbutton her pants.

My hands tremble ever so slightly as I slowly peel her pants down, revealing the most tantalizing, toned thighs I have ever seen.

Once her pants are off, I take a minute to drink in the sight before me. Every ounce of her soft, succulent skin is on display, save for the black thong I have yet to remove. She is a fucking goddess.

As I sit on my haunches between her legs, I bring her ankle up and place a kiss on the inside of it before resting it on my shoulder.

She squeals. "August, that tickles."

I cock an eyebrow at her before skimming my knuckles down the arc of her leg, making her quiver in their wake. My fingers reach her panties, and I halt my movement as my gaze locks with hers.

"Please, August." A breathy plea escapes her lips as she arches into my hand, tempting me to touch her where she needs it most. As she does, my hand skims her drenched thong. I pull her panties to the side and run my finger up her center.

"Fuck, you're so damn wet for me."

Not wanting to waste another second, I tear her panties off and sink a finger into her soft, warm pussy. It immediately clenches around me. My cock is now throbbing so bad it hurts.

Her pussy is swollen and aching for release. I know she's going to come fast. I add another digit as she lets out the sexiest moan while grinding her pussy onto my fingers. When I look down at her glistening, pink pussy—my fingers pumping her in and out, covered in her juices—I can't help but want a taste.

I've never really gotten into giving oral. Carson didn't seem to care for it unless another chick was doing it. The one time I tried, she pulled me up to fuck. Carson's kink was threesomes. She got off watching me fuck other girls hard. When it came to me fucking her, she always wanted it vanilla.

There was no way I was ever going to go down on some rando from a party, but looking at Gianna's pussy dripping with need shatters me. I pull back, and she whimpers at the loss of my fingers.

"Don't worry. You're going to come."

I lean down and press a kiss to her inner thigh before swiping my tongue up her center. She jolts up and leans onto her elbows, looking at me between her thighs. Fuck, that's a hot view. Her face flushes with ecstasy from my touch. I keep my eyes locked on her frenzied gaze as I stick my tongue between her folds and her head lulls back in complete euphoria. I swirl my tongue around her tight bundle of nerves before pumping two fingers inside of her and sucking hard. She explodes immediately. I keep pumping her slowly, letting her ride out the aftershocks of her orgasm.

When I pull my fingers out, I flatten my tongue against her pussy, making sure I don't miss a drop. I've never found the act of going down on a woman hot, but with Gianna, I want everything. I know these juices are the result of her enjoying me, and that's fucking intoxicating.

Her eyes are closed, and she squeezes her tits as I sit back on my haunches, staring at her, laid out before me, burning from the pleasure I gave her.

I unbutton my pants and pull my briefs down to release my cock. I stroke it hard as she massages her breasts, pussy glistening with arousal. Fuck, I need to be inside her.

Leaning down, I align my cock with her entrance, dipping it in slightly before running my head through her wet lips. Her eyes snap open in surprise. I come down on top of her, caging her in with my arms. "Are you going to take my cock, baby?"

She pulls my face to hers and kisses me like she might die if she doesn't. I reach down between us and line up to push in. Wanting to savor the feel of her, I move in slowly.

"Fuck, you're so tight. You have to relax."

She blows out a breath. "Yeah, okay, sorry."

"What? No, don't be sorry. You are so perfect. I need you to relax so you can let me in."

My words of praise seem to help, and I'm able to push in a little more. I know I'm big, so I give her a minute to acclimate before slowly pumping her. She screws up her face as if she's in pain. I lean in and kiss her neck before sucking on her lobe. That's when I feel her really start to loosen.

"That's it, soak my cock, you're doing so good." I push in deep, to the hilt. We both gasp, and I have to stop myself from losing it right then. Her brow is still furrowed, so I bring my lips to it and plant a kiss there before dropping featherlight kisses all over her face and picking up my pace.

Once her body relaxes, her little mewls pick up in an intoxicating crescendo. I start pumping into her at a piston pace, watching her tits bounce from the force. Her pussy starts to choke my cock, and I want to shoot my seed deep inside her. That's when it hits me. Fuck! I forgot a condom. I stop in panic, worry plastered across my face. *How did I forget a condom?* I always use a condom. Panting, I say, "I'm sorry, baby, I forgot a condom. Are you on the pill?"

Her face goes from one of concern to relief. "Yes."

Her voice is husky and sexy as fuck. I reach down and take her lips in mine as I slowly pump into her again. Her pussy clenches around my dick, and I know she's close. Pulling back, I search her eyes. "I want to come inside you. Say I can."

That's when she surprises the fuck out of me. Wrapping her legs around my waist, she leans into my ear, her voice laced with lust, and says, "Fill me up."

My dick twitches, and I quickly pump into her three more times before I feel her orgasm take root, and she begins to writhe beneath me. I follow her right over the edge as we both spiral into oblivion.

As we come back down, I pepper her with kisses, letting my hands trail over her body, and in this moment, I know she's mine. There will be no one else. I've never gone bareback in my life, and I never want to have anyone but her. She has ruined me for any other. Now all I have to do is figure out how to keep her.

"You're so perfect, Gianna. That was everything." I'm at a loss for words. I've never felt this way for anyone, but I want her to know how incredible she is. I don't want her to think it was just about the sex. She makes me feel real. Nothing is rehearsed. The way she responds to me is purely animalistic. It can't be duplicated. Her body comes alive under my touch as if it was made for me, and I'll be damned if I let that slip away.

She's about to speak but is cut off by a loud pounding on my front door. Our eyes widen, and she says, "Were you expecting someone?"

"No, the one person I was expecting is under me."

Then we hear, "August, open up, man!"

*Shit.*

It's Grant. You have got to be kidding me right now. They decide to come over tonight of all nights. Gianna quickly reaches for the blanket to cover herself.

"Calm down. It's locked. No one is going to see you."

I would literally kill them if they saw her like this. They start pounding again, and then Ethan says, "Come on, man, I got to take a leak."

These assholes are fucking up my night with my girl. I move to pull out and let Gianna clean up, but when I look down to watch my seed drip out of the first girl I've ever blown my load in, I see RED.

## SIXTEEN
### *Gianna*

For the first time in my life, I did something I wanted to do without overthinking it, and it was amazing. Sex with August was life-changing. While it may have been my first and only time, it was reckless, thrilling, and intoxicating, and I am so thoroughly screwed.

August reluctantly pulls out, and my body immediately feels the loss, and by the look in his eyes, I think he feels it too until he looks down. *Why did he have to look down?* His eyes snap up to mine in utter horror.

"Gianna, what the hell? Did I hurt you? Why didn't you tell me to stop?"

I quickly reach for the blanket hung over the side of the couch and pull it around me as I scramble for my clothes in hopes that he doesn't see my cheeks heat with embarrassment.

Clearly, I didn't think this through; otherwise, I would have considered the fact that I might bleed. *Shit.*

He pulls on his pants while I try to make quick work of heading toward the bathroom to clean up. Before I can get past him, he grabs me around the waist. "Talk to me, baby."

I pull my bottom lip into my mouth and close my eyes to

avoid his penetrating gaze. He is always so perceptive. Where are those skills now?

*Bang! Bang! Bang!* rings out through the condo, and he barks, "Hold on, fuckers!"

Then someone shouts, "Tell Carson to go fix her lipstick in the other room and let us in."

August pinches the bridge of his nose in irritation, and I take off toward the back of the condo, hoping to find a bathroom.

"Gianna, wait," he calls after me. Then, when I go to close the bathroom door, he stops it with his foot.

"They can stand out there all night for all I care. You're important to me and—"

I cut him off before he can finish. "It's okay. Let your friends in. I'll be out in a minute."

He briefly searches my eyes for reassurance that my words are true, and I give him my best fake smile. A smile that any one of my friends would see straight through. He seems to buy it, and I close the door.

Once the door is closed, I take a deep breath and let it out slowly before seeing my reflection in the mirror. The girl that was having sex with August felt like a powerful woman, a queen being worshipped by her king, but the girl in the mirror is a slut.

This is not me. I would never sleep with someone I've only known for a few weeks, and I can't even say I really know him. We haven't even talked about anything of importance. I don't know what college he went to, what he likes to do for fun, his favorite food or music. All I know is who he is to me, the CEO's son, future owner, and the man with the ability to fuck up all my goals.

Believe it or not, I'm very good at recognizing things that are bad for me, and August is one of those things. The problem is this one bad thing deep down inside feels so right, even though I know it shouldn't. I know girls like me don't land guys like him. Tonight, however, I chose myself, the guy I want, and the girl I want to be, but the sobering reality is that I don't have the luxury to be this reckless, and now I need to navigate a way forward before I lose everything.

The sounds of voices entering the apartment bring me out of my borderline panic attack. I look down to see how much damage there is, and it's not as bad as I expected. I assumed there would be a lot of blood, like a period, but it's more like the evidence of his ejaculation is coming out streaked with red.

Now that I think about it, he asked if he could come inside me, and when I gave him the green light, he came almost immediately. That explains why he looked down when he pulled out. The possessive freak wanted to leave his mark and see the evidence leak out of me. My insides clench just thinking about what we did. It was so good, and I'm so thoroughly screwed.

I quickly get dressed, minus my underwear since it was ripped from my body. Doing my best, I try to look normal instead of like someone who just lost their virginity. Taking a moment, I give myself a pep talk, "Only you can give people the power to make you feel small." These guys might have money and status, but that doesn't make them better than me. I put my lady balls on and exit the bathroom.

As I walk down the hallway toward the kitchen, a tall, attractive blond catches sight of me out of the corner of his eye, then he whistles.

"Damn, August, you didn't mention Carson brought friends."

My heart sinks once more at the mention of her name. They were high school sweethearts, they have history, and I can't compete with that. His words from earlier about their relationship should comfort me. However, I learned a long time ago actions truly speak louder than words. He can say it sucked all he wants, but the truth is he stayed with her for years.

"Fuck you, Ethan! You know Carson and I aren't together anymore," August yells.

Nearing the kitchen, I hear another voice chime in, "I think Carson believes you're still on a break, man."

Finally rounding the corner into the kitchen, I get a look at the other man and fuck me if he doesn't look just like Jake from *Twilight*. I stare at him for a minute too long, and he notices.

"Something catch your eye, princess?"

I'll play his game, knowing I need to come off completely unaffected even though I want to crawl into a hole and die.

"No, *Twilight*, I was team Edward. We're good."

The blond guy spits out his beer in laughter as I make my way toward the living room to collect my purse and find my phone. I don't want to stay here a minute longer.

I don't regret what I did with August. It was perfect, but that moment passed. We haven't talked about there being an *us*, and I'm not naive enough to expect there to be one just because we had sex.

I quickly share my location with Mason and ask if he can pick me up.

"Okay, she's a keeper, but since you already have a girlfriend, I'll be happy to take her off your hands, Auggie baby," says the blond playboy.

He is exceptionally handsome. Most women probably swoon over him, but I see straight through his type. The man is interested in one thing, sex. My eyes snap up to August as he rounds the island in one swoop and pins him up against the wall.

"You won't touch what is fucking mine. You're already treading on thin ice. Don't push me."

The disdain dripping from each word has me wondering if there's more to this confrontation than I'm comprehending. The two of them are staring at each other with such hate it's hard to believe they're friends. That's when *Twilight* decides to step in.

"Come on, bro! He was just fucking around."

August pushes him back before releasing his shirt. Before I know it, they're all staring at me. My eyebrows shoot up in surprise, not sure what to say. I swear August's eyes briefly soften in apology, but it's gone just as fast as it came, then my phone chimes. Wow, Mason got here quick.

"Well, boys, this has certainly been entertaining, to say the least, but my ride is here, so I'm going to head out."

I turn around to grab my purse off the table and start toward the door, but August beats me there and clips out, "I told you I'd take you home."

The ire in his voice admittedly surprises me. His friends showed up out of nowhere and are now nagging him about our relationship. If I leave, that gives him an out. He doesn't have to pretend to like me. He can talk shit about how he just 'hit it' and shrug off their derogatory comments instead of feeling obligated to stick up for me. I don't need his pity. I chose to have sex with him. He doesn't have to act like it was anything more for my benefit.

"Look, my ride is here, and your friends are here. It's no big deal. I'll see you at work tomorrow."

He crosses his arms and pins me with a murderous stare.

"Who's the ride, Gianna?"

Biting my lip, I avert my gaze to the guys who are now leaning up against the counter, beers in hand, watching this all play out. *Twilight* arches a brow at me as if to say we want to know too. *Bastards*.

I swallow hard and clear my throat, but before I can speak, August puts his hand up to stop me. "If you value the air in his lungs, you will not get in that car."

Now I'm mad. Who is he to threaten my friends?

"He's just a friend, August."

His jaw ticks and his eyes narrow on me. "A friend who wants to fuck you."

The nerve of this man!

"Well, we both know he isn't that lucky. Now, if you don't mind, I'd like to leave."

I meet the ire in his gaze with a fury of my own and quirk a brow at him, daring him to question the validity of what I just said. He may not have realized what the blood meant at the moment, but I think he does now.

A knock at the door breaks our stare down, and I feel like roots have grown out of the floor, cementing me in place. When I texted Mason, I fully intended to meet him at his car. My stomach sinks with the knowledge that he'll see August, and I feel sick knowing he's on the other side of that door.

August notices my sudden discomfort with the situation and quickly twists the knife by opening the door slowly. That's when I hear Mason mutter, "Is she fucking serious right now?"

And just like that, August throws the door open to reveal me standing here like a deer stuck in headlights.

Mason does a quick scan of the place, taking note of the two idiots at the island before raking his eyes up my body, no doubt checking for foul play before meeting my gaze. The desolate look in his eyes has my heart literally tearing in half. All I want is to throw myself into his arms and tell him how sorry I am, that I never wanted to hurt him this way. None of that matters now. I know I need to break things off with Mason. I can't be what he deserves.

Mason finally breaks the silence, his words laced with bile. "Gianna, let's go."

Before I can make a move, August casually steps in front of Mason's view. Then, putting his hands in his pockets, he says, "Leave, Croft."

My eyes widen in shock as I stare at the back of his head. How the hell does he know Mason's last name? Is he stalking me now?

"You know I can't do that." He steps to the side so I can once again see him and gestures for me to come with him.

I slowly take two steps toward the door, ready to walk around August, when he throws his arm out to block me before biting out, "I'll terminate the contract."

Mason shakes his head in frustration before meeting his eye.

"You're a prick. You know that, right?"

August casually shrugs. "I never claimed not to be."

Mason puts his tongue in his cheek before putting one hand on the doorframe and leaning in with challenge in his eyes.

"You already know she means more to me than that. You're just pissed that I'm the one she called to get away from you. Maybe next time you want to keep a girl, don't threaten her."

August turns around and glares at me hard. I confided in

Mason, now he's mad, but I don't owe him anything. Before either of them can say another word, I storm past both, shouldering August as I walk out the door.

I yell over my shoulder, "I'll get an Uber," as I quickly charge to the stairs in a rush to escape before anyone can stop me.

In unison, they both say, "Gianna, wait," but I'm done waiting. My heart is broken, my soul is shattered, and I want to go home. I need to get away from both of them.

I'm frantic to put distance between them and myself. I can't win in this situation. I lose all around. I either lose my heart, the boy who picked up the pieces of me and put me back together more times than I can count, or I lose the man who has awakened parts of me I didn't know existed.

August ignited a flame deep inside of me that burns only for him. Every piece of me hungers for him. From the minute our eyes locked for the first time, I was gone. He owned me whether I wanted it or not. We had an instant, undeniable chemistry. The only problem is I don't know how much of that rings true for him. As reckless as these feelings for him are, I can't ignore them. I feel like some lovesick teenager crushing on the first man she had sex with, when in reality, he's just not that into me.

Suddenly, my chest feels tight, my eyesight gets blurry, and I feel like I might faint. Putting my hands on my knees, I take deep breaths, trying to pull air into my lungs.

Then Mason's there on his knees in front of me, hands cradling my face. "Babe, look at me. I need you to calm down and breathe. I'm here. It's okay. We're going to be okay."

Suddenly, he's lying on the ground, and August is hovering above him, ready to strike. Then everything goes black.

* * *

I'm in a car when I wake up but not the right car. I can't avoid the tear that escapes and rolls down my cheek. August glances over at me and does a double take before pulling the car over.

"You're awake. Please don't cry, baby."

That's when the dam breaks. I can't help it. Tonight has been an emotional roller coaster with way too many ups and downs, and as much as I want to hold my shit together and not let August see me cry, the truth is, I want him to hold me again.

No sooner the thought passes than he's out of the car, opening my door, and pulling me into his arms. I let him hold me, and his woodsy scent quickly engulfs my senses, wrapping around me like a warm blanket, calming my racing heart. Our embrace is short because he pulls back to place his hands on my cheeks and wipe away my tears.

"Sit. I have snacks for you."

Snacks? How does he know I need snacks? I haven't had a fainting episode in a while, but he wouldn't know about my blood sugar issues. He opens the back door and pulls out a bag full of snacks and a Dr Pepper.

"I know you drink diet soda, but you need the sugar and calories after tonight."

My face flames with heat. Is he referring to our sex? Does he think I fainted because he wore me out? I drop my face to my lap to avoid his gaze, but that doesn't work for him. He grabs my chin and forces me to meet his eyes.

"I told you not to hide from me." His eyes search mine as if he is trying to read my mind. They finally settle on my mouth and he says, "Mason told me what to do before he got in his car and drove off."

I try, I really do, but the tears sting the back of my eyes and fall anyway. I hang my head in shame. I shouldn't have asked Mason to pick me up, and then he wouldn't have been hurt once again.

"Baby, I really need you to stop crying. My nerves are shot, and I need my girl back."

His hands grip the fabric of my pants as he puts his head in my lap. This beautiful man is acting as if I mean something to him. I gently run my fingers through his hair, watching as his shoulders slightly relax at my touch. My stomach chooses this moment to growl. He looks up at me and scolds, "Eat!" clearly agitated.

I nod in agreement and open the bag of snacks, finding a soft-baked macadamia nut cookie inside—my favorite. I take a bite and moan at how good it tastes. August is still standing outside the car door, watching me eat. Given the events of the last few hours, I shouldn't want him right now, but he's completely ensnared me. I'm trapped, and I don't want to get free. I want whatever attention he'll give me, and I know that sounds incredibly pathetic.

Trying my best to play it somewhat cool and not look like a complete lovesick fool, I reach for my soda and take a huge drink.

Once he's satisfied and sure I've eaten enough and won't pass out, he says, "I'm sorry. I should have fed you."

My posture slumps with defeat.

Damn, that's what he's sorry for? Out of all the things that have happened tonight, he's sorry he didn't feed me. That's when I realize I need to stop hoping he'll want me the way I want him. I need to bury my emotions that are screaming for him to keep me, and the only way I know to do that is by pushing him away.

"Can you please just take me home now?"

I turn and tuck myself into the car. He stands there for a minute, burning holes into the side of my head with his gaze before closing the door.

Once he gets in the car, I steal a glance at his hands gripping the steering wheel and notice his knuckles are trashed as if he got in a fight.

Oh God, that's when I remember the moment before I passed out. Mason was in front of me, and August knocked him back. Oh no, is Mason okay? Why couldn't he just let Mason take me home? I take out my phone to see if Mason has texted or called. He texted.

> Mason: Let me know when you get home.

Glancing over at August, I can tell he just read my text and who it was from as his knuckles are now white from gripping the wheel so tightly.

"Did you hurt him?"

He looks over at me and shakes his head. "No, I didn't touch him." I can see the look of disgust written across his face, like he wants to say more, but he's holding back.

"Why is your hand messed up if you didn't touch him?"

He looks at his hand as if he's just now noticing the dried blood across his knuckles. Yeah, that's right, you're fucking caught. Didn't touch him, my ass.

He sighs, shaking his head as if amused by my statement.

"You would think that, wouldn't you? It couldn't possibly be from something else."

"Then why don't you enlighten me, because the way I remember it, you knocked Mason to the ground before I passed out and—"

He cuts me off. "Yeah, and then you passed out on me. For the love of God, do you know what that did to me? I didn't fucking hit him. I punched a fucking mailbox. I knew hitting him would hurt you, and that's the last thing I wanted to do. I fucking panicked when I saw you pass out, Gianna. Mason calmed me down and told me what to do."

Mason comforted him after everything. What am I missing? I almost gave Mason my virginity yesterday. I told him I'd give him everything, and then he came over to find me with August, which I know ripped his heart out. And then he helped August care for me, and what, left?

Sensing my inner turmoil over his words, he says, "He knew I wasn't letting you go with him. I can't make you choose me, Gianna, but I'll be damned if I just let him take you without you at least hearing me out."

We drive in silence for a while longer until we reach the park across from my house, where he pulls into the parking lot. Again, I'm quiet because I'm not sure what to say. I know the words I want to hear, but I won't pretend this is some fairy tale where Prince Charming sweeps me off my feet.

I'm staring out the passenger side window when he puts the car in park and reaches over to grab my hand. When he interlaces our fingers, warmth from his touch envelops my entire body. It instantly puts me at ease and takes away all my anxiety, and that's what scares me. It would be so easy to fall for him, to get lost in him. Loving him would be as easy as breathing.

"Gianna, please look at me. You gave me something tonight, and I need to see your face when you tell me why."

Is he serious right now? He wants to talk about why I gave him my virginity. Who just says let's talk about sex? Fuck this. He's the one who said he wanted me to hear him out.

"I don't need to explain myself to you. You're the one who said you wanted me to hear you out, so start talking, or I can walk home."

He shakes his head and smiles as if what I said amuses him.

"Why do you always have to fight me? Why can't you see I'm just trying to understand you? Maybe I want to know that the girl who gave me her virginity did it because I mean something to her when her actions say otherwise."

My mouth is suddenly dry, my heart rate picks up, and my hands get clammy with nerves. Closing my eyes, I lean my head back against the seat and whisper, "You know you do."

He slowly blows out a breath as he shifts to lean over the console. Then, grabbing my chin, he angles my face toward him. "Look at me."

When I open my eyes, his beautiful golden-brown orbs are there imprinting on my soul, marking me as his. He is the other half of my soul, a part of me I didn't know was missing until I found him. It physically hurts to think he might not feel the exact same way.

"Why does it look like it pains you to say that?"

How do I answer this? Do I give him some bullshit response that leaves me protected, or do I open myself up and give him the power to break me? Isn't that what love is after all? Giving someone the ability to break your heart and trusting them not to. I'm not saying I love him, but at the same time, I can't expect something from him that I'm not willing to give myself, and that's honesty. So I answer with the truth.

"Because it does. I wasn't expecting you. I wasn't planning on finding someone who challenged my beliefs and who makes me feel empowered, fearless, and sexy with just one look. When you touch me, my world comes into focus. In those moments, nothing else matters because you are there. What hurts is the thought of you not feeling anything for me."

The next thing I know, his lips smash into mine, stealing the air from my lungs. Our teeth clash, and our tongues dance together, desperately seeking a depth that can't possibly be gained from a kiss alone. I want this kiss to consume him. I want him to be as hopelessly enamored as I am. I don't want him to let me go. He brings his hand to the base of my neck before pulling back to catch his breath. I'm sure he can see the vulnerability in my eyes from my confession, and a part of me wants to take it all back, but before I have a chance to let my insecurities take root, he puts his forehead to mine and says, "Promise me you are mine."

I calm my erratic breathing, put my hand to his cheek, and look him straight in the eyes when I say, "As long as you're mine."

His lips are back on mine, but this time his kiss is gentle and passionate as his tongue caresses mine, slowly melting my heart. Our tongues glide over one another in perfect harmony, and I'm aching for him to touch me everywhere. I want his hands on me. I grab his shirt and pull him into me as best I can, considering there's a center console in the way.

He smiles against my lips. "My girl is greedy. One taste, and she already can't get enough."

Then my phone chimes.

Of course my phone chimes because all our moments are stolen. I'm so tired of being interrupted whenever we are together that I could cry. That's what happens when I get angry or super mad—I cry. It's like an emotional overload.

Pulling out of my embrace, he thumps back into his seat. I don't think he's angry, just frustrated like I am. I retrieve my phone from my purse and see it's from my mom. Thank God because I don't think either of us could handle another emotional trip tonight.

"It's my mom. She's just checking to make sure I'm okay since it's late." What he doesn't know is that my mom never checks up on me. So tonight's text is very peculiar. I've come and gone as I pleased for years without question. The fact that I might be missed in general is even more perplexing, but my brain can't take any more drama tonight. I'm tapped out, especially with whatever is happening between August and me.

When I look over, I see him slightly relax at the revelation. He looks at the clock on the dash and says, "Yeah, I better get you home."

Because I can't help myself and I'm a glutton for punishment, I say, "I don't want to go home." Those words have never been truer. I want to stay with him. It doesn't matter where. Anywhere will do, as long as it's with him. With his head still lying against the head rest, he turns to me and reaches for my hand. Bringing it to his lips, he kisses each finger before interlacing them with his.

"Gianna, you have no idea how tempting you are. I'd love nothing more than to turn my car around and take you home, but since I plan on keeping you, I don't want to piss off your family."

I know he's right, and I'm so tired. It's only Monday and we have work tomorrow, so I drop it, but I can't hide the disappointment on my face.

"Pack a bag tonight and stay with me tomorrow after work."

I look over at him with a massive smile on my face. "Really?"

His face lights up like I've never seen. Although come to think of it, this might be the first time I've seen him smile, and my God, is he handsome.

"It wasn't a question, so yes, you're staying at my place tomorrow night."

And just like that, I'm ready to go home because tomorrow can't come soon enough.

## SEVENTEEN

### *August*

Yesterday was a total mind fuck! When I saw Gianna with the motorcycle guy at lunch, I almost lost it. I needed to get her alone and talk to her. However, when I decided to take her back to my place, I by no means thought the night would play out as it did. I had no idea I'd have the most mind-blowing sex of my life with the sexiest woman I've ever seen.

Our bodies were so in sync. The lust, longing, and desperate need to make her mine were irrepressible. I played her body like an instrument. She was so in tune with me, so responsive. My touch was her vice.

When I sank into her sweet heat for the first time, her pussy molded around my cock like it was made for me, sucking me into her tight as fuck core. I couldn't help but look down and watch my bare cock push through her swollen lips. I was a goner after that. Everything about her was hypnotic. Then to find out she was a fucking virgin, and I'm the only one who's ever been inside her was a game-changer. I was already hooked, but now she owns me.

Finding out I was her first and only partner wrecked me. If she thought I was a possessive prick before, wait until she meets the territorial, overprotective, controlling dick that I morphed into only seconds after taking her.

I was enraged when Ethan and Grant showed up right as we were coming down from our release. They never pop by like that during the week. Grant's a med student, so his coursework has him tied up with a book most nights, which is why I found last night's visit even more peculiar. While we just finished the semester, Grant still has boards and a summer full of excelled residency.

I'm almost positive Ethan is why Carson showed up Saturday night at a bar we've never been to, on the side of town she'd never dare visit.

What I haven't pieced together is why Carson came home early and didn't tell me, or how Ethan knew. But I have no doubt her appearance there was his doing.

My theory about his involvement was cemented when I saw his reaction to Gianna last night. He acted like she was one of Carson's friends when he knew damn well who she was, considering he wanted her for himself at the club. Perhaps Ethan brought Carson as a reminder that I still technically had a girlfriend. But that doesn't change the fact that he's covering something up. Why pretend as if he didn't know Gianna?

Grant acted indifferent to the entire situation, so I'm unsure if he's in on whatever this is or simply an unsuspecting accomplice. I know I have something Ethan wants, but what surprises me is that he's willing to sabotage our friendship to take what I've already claimed as mine. Friendships, relationships, even marriages are fickle things where I come from.

Everyone is usually in one for some sort of gain. Ethan's family is considered nouveau riche, whereas my family has maintained its good name and wealth over generations, solidifying our social affluence. Typically, new money will try to mix with old money to be accepted in established social circles, and that's what Ethan's family did with my uncle Eduard.

Eduard married my dad's sister. He doesn't come from money, so

I think he found a kindred spirit of sorts in Robert, Ethan's dad. The two became fast friends. That's how I met Ethan. While we went to the same school, we didn't hang in the same circles until Eduard started inviting them out for golf with my dad and me. I've always liked Ethan, but I know no one is as they seem in my world. Everyone always has an ulterior motive, and I think I'm about to learn Ethan's.

Maybe I'm wrong, and he thought I wasn't that serious about Gigi. I had just told them that I was done with her. But none of that matters anymore now. I know why I never made a move on anyone else while Carson's been away. It was because I was waiting for Gianna. No one caught my eye because they weren't her.

At the end of the day, something's going on, I can feel it, and my instincts are never wrong. What these assholes don't seem to understand is that I'm not fucking around when it comes to her, and I'll watch everything burn if that means she's mine. No one will take her from me.

\* \* \*

I'm late to work today. I fully intended on getting in on time, bringing my girl her coffee and a scone, but I let my thoughts run away with me this morning. Then I spent more time than necessary making sure my outfit accentuated my features. I want Gianna to be salivating when she sees me. I want her to want me. Last night she told me as much, but I can't help but feel she's not sold on being mine.

Today I'm wearing my light gray Bonobos suit with a white Oxford underneath and my black lace-up Louboutins. I want her panties wet from just looking at me. The problem is, she typically fights me for no good reason unless I'm touching her. Once my hands are on her, she submits. If I look hot enough, I'm hoping we can skip the banter and just be.

When I walk through the doors of Reds, I head straight back to her office. Well, she doesn't have an office, per se. More like she has a workroom where she makes up samples and a display room where they are kept once they have been made. The mockups are used in all departments for various purposes, but her job is to create, maintain, and ship them.

I smell her before I see her. She smells like warm vanilla and coconuts. Today she not only smells like summer, but she looks like it too. Silently, I stand in the doorway and watch her work while she's unaware of my presence. She's wearing a high-waisted, tight black skirt that hits right above the knee, black espadrille wedges that elongate her sexy-as-sin legs, and a fitted long-sleeved yellow top. Her hair is pulled into a high ponytail with soft curls spilling down her back. She is effortlessly breathtaking.

Knowing I need to pull myself out of my thoughts, I clear my throat to announce my presence. That startles her. She throws her hand over her chest in mock horror, and I can't help but smile.

"August, my God, you scared me."

If my smile could get any bigger, it did. I love the way my name sounds leaving her lips, especially when it's all breathy like it was just now. I stalk toward her to deliver her coffee and steal a kiss, but before I make it over, she slides around the work island, essentially putting it between us.

Setting down the coffee, I raise a brow in question. "Is something wrong?"

Her eyes widen, and her posture stiffens before she glances behind me. She's acting like a child who just got caught with her hand in the cookie jar. Then, tucking a fallen strand of hair behind her ear, she heads into the adjacent room. Without a word, I follow her, and she closes the door behind us, locking us in. If it weren't for the concerned look on her face, I'd be immensely turned on right now.

"I need to talk to you about something, but I want you to promise you'll hear me out and not get mad."

Since when does a sentence starting like that ever bode well for anyone?

Crossing my arms, I bring my fist up to rest under my chin, giving her my best relaxed look as if to say I'm listening.

"I don't want people to know we're seeing each other."

My eyebrows go up in surprise. I wasn't expecting her to say that. Most women want to be seen with me, but her admission is also one of the reasons I'm attracted to her. She sees me for me, not for what I have. Rubbing my forefinger across my lips, I try to find my words, but she beats me to it.

"Hear me out before you say anything."

Peering up at me through her thick lashes, I can clearly see that she's worried about how I'll react. Immediately, I assume she wants to keep it quiet because of Croft. My adrenaline starts pumping at the thought.

"I just started working here full-time, and I don't want people to treat me differently because I'm with you."

When I first found out how old she was, I had similar thoughts, but once I decided I was all in, I knew I'd simply flip the script. I'd protect her reputation at all costs. I'm instantly relieved at the conversation's direction. My body relaxes, and I reach her in two large steps. Pulling her into me, I place a kiss on top of her head.

"Gianna, first, we are together, there's no question, and secondly, my name will do nothing but open doors for you. This is a good thing."

She quickly pulls away and puts yet another table between us. She knows this infuriates me.

I say her name in a curt tone and gesture with my finger for her to return to me. But instead, she puts up her hand to say she's not done.

"I don't want handouts. I want to work my way up on my own merit. I want to earn people's respect and not be judged for who I'm dating. Dating you won't look good for me. I'll look like I'm trying to sleep my way up the corporate ladder. People will think I'm a slut, or simply young and naïve."

She drops her head and mumbles to herself just low enough that it's barely audible. "Maybe I am."

I'm going to act like I didn't hear those mumbled words because I don't want to get angry. I understand where she's coming from, but I don't care what other people think because I already know she and I are endgame. However, she has yet to realize that.

If I want her to see what I already know, I must give her time and space. I want to be the one she trusts and confides in. I want to be her everything, and that can't be forced. Closing my eyes, I take a deep breath. "I'll give this to you for now, but just so we're clear, you are not my secret."

She visibly relaxes and then comes around the table to throw her arms around me in an embrace.

"Thank you. This means a lot to me."

I pull her chin up so she's looking at me.

"That's the only reason I'm agreeing to this, and, Gianna, make no mistake, this is temporary. Everyone will know you're mine." I lean down to finally get the kiss I've wanted since the moment I walked into the room, but she pulls back yet again. "Gianna, please just let me kiss you."

She's giving me a nervous smile, so I run my hand tenderly down her back in reassurance.

"One last request?" Her tone is meek this time, which is a new one for her.

Because there's nothing she could ask that I wouldn't give, I say, "Anything."

"If things don't work out between us, promise me you won't fire my mom or me. I really need this job, August."

My eyebrows shoot up in surprise. Those were not the words I expected. I'm not sure what hurts worse, the fact that she doesn't see this ending well or that I gave her the impression that I'd ever be so cold. My hesitance to respond has her nervously fidgeting in my hold to get away, which only makes me pull her tighter.

"Baby, I can promise you that I'll never do anything to hurt you."

When I look down into her eyes, she whispers, "Okay," before I finally taste her lips. Her body melts against mine, her sweet mouth parts, and my tongue finds hers briefly before she pulls away. I let out a frustrated growl at her abrupt retreat as she dares to smile.

"Save all that for later, not here." She throws me a wink before retreating to the door.

This woman is my fucking kryptonite. I have never felt such an innate, all-consuming connection to a woman in my life. I need her like I need air to breathe. I wake up thinking about her and go to bed dreaming about her. Since the minute I laid eyes on her, she has become my everything.

* * *

This day has gone by so slowly. While I've been in meetings all morning, my head has been consumed with thoughts of seeing Gianna tonight. It's now lunchtime, and if I could, I would have met her at the coffee shop, but my uncle Eduard wants to talk about possible marketing strategies for brand growth.

It's times like this that I wish I were interested in this shit so my time didn't feel so entirely wasted. The only bright side to starting my legacy at Reds has been her. I'm doing this for my dad because it's what's expected of every son in my family. For the past four generations, every son has taken over, but this isn't me. It's not what I want.

I'm waiting by my car for Eduard when he finally decides to show up.

"Sorry I took so long. I was going over my calendar with Lena."

Lena is his personal secretary. He's the only salesman with a personal secretary. It's just one of the many perks my dad affords him, but lately, I've wondered if anyone else has noticed that Lena seems to be in his office more than not. The man is shady. I've never trusted him. He does what suits him, and I'm almost certain he isn't faithful to my aunt. I feel like he's an opportunist. He saw a woman with a trust fund and leeched on.

Shrugging my shoulders, I say, "No big deal. Where do you want to go?"

He walks around to the passenger side door of my car. "You're driving, so you pick."

Of course I'm driving. The dick thinks I'm his chauffeur. I hop into the driver's side of my Mercedes G-Wagon, and no sooner I start the engine than he's saying, "Your aunt has been wanting a new vehicle. You like this?"

He's rubbing the leather interior of the captain's seat and checking out the back seat. I give him a half-smile, trying to play it cool as if I didn't notice him checking out the roomy rear.

"Yeah, I like it, but I thought Aunt Sara likes cars?"

Shrugging off my comment as if her wants don't matter, he says, "She likes whatever I like."

I fake a laugh and internally seethe. I decide on Ruth Chris Steakhouse, knowing he wouldn't expect anything less than an expensive lunch when he's probably putting it on the company card. When the waiter approaches, he orders a glass of wine, knowing he shouldn't have a drink at lunch. It's against company policy.

We work in a manufacturing facility. If anything were to happen at work, there would be a lawsuit and unwanted attention brought to the company by OSHA and the FDA. He's such a prick.

"So how are you liking your first official week at Reds?"

"It's been good just getting my feet wet. I have a ton of ideas for marketing campaigns and new product avenues for us to explore."

"Well, I'm sure you'll take the company to new heights as long as you stay focused. Just make sure you keep your head out of the samples."

I almost choke on my water in surprise. What is he talking about? Keep my head out of the samples? Before I can question him, he continues with the seediest-looking grin on his face.

"I've seen you talking to Maria's daughter. She's a hot young piece of ass, but she's not right for you and will only bring down your reputation. Your best bet is to stick with Carson. Her family comes from a sound background that will look good on your father's campaign trail."

Is this guy fucking serious right now? Who does he think he is telling me who I can and can't date? I'm about ready to tell him off when it hits me. How would he know I have anything going on with Gianna?

She told me not to tell anyone, and we only officially hooked up last night. I try my best to school my expression and keep it neutral, not to give anything away, when all I really want to do is punch him in the face for talking about my girl like she's some piece of trash. He's the fucking gold-digging leech in the family.

"I'm not sure what you're talking about, Eduard. I was in training with her last week, so naturally, we ran into each other. I'll be at the fundraiser with Carson."

My eyes stay locked on him to ensure I don't miss one second of his reaction to my words. He holds my gaze, but I see his fist clench in my peripheral, and there it is, the sign I was looking for. He's hiding something, but what is it and what could it possibly have to do with Gianna?

"I must have read it wrong. I'm glad to hear you're not slumming it."

Now I know he's trying to get a reaction out of me. But how would he know those words would provoke me unless he knew I was lying about my relationship? I roll my lips. "Yeah, maybe you should get a new source."

I want him to know I'm onto him. I won't let him think he's got me by the balls for one minute, not to mention I don't care what anyone thinks about my relationship, but I gave Gianna my word, and I plan to keep it. I'm not going to out our relationship until she's ready.

The waiter comes at just that moment with our food, and for a split second, I see rage cross Eduard's face, but it's gone just as quickly as it came. He has a reputation for getting what he wants through manipulation and fear. People at work fear that if they don't do what he wants, then, because he's family to the owner, they'll get fired.

If the fear tactic fails, he uses manipulation, playing with people's emotions and making them question their choices. I've always seen right through him, and he knows it. That's why he's mad. He's not getting his way with this fake lunch, but what I haven't figured out is what he wants.

The rest of the lunch is uneventful as he tries to discuss work with me to save face, but it's a lost cause, and he knows it. I pay, and we leave.

*** 

It's just past five when I get home, and I'm wondering if Gianna is standing me up. I know she gets off work at four every day, and I only live fifteen minutes away.

Last night when I asked her to stay with me tonight, her eyes lit up like a kid on Christmas. I couldn't keep the smile off my face in return, knowing that spending the night with me made her that excited.

I need her badly. My nerves are shot after the lunch I had with my uncle this afternoon. There's no reason Gianna's name should be leaving his lips. He's up to something, and I haven't figured it out.

Heading for the wine fridge, I grab a bottle of red wine and pour two glasses before turning on some R&B. Miguel's "Adorn" comes through the speakers just as I hear a soft knock on the door. I can't help but smile knowing she is on the other side of the door.

When I open it, she's there with a bag slung over her shoulder. Bending down, I swoop her up into my arms and spin her in excitement. She lets out a squeal before I set her down. I quickly close the door, making sure to lock it before turning to say, "No interruptions!"

She laughs. "Yeah, those fuckers seem to be obsessed with us."

I swiftly cut the distance between us and sweep her into my arms again. I just want to hold her. She wraps her legs around my waist, and I walk her to the kitchen island, where I set her down.

Just touching her calms me down and settles all my inner turmoil. Burrowing my face in her neck, I inhale deeply before planting open-mouth kisses from her shoulder to the spot behind her ear she likes. I lightly suck when I feel her pulse beating beneath my lips. Goose pimples break out over her skin, and I move on, leaving a trail of kisses across her jaw before reaching her mouth and taking her silky soft lips with mine.

I gently tease her lips open, seeking out her lush tongue. She fists my shirt in her hands, pulling me closer, and that's all the encouragement I need to grab her hips, pulling her forward so that I'm firmly planted right between her creamy thighs. Her skirt has ridden up to her waist, and I can feel the heat from her center between us.

She slowly releases her hold on my shirt, trailing her fingers down my stomach until she reaches my belt. She glides her hands along my waistline from front to back, sending white-hot pleasure up my spine. I moan into her mouth as her tongue plunges into mine with long, delicious strokes. Her hands move under my shirt, exploring their way up my back, racking my body in shivers. I can't help but smile at how my body responds to her. Never has a woman made me feel this way.

"What's funny? Why are you laughing?"

Shaking my head in amusement, I kiss her forehead sweetly in reassurance.

"Nothing's wrong, baby. You're so fucking perfect it's scary."

She's still looking at me with concern etched on her face. Stepping out of her thighs, I fix her skirt before reaching behind her to hand her a glass of wine.

"I want you so bad. I want nothing more than to feast on your sweet pussy right here on my kitchen counter while you scream my name, but I also want to date you. That means I need to wine and dine you."

Her face flushes with embarrassment at my brash comments, and I love it. I like to make her squirm. While she may seem uncomfortable with my vulgar words, I know they make her pussy wet. I want her wanton and begging when I let her come later.

I watch her take a sip of her wine, and I smirk. Her eyes narrow in question. "Now what?"

"It's nothing, really. I just think you're cute when you blush."

The doorbell rings, and she shoots me a suspicious look. "Don't worry. It's just dinner." She hops off the counter as I go to the door to grab the food.

Making my way back to the kitchen, I notice she's texting on her phone, which reminds me of my lunch with Eduard. Since I spent the afternoon racking my brain for any potential connections, all I could come up with was maybe Maria had said something to him.

"I ordered sushi. I probably should have asked if you liked it first, but if not, I have frozen pizza we can throw in the oven."

She smiles. "I'm not picky. I like trying new foods, but I happen to love sushi, so we're good."

Gianna helps me lay out the food on the island before us, and we sit to eat. I can't help but think how mundane this is, eating a meal with her in my kitchen, but how at this moment, there's nowhere in the world I'd rather be.

"I have something I need to ask you. What does your mom think about you seeing me?" With this question, I figured I'd kill two birds with one stone. One, I find out what her family thinks about us dating, and two, I can deduce if Maria mentioned something to Eduard. She stops chewing her food and then looks at me wide-eyed.

"What do you mean what does my mom think? I haven't told my parents about us. There wasn't an us until last night."

I don't know why those words burn as much as they do, but fuck if they aren't a knife to the heart. She's been mine since the moment I laid eyes on her, but the sobering truth is those feelings haven't gone both ways.

"What did you tell your mom last night after I dropped you off?"

Hopping off the stool next to me, she walks over to the sink and pours out her wine, only to fill the glass with water. She almost drinks the entire glass before gently setting it down as if my question made her nervous.

"Sorry, I had too much wine first and not enough food."

Holding her gaze, I wait for her to answer my question, and when she doesn't, I rephrase it. "Gianna, who does your mom think you were with last night?" I'm currently sitting on my stool with my chin resting on my hand, feigning nonchalance, but inside I'm boiling over.

She fidgets with her sleeves before answering. "I told her I was with Mason, which wasn't a complete lie."

Calmly, I get up from my stool, walk over to the bar in the corner, pour myself two fingers of Macallan, and shoot it back in one go.

When I turn around, I find her looking at me with her arms crossed over her chest like she's mad at me.

"We talked about all this at the office this morning. You agreed we wouldn't tell people about us yet." She's not wrong, but I assumed she'd at least tell her mom. Don't girls share everything with their moms? It pains me to know that she doesn't want to tell anyone about us. While I understand it, that doesn't mean it doesn't feel like a punch to the gut that my girl doesn't want to claim me the way I do her. Then, as if to rub salt in the wound, she adds, "My mom knows Mason. It's not uncommon for me to come home late when I'm with him."

Closing my eyes, I grip the edge of the countertop hard in an attempt to calm the raging inferno building inside me. Unfortunately, she realizes a second too late that she chose the wrong words to say to me.

"Oh my God, August, I'm so sorry. That came out wrong." Then, rushing over, she throws her arms around me from behind. "Please don't be mad at me."

I push off the counter and peel her arms off me, needing the space. I don't want to touch her when I feel this way. "Sorry if hearing that Croft is the better boyfriend for you doesn't elicit the response you expected." I can't keep the venom out of my tone, and honestly, I don't want to.

Her hands fly to her mouth, her face stunned by my reaction. I can see the apology in her eyes before she drops her head and starts toward the couch, where she left her things when she came in. "I'm sorry. Maybe this is too much too soon. I shouldn't have come here tonight."

Fuck, I scared her. As much as I want to stand my ground on this, I don't want her to leave. "Gianna, I didn't mean to—"

She puts her hand up to stop me as she picks up her bag. "August, I never meant to hurt you, but you must understand how insane this is. We've known each other for less than a month. I'm trying, I really am, but where I come from, there's no knight in shining armor, no frog that turns into a prince. There's no happily ever after where any of this is my reality. Clearly, this is overwhelming for both of us." She starts walking toward the door, but I grab her wrist before she can make it there.

"Gianna, I can't let you leave. I'm not sure why you're fighting this. You've been fighting me since we first met, but you can't deny our chemistry. You feel it every time I'm near, every time we touch, every time our eyes meet, and you see into my soul. I scare you because I've done in just a few weeks what no man ever has. I make you feel alive. I've awakened a part of you that you didn't know was there, and I know this because you've done the same for me."

Her eyes are fixed on the floor, and the hand gripping her bag is white-knuckled with tension that I'm sure is swimming through her body. She knows my words ring true, but she's fighting her inner dialogue. A part of her wants to run, and I don't know how strong that part of her is. I gently squeeze the wrist I've been holding on to and try to bring her out of her thoughts and back to me. When her eyes find mine, they're filled with sadness.

I let my hand slip down to hers and interlace our fingers. "Don't make me the villain before you give me a chance to be the prince."

Those big green eyes snap to mine in a deep, penetrating gaze. Her breathing is shallow, and it's as if she's focusing on those breaths, trying to stay cognizant of her emotions and not get swept up in the heat building between us. Like me, she feels the undeniable pull, the overwhelming sense of completeness.

I gently pull her into me, keeping those big eyes locked on mine before whispering, "Stay."

She takes in a shaky breath and nods her agreement. My free hand slowly slides up her arm to where her bag is still clutched in her hand, and I gently lower the straps off her shoulder and let it drop to the ground.

Breaking our gaze, she lays her forehead on my chest. "Promise me, promise me this is real."

I bring my hand under her chin so that I can look into her eyes when I say, "Let me show you."

Bending down, I cover her lips with my own in a gentle, cautious embrace. Her lips are so soft, so pliant against mine, and I want to deepen the kiss, but I hold back, not wanting to push for more if she's not ready. Her lips part, and then her tongue seeks entrance that I'm more than willing to give. As our tongues hungrily dance together, her hands find the hem of my shirt and make their way around my waist. Her fingers lightly graze my back, leaving a trail of heat in their wake. Throwing caution to the wind, I reach down with both hands and grip her plump ass, squeezing gently before lifting her up.

She wraps her legs around my waist before breaking our kiss to place one behind my ear and whisper, "Take me to bed."

## EIGHTEEN

### Gianna

Moments ago, I was ready to leave. I'm still not convinced that trying to date August is a good idea. He calls me his and talks a good game, but words mean nothing to me. My entire life, I've been lied to by the people who are supposed to love me the most. I've watched more people than I can count go back on their word simply because they changed their minds. Words are empty, but that hasn't stopped me from asking for assurances from August and hoping they stick. At least this time, if I fuck up my life, I'm doing it on my terms.

I learned to guard my mind, heart, and body a long time ago. People are always looking to take advantage of you. They'll take until you have nothing left to give. I watched my parents take from me as a young child. My mom would give me money for lunch or a field trip, only for it to be gone by the time I got to school. My piggy bank money was stolen, and my gold coin collection from my grandma was pawned. Robbed time and time again, only to be told they're sorry and it won't happen again. It became a broken record, and they weren't the only ones. All the adults in my world were lying, stealing, or dealing for their own gain.

That's why I feel like I'm always on edge with August. How am I supposed to believe this gorgeous man when he tells me he wants me and that I'm his, when everything I always wanted was taken from me? I'm always waiting for the other shoe to drop. I've already given this man my body, and I'm fighting hard not to give him anything more because he might be the thing that finally breaks me.

The problem is, if August is breaking me, it feels too good to let him stop. Before it's all said and done, I think I'll let him shatter me if it means I get to have him just a little while longer.

August walks me down the hall toward his room as he sucks on the tender spot behind my ear that he knows drives me crazy. His erect cock presses against my core, and my pussy drips in anticipation. There's no denying that when his hands are on my body, it comes to life. When his mouth is on mine, he steals my breath, and when his cock is buried deep inside me, I'm his. I can't stay away, and I don't want to.

We reach his bedroom, where he lays me down on the bed and kisses me hard and deep. I buck my hips into his erection and moan when the tip nudges my clit. He breaks our kiss, panting, his lips a hairsbreadth apart from mine.

"Tell me what you want. Are you sore?"

God, this man can be so infuriating when he's demanding and jealous, but when it comes to pleasuring me, he's a giver, making sure my body gets what it needs, so I spur him on.

"Someone was talking a good game earlier about spreading me out on the counter and making me scream his name."

He smiles against my mouth before retreating down my body.

"You want me to eat that pretty pussy, baby?"

Fuck me if those words don't make my pussy throb.

"Tell me, when I pull this skirt off, will your panties be soaked for me?"

Why is it so hot when men talk dirty? Shouldn't I feel cheap? He stands up to pull his sweater over his head, revealing his toned, tight stomach and delicious deep V. The man is a fucking god. I'm hit with the need to rub my fingers down his delicious abs, but before I make contact, he tsks, knocking me back, only to crawl up my body and grind his erection against my core.

"Stay put. No touching, or I'll have to tie you up."

*Would he seriously tie me up?* Not wanting to find out, I watch as he undoes his belt, and his pants drop to the floor. He's wearing black boxer briefs, and the tip of his cock is peeking out of the waistband, teasing me.

Following my line of sight, he shoots me a cocky grin. "Like what you see, baby?"

I swallow hard and lick my lips, dying for just a taste.

"You want my cock in your mouth?"

I nod swiftly and look into his eyes, seeking permission, only to find them black with desire. He wants me to suck his cock, and while I've never done that before because I felt like doing so would make me a slut, doing it for him feels empowering.

"This cock is yours. You can have it any way you want it, but right now, I need my mouth on your pussy."

Dropping to his knees, he lifts my leg and places a kiss on my inner ankle before removing my wedged sandals from my right foot and then my left. As he makes his way back up, he slowly trails his fingers along my overly sensitive skin, sending a pulse of need straight to my core. I may come before he even takes my skirt off at the rate he's operating. Reaching for my waist, he grabs my skirt and peels it down, taking my panties with it while slowly kissing his way down my stomach in his descent. His open-mouth kisses feel divine against my overheated flesh, making me ache with the need for those lips to be on my clit.

Seeking some sort of release, I grab my breasts and squeeze. My nipples are hard, and when they rub against the lace of my bra, I can't help but throw my head back in sheer ecstasy. I can't take any more foreplay. "August, please stop teasing me. I need you."

My face immediately flushes from my voiced confession. His body is on top of mine faster than I can blink, his face right next to mine, his eyes locked on me when he says, "Baby, you have me."

Our lips collide in a passionate embrace, and I feel like I've just given him a sliver of my heart. I confessed out loud what I've felt in my heart and tried to bury it deep. Not only do I want this man, but I also need him, and that fucking scares the shit out of me.

A tear rolls down my cheek, landing on the hand he has cupped around my face. When he looks at me, I know he must sense the depth of my words because he rasps, "You have no idea how much I need you," before quickly pulling my shirt over my head and removing my bra. He stands to slide his underwear down, and I admire the sight of his large cock that reaches to his belly button. Fucking hell. How did that fit last night? I slam my legs closed, seeking friction and trying to ward him off.

Never taking his eyes off me, he slowly glides his hand up and down his shaft until a bead of pre-cum glistens over his head. Biting my lip, I twist my nipple, desperate for him to touch me where I need it most.

"If you want me. You have to open up."

I shake my head, and he smiles before reaching down to pry my legs open. Once I'm spread out before him, he smacks my pussy, and I cry out in pleasure. The next thing I know, his mouth is on my clit, sucking it into his mouth, and I fucking see stars. I come so hard, so fast, and he barely touched me. How embarrassing.

Before I have time to overthink it, he says, "I love how your body responds to me. You're so attuned to me, so eager, so mine."

He reaches up and grabs my hips and slowly pulls my ass to the edge of the bed, where he lines his cock up with my entrance and dips the head in. My pussy spasms immediately from the intrusion. "Fuck, baby, your greedy pussy is trying to pull me in." Then he pulls out and runs his throbbing cock through my wet lips, rocking into me, applying just enough pressure to torment me.

"August, please."

His eyes snap up from where he's been watching his dick run over my clit and soften with a promise to give me what I want. He must know how much I need him inside me to feel the soul-crushing, irrevocable connection we share. That connection is almost as good as the sex. Closing his eyes, he says, "I know, baby, I know," and then he's pushing into me one delicious inch at a time.

My body struggles to relax at the intrusion, but he leans down over me, cradles my head, and whispers, "Let me have you." His words immediately melt me to my core, and my body relaxes around him, letting him sink in to the hilt. We both moan in complete rapture as our bodies join together. He looks down at me, jaw slack, eyes hooded with lust as he takes my mouth and swipes his warm tongue against mine, stealing pieces of my soul with each sultry caress.

"You're mine now, Gianna. Do you understand? I'm the first and last that will ever have this. You have no idea what it does to me, knowing I'm the only man who's ever been inside you." Then he pulls out before slamming back in so hard it takes my breath away. Closing my eyes, I breathe through the sting as he stretches me. He takes a nipple between his fingers and gently tugs it while sucking the other in his mouth, and I feel my body release. "That's it, baby, soak my cock." His dirty words stir a fire in me that I didn't know existed. He makes fucking him feel so right, so natural, and I can't help but surrender to him completely.

He's standing, plunging into me repeatedly, watching where our bodies connect, wholly entranced, and I can't help but feel every word he's said to me is true. He wants me, he desires me, and I'm his. My orgasm is building, and I'm on the verge of coming when he reaches down to rub slow circles over my clit. "I can feel you clenching. I want you to come on my cock. Milk me."

I shatter beneath him, and when he slams in hard, I feel the jerk of his cock as he fills me up before falling on top of me.

Chest heaving and glistening with sweat, he kisses my neck and murmurs between ragged breaths, "You're so perfect, Gianna. Promise me I can keep you."

And I'm a goner.

* * *

Something startles me awake, and my eyes fly open while my body remains frozen in fear. Looking around the room, I briefly panic before realizing I'm in August's room, and he's currently wrapped around me, spooning me from behind. His arm is tightly wrapped around my center as if he was scared I might slip away during the night. I hear his light breathing on the pillow behind me, and I try to calm my racing heart. Knowing that August is with me comforts me, but something startled me awake.

No sooner my heart settles than I hear something crash to the ground outside the glass doors that lead out to the wraparound deck. I turn in his arms, expecting him to wake, but he must sleep like the dead because he doesn't flinch.

I gently nudge his chest and whisper, "August, wake up."

Then, sitting straight up in bed, I clutch the sheet to my chest and focus my eyes on the sheer curtains that run the room's length. They obscure the view to the deck so that you can't see in or out, but you can see shadows. The lighting that runs beneath the glass panels of the decking casts just enough light that I can make out the outlines of the potted trees and deck chairs. I sit frozen, waiting to catch movement, so locked in alarm that I don't even feel August move until he's kissing my shoulder. I scream and clutch my chest in absolute horror. August throws his arms around my body, holding me tightly.

"Baby, I'm here. Calm down. Everything's okay."

He kisses my shoulder again, and I know he can feel my body trembling against his. I press my palms into my eyes and take a deep breath before saying, "I thought I heard someone outside."

Without question, he jumps up and pulls his boxers on before grabbing a bat resting next to his nightstand. Making his way to the sliding glass door, he slowly peers out the curtains, scanning the deck. When he's satisfied that there isn't an immediate threat outside, he exits the bedroom to check the living room.

I'm still trying to determine if being here with him is what startled me awake or if something was indeed out there. Then it hits me. He didn't even question my claim, and he had a bat next to the bed as if prepared for this moment. So either he is my knight in shining armor, valiantly rushing to protect me, or this has happened before, which is terrifying.

Finally, he returns, sets the bat back in its spot, and climbs back under the covers with me. Then, pulling me into his arms so that we're spooning again, he says, "It must have been a raccoon or something. A potted plant was knocked over."

I let out a breath I didn't realize I was holding. But still, I can't relax. I need to know why he has the bat. "Why do you have the bat next to your bed?"

He pulls my chin toward him to take in my expression and read the direction of my thoughts. His eyebrows furrow with concern.

"I've always kept a bat next to my bed. Gianna, you're safe with me. My place is locked up, and I have a security system. It's just you and me in here." The tension in my body slowly leaves, and I relax into his hold. I suppose he's right. My dad keeps a bat in the hallway closet for the same purpose. I'm just letting fear cloud my judgment. "I'll always protect you, Gianna. You don't have to be scared."

Pulling my hair over my shoulder, he kisses his way up to my neck before wrapping his arm around me. Slowly, his fingers trail up my stomach with a tantalizing promise of pleasure. When he reaches my chest, he grabs my bare breast in his hand before dragging his thumb over my erect nipple. He groans and pumps his hard cock into my ass.

"Baby, I love having you naked in my bed. I could get used to this."

I arch my back so that my breast pushes more firmly into his hand, and my ass rubs up against his stiff cock.

I don't know what time it is or how long it has been since we fell asleep, but I want him again. Reaching behind me, I do my best to free him from his briefs and take his thick, silky shaft in my hand. He pumps into my hand as I slowly stroke him, and when he pinches my nipple, my pussy starts to drip with arousal. I need him inside me. Arching my back, I push my ass out so that I can slide his cock through my soaked folds. He hisses when he feels how wet I am for him. I line him up with my entrance, and he slides in deep with one pump. This angle is new, and it feels so very intimate. He's giving me long, slow, teasing strokes, hitting my G-spot every time. With every thrust, he tightens his grip around me, pulling me down on his cock so he can go deeper.

What's happening between us now feels like more than sex. It feels like every pump is an unspoken promise that he wants me, a vow that I'm his, an assurance that this is real. My thoughts become hazy, and my body starts to tremble from the orgasm threatening to tear me apart in the best way. I can hear his ragged breaths behind me, and his body tenses as he tries to hold back his own release.

With a shaky breath, he says, "Baby, you feel too good. I'm not going to last." He strokes over my G-spot two more tantalizing times before my pussy clenches him hard. We cry out our release in unison as our bodies are racked with an orgasm at the same time.

Fuck me. I didn't know sex would be this good, but something tells me it's more about the man than the act. We drift back asleep, him still inside me, without speaking another word. While I know we are nowhere near saying the L-word, I can't help but feel what we just shared wasn't far off from love, and I think he feels it too.

\* \* \*

When my alarm goes off, August groans. "Make it stop."

Pushing out of his hold, I reach over to the nightstand to grab my phone before remembering my phone's not in here.

Last night he carried me to bed. I smack him and say, "It's your phone."

He reluctantly shuffles over to his side of the bed and silences his phone. I move to get up and start getting ready, but he pulls me back. "Not so fast. I'm not ready to let you go."

I laugh. "Well, that's too bad. I'm too new, and I can't be late. They'll fire me."

He tightens his grip on me. "Well, I own the company, so I think it'll be okay."

I slap his arm. He knows I don't want things to be that way.

"August, I'm serious. Let me up."

"Fine, for now. I won't make you late, but I can't make promises for the future." He gives me a quick kiss on my back and lets me up. Realizing I have nothing to wear to the bathroom, I fling my arm over my boobs and quickly go stark naked to the en suite. Of course August doesn't miss the opportunity to take advantage of the view. "Now that's a sight I can get used to."

I throw a glare over my shoulder before quickly closing the door. My jaw drops once I look at his master bath. Shit, I might be late. This bathroom is amazing. The ceiling is vaulted just like the rest of the condo and lined with cedar beams. The walk-in shower is encased in gray stones that run up the wall to the ceiling. His bathtub is big enough to fit four people, at least, and looks like it was carved out of slate. The room looks like it could be a luxury suite bathroom in Aspen at some ski lodge. I could light candles and spend hours in here.

I quickly pull my thoughts back to the task at hand, shower, and get dressed so I'm not late. When I finish showering, August walks in with my bag and looks like he has freshly showered himself. My heart sinks a little at the fact that he didn't try to join me, and he must see it because he says, "Don't look so disappointed, baby. I knew if I joined you, we'd be late."

He drops a kiss on my forehead and leaves me to get ready. Why does he have to be so perfect? Grabbing my bag, I quickly brush out my thick blond hair and add Moroccan oil so it doesn't frizz. I hadn't planned on washing my hair, but I smelled like sex. My makeup takes me no time since I only wear eye makeup. I throw on my vintage black twill romper and wedges from yesterday, and I'm ready to go.

Typically, a romper wouldn't be work appropriate, but this one almost doesn't even look like a romper. It has a puff shoulder sleeve that cinches right above the elbow and a relaxed silhouette with a belted waist. I think it has a classic utilitarian look. I was stoked when I found it brand-new from Goodwill.

August must approve because when I come down the hall, he stops mid-stride to check me out from head to toe. Well, I thought he liked it until he didn't say anything.

"What's wrong? Do I look okay? Is this not appropriate?" I can feel my self-conscious anxiety setting in.

Snapping out of his daze, he says, "You look great. That's the problem. Maybe tomorrow you can just wear one of my shirts."

I quirk a brow at him. "Tomorrow? Are you expecting me to sleep over again tonight?"

He rounds the kitchen island and pulls me into his arms. "Gianna, I want you to stay with me every night."

Then he leans down and plants his lips on mine in a slow, savory kiss that robs me of my breath before pulling away with a smirk. He knows what he's doing. He's trying to get me hot and bothered so I give in to him and say I'll come over tonight. Well, two can play that game. If he's going to make me work for it, so is he. I let him walk away without a response and try to seem as unaffected as possible by his handsome good looks, delicious cologne, and tantalizing kiss, but then he has to go and grab two thermoses from the counter.

"Ready to go?" He signals to the door, holding a thermos out to me.

I can't help the big, goofy smile that breaks out over my face at the gesture.

"You made me a coffee?" I don't even try to hide the excitement in my voice. This man melts me. His eyes sparkle at my reaction, and he immediately blushes while trying to stifle a smile. I can't help but poke at him. He takes every opportunity he gets to make me feel uncomfortable, so it's payback time. "August Branson, are you blushing?"

He tries to save himself by saying, "You caught me off guard. I wasn't expecting such a reaction to coffee, but if it makes you this happy, I'll gladly make it for you every time you wake up in my bed."

I know it's a small gesture, but it feels like we're genuinely a real couple. I like that he wants to take care of me. Those little mundane tasks that most people take for granted light me up because they are ones I haven't had the luxury of having.

* * *

I'm just about to pull into Reds when my phone rings. I see it's Vivian, and my phone's about to die. She never calls. If she does, she typically texts first to ensure I'll answer.

"Hey, Vivian, my phone's about to die, so if I lose you—"

She cuts me off. "Gigi, you have to come straight to the hospital. Mason's been in an accident. We're at St. Mary's in—"

My phone dies. *Are you fucking kidding me?* My heart drops into my stomach, and tears immediately stream down my face. I must get to Mason. A million thoughts go through my mind. What kind of accident was he in? Why was Vivian notified before me? Oh God, what if he doesn't make it? Tears threaten to choke me, and I try to focus on my breathing so I don't have a full-on panic attack.

I haven't spoken to Mason since Monday, when he found me with August. *What if I never get to tell him how sorry I am?* He's my best friend, and I hurt him in the worst way, and now I may not get the chance to make amends. I hadn't called because I was giving him space, and honestly, I also needed the space. We needed to talk about what happened with August and what almost happened between us on the bluff.

Before it happened, I hadn't put much thought into losing my virginity, but looking back, I know I always hoped I could give it to Mason. I'm not sure if he's still a virgin. I know he has messed around with girls. We were never an official couple, but there was always this undeniable attraction between us. Different from what I have with August but still potent. I always found Mason handsome, and I was hooked once I got to know him. He was the perfect guy to laugh with, talk on the phone for hours, and dream with.

Mason's parents divorced when he was ten because his dad was a workaholic, and his mom had *needs*. Basically, she wasn't getting enough dick at home, so she started stepping out on his dad. His mom prioritized dating, which left Mason home alone a lot. He was never bitter, per se, but we'd talk about the future and all the things we'd do differently than our parents.

Mason was adamant that he never wanted his children to go through the loneliness that he had. Yes, children plural. He was always resolute that he would have multiple kids. He hated being the only child. While I wasn't an only child, I could relate to feeling alone. What was the point of talking to parents who were cracked out of their minds? When my parents weren't completely blown, they'd feed me bullshit lies to make up for their poor parenting while they were high.

When we were young, we'd talk about running away together and starting over, doing things our way. We both had it all figured out. As we got older, we realized we had to have solid goals and not childish dreams.

Before his dad's IT company took off, he wanted to be a coach. He played soccer his whole life and loved it. Mason loved the discipline, loved the friendships, and loved the game. It fulfilled him. However, when the company took off, I think Mason started seeing his dad differently.

He was no longer a workaholic, absent father. Instead, he was a man on a mission, dedicated to his dreams. His father had a vision and worked hard to make it a reality, and I think a part of Mason admired that. The other part is more of an assumption on my part, but I think he believes working there with his dad will bring them closer.

\* \* \*

Finally, I arrive at the hospital and try to pull myself together before entering. I need to be strong for Mason and his family. I don't know what I'll do if I lose him.

Once inside, I find Vivian, and she explains that Mason was in a bad car accident last night around midnight. He was driving home from a friend's house when the brakes stopped working. His car ran off the road and straight into the river. Luckily, someone behind him saw the entire accident and called 911 immediately. He's been in surgery since he got in last night, so she doesn't have any more updates.

I clutch my stomach and feel like I'm going to be sick. Vivi pulls me over to a chair and lets me cry into her shoulder until I can't cry anymore.

Hours later, the doctor tells us that he's stable, but he's not out of the woods. He had a collapsed lung, five broken ribs, and internal bleeding. The reason surgery took so long was due to the internal bleeding around his collapsed lung that they couldn't stop. In addition, he has swelling on the brain, which they said is typical for the injuries he sustained to his upper body when the airbag hit, plus he was underwater for at least two minutes when the car finally sank.

While I sit and listen to the doctor's account of his injuries, I need to excuse myself to the restroom. When I reach the bathroom, I take the first stall and fall to my knees, heaving my guts up until there's nothing left. I feel like this is all my fault. If I had told August to go fuck himself Monday night, I wouldn't have given him what belonged to Mason. Mason would have been with me instead of sinking to the bottom of a river. I fall to the floor, a sobbing mess.

As I make my way back out to the waiting room, Mason's mom pulls me into a hug.

"Gigi, sweetheart, they're allowing Johnathan and me to go back, but I told them you'd be joining us. Mason would want you there."

I hug her tightly before nodding and following her back, praying her words are true. The way things were left between Mason and me would suggest differently.

When we get to his room, he's hooked up to tons of machines. The doctor explains that the breathing tube will be removed in the morning, once they're confident his lung is strong enough. He's also in an induced coma to help his body and brain heal. Depending on how the next twenty-four hours go, they will reevaluate waking him up.

As I take in his bruised body, I'm overwhelmed with emotions. He looks so peaceful yet so broken. Mason had a smile that would brighten the rainiest of days and a way of making light in the darkest of times. I wish he were awake now so that he could do just that.

He's always been there for me through thick and thin, and I'm not leaving his side until he wakes. I'll be here for him for as long as he needs me because I know that no matter how much hurt I've put him through, he would do the same for me.

\* \* \*

My arm has fallen asleep, my back aches, and my head is pounding. Someone is tapping my shoulder.

"Miss, miss, we need you to wake up."

I snap my eyes open and realize I'm slumped over in a chair, leaning against the hospital bed, holding Mason's hand. I quickly straighten and immediately regret my haste. Everything hurts, and I groan in agony.

"Sorry, miss, but we need access to this side of the bed to do our charts. His parents said you have permission to be here no matter what. But maybe you want to grab a coffee and freshen up? He won't wake while you're gone. We can promise you that."

I look at Mason's face and notice some of his color has returned. I nod to acknowledge her words and head toward the door.

Somehow, I manage to make my way down to the cafeteria, placing one foot in front of the other, completely numb. I order a large coffee before pulling my phone out of my purse to check the time. That's when I remember it's dead. Oh shit, it's been dead since yesterday when Vivian called. Crap, I didn't call into work. I need to call my mom and August. I say his name aloud with a mix of sadness and angst.

He's probably so pissed. Before I can finish the thought, big arms wrap around me, and the scent of leather and cedar invades my senses, instantly quieting all the noise. I immediately start crying again for all new reasons. He holds me until the sobs that have immobilized my body subside. Then he pulls back to look at me.

"Gianna, do you know how fucking out of my mind with worry I've been?"

I nod in understanding as he guides us over to a table, where he takes a seat and pulls me onto his lap.

"When I didn't cross paths with you at work, I assumed it was just because you were busy, and when you didn't return my texts throughout the day, I figured your phone must have died, but once the night hit and your phone never came on—" He puts his head into my neck and inhales deeply. "I didn't sleep at all last night. I went into the office, found your mom, and asked her where you were. I'm sorry, but—"

I cut him off. "My mom knows I'm here?"

He gives me a perplexed look. "Yes, why wouldn't she know you're here?"

I shake my head. Of course she knows I'm here. Vivian or Chloe, Mason's mom, must have let her know.

"I'm sorry, August. I got the news when I was driving in yesterday, and my phone immediately died. I came straight to the hospital, and I've been beside myself."

My voice cracks, and I close my eyes to focus on breathing so I don't cry again.

"Baby, whatever you need, I'm here for you. I know he means a lot to you."

Is he serious right now? He's not upset that I'm sitting in a hospital crying over Mason? He's gently rubbing his hand up and down my back, offering comfort, but I know this must be taxing on his emotions. If there's one thing I know without a doubt, it's that August is a possessive man. There's no way in hell any of this is okay with him. His brow is furrowed with mixed emotions, and his face is pale like all this makes him physically ill. He must know

I'm on to his newfound acceptance of Mason because he looks away and says, "I brought you something." Essentially shutting me down before I can question him.

He pulls a phone charger out of his pocket and places it in my hand, and I smile.

"Thank You."

We sit there in silence a bit longer, me on his lap while he holds me. That small and simple act brings me so much comfort and peace, and I know he needs it just as much as I do. I cling to him, scared to let him go because I know I'll push him away as soon as I do. Mason deserves all of me, he needs all of me, and I can't be what he needs if August is in the picture. August makes me weak, I lose all control, and my rational thoughts go out the window. He fills a part of me I didn't know I was missing, and as much as I don't want to lose that, I'll sacrifice that part of me to ensure the man upstairs is whole.

Pulling away, I move to stand, but my legs start to shake as I do. I quickly sit in the chair opposite August and lay my head on the table. *Damn it.* I need to eat. August quickly grabs my hand. "Tell me what to do."

"I need something to eat."

Running over to the breakfast bar, he grabs muffins, granola bars, and juice, ensuring I have them all before running back to pay. God, why does he have to be so good to me? Why can't he do something shitty so that I can hold it against him? Why can't I hate him?

I need to eat so I can think clearly—damn low blood sugar. Grabbing the orange juice, I start chugging, knowing that the sugar will quickly enter my system and breathe some life back into me. With each bite I take, my hands tremble.

August looks on with a mix of panic and anger in his eyes. "I know what you're going to ask of me, and after this little show, it's not going to happen."

I simply stare at him, still too weak to argue. August sits in silence, watching me eat while deep in thought. Finally, once I've finished the muffin and get half a granola bar down, I have enough strength to say, "You can't be here." I figured he would be stunned by my claim, but he looks at me unfazed. That's when I realize those were the words he was expecting. As much as I don't want to hurt him, I need to. He can't be here with me. I don't want to explain who he is to close friends and family, and God forbid Mason wakes up and he's here. Closing my eyes, I choose my next words carefully. I choose the words that I know will hurt the most. "Let me clarify. I don't want you here."

I know I could have chosen different words, but I still have to endure his presence at work. I'm trying to remain somewhat neutral in hopes he won't have any knee-jerk reactions and choose to renege on his word that he won't have me fired. The words hit their mark because I see for a brief moment he's hurt, and fuck if those words didn't taste like poison coming out. He needs to leave. He can't be here when Mason wakes up, and I may as well get all the breaking done at once.

Mason is upstairs broken, counting on me to put him back together as he has always done for me. August's eyes lock on mine as if he's peering into my soul, looking for the truth in my words. I hold his gaze, not wanting to give anything away, and then he says, "Goodbye, Gianna," and walks away.

Watching him walk away from me hurts, and I know I'll live with an ache inside of me where he should be. I want to run to him and tell him I didn't mean it, for him to pull me into his arms, call me baby, and tell me I'm his. That's when I realize that part of me hoped he'd fight for me. But in the end, he does none of those things, and I'm left cold and empty.

## NINETEEN
### *Gianna*

It's been a little over a week since Mason has been in a coma. The doctors stopped giving him the meds that were keeping him under on Sunday. It's now Friday. They say that everything looks good. His bruising is almost all gone around his face, and the swelling has gone down. He's starting to look like himself again, just peacefully sleeping. They seem confident that his brain has healed and that there should be no long-term issues, but the brain can't be rushed, and we won't know anything for sure until he's awake. He'll wake up when his body is ready. It is doing what it needs to do to heal.

I haven't been back to work since the accident happened. I fully expected to be fired since I just started, and the work I do can't be done remotely. But for once, my mom must have stepped up for me and pulled some strings because they've been sending me odd tasks from multiple departments to work on while I'm at the hospital. She's probably hoping this act of generosity will earn her some gratitude cash. I know my parents seem to be on the right track, but my mom has never just done something for me out of the goodness of her heart. There's always an ulterior motive.

The only person I've checked in on at home has been Elio. I

call him every night to make sure everything is okay. He never really received the beatings, the hate, and overall disdain that I've endured from our mother for merely existing, and for that, I'm grateful; but because I've been absent, I can't help feeling that he'll turn into her punching bag if I'm gone too long.

This entire event has been a sobering experience for me. Why does the worst possible scenario have to occur to make you see what's been in front of your eyes all along? I've always wanted Mason, but when he confessed his feelings for me, something I had dreamed about for years, I couldn't see past August. The saying that you don't know what you have until it's gone has never felt more authentic.

Everything between us is so easy, so natural. We fit together. I only hope when Mason wakes up, I'm not the biggest mistake he ever made. After all, he was ready to walk away from me last week, and because I selfishly couldn't bear the thought of losing him or breaking his heart, I asked him not to. I told him I'd give him everything I had, but then I went and gave it away. All I gave him was heartache.

I was ready to walk away from Mason to have August. What hurts the most about all of this is that I still want August, but I know those are narrow-minded thoughts. Choosing August meant giving up on a man who's been by my side through thick and thin, held me through my tears, kissed away my pain, and now offered me his heart. I can't toss all that away. Mason deserves my best, so that's what he'll have.

Today I'm going into the office to drop off all the work I've done over the past few days and collect a few more projects. While I hate leaving Mason, I know I can't afford to lose my job, and I'm lucky they are working with me. Reaching for his hand, I take it in mine and squeeze. "Babe, I have to go to the office, but I promise I'll be right back. Maybe when I get back, you can wake up for me so I can see those big blue eyes and that handsome smile."

I kiss the back of his hand and lay it back down on the mattress before running my fingers through his blond locks, ensuring they're off his forehead. He likes having his hair longer on top and shorter on the sides, but he hates when it falls on his face. I place another kiss on his cheek and then head out.

* * *

My heart starts racing when I pull into the parking lot at Reds. My mind has been so focused on Mason that I didn't even think about how I might run into August. My chest tightens at the thought. It's been over a week since we last spoke at the hospital. Neither one of us has reached out, and I guess that means we are officially over. *So why does that thought hurt so much?* I know I pushed him away, but I guess a part of me didn't think he'd leave so easily, but maybe the feelings I hoped existed never really did.

I've thought about the night of Mason's crash almost every night, and it makes me sick. I was having sex, wrapped up in another man's arms, when the one who needed me most was dying. What rips me to shreds is that I don't regret one minute I spent with August. There's nowhere else in the world I wanted to be. The time spent in his arms was pure bliss, and the last time we had sex, it felt like so much more than that. To be honest, every time with him was highly passionate, intimate, and irrevocable. A part of him is imprinted on my soul and being here at Reds is too much.

I need to get in and get out. I quickly scan the parking lot for his G-Wagon or BMW, and my stomach twists when I don't see either. Part of me is relieved, while the other is disappointed that I won't accidentally run into him.

Once inside, I greet the receptionist and head back to my office. My boss left me a note saying she was out to lunch. Duh, it's lunchtime. That's why he's not here. I swiftly drop off the completed work and pick up the envelopes full of cutouts to be completed. Relief floods through my veins when I hit the lobby. Somehow, I managed to get in and out without running into a single soul. I didn't want to explain my absence and relive the nightmare ten times with nosey coworkers. I just want to get back to Mason.

Once the fresh spring air hits my face, I instantly relax until I look up and see August's blond friend standing in front of his car, looking my way. I give him a clipped wave and hurriedly head to my car. He must be waiting for August, which means I need to get out of here.

When I get to my car, a voice calls out, "Gianna, wait up."

I look over my shoulder, and sure enough, he's jogging up behind me. The man is truly striking. He has blond hair and blue eyes, just like Mason, except where Mason's eyes are pale blue, his are a dark stormy blue. Both men are probably the same height, but where Mason is lean and toned, this man has defined muscles that visibly stretch his polo shirt and tight-fitted jeans. This man has a gym body rather than an athlete's body. Mason has that boy next door, melt-your-heart look with an inviting smile, whereas this guy looks like he wants to rip your panties off and fuck hard, a total playboy through and through.

When I snap out of my daydream, I realize his smug ass was watching me check him out, and now he has a smirk on his face as if to say, like what you see?

"I'm sorry. I didn't catch your name the other night. Who are you?"

"Ethan Grand. I'm surprised August didn't mention me."

I quirk a brow. "Is there a reason he should have?"

He looks me over from head to toe. "I suppose not, just surprised, seeing as how we're best friends."

I look at him, baffled by this entire exchange, not sure what his purpose for talking to me is at this point. "Well, I'm kind of in a hurry to get out of here, and I'm not sure where August is so—"

Holding his hand up, he cuts me off. "Oh, princess, I didn't come here to see August. I came to see you."

My eyebrows shoot up in surprise. Why would this man come to see me? I didn't even know his name until five seconds ago.

"Don't look so surprised. I know I'm not the only one trying to score a date with you."

"Excuse me, score a date with me?"

"Yeah, see, I have this thing I need to go to tonight, and I need a date. Then I remembered there was this hot girl at August's place last week, and since he has a girlfriend, she must be free."

I try hard not to react to his words, but they fucking hurt even though they shouldn't. I'm so done with this conversation. I turn to open my back door and put my work inside when I notice a Christian Dior garment bag lying on the back seat and a matching shoebox on the floor.

Now I'm so mad I could scream. I turn to face Ethan. "Is this funny to you? Am I some sort of sick joke? I'm not a fucking idiot. While I may not have known your name, I know your face, and you can get any girl you want. So why are you slumming it?"

He steps in closer, leans down so that his mouth is a hairsbreadth away from my ear, and says, "Princess, I can't get another you."

Those words make bile rise in my mouth because I realize I was played. Those were the exact words August said to me when I thought he wanted me. These cocky rich motherfuckers think they can use people. Well, I am not the girl.

"Get that fucking dress out of my car. I'm not going anywhere with you."

He puts his hands in his pockets and casually says, "How's your dad liking his new job as lead foreman on the new Grand Media building downtown?"

"Are you threatening me?"

"Wouldn't dream of it. I'm just making small talk with my date. I'll pick you up at six tonight." Then he turns on his heel and walks back to his car. I glare after him as he casually strolls back, wishing like hell I could burn him alive with my gaze. Then, before he drops into the seat of his Bugatti, he says, "I think it goes without saying you won't be mentioning a word of this to August." He shoots me a wink and then drives off.

How the hell did I get caught up in whatever the fuck this shit is? I never wanted to be on anyone's radar. Now I have another hot as sin, rich as fuck guy talking to me. The difference this time is I'm not going to get played. Fool me once, shame on you. This bitch doesn't get fooled twice. They want to play. Let's play!

\* \* \*

I return to Mason's side after my run-in with Ethan. He's still asleep, but the doctors think he can hear us. I hope he can hear everything because then he knows I haven't left his side and he means the world to me.

Over the past week, I've told him everything. All our highs and lows, how much he means to me, and how I promise to be better. How I promise to be what he needs. I begin to tell him about my run-in with Ethan and how I must leave his side tonight to be his date, but before I can ask him not to wake without me, there are five nurses in the room.

"Gianna, we must ask you to step back while checking his vitals." I immediately drop his hand and step away.

"Did something happen? Why is everyone in here?"

"Well, something caused his blood pressure to rise, and his heart rate dramatically spiked, so we are checking him out to see what might have caused that."

I nod and watch as they run tests. Why, tonight of all nights, when he's on the brink of waking up, do I get pulled into this crap? Once the nurses are done looking him over and leave the room, I say, "I'm sorry, babe. I promise everything will be okay. I wouldn't leave if this weren't necessary. Please wake up soon. I need you."

I squeeze his hand and wait a moment to ensure nothing else happens. He doesn't move. Instead, he lies asleep peacefully, so I take a deep breath and leave the room.

\* \* \*

Once I finally return to my house, I have roughly an hour before Ethan picks me up. I don't want to even think about how I'm going to explain this to my parents.

When I walk through the door, Elio is there.

"Hey, Gigi, how's Mason?"

I can tell my brother is genuinely concerned. Mason was

somewhat of a big brother figure to him. He would come over, throw the ball around with him, and play video games here and there.

"He's getting stronger every day, but he's not ready to wake up."

"I'm surprised you left his side, Gigi."

I close my eyes and pull in a deep breath through my nose to keep myself from reacting to those words.

"I didn't want to leave him, believe me. If I had a choice, I wouldn't, but I have somewhere I have to be tonight." He nods, seemingly content with my response.

"Where's Mom and Dad?"

"Dad is working late and said he'd be home around seven tonight, and Mom stopped to pick up Chinese by the old house, so she'll be home a little later."

"Damn, I love Hunan's. I wish I didn't have to go."

He laughs. "I'm not sorry. More for me."

I hurry down the hall toward my room, but before I make it in, Elio calls.

"Hey, Gigi."

I turn back to look at him.

"I miss you, just so you know."

My eyes soften as I take in his sandy-blond hair and big brown eyes. He's here alone a lot without me coming home at night. I know my dad has been working late to make extra money, and my mom has been doing physical therapy after work to help her recover from her fall a few weeks ago. But in my world, lonely is the better evil.

"I'm sorry, Lo. I promise I'll be around more as soon as Mason is better."

He nods in understanding, and I enter my room. I throw my dress and shoes on the bed and hurry to the shower.

After I've showered, I head over to the garment bag and open it up to see how I should style my hair and makeup. The man bought me a Christian Dior dress and matching black heels. This dress probably costs more than all the clothes I have ever owned in my entire life combined.

It's a black vintage Dior dress with drop sleeves and silk embroidery. At first glance, I thought it was lace, but when I picked it up to hold it against my body in the mirror, I knew it was silk.

My hair must be classic to match the dress, so I style it in soft curls pinned back to one side and add a soft smokey eye for makeup.

As I put the finishing touches on my makeup, I hear his car pull up outside.

I steal a glance out my bedroom window, and sure enough, his black Bugatti is sitting right outside my house. That car is fucking sexy as hell but so out of place in this neighborhood. His car cost more than every house on my cul-de-sac combined. I roll my eyes at the ridiculousness of this entire situation and decide it's time to put on my dress.

The dress is absolutely breathtaking. At first glance, I thought it was all black, but the embellished silk layer has a deep merlot hue. Underneath is a black, fitted, silk slip dress that hits me mid-thigh while the see-through wine-colored embroidery layer continues to the floor. It's super sexy but very elegant and classic at the same time. The shoes are five-inch heeled sandals with a thin leather ankle strap and toe strap.

When I check my reflection in the mirror, I know I look good. It's incredible what an expensive dress can do for your confidence. I'm about ready to walk out the door when I hear Lo.

"Gianna, you are not going to believe what kind of car is parked out front."

Shit, he noticed. I'm heading down the hallway when Elio sees me and does a double take.

"Gianna, you look beautiful. Where are you going? Wait, is that Bugatti here for you?"

Before I can answer any of those questions, the doorbell rings. I throw my head back to the ceiling and groan. Why did he have to come to the door? This isn't an actual date.

Elio rushes down the stairs, eager to see who's at the door. He throws it open, and Ethan stands there looking devilishly handsome and sexy. He's wearing all black, just like me: black suit, black shirt, black bow tie, and black pocket square. The only color is in his cerulean blue eyes.

Elio stares at him, completely awestruck. "Gigi, why is Ethan Grand at our house?"

He doesn't even turn to look at me. Instead, he just continues staring at Ethan while Ethan's penetrating gaze is locked on me at the top of the stairs. I put my hand on my hip, exasperated by this entire exchange.

"Elio, how do you even know who Ethan Grand is?"

He finally breaks his stare away from Ethan and looks at me like I'm an idiot. "Gigi, you can't be serious. Everyone knows who Ethan Grand is."

I quirk a brow at him. "Well, I didn't know who he was."

He laughs. "Yeah, well, that's because you live under a rock."

"Okay, Lo, I think that's a bit extreme. I don't watch the news. It's too depressing. That doesn't mean I live under a rock."

I descend the steps, and Ethan's eyes stay glued to my every step as if he's astonished. Just another one of his playboy moves, I'm sure. Make the women think you only have eyes for them, buy them fancy clothes, pick them up in your sexy car, and show them the world. Their legs will be wrapped around your back by the end of the night. Too bad I'm on to you, Ethan Grand.

As I stand in front of him, I clear my throat to snap him out of his act. He turns toward the street and sticks his elbow out for me to take, which I do.

We're walking down the driveway when Elio calls out, "So should I tell Mom you're out with America's most wanted bachelor or...?"

I throw him a scowl over my shoulder, and he laughs before closing the door. Ethan chuckles to himself at my expense.

"I'm glad you find fucking up my life amusing."

We reach the car, he opens the door, and I slide in, but before he closes the door, he leans down and says, "You better watch that mouth tonight, princess. I like it dirty."

I don't even have a chance to process those words before he shuts the door, sealing me in with his intoxicating scent. The man smells divine, looks like sex, and happens to be dripping with money. I'd like to think I'm not a shallow person, and those things don't matter because they really don't, but they also don't hurt.

Once he's in the car, he gives me a mischievous glance and then floors it out of my cul-de-sac. The black leather of my seat is warm and soft like butter, which I can appreciate since I'm wearing a silk dress. The inside of the car is wrapped in black leather, and soft ambient lights run along the footwells and doors. When we get to the highway, he lets loose, and I can't stop the smile that takes over my face.

He notices and smiles. "You like to go fast, princess?"

Why do I have to be enjoying this? I'm supposed to be mad at him. He threatened my dad's job. He's using me to get to August, and being with him means I'm not with Mason. I try to school my expression and not look as pleased as I am because I shouldn't be.

"You know, princess, I don't have to be the bad guy if you don't make me one."

He's right about that. But if I'm going to be stuck with him for the night, I may as well try to enjoy myself. It doesn't matter that he's using me because I'm using him. I know if I'm seen with Ethan, it will get back to August, and maybe that will hurt him. If not, at least it will piss him off.

Either way, I need to figure out Ethan's purpose for inviting me out tonight because I sure as hell don't buy that he wanted to take me on a date.

I've decided I'm not going to figure it out by glaring out the window, so I ask, "Where are you taking me tonight?"

He keeps his eyes on the road. "We are going to a black-tie fundraiser."

Of course his response is short and to the point, giving nothing away. "Why did you ask me not to tell August?"

He runs his forefinger over his lips, contemplating his next words.

"Maybe I'm tired of his crap. Maybe I want to be an ass, or maybe he has something worth stealing." He looks at me and holds my eye for a beat before looking back at the road.

"Ethan, you can stop with the over-the-top flirting. I know I'm a pawn in some revenge scheme you're playing against August, so you can drop the act."

He rubs his thumb along his bottom lip. "Princess, I don't have to pretend to be attracted to you. Every man in the room will want the girl on my arm tonight."

Of course his words send heat coursing through my body. What woman wouldn't be flattered by those words? But I have to remind myself this is all part of his plan. Once I get out of his sexy car and away from his seductive scent, I'll be able to react appropriately and not be fazed by his sweet talk.

We finally arrive at the Ritz Carlton in the Central West End. He gets out and hands the valet the keys before coming around to open the door for me and help me out. Upon exiting, his eyes roam over my body, taking in my dress.

"It's a stunning dress, thank you."

I wrap my arm through his before he leans in and says, "Princess, I wasn't admiring the dress, but I'm glad you like it."

My face immediately heats, and he laughs before ushering us into the hotel. Suddenly, I'm incredibly nervous. My heart rate picks up, and I get butterflies in my stomach. I stop, paralyzed as if the floor grew roots and wrapped around my ankles.

Ethan looks over at me with furrowed brows. "What's the problem? We are here to see and be seen."

"Yeah, that's the problem. I don't want to be seen."

He looks amused by my comment. "I'm going to need you to have thick skin for me tonight, and remember, I'm not the bad guy unless you make me out to be one."

"Ethan, what does that even mean? You are the bad guy. This is the last place on earth I want to be right now."

He doesn't bother answering. Instead, he pulls me through the double doors and into the grand ballroom.

The space is elegantly decorated. A bar is stationed across the room, adjacent to the doors that run the room's length. There are at least one hundred tables draped in black cloths, with huge red floral centerpieces. The white walls are lit in deep shades of red, and toward the front of the room, there's a stage with a pedestal flanked by the Missouri State flag and the United States flag. We must be at a political fundraiser.

That's when it dawns on me that the only political figure I can think of that would be close to Ethan is August's dad. We are at a political fundraiser for Augustus Barron Branson. The Branson family has been involved in politics for years. They are longtime donors to the Missouri Republican Association, but recently Augustus decided to throw his hat in the race for a Senate seat. He figures he can appeal to middle-class Americans with his blue-collar manufacturing roots. Then it hits me. This means August will be here. Earlier, I was all gung-ho for this plan because I thought being seen with Ethan meant mingling with friends and word filtering back to August that we were together. But I hadn't mentally prepared myself to actually see him.

As soon as the thought crosses my mind, I spot him at the bar, and my heart sinks. He's standing at the bar with a beautiful blonde, the same blonde who showed up at the club. His hand is placed on her lower back as she leans into him to say something. They look perfect together, the epitome of upper class, with their flawless outfits and perfectly manicured hair and makeup. They were high school sweethearts, and I was foolish to think I could compete.

We made promises to each other, delicate vows in moments that I thought were filled with heart-wrenching, passionate honesty. But standing here now, I know they were empty. Promises are supposed to mean something, but sometimes they are just words.

Ethan follows my line of sight, and I try to look away quickly so he doesn't see the hurt in my eyes. "Princess, remember that tough skin I warned you about."

"Why did you bring me here? Why do you want to hurt me?"

He narrows his eyes at me in question. "Am I the one hurting you?"

As soon as the words leave his mouth, I know he's right. He technically isn't hurting me, but he knew where he was taking me tonight, he knew August would be here, and I know Ethan knew he'd be here with her.

"Don't act like you didn't know he'd be here with her."

"I haven't pretended anything with you, and if you must know—" He's cut off mid-sentence when Augustus Barron Branson comes over to hug him.

"Ethan Grand! How are you doing, son, and who is this lovely woman you have on your arm tonight?"

I smile, taking in his handsome features. Augustus is an older version of August. His hair is starting to gray around the edges, and his kind eyes are beginning to wrinkle, but you can tell he keeps himself fit for his age. I met him a few times over the years when I was young as my mother was his father's personal assistant. My mother would occasionally bring me to work when she couldn't find a babysitter. I'm sure he doesn't remember me, but he was always so lovely, and he'd even pay me for helping out, which was a big deal for me. I can't help but smile at the memory.

"This is Gianna Moretti. We met through August."

Augustus smiles and reaches out to shake my hand. "Young lady, you have grown into a lovely woman." Then he turns to Ethan and says, "Son, you'd be a damn fool to let her go," and walks away.

Ethan smirks. "Let's get a drink, shall we?"

I take his arm. "Yes, but at the other end of the bar, please."

He smiles. "Your wish is my command."

## TWENTY

## *August*

It's been over a week since I last spoke to Gianna. I haven't slept, I barely eat, and the only thing I'm running on is protein powder and whiskey. Work sucks because she's not there. When I leave the office, I head to the gym and work out until I physically can't anymore, letting out all my frustration. When I found out where she was and why, I knew she wouldn't want me to stay. Hell, she probably wouldn't want me there, period, but I had to see her. Consequences be damned. I know Croft is important to her, but I don't believe that she doesn't feel anything for me. The night before, we practically made love, as crazy as that sounds.

When I walked into that hospital and found her looking broken as hell, I pulled her into my arms and held her. I know she was happy to see me, I could feel it in the way her body relaxed into mine, but I also know my girl is stubborn. For this reason, I was prepared to stop by, check on her, and offer her support in whatever way she'd let me. Of course in the back of my mind, I was hoping she'd want me to stay, but I was prepared to leave.

Then she almost passed out on me. It took everything I had not to take her home with me once she ate. She was sacrificing her health to stay by his bedside, and I'm not going to lie and say that didn't tear me up inside. I'd give anything for her to care about me that way. What I hadn't prepared for was her asking me to leave because she didn't want me there. After the night we shared, I thought we were past pretending we didn't want or care about each other. But when I looked into her eyes, they were laced with regret, hurt, and sadness, as if I were the source. I couldn't bear to be the reason for her pain, so I did as she asked and left. I wasn't expecting her to completely cut me out of her life. There have been no texts, calls, or messages. I was nothing.

So you could imagine how livid I am to see her at the end of the bar on the arm of Ethan *fucking* Grand, my alleged best friend. He has his hand on her waist while he leans into her ear, saying something that makes her laugh out loud. If every guy at the bar wasn't already staring at her, they are now. She is the most beautiful woman in the room. Her long dark-blond hair is pulled over one shoulder in soft curls, and her dress leaves enough skin on show to make you salivate without being too risky. Tonight, she is elegance personified, and I'm furious.

This isn't happening. There's no way he showed up here with her like she is his to flaunt. I make my way to the end of the bar in no time flat and stand right in front of them just as the bartender sets down two shots and two martinis. Ethan spies me first and gives me an arrogant half-grin before Gianna notices my presence. When she does, she looks at me, her expression void of any emotion. *What the fuck is that about?*

"Gianna, why are you here?" I know Croft hasn't woken up yet, and she hasn't left his side. So the sight before me doesn't make any sense.

Before she can answer, Ethan cuts in. "Well, isn't that obvious, August? She is my date."

My eyebrows shoot up in surprise, and I cross my arms to keep myself from punching him square in the jaw right there on the spot. "Date? You have some nerve bringing my girl here on your arm—"

Gianna cuts me off. "I think your girl is at the other end of the bar, wondering why you're down here making a scene."

My eyes are fixed on her face, waiting to see a crack that says this isn't what it looks like, but it never comes. Instead, she stares back at me, indifferent to the entire exchange. Ethan takes that moment to place his hand on her waist. I put my hands on my hips and take a deep breath so I don't strangle him.

"You better fucking remove that hand before you lose it."

The asshole dares to laugh. "Maybe you should let Gianna choose whose hands she wants on her."

Before I can respond, Carson walks up and wraps her arm around my waist, effectively tucking herself into my arm as if we're some cozy couple. She knows damn well the only reason she's here tonight is that our families set this up months ago. Her parents bought a twenty-thousand-dollar table, and since we had been dating, it was only fitting that she'd accompany me.

"Auggie, you left me all alone." *Why the fuck does she keep calling me that?* The only person who has called me that is Ethan, and he does it out of insolence. Before I can remove her arms from my waist, she shocks the hell out of me. "Oh hey, Ethan, who's the flavor of the week?" What the hell? Has she always been this spiteful toward other women, or is this a new development since she's been away?

Gianna doesn't even flinch at her words. Instead, she picks up her shot, tips it back, and says, "Oh, I'm not his flavor of the week. He's my sugar daddy."

*Is she fucking serious right now?*

I watch in horror as she turns into him, grabs his suit lapel, and says, "Come on, Daddy, I'm getting bored."

His eyes sparkle with delight like he's enjoying every second of this exchange. Then, giving me a cocky smirk, he shoots his shot, grabs his drink, and walks away with her in tow. I'm just about to lunge at him and knock his ass out when Eduard appears out of nowhere.

"August, it looks like your dad is getting great support tonight! This is an amazing turnout." He claps me on the shoulder and squeezes it before addressing Carson. "Carson, sweetheart, it's always a pleasure seeing you here on August's arm." He leans in and kisses her cheek.

"Eduard, I was at the salon this morning, and when I walked out, I saw you getting into a brand-new Ferrari Aperta. Lucky man, you."

My eyes widen in surprise. My aunt has a decent trust fund, and Eduard makes good money working for my dad, but not two-million-dollar Ferrari good. Last month they went on a month-long trip to Europe, and they just bought the most ostentatious house of anyone I know. They're either investing well, or they're blowing through her inheritance.

"Well, you only live once," he admonishes.

I fucking hate pompous small talk, not to mention this entire exchange is incredibly bizarre. Eduard never makes small talk with Carson or me because he has nothing to gain from us. This entire interaction only reminds me that he's up to something. I excuse myself to find Gianna. There's no way she's willingly here with Ethan.

"If you guys will excuse me, I need to use the restroom."

I swiftly start walking away before they pull me into more trivial commentary, and God forbid Carson tries to follow me to the restroom. Once I'm clear, I quickly scan the room and see that Ethan is making his rounds and is currently stuck talking to his dad's board of directors. If I walk over there and steal Gianna, I know he won't be able to stop me because he'll have to keep up appearances with the board.

"Gentlemen, if you'll excuse the interruption, I'm just going to steal Gianna away for a moment."

Ethan sets his jaw and glares daggers at me, and out of my peripheral, I see him squeeze her hip. If that was a silent message, I wouldn't know because her gaze gives nothing away. When I extend my hand to her, she gives the men a curt smile before saying, "If you'll excuse me," and then she takes my hand.

Her hand in mine feels so good, and I can finally breathe even though I want to murder someone. I promptly pull her aside to a quiet, empty table. I search her expression for answers, but she won't meet my eyes.

Finally, irritated by my stare, she says, "What do you want, August?"

"What do I want? Does that mean you care now?"

She finally gives me her eyes. "That's rich coming from you, considering you never cared. Just leave me alone and go back to your girlfriend."

"Is that what this is about? Do you still think I'm with Carson? I haven't been with Carson for months, Gianna. I'll fucking kiss you right here, right now, in front of this entire room, so there's no question who you belong to." I step into her, seeking approval, but she nervously looks around me, searching for Ethan. I'm entirely enraged, and I don't want to take my anger out on her and make things worse, but before I can say another word, she moves to walk around me. Grabbing her wrist, I halt her movement. "You'll let him, of all people, parade you around as his flavor of the week, but I had to keep you as a secret?"

She closes her eyes and swallows hard as if readjusting her mask for the night. "You played me. At least with Ethan, I know what I'm getting."

She yanks her wrist out of my hand and hurries off toward Ethan, who has started walking our way. When she reaches him, he rubs the sides of her arms and looks up at me like checkmate, motherfucker.

*What the hell is going on? When would they have even talked?* I'm missing something big, and I can't place it. Everyone starts taking their seats for dinner, and I notice Gianna excuse herself and head for the doors. Ethan seems to be in a deep conversation with his dad, so I quickly slip out in search of Gianna.

She walks into the women's bathroom, and I make sure no one is watching before I follow her in. Once inside, I instantly scan the room to ensure we're alone before locking the door. Gianna is bent over the sink, running cold water over her forearms, so she hasn't noticed my approach. However, when she shuts off the water and looks in the mirror, her gaze locks with mine, her breath catches, and her skin prickles with goose bumps.

"Why can't you just leave me alone?"

I can tell she's flustered, but I don't understand what's happening. All I know is I need her. I put my hands on her shoulders and squeeze before placing a kiss on her neck.

Her body shudders, and she whispers, "Please don't."

"Tell me what this is, Gianna. I'm going to need you to open that pretty mouth and use your words unless you like being treated like the flavor of the week."

Turning around, she slaps me hard across the face. "You have no right to talk to me like that. After everything."

I grab her wrists and back her up against the wall, fury all over my face. "After everything? Are you referring to when you went MIA for twenty-four hours, only to show up in a hospital crying over another man after the night we had together? Or when you told me you didn't want me by your side, or how about tonight when you showed up on the arm of Ethan Grand to my dad's fundraiser?"

Her chest is heaving, and her breasts are brushing against my chest, making her nipples pebble. She continues to glare at me, not saying a word.

"Fine, have it your way."

I bend down and crush my mouth to hers, plunging my tongue into her mouth to remind her of all the pieces of me she's missing. It takes her a minute, but then she's kissing me back feverishly like she's missed me this past week as much as I've missed her. I pull back and bite her plump bottom lip before releasing her completely. She steadies her breathing before bringing the back of her hand to her mouth and wiping her lips. Which only serves to further piss me off. She doesn't get to wipe me off. Then, standing at the sink, she opens her clutch to reapply her lip gloss.

"I'll make you a deal. If you want me to leave you alone, then you have to prove it."

Narrowing her eyes at me in the mirror, I can see her contemplating my words. "Okay, what shall I prove?"

I smile at her. "Easy, baby." Bending down on one knee, I catch the bottom of her silk dress, trying not to let the fact that I know Ethan bought this for her ruin my moment. I slowly slink my hand underneath her dress, running my fingers from her ankle up the inside of her leg, where I stop when I get mid-thigh. "Your lips tell lies, but your pussy won't. The deal is, if you're not wet for me, I'll leave."

Her body trembles and I already know what I'll find.

"But if you are, I take what's mine." I kiss the back of her exposed thigh where my hand is before continuing my way upward excruciatingly slowly, ensuring I don't miss a second of how her body responds to me. Her legs are shaky, her hands are white-knuckling the marble counter, and her eyes are closed when I glance at her in the mirror.

When I reach her center, I hook my finger through her thong and pull it to the side so I can stroke her straight down the middle of her plump, silky folds. I'm unsure if she means to, but she ever so slightly opens up to give me more access. Ultimately, it doesn't matter because what I find confirms what I know in my heart. She's mine.

"You're not just wet. You're soaked." I tease her opening with my finger, and she pushes back on it, impaling herself on my hand. Immediately, she gasps, and I curse.

I make quick work of unbuckling my pants, and my cock springs out with pre-cum already leaking from the head, ready for her. I run my free hand up the center of her back until I reach her shoulders, where I push her forward before gathering her silk dress around her hips and exposing her perky little ass.

"Fuck me! Do you know how sexy you look, dripping wet for me with this perfect ass in the air wearing black heels?" I smack her ass hard before I brace myself on her hips and slam in hard. The air leaves my lungs in a rush, and I'm pissed. I pull out to the tip and slam back in just as hard, and when she whimpers, I lose it. "Is this what you want, Gianna? You want to be my slut, a quick fuck in the bathroom, instead of my queen?"

She doesn't respond, and that doesn't work for me. I grab her long blond hair over her shoulder and wrap it around my wrist, pulling her head back so she has no choice but to watch me take her in the mirror. Pounding into her, our eyes meet, and I see she's just as furious as I am. I don't know what Ethan has said to her, but she hates me right now even though her body wants what I'm giving her. She's treating this like the quick fuck it is so she can be done with me. I keep my eyes on hers, matching the ire I see there with each hard thrust. Fuck this. She doesn't get to walk away.

I feel her pussy starting to clench around me, and in a last-ditch effort to bring her back, I say, "What is it going to take?"

Slowing my thrusts, I release her hair, move my hand to the base of her neck, and pull her flat against my chest.

"Why are you testing my limits when you already have my devotion? Why do you want my hate when I'm only trying to love you?"

Her eyes stay on mine as her orgasm tears through her body, and I know my words triggered it. I pump her through the shockwaves, racking her body as my own release hits me. There's no way she doesn't feel anything for me. As much as she might want to hate me, she doesn't. She's mine, and I'm done doing things her way. Slowly, I pull out of her. Seeing her juices all over my dick, I grit my teeth and tuck myself back in. This is not where I wanted to do this. She should be at home in my bed, spread out before me to worship. I wanted to let her heart figure out what her body already knows, that she's mine, but then she showed up with Ethan. When I look up, I see she has already started trying to fix her makeup and that just-fucked hair, but that afterglow she has isn't going anywhere, and I fucking love it. Ethan won't miss that.

Suddenly, there's a loud pounding on the door. "Gianna, are you in there? Time to come out."

It's Ethan. Her eyes go wide in the mirror, and panic briefly flashes across her face, but she quickly recovers. "I'll be out in just a second. The martini got to me."

I smirk, finding it comical that she thinks she'll be going anywhere near Ethan.

Her livid eyes find mine. "I'm glad you find this funny. We had a deal. You got what you wanted. Now get the fuck out."

I stand there holding her gaze as the rage I've felt all night threatens to explode any second. When she sees that I'm not leaving, she starts toward the door but doesn't even make it two steps before I have her pinned to the wall. She tries to fight back, but I pin her with all my weight so she can't move, and when she goes to speak, I cover her mouth with my hand.

"What's funny is that you think you're leaving here with another man. The deal was I'd leave if you weren't wet for me, but we both know not only were you soaked, that pussy was starving for my cock." When she closes her eyes, I continue, "I said I'd take what's mine, and you, Gianna, are mine. Have been since the first day I laid my eyes on you."

Leaning into her, I kiss her neck as a tear rolls down her cheek. I can feel her body tremble beneath me, and it's then I know that she's scared. Good, because I want answers. "I don't want to hurt you, but I will if you don't start talking."

Her eyes snap open and find mine as if to verify that my threat is real. I know my expression is void of emotion because I'm on the brink of losing it. I don't want to do this to her. I don't want to scare her. I don't want to be the reason for her distress, but I'll be her worst fucking nightmare if that's what it takes to make her open up to me.

Finally, she relents, and I drop my hand from her mouth, but I keep her pinned in case she thinks about running. Her tongue darts out to moisten her dry lips, and on bated breath, she says, "Ethan threatened me."

My brain doesn't even have time to process her words. Instead, I see red and throw my fist into the wall beside her head. She yelps in surprise. "Are you fucking serious right now? Ethan threatened you, and you didn't think to come to me?" He was already dead to me, but now I'm going to kill him. I release her because I'm furious with her, and I will never put my hands on her when I feel that way. After everything, she still doesn't see me as someone she can trust or count on, someone who will protect her.

Ethan pounds on the door. "Open the door, princess. Time's up."

I immediately close the distance between myself and the bathroom door, pull it open, and throw him into the bathroom. Catching him off guard, he trips, enabling me to land a swift kick to the ribs before I fucking lay my fists into his face. I land blow after blow to his face, and he never gets the chance to take a swing. Gianna is screaming, trying to pull me off him.

"August, stop. You're going to kill him." She's right. I am going to kill him, but not here. I want him to know I'm coming.

Reluctantly, I let her pull me back. If she weren't here, I don't know that I could have stopped. I stare at him, lying there like the pathetic pretty boy he is, before saying, "You came after my world. Now I'll destroy yours."

Sitting up, he wipes his bloodied lip and shrugs. "We'll see."

I lunge to round on him again, but Gianna throws herself in front of me. "Let's go, August. Now."

Her eyes are pleading with mine. Anxiously running my hand through my hair, I contemplate my next move before grabbing Gianna's wrist and pulling her out of the bathroom. I'm so fucking livid. My girl doesn't trust me to protect her, and my best friend just threw everything away. Of course he wants Gianna. Who wouldn't? But if he's willing to fight me, there must be more to this than just a quick fuck because he knows I won't lose. I'm just not sure why he's risking everything over her, especially when I'm now sure he's fucking Carson. It's the only thing that makes sense.

The night she showed up at the club after I laid into Ethan wasn't a coincidence—hell, Ethan all but confirmed that when he showed up at my place out of nowhere and acted like he had no idea who Gianna was. Then tonight, when Carson called me Auggie, a name only Ethan has ever used to rile me up, it could only mean one thing; it's him. If she thought her vile comment went unnoticed, she's not as smart as I thought. That comment slipped because she was jealous of the fact that Ethan had his arm around Gianna. I couldn't care less that they are fucking. What I can't figure out is what Gianna has to do with any of this. Why pull her in?

Lost in my thoughts and rage, it's not until we hit the parking lot that I realize Gianna has been struggling to keep pace with my stride in her heels.

"August, please stop pulling me. You're hurting my wrist and walking too fast."

Then, turning back, I yank her into me before bending down and throwing her over my shoulder. I know I'm a little rough, but I'm doing the best I can given the rage threatening to consume me.

"August, put me down right now."

I slap her ass hard. "Not going to happen, baby."

When I reach my SUV, I deposit her in the passenger seat before pulling her seat belt across her lap and slamming the door. I waste no time tearing out of there and heading toward my house.

"August, please just take me home."

I don't respond. There's no way I'm taking her home. She's not safe at home. I'm not sure what Ethan wants, but I know he has no problem using Gianna to get it. She'll be staying with me indefinitely until I figure this out. In a clipped tone, I grind out, "You can't go home. Maybe if you had come to me before tonight, that would have been an option, but it's gone now."

Shaking her head, she stares out her window in silence. That's fine with me. I don't want to talk to her right now anyway. It will only lead to words I'll regret later. When I pull onto the heavily wooded road that leads up to my house, she finally snaps out of her thoughts and notices we aren't going to my condo.

"Where are you taking me?"

The unease in her tone isn't lost on me. I threatened her tonight, not to mention I came damn close to hitting Ethan one too many times. It amuses me as much as it burns me that she really thinks I would harm her. While I do plan on punishing her for her little stunt tonight, I would never hurt her. Any punishment I ever serve her will only bring her pleasure. We pull up in front of my log home, and I exit the vehicle without saying a word. She crosses her arms when I open her door and glares out the front window.

"I'm not going anywhere with you, August."

I'm not in the mood for games. Reaching into the car, I unclasp her seat belt and start to pull her out. But of course she'd start hitting me. "Stop fighting me, Gianna. What do you think I'm going to do?"

She scowls at me. "Just don't touch me. I'll follow you on my own."

I raise a brow in question, unsure if I can trust her, but I let it go because there isn't anywhere for her to run anyway.

The property is dark. There are no lights on, and it looks deserted. I don't usually come here, and no one knows I own it. I've always wanted a property like this, tucked away in the woods with no one around for miles, where I could breathe. Where I grew up, no one moved right of the I-70 corridor. It's considered low class. Growing up and being expected to walk, talk, and dress a certain way gets old quickly. Here, I could escape, but after installing the security system on the property, I locked it up and haven't been back since. I told myself I wouldn't come here until I was ready to be who I wanted to be.

Tonight's events forced my hand, but I knew I'd end up here eventually. I just didn't realize my dream girl would be with me. While the circumstances surrounding her being here aren't ideal, it feels exactly right. It's as if I wasn't meant to return here until I had her. Opening the front door, I flip on the lights, and everything is as I remember. The smell of cedar wood overwhelms your senses, and your eyes are immediately drawn to the wall of windows that make up the rear of the cabin. The view of the Ozark Mountains takes your breath away. Gianna follows me in and walks straight to the back windows, and I can tell she's just as captivated as I was when I first found this place. It's like it becomes a part of your soul, grounding you by showing you how small you are in this big world.

As much as I want to take in the view with her, I need to

make sure we are safe. So I head over to my office located off the main living room and ensure my security system is up and running. I'm bent over my desk, checking all the monitors, when movement catches my eye. Looking up, I find her standing in the doorway with her arms crossed over her chest, seemingly shaken and unsettled.

"Where are we, August?" Her voice is filled with apprehension.

"This is where we'll be staying. I bought this house a few years ago. No one knows about it, so we'll be safe here."

She walks over to my desk and throws herself into one of the wing-backed leather chairs. "August, I can't stay here. I need to get back to the hospital, and I live with my parents. While they have their problems, I've never been unsafe."

That had to be the worst sales pitch of all time. "Gianna, you can't go home. This just became a game to Ethan, and I don't know what he's after. I don't buy it for a second that he just wanted a date with you, and to top it off, he threatened you. The only way I can keep you safe is to keep you with me." Coming around the desk, I loosen my tie and prop my ass against the front, grip the sides with my hands, and cross my ankles. I'm trying to seem as non-threatening as possible. "What's the real reason you don't want to stay with me, Gianna? You know I'm not going to hurt you."

"You're right. You're going to fucking break me into a million pieces that I'll never be able to repair when you decide you're done playing with me."

My breathing picks up, and my heart starts racing because if I have the power to break her, then that means I hold a part of her together. A piece of her is all I need. Dropping to my knees before her, I take her face in my hands. Her eyes are glassy, like she's about to cry, no doubt because tonight has been overwhelming.

"I'll never let you break when all I want to do is make you whole."

A tear slips down her cheek, and I kiss it away before dropping my mouth to hers. Her plump lips are pliant against mine as she lets me own her mouth completely. I part her lips and brush my tongue against hers and release a deep groan as her taste explodes in my mouth. Her hands make their way up around my neck, her fingers curl into my hair, and my body instantly relaxes. My girl is in my arms where she belongs, kissing me.

She breaks our kiss and stares at my chest, not wanting to meet my eyes before saying, "I'm sorry. I shouldn't have pushed you away, and I should have told you about Ethan, but you hurt me too."

I take a deep breath and wait to see if she'll elaborate on that last part.

"When I pushed you away, you actually left. You didn't even put up a fight. At first, I thought that was what I wanted. That it would make me happy, but as I sat in that hospital room for a week alone with my thoughts, I realized maybe you didn't think I was worth fighting for, maybe I liked you more than you liked me, maybe you got all you were looking for."

I cup her face in my hand, but she pulls away.

"I need to finish this so that you know."

I nod, drop my hand, and push up to take the seat beside hers.

"When Ethan approached me, I was on my way back to the hospital. In so many words, he said if I didn't go with him to this event, my dad's job would be in jeopardy. My family just recently lost everything they had. We were homeless. I couldn't afford not to do as he asked, but when he used the same pickup line you did, my heart sank. Everything I thought about how you might have used me was suddenly confirmed when he said, 'Princess, I can't get another you.' So I decided to play the game. I knew whatever he might have planned involved you, but I wanted to get back at you for hurting me."

I stop her before she can turn this moment into another fight. Every time we take two steps forward, I swear we take ten steps back. "Gianna, this has to stop. His choice of those words was a complete coincidence. What we have is ours, and if any part of you wants me, you need to stop pushing me away. You have to let me in and talk to me."

I push myself out of the chair, furious that he was able to corner her and make her feel like she meant nothing to me. I run my hands through my hair before dropping in front of her again. My hands run up her thighs because I can't keep them to myself. I need to touch her, and I need her to hear my words so she doesn't ever question my heart again.

"Gianna, you can't kiss me like your next breath depends on it and tell me I have the power to break you, only to then stand here and accuse me of playing some game with you. You know what we have is so much more." She sits perfectly still, barely breathing, with her eyes glued to my every move. I already know what she hasn't seemed to figure out. If I'm touching her, she's mine. She can't refuse me. I choose the following words carefully. "We're finishing this tonight. No more hiding, no more secrets, let me in."

She hesitantly bites her lower lip in thought and then says, "Okay."

I stare at her, completely frozen, almost scared to move because my mind isn't sure if she really just conceded. Could it have happened that easily? Smiling, she brings her hand up to cup my face. "I don't think I stopped being yours. I was trying to convince myself that I wasn't, that you weren't and aren't good for me."

Just as I'm about to lean in and kiss her, my phone alarm sounds. "Damn it," I hiss out as her eyes widen in horror at the potential threat.

"Oh my God, is someone coming?"

I bury my head in her lap and shake it because, for whatever reason, I can never catch a break when it comes to her.

"No, Mason's awake."

I feel her tense under me before she pushes my shoulders up. "What do you mean he's awake? How do you know he's awake?" Now she's panicking. I grab her hands and pull her with me toward the door.

"Come on. I'll take you there."

Once we're in the car and en route to the hospital, I grab her hand and intertwine our fingers. Touching her calms me and makes me feel grounded when everything around me seems out of my control.

"When I left the hospital that day, I didn't stop watching you. I didn't stop caring about you. I left because you had just been through something traumatic, and I was trying to give you the space you needed to process. I had eyes on Mason at the hospital to make sure I knew his progress and, therefore, your state of mind."

I glance over to see how she's processing my confession. From a simple squeeze of her hand, relief floods my system.

"I get that. My highs and lows were based on his progress." She goes back to staring out the window before asking, "Did you have something to do with my newfound workload?"

I pick up our joined hands and kiss hers. "Yes, but I was very discreet about it. I wanted to make sure you didn't lose your job since you just started and didn't have personal time to use."

Her eyes get glassy. "Thank you."

Pulling into the parking lot, I can tell she's nervous. She doesn't jump to race inside like I thought she would. Instead, she stays seated, fiddling with the silk designs on her dress.

"Tell me," I say.

"I know you don't want to leave me, but I haven't spoken to Mason since the night he showed up at your apartment."

*Fuck.*

I wish I had known that last Wednesday when I walked out. Everything makes so much more sense now. That one little confession almost justifies all the grief I've endured. She felt guilty about being with me and still does. I know he means something to her and vice versa. They have a bond, and I don't know how deep it runs. I don't know the depth of their relationship. While I know they haven't slept together, I also know that he wants her as more than a friend.

"Can you let me do this on my own?" Her eyes meet mine, and I see the sadness and regret. There's no way I'll refuse her this, even though it kills me. She's opening up to me and being honest about what's going on, and it doesn't hurt that we are now officially a couple.

"I'm going to walk you in, but I'll wait in the cafeteria."

She nods, and we exit the car. When we reach the elevator, I pull her into me and hold her tight. She holds me with just as much intensity, which offers me the comfort I didn't know I needed. Knowing she's as emotionally invested as I am makes this easier to swallow. But I hate that I'm letting her go up alone tonight of all nights. I had to steal her from one man just to take her to another. I pull back from our embrace and lean down to kiss her lips.

"Text me when you get to his room and when you leave."

She checks her purse and pulls out her phone. "Okay, I can't promise I won't be too long. There are things I need to say."

I nod and hit the elevator button. It immediately opens, and she enters, taking a piece of my heart with her. It's then I realize I'm in love with Gianna Moretti.

## TWENTY-ONE
### Mason

It's ten o'clock at night, and I've been awake for a little over eight hours. I've been in the hospital for ten days. For the most part, I remember the last six. My family has been in and out, while Gigi hasn't left my side until today. The hardest thing about being in a coma, at least for me, was that I could hear everything going on around me, but I couldn't move my body. It was incredibly frustrating but also very enlightening. It turns out you can learn a lot about the people in your life when they don't know if you can hear them or not.

My parents, for example. They have never had a good relationship. My mom would always tell me that my dad cared about his work more than us, which I assumed is why she started cheating, seeking attention from men who would give it to her. The part I didn't know was that my dad threw himself into his work because he knew my mom was having affairs long before he ever officially divorced her.

Eventually, he left her because he didn't want to give her any piece of what he had built when she couldn't support him and be faithful. He stayed for me until he couldn't. For some reason, I always thought he walked in on her with another guy and couldn't stand to look at her. I never knew that it was happening for years or that he was trying to keep his family together for me. My dad cared for me more than I realized and still does.

The night of the crash, I was driving my dad's new Audi while mine was in the shop for repairs. He had the car excavated from the river with the intent to sue the manufacturer for faulty brakes. But as it turns out, the brakes were tampered with, which was a game-changer for me.

The night Gigi called me for a ride home broke me. I had no idea she was with August. We had been making progress on our future as a couple, and I thought we were happy. Literally the night before, we almost had sex. She almost gave me the only part of her I've never had, so finding her with him was confounding.

While I've been laid up in this bed, Gigi has sat by my side and confessed many things. One of them is how much she loves me and would do anything to take it back, not just the sex but everything. Yes, she confessed to giving August her virginity, which crushed me because she almost gave it to me, and that night we shared on the bluff meant the world to me. I hadn't realized she was all I ever wanted until that moment.

Over the years, I've taken Gigi for granted. I've always known that she wanted more from me, from our relationship, but instead of taking the love she so freely offered, I made excuses. The truth is, I didn't want to let her in. She was too good for me, and I wanted to stay broken. I wanted to party, hook up, use, and be used in high school. Gigi saw the side of me I wanted her to see. She saw the man I wanted to be. Maybe, in the end, I'm getting what I deserve. Before the accident, I thought it was possible that I wasn't the better man. After all, I have my own ugly truths, one of them being where I was the night of the accident, but now I can't just walk away.

Consequently, when you're stuck in a vegetative state, you have a lot of time to think. I've drawn many conclusions about the accident and who may have been involved over the past week. I've listened and taken note of all my visitors and formulated a plan of action for the moment I woke up.

\* \* \*

Sitting in my hospital bed, I'm fully clothed and ready to check out. Unfortunately, there's no chance I'll be discharged today or even tomorrow. I'm sure there are multiple specialists and tests to run in my near future, but I'll be damned if I'm lying around in one of those hospital robes.

My dad had brought clothes up the day after I was admitted. He said it was his way of knowing I'd come home, that I'd wake up. Getting the clothes gave him peace of mind.

Coincidentally, after I woke up earlier today, Vivian stopped by to visit. I asked her and the nurses not to alert anyone to my awakened state, especially Gigi. I needed to get Vivian on my side to help me keep Gigi safe.

One of the nurses who has been on my rotation every day since I arrived is feeding information to August. The woman had the boldness to call and update him while in my room. That's one of the reasons I don't trust him. Why keep tabs on me? When I woke up, she was in the room, and I told her if she notified August before I was ready, I would have her fired for violating my HIPPA rights.

About an hour ago, I gave her the okay to notify him, and I'm almost positive he's with Gigi. In fact, I'm counting on him to be the one to bring her here so that I can see his face when I steal her away.

I'm just getting ready to sit on my bed after using the restroom when Gigi opens the door. Her emerald eyes lock on mine, and I remind myself to breathe. She looks breathtaking in the black dress she's wearing. I'd give anything to go back in time and ask her to be mine years ago, but I was selfish. Back then, I wasn't thinking about the endgame. We both came from wrecked homes, so we ran away together in our dreams. She was the dream I wished could be real. There was no way she could be my reality, or maybe that was just the lie I told myself so I didn't ruin the one good thing I had. Now all my excuses seem utterly stupid. I should have just told her how I felt.

"Gigi, you're here! Did you get my texts?" Vivi anxiously breaks the deafening silence.

Looking down, she checks her phone, likely searching for a message I know she didn't receive. I asked Vi not to send her one. She's trying to cover her tracks and not look like a bad friend. Turning her attention to Vivian, she furrows her brow, no doubt feeling guilty about not being here when I woke.

"No, I didn't get them. I probably didn't have service or something." Walking farther into the room, she hugs Vivian before bringing her eyes back to mine. I can tell she's nervous and apprehensive. She's probably wondering if I indeed heard all of her confessions or if I'm mad at her, considering the last time we saw each other, she was with him and not me.

I clear my throat. "Vi, can you give us a minute alone?"

She nods. "Of course. I'll just wait outside."

Gigi remains frozen, eyes locked on mine like she has a million things to say and has no idea where to begin. Finally, deciding to show her a little mercy, I release her from her grief and uncertainty.

"Babe, come sit with me."

I pat the bed next to me and slowly scoot over to make room for her. She doesn't immediately move, and I know why.

"Yes, Gigi, I know. I heard every word."

One tear falls down her face, and her bottom lip starts to tremble. I already know she's sorry. Now she needs to hear what I have to say.

"Can you please sit with me and hear what I have to say?"

She nods and slowly makes her way toward my bed to sit on the edge. Shaking my head, I motion with my finger for her to come here and lie beside me. She quickly presses a button on her phone and then lies down beside me. Taking her hand in mine, I lace our fingers together, and she lets out a shaky breath before laying her head on my shoulder.

"Mason, I was so scared. I thought I was going to lose you."

I pick up our joined hands and kiss the back of hers.

"I know, babe, and I know you haven't left my side since I got here apart from tonight, and I also know why you left."

Her body goes rigid beside mine.

"I know Ethan threatened you, and at the moment, I tried so hard to wake up and stop you. I wanted to protect you."

Then, pulling her head from my shoulder, she faces me. "Is that why your heart rate accelerated?"

I can't help but laugh. "Yeah, babe, that's why."

She turns around, and her shoulders slump. "I swear I'm not trying to continually fuck you over, but recently I feel like that's all I'm doing. You have to think attempting a relationship with me was a huge mistake."

"Babe, shit happens. I don't blame you for any of this. I know you regret what happened, and if I'm honest, I also have regrets."

Nodding, she returns her head to my shoulder.

"Do you remember when we were younger, and I sang you the song 'Freshman' by The Verve Pipe?"

She chuckles. "I could never forget. It was the first and only time a guy has ever sung to me."

"That song resonated with me back then. At the time, I told you it was my favorite song and that I liked it for no particular reason, but the truth was, it reminded me of you. We thought we had everything figured out. We talked about our futures and how we'd do things differently. We rarely talked about our relationships with other people, and back then, I didn't think it would be you and me. I knew you felt something more for me the first time we kissed, but I didn't want to be responsible for breaking your heart or committing to you when I thought we were too young."

I feel her take a deep breath as she lets my words resonate. Gently, I rub my thumb over the top of her hand. "I know August means something to you, babe, but I'm hoping I mean more. I still want everything."

She turns to look at me with those big green eyes, and I grasp her chin between my forefinger and thumb. I want to kiss her so badly, but I won't. I'll put the ball in her court. I'm not going to cross the line. She'll have to make the first move.

"I don't want you to say anything right now. Just think about what I've said."

Movement outside the window to my room catches my eye, and sure enough, I see August just like I was hoping, and fuck me if his timing isn't perfect. Gigi is in my bed, looking all too comfortable. His murderous glare bores into me, and I smile, knowing he won't do shit. The night I showed up at his place to get Gigi, I discovered she was his weakness. He didn't touch me because he knew it would hurt her. I can't help the smile that breaks across my face. Gigi notices and furrows her brow at me, probably wondering why I'm smiling, until August barges into the room.

Immediately, she startles from his loud entrance, and her eyes go wide in surprise. I take this moment to slide the phone she placed down under the covers.

"Didn't trust she'd come back down the way she came up?" I raise a brow in question to August. He shakes his head and sets his jaw. I can see he is pissed. *Good.*

Gigi looks back and forth between us. "How did you know he was here?"

"I told you I heard everything. Your attire and the fact that you sent a text when you entered the room only confirmed what I assumed."

August cuts in, "Well, I'm glad you're so alert. I was worried if you were still in a vegetative state, I would have to wait longer for answers as to why you were at my place the night of your crash."

I couldn't have planned this better if I had tried. The man is eating out of the palm of my hand, and he doesn't even know it. Gianna is a blind spot for him, so she must go. But of course Gigi is now wide-eyed, staring at me with a mixture of regret, hurt, and curiosity, waiting for a response. I only wish I had all the answers to give her, but I don't. I need more time, and I need her to leave for my plan to work. I'm counting on her trust in me to outweigh her need for answers for the time being.

"Gigi, can you give us the room, please?" I ask.

"I want to hear this, Mason. I deserve to know."

She's right. She does deserve to know, and she has always been able to rely on me to give her the truth. I'm counting on that foundation of trust now when I give her a pleading look.

"Babe, do you trust me?"

Out of the corner of my eye, I see August clench his fists, probably pissed at my term of endearment for Gianna. Well, he can fuck off. I've called her that since I met her.

"Fine, I'll get coffee with Vi."

I squeeze her hand before she hops off the bed to exit.

Of course August can't just let her walk past. Instead, he stops her and pulls her in for a hug before placing a kiss on her forehead, all the while keeping his eyes pinned on mine. August is trying to make a point of demonstrating that she is his again. Too bad for him that's not a done deal as he thinks.

Once she's out of the room, August makes no time rushing to my bed to pin me.

"What the fuck are you playing at, Croft?"

"Real tough, August, pinning a guy who just woke up from a coma."

He releases my shirt and steps back.

"Why were you at my house?"

"The better question is, why did your so-called friend Ethan ask me to show up and place a camera on your back door? Something he could have done more discreetly himself." I watch his face closely, looking for any sign that he may have expected such a dupe from his so-called friend.

Clearly, he must know that Ethan is up to something. I know she showed up with him to the event tonight, but August ensured he didn't leave with her. His friend has crossed him, and from the way he grinds his teeth and meets my gaze, I'm sure he doesn't know why.

Before he can spin me some more bullshit, I let him in on another bit of information I learned while in a coma.

"I was driving my dad's car that night. Someone tampered with the brakes. Weird how that happens right after you threatened to come after our contract."

He punches the cabinet he's standing next to and leaves a dent. That burst of rage answers my question. It wasn't him. He had nothing to do with the brakes.

"So that's it, you're going to try to steal Gianna back from me by making it look like I set this up?"

And that's how I know I made the right choice sending Gigi away. As much as I hate to admit it, I'll need his help to figure out why Gianna is caught up in this mess. Whatever game is being played can't get solved if she's around. He's too fucking blinded by her to see the big picture. I know my next words are going to set him off.

"I don't have to steal her back, August. She's already gone."

He stops pacing and meets my eye.

"What the fuck do you mean she's already gone?"

"Easy, she's gone, as in you won't see her until I know she's safe."

He rushes over as though he's going to punch me, and I spread my arms wide.

"Go ahead, fucker. It's not going to bring her back."

"She's my fucking girlfriend, Mason. You think I don't want to protect her?"

I pretend like I didn't hear him call her his girlfriend.

"I'm not sure what I think about you right now. You were quick to throw her away when you found out who she was to your family, but then something changed, and you pursued her even though you had a girlfriend and knew she couldn't say no to you because you were her boss."

"Is that what she told you?" He holds my gaze, indeed waiting to see if those are my words or hers.

"You know what, I know they're your words. Gianna couldn't say no to me for reasons you know nothing about. I didn't use her, and she knows that. You think you are better for her because you've known her longer, and that's bullshit. You'd already be a couple if you were the better choice."

This entitled prick thinks that just because he claims something is his, it makes it true.

"I'm sorry that you have some god complex from growing up as a spoiled brat and having everything handed to you, but I love Gigi, and I know she loves me. I've listened to her tell me as much the entire time she's been at my bedside. The fact that you're too stupid to realize we're endgame is your problem."

I'm waiting for him to blow up, to punch me for that last sentence, but he doesn't. Instead, he crosses his arms over his chest and runs his forefinger along his lips.

"Mason, there's a difference between loving someone and being in love with someone. I don't doubt she loves you, but I'm almost certain she's in love with me. If you want to sway her into thinking her feelings for you are the real deal and accept that she settled for you out of obligation, I can't stop you."

"You're giving up on your girlfriend that easily?"

"Not at all. I just thought it's only fair I get in your head the way you're pathetically attempting to get in mine. We both know I got a piece you never did."

Jumping out of bed, I forget I'm still hooked up to the damn machines. I rip all the shit off and start walking out. Forget this. I don't know why I thought I could stand to be in the same room with this asshole. As I walk down the hallway, no one even questions me. I guess they don't recognize me awake and dressed, and that's fine with me. Passing the elevator, I opt for the stairs before anyone notices.

August is hot on my heels. "Where the fuck are you going, Mason?"

"I'm going to get Gigi, and you can stay here and figure out who the hell in your inner circle is fucking up your life and hers."

He pulls me back and slams me into the wall. "I don't think you get it. I fucking love her. Stop fucking around and wasting time because your ego hurts from the reality I just hit you with."

I punch him in the face hard, and he spits blood. "Now we're even, prick." I'm not some little bitch who will roll over and take orders from him. I have just as much to lose, if not more if I fail her. Not to mention, he deserved it.

Keeping my pace, I head downstairs until I'm outside. I didn't realize I didn't have a car in my haste to get out. *Shit.*

August shoulders past me as he walks, calling out, "Let's go."

# Part Two

## TWENTY-TWO
## *August*

Croft can organize stealing my girl while he's sleeping, but the dumbass didn't remember he doesn't have a car here.

"Where to?" I bite out, pissed that he punched me. There's no way I'm hitting a guy who literally just got out of a coma—no matter how much I might want to.

"My place." He hits a few buttons on the dashboard, connecting his phone to my car's navigation system before inputting his address into the GPS on his phone. Once the map pulls up on the dash, he presses his lips together and shakes his head in annoyance before his face settles into a scowl as he glares out the front windshield. We drive to his place in silence. The tension in the air between us is thick with malice.

I'm so fucking furious right now I could murder him. The only reason he's not dead is that it would hurt Gianna, and I bet he knows it. I showed him my cards that night he showed up at my house. When I didn't punch him, he knew it was because of her. He thinks Gianna is my weakness, which couldn't be further from the truth. Mason is only seeing what I want him to see. I grew up mastering the skill of deception and allowing people only to see what I want to show them. Wearing a mask is second nature to me.

I'm supposed to be cocky, arrogant, and self-serving. Isn't that what all rich boys are? Automatically, I'm entitled because I inherited my wealth. I have no idea what hard work is because I've had everything given to me.

That's what people don't understand. Wearing a mask is hard. Fitting into someone else's mold for your life about how you should walk, talk, and dress is brutal. It takes talent to learn how to see through the masks people wear. Someone is always trying to use you for money, social status, and even marriage.

Patience is critical in this life. You must be able to wait out your opponent, make them think they have you figured out, and then strike. He can think Gianna is my weakness all he wants because at the end of the day, she's my strength. She has tested my limits, pushed me to fight for what I want, and I'm done playing the part. I'll embrace who I've always been and fuck what anyone else thinks.

Once I pull up to his condo, I realize it's not far from mine. I'm surprised that he can afford the area.

As we walk up the steps, I ask him the question that's been burning in my mind since he said Ethan asked him to set me up. "Why did you help Ethan?"

"Isn't that obvious?" Mason all but spits out.

I shrug as we continue walking. I have an idea, but I want to hear his reasoning.

"Ethan *fucking* Grand asks me to do something he can do himself. Being your best friend, he has more access to your life than I do. I was curious. Not to mention it involved Gigi, and she's important to me. He didn't just ask me to place the camera at your door. He asked me to place a tracker on Gigi's car. I wanted to help him. I wanted him to use me so that I could figure out what he was up to and why Gigi was involved."

I'd assumed he'd want to help Ethan if it in any way benefited him in winning Gianna back, but I wasn't expecting the rest of the bullshit he just spewed. My fists clench at his admission, and I pull him back by his shoulder, giving him a murderous glare. "You fucking put a tracker on her car that he has access to?"

He pulls out of my grip. "Yes, I did, but that's why we're here. I rigged it so that I could track him through the device."

I take a deep breath to try to calm my nerves, reminding myself to have patience. As he opens the door, I notice the entire condo is empty. When he starts down the hall, I call out, "Mason, what the fuck is this? Why does it look like no one lives here?"

I'm standing frozen in the front entry as he storms through the space, clearly on a mission.

"I just moved in, asshole, and I've been a little tied up."

I can't help but smirk, even though I know it's sick. Following him down the hall, I find him in his office. "You weren't too busy to set up an office?"

Unlike the rest of his place, his office is completely set up. It looks like some crazy, high-tech, undercover-agent-type shit.

"This was all I managed before my stint in the hospital, yes, and I'm glad I had my priorities straight."

The office is imposing. It's different from the offices I've grown up frequenting, with bookshelves lined with books you've never read, leather couches, and cigar boxes. Mason's office is a black cave with multiple computer screens and gadgets that I couldn't begin to tell you what they were. I researched his dad's IT company when I discovered who he was. The company started small, helping businesses set up firewalls and web filtering solutions to keep employees off websites they shouldn't be tapping into at work. Over the years, he added employee monitoring software to his portfolio, and now his recent acquisition of the security company Reds hired makes sense. Mason joined his father's company six months ago and is clearly a hacker, which also makes sense. If you offer security solutions, you need to ensure they can't be hacked. I will say I underestimated his tech skills. Feeling somewhat intimidated, I strike.

"You know that tracker is how he found her, right? He tracked her to work and got her alone when he knew neither of us would be with her."

When I meet his gaze, I can tell he's furious. He keeps rubbing it in my face how all of this is my fault, and I'm the one who put

Gigi in danger, but he's the dumbass who put a fucking tracker on her car and led Ethan straight to her.

He clicks his tongue. "Yeah, I didn't plan on being laid up."

"That's precisely my point. You have no idea what you're dealing with."

"You know what, August, if she were with me, she wouldn't even be in danger. I have the means to provide for her, protect her, and keep her safe."

His comment doesn't faze me. I expected that lame-ass reply from him because he doesn't get it, not yet, but he will.

"This coming from the guy who just had his car pulled out of the river because someone sabotaged his brakes and who spent the past week in a coma. You still don't know if the accident is related to my involvement with Gianna or not. It could have been a business rival or client contract that came after your dad and got the wrong guy. At the end of the day, your company is expanding, your wealth is growing, and that means the number of people who want to come after you is multiplying. This attack was just the first of many, trust me."

He shakes his head and puts his tongue in his cheek while typing away on his computer. "If you have so much more experience, please enlighten me on how this happened and why you weren't prepared."

I'm about done playing this song and dance with him. Walking over to his desk, I slam my hands down and lean into his face. "Let's get one thing straight. I didn't lead Ethan to her. You did. The minute he showed up with her, I was on his ass, and I made damn sure my girl didn't leave with him. We were at my safe house when you woke up, and I brought her to see you. You took her from me, and since you are so out of your depth here, let me make something crystal clear. If something bad happens to one hair on her head, it is your doing, not mine. But know this: I will literally kill you if something goes wrong."

He swings around in his chair and punches one of the screens behind him, sending it crashing to the floor. Good, I hope he's mad. I hope he feels all the anguish I feel knowing Gianna isn't here by my side for me to watch over.

"I'll serve myself to you on a fucking platter if she gets hurt."

I pull back and start pacing the room, debating whether or not walking out is best, but I'm curious about what that tracker shows. Of course I already knew Ethan was involved, but he's not the only player in the game, and I have a sinking suspicion I know who the other players are.

Finally, Mason says, "Here it is, all the places Ethan has frequented over the past week." He reads aloud, "Reds, Grand Media Office Suites, Lost Valley Golf Course, and the Bradbury Estate."

"Fuck." I run my hands through my hair out of frustration. Tonight only solidified what I was starting to suspect: Carson and Ethan are hooking up. This evening, when Carson went over the top to make it look like we were a couple in front of Ethan and Gianna, I should have opened my mouth, but I was too distracted by Gianna's presence to give two shits about their affair. The problem is, I can't place what Gianna has to do with any of this.

"Care to share with the rest of the class what put that scowl on your face?"

"The Bradbury Estate is my ex's house," I clip out before Croft nearly doubles over into a fit of laughter.

"That's perfect. Your ex is fucking your best friend. Maybe Ethan isn't so bad after all."

I'm pissed, not because they're hooking up, but because I'm not sure what Gianna has to do with it. "I don't give a shit if they're fucking. The part I'm missing is what Gianna has to do with any of it."

Mason leans back in his chair and drums his fingers on the table, clearly mulling over my words. "Either you've been really shitty to them and they want revenge, or it's all a distraction."

Sitting up with a renewed sense of purpose, he starts typing in something on the computer. "Ethan goes to her place every night."

I can't help but glare. If he's trying to get me riled up, it will not work. I literally couldn't care less.

"Relax, I'm saying you need to go on a date."

"Are you fucking kidding me? I'm not going on a date with her so you can use it as leverage with Gianna."

"And that right there is exactly why I sent Gigi away. You're so consumed with losing her that you're not looking at the big picture. You going on a date is supposed to be reconnaissance. I couldn't tell her about any infidelities you chose to partake in even if I wanted to."

He pulls a phone out of his pocket and tosses it on the desk. The light pink case immediately catches my eye, and I know it's Gianna's. My chest tightens at the thought that I can't reach out to her right now, but knowing he can't either is somewhat gratifying.

This begs the question: "How are you in contact with her then? What about her parents?"

He sits back in his chair smugly as he laces his hands behind his head. Mason believes he has everything figured out. Hell, part of me hopes he does because the sooner we figure this shit out, the sooner I get my girl back.

"I took her phone so she can't be traced. Her parents don't know that I'm awake, at least for now, so I'm hoping to have a few more days to figure things out while they assume she's with me in the hospital."

What's fucked up is that's a good plan. Gianna hasn't left his side, and I've also been having her work sent there. "Did she leave with that girl?"

Mason looks up from the computer and shakes his head. "Seriously, you don't know her name? I can't believe you're my competition."

"That doesn't answer my question, Mason." I completely ignore the second half of his remark because he has no idea what we share.

"Yeah, well, it answers mine. Her name is Vivian. She's been

Gianna's best friend since they were six. Vi is with her, but they are not staying at Vi's place."

I do my best to bite my tongue at his insinuation that I know nothing about her. But it pisses me off that he's right, and I don't like feeling bested. I know what we have when we're together can't be replicated, and she'll have all my tomorrows if she wants them. Most of my moments with her have been intermittent, interrupted, or flat-out stolen. I plan to rectify all of that once I have her back.

What infuriates me is I want to know everything. I want to be her world, but we just met, and when we're together, we fuck more than we talk. We haven't been alone enough to have organic conversations about our pasts, but I know that her past, my past —neither one matters because she's my future. Fuck spying. I'm getting answers.

"Can you see where Ethan is now?"

His eyebrows rise before he narrows his eyes at me, attempting to follow my train of thought.

"Yeah, the app connected to her tracker is used via his smartphone, so as long as he has his phone, I can always find him." A few clicks later, he announces, "He's at the Bradbury Estate."

*Perfect.* "Time to go."

## TWENTY-THREE
### *Gianna*

We've been in Florida for a week. It's been a week since August asked me to be his girlfriend and a week since Mason woke up and told me he wants everything, even after all my admissions. My heart has never felt more torn, and I've been through some earth-shattering shit.

When I left Mason's room, I expected to grab a coffee with Vivi, but as we walked down the corridor back to Mason's room, Bryce showed up. It was so unexpected. I didn't think he'd be back so soon. He just left a little over a week ago, and he and Mason had no relationship. They had met a few times through me and knew of each other, but no friendship. So when he showed up at the hospital, I found it odd, but I was too excited that he was there to dwell on it. All I could do was wrap my arms around him in a big hug, happy to see him.

Bryce explained he returned to grab a few things from his mom's house and stopped by mine on his way out. That's how he found out what had happened and where I had been spending all my time. At the time, I bought it, but now I know better. He was back for me. Vivian and I followed him to his car, where he claimed he had left his phone. I was under the impression he wanted to show us pictures of the shop. Sitting in the passenger seat, scrolling through photos, is the last thing I remember. My friends drugged me.

Vivian was in on everything. She slipped the sleeping pills into my coffee and decided to tag along for the kidnapping. Yes, I say kidnapping because there's no way in hell I'd leave my job and family or let Mason run my life. I was furious when I found out he orchestrated this. I mean, who the hell directs this kind of thing from a coma? Before I left the room, he'd asked, "Do you trust me?" That should have been my red flag, but silly me, I assumed he was trying to ease my concerns about starting a fight with August.

Once I was out, they drove straight to Florida. I didn't wake up until we were crossing the state line. That's when Bryce filled me in on everything. He explained Mason's theory that I'm in danger because Ethan is plotting against August and using me as bait. First, Ethan had Mason install a tracker on my car, and then the brakes on Mason's car were tampered with. It would appear that Ethan used Mason and then tried to tie up loose ends by getting rid of the evidence, i.e., Mason. At this point, I think everything looks coincidental at best. I believe Mason is overreacting, but Bryce, Vivian, and, surprise-surprise, Aiden all agree it seems too suspicious not to be more than a revenge plot against August.

Since I was forced down here, I'm now living in the same house with my longtime crush, and let me tell you, some crushes are meant to stay just that. I never really talked to Aiden in the past. I only admired him from afar and dreamed about what being his girlfriend would be like. But now that I live with him, I'm glad those dreams never came to fruition. He's a moody son of a bitch, and I don't care what anyone says. I know he holds a grudge against me for August punching him at the club.

Saying the guys' place is small would be an understatement. The actual living space is minuscule. You walk into a living area/kitchen combo with a tiny hallway that leads to two bedrooms and a cramped bathroom. Bryce gave Vivian and me his room while we are staying here. He's been sleeping on the couch.

I felt so terrible when we arrived that I refused to stay and put them out like that. That's when I got another huge surprise.

Apparently, Mason didn't know how long it would take to settle things at home, so he paid the guys' rent for the next two months. As if that wasn't a huge shock, Bryce then handed me an envelope filled with cash to the tune of ten thousand dollars. Where he got all this money from is beyond me.

I went into the bedroom and cried for hours, a million different things running through my head. Mason knew I gave my virginity to August, knew I was with him the night of his crash, and knew I'd show up with August at the hospital, and he still loved me through all of it. How can I be so cold, so callous, so heartless? I've been beating myself up over the events that have led me here because they weren't part of my plan, but I've learned that sometimes the things we didn't plan for are what we need most. Sometimes no plan is the best plan.

* * *

"Gianna, let's go. We said we'd help the guys at the shop today."

I hear Vivian call me for about the third time since we've been up. Today we decided we should do something productive instead of staying holed up in the house thinking up worst-case scenarios of what's going on back home. At first, Vivi and I were too scared to leave. Then when we thought about leaving to go to the beach, we felt like assholes for treating this like some sort of vacation while Mason—and, I assume, August—are working to figure out who's potentially after me. I'm not able to have contact with anyone back home. Vivian willingly left her phone back home and pulled out enough cash to live off while she was here. She said there was no way she was letting me do this alone. Mason only asked her to help get me to Bryce's car, but she insisted on coming. So here we are.

"I'm coming, but my hair got stuck in my swimsuit ties twice," I yell back. It's a surf shop, so we figured we'd wear swimsuits under our cut-off jean shorts and tank tops. When I come out of the bedroom, I find Vivian standing in the kitchen with her hand on her hip, glaring back at me like I have two heads.

"What, is there a problem with my outfit?" I quickly do a double take of my outfit. I've lost a little weight from stress, and I'm pale, but other than that, I don't think I look that terrible.

She shakes her head. "It took you twenty minutes to put on a swimsuit, shorts, and tank top? You're not even wearing any makeup!"

That's the thing about best friends. They know you better than you know yourself sometimes and call you on your shit when it's needed. For example, Vivian knows I spent eighteen out of the past twenty minutes overthinking, considering leaving the house, and worrying about my heart.

"Gigi, I need you to open up to me and stop bottling everything inside. I know you're worried about Mason and August, but sometimes talking it through and saying the words out loud is the best medicine. I can listen if that's what you need, or I can give you feedback, but either way, you need to work through this. It's not healthy the way you are handling things."

Closing my eyes, I nod in agreement. "Okay, let's have lunch on the beach today and talk."

She smiles and then comes over to give me a big hug. The smell of her coconut lotion surrounds me, and I can't help but laugh.

"What's funny?" She looks down, checking herself out to ensure nothing is out of place.

"Nothing. I know we both always use coconut products, but now that we're living by the ocean and working in a surf shop, it feels a little cliché."

"Hey, I think our love for all things beachy has finally manifested itself, and we landed where we were always meant to be."

I can't help but laugh. "I guess that's one way of looking at it."

\* \* \*

We've been working at the shop all morning. We started by helping the boys organize and set up inventory software, something I was familiar with from working at Reds. The place has been hectic so far, and I'm impressed. While the guys were helping customers, Vivian was able to cover the register, and I managed the back of the house. I figured the less I was seen, the better, just in case.

"Bryce, it looks like the skateboard sales outweigh the surfboard sales," I hear Vivi yell out. That must mean the shop is empty, so I come out from the back to find Vivi standing at the register, her long brown hair blowing in the breeze. The front of the shop has sliding doors that push open and disappear into the walls. Overall, I'm still unsure how the guys are pulling this off. Bryce didn't win that much money on his scratch-off ticket. Maybe Aiden has money I didn't know about, or they took out some big loans.

"Yeah, I knew they would. When we took over the shop, they only sold surfboards, but skaters like to skate up and down the boardwalk and around these beach shops. I was surprised they limited their inventory the way they did. Down the road, I plan to order snorkel gear and pair up with someone to offer scuba lessons."

"Bryce, when did you get so business savvy?"

He eyes me up and down, his gaze lingering on my stomach before I snap my fingers.

"Eyes up here."

He laughs. "I've always been business savvy. Maybe you've just been too focused on other things to notice," he shoots back sarcastically before storming out of the shop.

Shocked by his apparent displeasure with what I thought was a lighthearted comment, I awkwardly turn to Vivian to see if she read the situation the same way I did, as a complete overreaction. But instead, she rolls her eyes, clearly exasperated with the situation.

"Let's take that lunch break."

That's when I notice Aiden sitting on the floor in the corner, unpacking a box of surfboard wax with a scowl on his face. What the hell did I do to piss everyone off? I throw the clipboard I used to take inventory on the counter and walk out.

Vivian and I are finally sitting on the beach, eating street tacos and drinking Coronas. Yes, we are drinking beer at lunch. Why not?

"Maybe we shouldn't help out at the shop," I suggest. "Maybe living under the same roof and working with them is way too much time spent together."

Vivian finishes her taco before pulling her tank top over her head, revealing her yellow bikini top and naturally toned stomach. I swear some girls are just blessed with fit bodies they don't have to work for. The girl just ate tacos and doesn't even have a pooch. She pulls her hair up into a messy bun and then lies down on her towel, not a care in the world.

"You don't have to ask me twice. I felt like we should be soaking up the sunshine this entire time. I'm just following your lead."

"So you agree Bryce's reaction was probably because we're spending too much time together?"

"Nope, not at all." She slides her glasses over her eyes.

"Care to elaborate?" I ask. Typically, she'd speak her mind, but I think she's been biting her tongue, waiting for me to show signs that I'm ready to open up.

Sitting up, she grabs her beer and takes a long swig. "Well, if you're in the mood for a dose of reality, sure. But I don't want to make you cry or add to your already abysmal mountain of guilt."

I nod and take a sip of beer. "Let's hear it."

"Well, you told me Bryce left for Florida because of you. He said he wouldn't get over you if he stayed in Missouri, hoping you'd change your mind. Then you come here, and he's supposed to look after you and play house, only to hand you back to another man."

Yep, that's definitely a guilt trip, but I didn't ask for this, and at some point, I have to stop feeling dejected. Being angry that the plans I had laid out for my life didn't work isn't getting me anywhere.

"What would you do if you were me?"

Leaning on her elbows, she smiles. "I'd do exactly what we're doing right now. Lie on the beach, eat at food trucks, swim in the ocean, enjoy beach bonfires and sunsets. We only live once, and life is too short to be spent crying over spilled milk. We can't change what's happening. Mason loaned you money, and I know you hate that, but you can pay him back in time. Bryce offered to help. It's not your fault he wants more. I think you just need to roll with the punches like you've done your whole life and leave the feelings out. Don't get me wrong, if you want to run away, we can do that."

I laugh a deep belly laugh, and it feels good. I couldn't tell you the last time I laughed that hard. That's the thing about my best friend. She is down for whatever and gives zero fucks about all the what-ifs. I can waste entire days dreaming up all the adverse outcomes from one choice while she just says, fuck it.

Once I'm done laughing, I say, "Thanks for coming with me."

She smiles. "Wouldn't miss this shit for the world."

"Vi, I've been meaning to ask. Where do you think Mason came up with all this cash?" I know his dad's company is doing well, and Mason got an Audi for a graduation present, but I feel like I'm missing something.

Pulling in a noticeable breath, she sits up and straightens out her towel. "The only reason I know where he came up with the money is that he told me right before he let me in on this little trip he was sending you on. I don't want you to think I was hiding it from you. I was just waiting for the right time to bring it up. You already know Mason is working for his dad now. That's nothing new, but recently, they acquired a security company per Mason's insistence that it would fit well into the company's portfolio. His dad took the risk, and it paid off. Now Mason is in charge of that side of the company and part owner. I'd imagine that came with a nice salary."

I know my eyebrows must be touching my hairline while my

mouth hangs open in shock. Mason has always been super smart. I shouldn't be so surprised. "Wow, that's amazing. I'm just confused about why he didn't tell me." Not only am I confounded, but I'm a little hurt. That's all great news that I'd think he'd want to share with me.

Vivi doesn't miss the disappointment hearing those words from her instead of Mason causes, since she quickly adds, "Gigi, I think he wanted to tell you this news himself. In fact, I know he did. I think he knew I'd question the money, and that's the only reason he offered up any details to me. You've had a lot on your plate, and he was waiting for the dust to settle before he shared that news with you." She might be correct, but it's also not the first time Mason has kept part of himself from me.

After a few minutes of silence, she asks, "So when are you going to lay the heavy on me?"

I frown because I know what she's asking, but I don't know if I'm ready to speak what I feel out loud.

She shrugs. "Okay, so you're not ready to talk, I get that. Do you want to know what I think?"

Over the past week, I'd opened up about everything that had happened between myself, Mason, and August, but I never addressed how I felt or what choice I'd make when this was all over. Yes, I told August I was his girlfriend, but does everything happening now change things? I'm still deciding.

Reaching for my beer, I see that it's empty. "Sure, tell me your thoughts, but we need some drinks first." I shake my empty bottle at her.

She smiles and bounces up. "I'll be right back." She trots off to the food truck that had the beers.

This place is truly perfect. Maybe being here is exactly what I didn't know I needed. I would never let myself do something like this, namely because I couldn't afford to, but I might as well take advantage of it since I'm here now. Mason sent me away with one rule: no communication with anyone back home. He didn't say you must work, have zero fun, and definitely avoid the beach.

That's it. My mind is made up. My ass will be parked on the beach daily until I can't stand it anymore.

Vivian makes her way back with two huge margaritas in hand. The fake IDs Mason made us months ago so that we could get into bars will come in handy while we're down here. I'll spend my days lounging on the beach, drinking away any fucks I have left to give. I'm beyond grateful that Vi tagged along. Without her, I wouldn't have my purse, which contained some very important essentials like my wallet and birth control pills, but paramount to that, I wouldn't have her emotional support.

"I thought this conversation could use something a bit stronger."

Rolling my eyes, I get comfortable on my beach towel. We sit silently, looking out over the waves and sipping our margaritas, letting the sun recharge us.

A few minutes later, Vivi is ready to talk. "You know I've always said you and Mason were endgame. Since we were kids, there's always been something between you two. I know he was your first kiss and vice versa, among other things. When we were younger, we used to talk about the crush you had on him. I remember we literally spent one entire summer trying to concoct ways to get him to be your boyfriend." She smiles at me playfully.

Wow, I had completely forgotten all about that. The summer we shared our first kiss, I became obsessed with trying to get him to be my boyfriend. While I never told him that's what I wanted, I remember hanging on to his every word and overanalyzing every hangout and every call. To say I was infatuated would have been an understatement. But of course nothing ever happened, and I guess at some point, I just accepted the attention he did give me for what it was. I never felt he used me for our make out sessions, heavy groping, and dry humping. In those moments, I felt like I was his everything, but why were we nothing more if that were true?

"When you told me about August and the instant chemistry you felt for him, the deep soul connection you have with him as if your inner self recognized him before you did... I can't help but feel like maybe he's the one. Maybe all this had to happen so that you could finally be free. I think subconsciously, you have always been holding out for Mason, waiting for him to reach for more because you always wanted that deep down. Now that he's offering it, you're struggling with walking away from something you always wanted for something new and unknown. In the end, there are no guarantees with either choice. Either relationship could succeed or fail. I know you're not blind to Mason's secrets either. I've told you about the side of him you don't get to see. When we crossed paths at school parties, he'd be fucked up, and he always had some slut on his arm. Again, I know you guys have never been exclusive, but you shouldn't feel bad about not holding out for someone who didn't hold out for you. Even if the sex thing isn't a deal-breaker, maybe the fact that he never talks about that side of him should be. I think you know in your heart what you want, but you feel guilty for wanting it. My advice is to always be authentically you because, ultimately, not everyone will like you anyway. The least you can do is like yourself."

She's not wrong. Meeting August has been a catalyst for change. He has shaken up my whole world and pushed me outside my comfort zone. I thought I had my future figured out. I did all the right things, colored inside the lines, got good grades, and got a job that would help support my dreams. I would attend school at night and work during the day to pay for it. Once I had my degree, I'd land my dream job, and then I could start dating. Not before because that would be a distraction.

I swore myself off August because he was bad news. The son of my company's owner, rich, arrogant, brash, and off-limits. He and I could never be. It would ruin my reputation, I'd lose my job, and all for nothing because he'd get tired of me. He can get any girl he wants, and I'm a nobody from nothing, easy to forget. I was willing to bury my feelings for him and walk away, but he fought me at every turn. Even after August found out who I was, he still couldn't stay away. He still looked at me with a fierce hunger in his eyes like he didn't want to keep his hands off me, like being apart caused him physical pain. From the start,

August knew what he wanted: me. Nothing else mattered if I was his.

"You and August tried to push each other away, but neither of you could resist the other, and I think that's because you are not meant to. The best things in life come to us when we least expect them. Don't pass up your future because you can't move on from your past. Mason had a long time to make his move, and he didn't. As much as that breaks even my heart, there's a reason for that. Don't get me wrong, I know he loves you, but maybe not enough, or maybe not in the way you need to be loved."

There's a lot of truth to what she's saying, and I can't say for sure why Mason never made his move. Sure, he gave me reasons like we were young, and he thought we had time, but a part of me believes it was more than that. The night Mason finally admitted he wanted more, he sincerely looked broken by the fact that I wasn't jumping at his offer. It was as if the roles were suddenly reversed, and he was the one wanting me with all he had, and all I could do was pause.

I'm hard to love, I'm a mess, and I know I was emotionally unavailable. I knew I had a lot of baggage with my family drama, and that's why I'm sympathetic to the role he played in my life. When I found out about Mason's drug use at parties, I was upset, but I never called him out about it. I hoped maybe he'd tell me himself, but I think because he knew how drugs royally fucked up my entire life, he kept that part hidden from me. As far as the girls, we never asked for details about the other people in our lives. Mason knew about all my secrets, but that's because I openly shared them with him, but I never pressed him to share with me. Looking back, I know it's because I would have been hurt. Knowing that other girls had something I didn't stung, but again, I was willing to take what he gave me. However, when we were together, I felt cherished. Mason was always trying to fix me and make me feel better because he knew things were so shitty at home. He was my happy place. Even on the night that I almost gave him my virginity, his words were, "Babe, I want to make you feel good."

That's what he always did. He made me feel good, but what about him? What value did I add to his life? When I found out about the wreck, I rushed to his side, and I was ready to be his. I would commit and give him what he asked for, what I thought I always wanted. Being with Mason would be easy, but that doesn't mean we are good for each other. While we love each other, it's not the right kind of love.

The love I've always dreamed about accepts every part of you. It has no reservation, pause, or limit on when it should materialize. It just is because there's no choice. I know this now because there was never a choice with August. He consumed me from the moment I met him. Even when I tried to push him away, I couldn't because my heart knew what my mind wasn't ready to accept. I was all in. I was his. August knew what he wanted and wasn't afraid to take it. He was always so sure that I'd be his. He told me as much from the beginning, and every time I heard it, I believed it a little more, and now I know it's true.

Taking a deep breath, I lie back on my beach towel and put my hands behind my head. When I close my eyes, I inhale the salty sea air and let my lungs expand with resolve, knowing that on the exhale, I am releasing all the doubt, fear, and insecurity that I've been carrying with me, telling me I don't measure up. I know there's no more question about who my heart wants, and I'm done being divided.

"I don't think you're wrong, Vivian, but it doesn't mean it makes anything easier."

In the end, none of this is easy. Matters of the heart never are. Vivian lies back on her towel, and we spend the rest of the afternoon lounging on the beach until the shop closes and the guys pick us up to head home.

## TWENTY-FOUR
## Mason

Last Saturday, August and I went to the Bradbury Estate to confront Carson about what she knew regarding Ethan's newfound obsession with Gigi. Unfortunately, that was days ago, and I haven't seen August since. When we arrived at the estate, I told August I'd hang back in the car. I didn't need to be in the house when he confronted her. She didn't know me, and my presence would only guarantee no helpful information would be shared. What I wasn't counting on was him not walking back out.

That night, after too much time had passed, I decided to case the house. Looking through the windows, it appeared as though no one was home, but the lights were on. Once I made my way around back, Ethan's ostentatious Bugatti Chiron caught my eye. That's when I decided to high-tail it back to the car and see if I could hack the security system.

Hacking the home security system would be child's play. While looking through the windows, I caught sight of one of the cameras mounted under an eave, and it's a brand that notoriously gets hacked just because techies know they can do it and fuck with people. It would only take me a few minutes, and I could easily access it from my phone. My hope was that there would be cameras inside as well so I could get eyes on August. To my delight, there were. Once I had the feed pulled up, however, I saw nothing. The house was empty. Knowing that wasn't possible, I then had to hack into the servers that stored the footage so I could rewind the feed. Hacking into servers is a lot easier with a computer. It took me longer to do that from my phone, but I've been honing my skills for years. After about thirty minutes, I finally got in and rewound the feed to the time when August would have entered the house. *Bingo.*

When August arrived, he and Carson disappeared into the kitchen. Watching the playback, I couldn't hear what words were being exchanged. After another twenty minutes, I was able to get the audio pulled up.

*Carson poured two whiskeys and slid one across the island to August.* "I must say, August, I'm surprised you showed up here tonight. After all, you left with your trophy."

*The spite in her tone made me want to choke her, and I would never dream of touching a woman.*

"Carson, you are the one who left for six months, claiming you wanted a break. You wanted time apart to make sure we were right for each other. We both know that was bullshit. I don't understand why you're upset. I moved on, and so did you."

*She sipped her whiskey before swirling the ice in her glass with her finger.* "August, you really are clueless, aren't you? It almost makes me feel bad for you."

*August threw back his entire glass.* "Well, why don't you enlighten me? Did you think I was here for any other reason?"

"I couldn't care less about your new toy. You'll tire of her in time. We both know your tastes are darker than what most girls care for. Do you think you can honestly have a monogamous relationship after me? You can't truly believe she's the type of girl who will bring others to the party?"

*I couldn't help but let my mind wander on that comment. What the hell kind of taste was she referring to? There was no way in hell Gigi would be down for multiple partners. I* doubted she knew about this side of August because a girl like Gigi, who took dating and relationships seriously, wouldn't sleep with August knowing this information. I was about to drive off and say, fuck it, when I caught movement behind August in the hallway. Someone was hanging back in the shadows, listening.

"Carson, we both know that shit was your idea. Excuse me for not complaining. I'm not here to rehash our sex life. I think you know why I'm here."

Turning away from August, she fluffed her blond hair in the mirror hanging on the wall as if his words didn't bother her in the slightest.

"As a matter of fact, I do know. You're here because you want to know why I'm fucking Ethan. Well, that's really very easy. It was always Ethan. We've been fucking for years, but I wasn't convinced it would work out, and I needed a backup plan. That's where you came in. Your name holds more status in our social circles. It's established, respected, and you come from old money, not new money like Ethan. We all know how new money is viewed. I had to make sure the funds wouldn't dry up."

August slammed his hands on the island. "Are you fucking serious, Carson? This is all about money? You really are a stupid bitch."

Throwing her hand over her chest, she feigned offense. "I'd be offended if I didn't already know that everything revolves around money, August, and the thing is, Ethan is about to have a hell of a lot more than you."

At that moment, Ethan emerged from the shadows, stepped up behind August, and stabbed a syringe into his neck. He let August drop to the floor before rounding the island to Carson.

Then wrapping his arms around her waist, he pulled her into his crotch and said, "You did great, my little slut. I want his brain spinning while he's tied up in the basement."

He started biting his way down the side of her neck while pulling the front of her strapless evening gown down. Huge fake tits spilled out, and he squeezed them hard. Throwing her head back, she moaned loudly before he took a nipple into his mouth. For a few fleeting moments, I was stunned. They were about to get it on with August lying passed out on the floor next to them, but before my mind could pull out of its stupefied haze, Carson pulled back and slapped Ethan across the face.

"You know you didn't have to be so friendly with her tonight. I didn't like watching you paw all over her like some lovesick puppy."

I hadn't seen that coming. Ethan's chest was heaving, and his face looked cross. I'd never seen a man hit a woman, but he seemed close. Carson was either really stupid or had brass balls because she met his gaze with a furious scowl before pulling her dress back over her tits.

Picking up her whiskey, she headed out of the kitchen. I didn't miss the outrage on Ethan's face or the wrath in his tone when he called out, "You know they can't be together. It jeopardizes everything."

I was on the edge of my seat, wondering how this would play out. I knew August hit him. I could see the evidence of that on his face. Add in Carson being a cock tease. The man was about to lose his mind.

Carson was out of view, but I could still hear her. "Keeping August away from her didn't require you to be handsy. That's your problem, Ethan. You're too short-sighted. Tonight you acted like you would run off with her instead of helping Daddy steal her money. This isn't some game. If you want my help, you better get your priorities straight."

He placed his hands on his hips, shook his head, and then looked down at August's body lying on the floor. He gave him a swift kick to the stomach before dragging him down a set of steps off the kitchen.

I quickly flicked through all the cameras but found none in the area where he was hauled off. That's when I came across the feed of the wine cellar. Most wine cellars are in basements, so I turned up the volume and played back the tape to see if I could catch any sounds that might help me figure out where he was in the house.

Slowing the feed, I heard a loud bang that sounded like a door *being slammed open, followed by grunting. Ethan was tying him up. Then he started talking.*

"*You always had to be the best at everything. The golden boy who could do no wrong with the cemented family dynasty. You always get everything you want. Not this time. I'm more than happy to take it from you now. Your little whore stands in the way of me becoming a billionaire. I never wanted Carson, but fucking your girlfriend felt good. It's funny that you thought you'd be burning my world down tonight. I can't wait to see your face when you find out Gianna is gone, and you'll never get her back. This time, you don't win, August.*" *A door slammed again, and it went silent.*

\* \* \*

The night August got himself tied up in Carson's basement, I wanted to head straight for Florida, grab Gigi, and run, but I knew that wasn't the right choice. I still had too many questions, and running wouldn't bring me closer to getting the answers. As much as I don't want to rescue August from the Bradbury Estate, I need to. I can't have that on my conscience, not to mention I don't know that Gigi would ever forgive me if something fucked up happened to him.

Somehow, Gigi is a roadblock to Ethan's financial gains, which is mind-numbing. Her family has zero money, and her parents have been drug addicts for decades. There's also the fact that the brakes on my car were tampered with. While I don't believe August was involved, I haven't ruled out Ethan as a suspect, and I want revenge. These entitled pricks think they can fuck with people and get away with it because they have money. That stops with me. I'm no one's puppet.

On Saturday, Ethan threw August in the basement. By Sunday afternoon, he was awake. It wasn't until Tuesday that anyone went downstairs to check in on him.

"Oh, goodie, you're awake. Did you miss me?"

"Fuck off, Carson. What do you want?"

"August, I already got what I wanted, and you no longer have anything I need. Now I'm just here to tease you and break you."

"Now the slut outfit makes sense. Too bad I'm not interested in what's between your legs. Haven't been for a long time."

I hear her tut, "You really sound like a scorned, jealous man, August. Ethan told me all about how you stayed celibate while I was away. I must say, that was very chivalrous of you, but I've only ever had eyes for Ethan."

There's a moment of silence, followed by what sounds like rustling before I hear August yell, "What the fuck are you doing? I'm not fucking you."

"Now there's an idea. I bet your trophy would hate to find out that I rode your cock. Maybe I'll do that and make a video just for funsies."

"Carson, I swear to God you better get your hands off my dick!"

*What the fuck is going on?*

"Well, I don't plan to untie you anytime soon, so unless you want to piss all over yourself again, I suggest you do it in this jug."

August lets out a frustrated growl.

"This entire fucking setup has gone too far. What the fuck is your plan?"

I hear what sounds like him pissing into a container.

When it stops, she says, "Now fucking drink this water. If my plan was to kill you, you wouldn't be sitting here tied up in my basement. This isn't about you, August."

"Then why don't you fucking explain it to me?" There's no way she could miss the ire in his voice because. While I can't see his face, his tone is dripping with palpable hate.

I hear what sounds like the shuffling of papers before Carson chirps, "Look, August, as much as I'd love to tell you everything I know, that's just not going to happen. Besides, we both know the only reason you're really mad is that I've been fucking your best friend."

My eyebrows shoot up in surprise because after what I've witnessed from her, I know she's not that stupid. Carson is clearly trying to get a rise out of him. She's playing with fire and not just with August. If she doesn't plan on killing him, I'd be worried about what happens when he gets untied if I were her.

I can't see anything, but I'm pretty sure I hear August let out an exasperated sigh.

"Carson, you must think I'm a damn fool. Do you think I didn't know you were fucking around on me? Hell, I knew you were whoring yourself out before you ever left. What I'm trying to figure out is why Ethan? There's no way in hell you can hold that man's attention, and you fucking know it."

Something is tossed across the room. "You're fucking wrong, August. Ethan and I have been together for years, and he's ready to make it official."

I hear him chuckle before saying, "Oh yeah, Carson, and why is that? Why now? I'll tell you why. He's using you to do his dirty work. Since I moved on from you, his extracurricular activities with you no longer aid him in ruining me. Since you are no longer the leverage he needed to hit me where it hurts, he decided to go after Gianna. He didn't give two shits whether I found out about the two of you. For him, it was just icing on the cake. You know he wants her. You saw it in his eyes the night of the fundraiser. It's why you couldn't hold your tongue."

There's another loud bang like something was thrown across the room again before Carson says, "It doesn't matter if he wants her or not because she ran off with her boyfriend. How does it feel knowing your new obsession has her legs spread wide for another man?"

The door slams, and I know he's sitting there alone. I wait to see if she'll come back, and when she doesn't, I hear him let out a gut-wrenching shout. At that moment, I feel for him. I know the love he confessed to having for Gigi is real. He's devastated because he believes she is gone.

\* \* \*

On Wednesday, I'm digging through Ethan and his father, Robert Grand's, finances, trying to find a link to Gigi or her family. That's when I see that Grand Media is about to go public. The fees to take your company from private to public are steep, so I'm still trying to figure out how Ethan is profiting. I'm just about to log off my computer and grab a bite to eat when I hear voices on the security system at the Bradbury Estate.

"How much longer will we keep him tied up in the basement, Ethan?"

I quickly pull up the video feed to see if I can get eyes on them. They're in the great room. Carson is wearing a silk robe with lingerie underneath, no doubt trying to catch Ethan's eye. She hasn't left the house since August has been tied up in the basement. It's now the middle of the day, and there's no reason for her to be wearing that outfit.

"What are you wearing, Carson?" Ethan is standing with his hands on his hips, looking irritated by her antics, which is surprising. She clearly wants to fuck, and he doesn't seem the least bit interested.

"Are you jealous that maybe August has seen me like this today?"

A laugh bellows out of him, followed by a sigh as he runs his fingers through his hair, clearly agitated. "Carson, not only has he seen you completely naked, but he has fucked you, so no, I'm not jealous." Ethan continues to pace back and forth, lost in thought, completely oblivious to the rage written across Carson's face. Considering she could blow up his plan, he'd be stupid not to toe the line with her.

"What has you so stressed out that you don't even recognize when I'm trying to get laid?"

Ethan screams, "I can't find her," before closing his eyes and leveling his tone. "I've been looking all over. It's like she disappeared out of thin air. All signs point to her running off with that idiot who crashed his car into the river, but I can't just leave it to chance that she won't potentially show up out of nowhere and ruin everything."

That's interesting. His word choice makes it sound like he has no idea that my brakes were tampered with. If he's not behind the accident, then August was right. My dad has enemies.

"You are really starting to piss me off. Don't tell me you're obsessed with her now as well."

"Don't be ridiculous. We obviously can't knock off August, but we could set it up so that Gianna has a happy accident."

That snaps my attention back to the screen.

Carson slowly walks across the room to where Ethan stands and rests her hands on his chest. "What about her parents? Gianna isn't the only one who would get the money. Her dad is still in play as well. Shouldn't we take him out?"

Ethan keeps his eyes locked on her as she drops her robe. "No, Ed is watching them. They have no idea about anything. We don't need this to get any messier than it already is. Her family has been in the dark for years. Things will only get spoiled if she starts talking to August. He would figure out everything."

She runs her pointer finger down his chest until she reaches his belt and starts undoing the clasp. "So you're only worried about finding her so that you can get rid of the problem?"

His cock is free now, and she pumps it once before he hisses. "You already know the plan. Now be a good little slut and suck my cock."

She smiles and drops to the floor before taking his cock into her mouth. He throws his head back in bliss as she deep throats him and fuck me if I'm not getting a semi. It's like watching live porn. I quickly click out of the screen showing the video and walk into the other room.

Pacing my living room, I try to clear my head and devise a plan. August is trapped in the basement, and I need to find a way to get in there and talk to him. That's when I remember the new technology I'm testing that came with our latest securities acquisition. I started hacking in high school. At first, it was just because I could. My first hack was into the school's computer system to change my C- to an A+. I never got bad grades, but we had a surprise test on a Monday, and I had spent that past weekend high as a kite on a bender. If I wasn't with Gigi, that's how I passed the time to forget how much everything else fucking sucked. Needless to say, once I was in the school's system, I started seeing what else I could hack into.

Hacking became an obsession until it also became the way I thought I might be able to reach my dad. He buried himself in his work to escape his life, which worked for him. Maybe it would work for me too. I could kill two birds with one stone. Earn my father's respect and find an outlet for the darkness I could never seem to escape.

Heading back into my office, I find the device I'm looking for when suddenly I hear grunting sounds, followed by, "Thanks. I can't stay. I just thought of something. I guess your stress-release tactics work well."

I laugh and shake my head. August had the guy nailed to a tee when he said Ethan was using her. At first, I wasn't sure Ethan wasn't equally interested, but now it's clear as day. How she doesn't see it is beyond me. On my shelf, I find the gadget I'm looking for. It's the size of a marble and as light as a microchip. The device is similar to a drone. You can send it where you want, and it'll transmit video, but it also has two-way audio. I can hear and speak through it. My plan is to take it to the Bradbury Estate and get it inside to talk to August. They clearly don't want Gigi talking to August because he would catch on to their plans. That means I need to speak to August so I can figure out what they have been trying to prevent.

* * *

It's now Thursday, and I've been hiding in a bush for an entire hour, waiting for the cleaning lady to leave so I could get the gadget into the house. I'm able to connect to it via an app on my phone. Time flew by last night while I messed around with it, ensuring I knew how to use it before coming to the estate. The gadget is impressive. It makes zero noise and is so tiny you'd never notice it unless you were specifically looking for it.

Today, I lucked out with the cleaning lady. Unfortunately, since I've only been surveilling the house since Saturday, I don't have any precise schedules, and I'm sure since they have August tied up in the basement, the typical staff hasn't been around. After I have the gadget inside, I waste no time maneuvering it through the kitchen and to the downstairs door. The device is small enough that it will roll right under.

Of course once I reach the basement, it's enormous and looks to be completely finished. Scanning the area, I try to locate the wine cellar as it is the only room on this level with a camera, and August must be close to it. It feels like I've been searching this level for an hour when I finally spot a wall filled with wine. The closer I get to the wine cellar, I hear moaning, but not just any moaning—ecstasy-filled moans.

If I find him in that room fucking Carson, I'm out. I don't give a fuck. Gigi deserves better than a man who would cheat because shit got hard. Gigi had a hard life, and Lord knows loving her isn't always easy. I know she has always felt like she was a burden to me because most of the time when we'd get together, it would be after she had a rough incident at home. Coming to me in a moment of need made her feel like I thought everything was always about her problems and needs. I could never get her to understand that I loved being her safe place. I wanted to hear her problems and take them away. When you're in a relationship with someone, don't you want to be the person they run to when they're scared? The person they celebrate with when they're happy. Don't you want to be their everything? Yes, technically, we weren't a couple, but I liked having those moments with her.

Whenever she would start to overthink things and feel insecure, I'd kiss her. Kissing her made her relax. Her tangents would stop, and I could show her how much I cared, how much she meant to me. Being intimate with her was a prize. Gigi is not a girl who gives that part of herself freely. I earned every kiss, every touch, every delicious moan.

A loud outburst jerks me out of my trip down memory lane, and I remember I'm supposed to be finding August.

"Fucking get out of here, Carson. Go put on this ridiculous act for Ethan."

Once I find the room the voice came from, I roll under the door, and that's when I see that August is tied to a chair. He looks like shit. The stress of the last few days has aged him incredibly. Dark circles frame his eyes, his five o'clock shadow is now almost a beard that's taken over his face, and they most definitely aren't feeding him.

"Fuck yes! Don't stop."

When I turn the camera in the other direction, I see Carson on a desk, completely naked, riding another girl's face. Grabbing her fake tits in her hands, she squeezes them before trailing one hand down her stomach to her pussy where she parts her lips and climaxes all over the other girl's face. When I say climax, I really mean squirt. The woman is a grade-A porn star squirter, and that's a turn-off for me. Of course it could just be the woman. Carson wants to kill Gigi, and her fake tits and lips repulse me, but I digress. I'm not sure what the hell August ever saw in this woman. She is vile from the inside out.

That's when August says, "You always did come hard for the girls."

"I never heard you complaining." She stands up and puts her silk robe on.

"You're right. That's because I was usually fucking the other girl."

Carson walks across the room and slaps him hard across the face. "You better watch how you talk to me, August. I might just do what Ethan doesn't have the balls to do." Then she turns on her heel, and they walk out.

He sits frozen in his spot, listening intently to ensure they are gone. Once he's convinced they aren't coming back, he starts to mess with his restraints.

"August, it's me, Mason."

He goes still and looks around the room. "Great, now I'm losing my fucking mind."

"You're not losing your mind. Look down. See the ball on the floor?"

He looks down and then spots it. "Son of a bitch. I thought you took off the moment I didn't come out of the house," he says as he continues to fiddle with his restraints.

"Yeah, well, trust me, the thought has often crossed my mind, but Gigi is in real trouble. They plan on killing her." .

His eyes close and he grinds his jaw. "Then why are you here saving me?"

"They can't find her, and I need answers. If I could run away with her and know that it would save her, I would have, but I think they would hunt her down until the job is done. There's also the fact that I don't think she could say goodbye to her family forever."

He opens his eyes and nods in agreement.

"Who is Ed?"

His eyes widen, and he takes in a deep breath. "I fucking knew it. Ed is my uncle."

Suddenly, he throws himself backward in the chair, and I watch as he jiggles each wooden spindle free and slips the knots. He must have been working on loosening the spindles the entire time he's been down here. That, or until he found out Gigi's life was on the line, he didn't have a real reason to escape.

"Do you have eyes on the house?"

"Yes, Carson hasn't left the house since you've been locked up here, and there isn't any staff on the premises."

"Where are you?"

"I'm down the street in a car."

He nods as he works to untie the knots around his ankles. "Can you tell me where she is now?"

Without pause, I pull up the camera feed and flick through the rooms I have access to. "The brunette is leaving. Carson is in the great room."

"Great. Pick me up in ten minutes." He stands up, cracks his neck, and exits the room.

Using the gadget, I follow after him and ask, "What are you planning to do?"

He looks down at the ball. "What would you do?"

*Shit.*

"August, listen, I know you want revenge, but don't do something stupid. Get out of the house, and we'll figure it out."

"Fuck that, Mason. They want to kill Gianna, and no one lays a hand on my girl. I won't risk it."

Punching the steering wheel, I rush out of the car toward the estate.

## TWENTY-FIVE

*August*

Heading upstairs, I take the steps two at a time. We've dated since high school, so I know this house like the back of my hand. When I thought Mason and Gianna had run off together, I was fucking devastated. I threw myself a pity party for a few good hours before realizing that if she did run away with him, at least she wasn't near Ethan and Carson.

Ethan tied me up tight as fuck to a wooden chair with spindles, making sure to knot each spindle. It took me the first two days just to loosen the knots enough to move my hands and make any headway with loosening the spindles. My plan was always to escape, but once I thought Gianna ran off with Mason, I figured I'd draw out my captivity and try to get more information. Carson's show today and Mason's revelations were the final straw. I was done playing weak and helpless.

I've spent years dealing with Carson's fake, social-climbing antics. For the most part, I thought it was all superficial bullshit, but now I know she has a black heart. She'll do anything and pay any price if it gets her ahead. I never thought she had any true loyalty to me, but I didn't realize she had a deep-seated hate.

Never had I thought the day would come when I would kill someone, but I've also never wanted to kill someone more than I do at this moment. Reaching the top of the steps, I slam the basement door open. Walking through the kitchen, I knock a crystal vase on the island to the floor, shattering it into a million pieces. I want the bitch to hear me coming. Once I reach the living room, she stands there with a smirk.

"See, I knew you liked my show. Too bad I'm not in the mood for seconds."

My eyebrows shoot up in surprise. *Is she serious right now?*

"Carson, my God, what is wrong with you? I did not just come out of the basement that I've been locked in for a week to have sex with you. I'm here because I'm done dealing with your bullshit. There's no way I'm letting you lay a finger on Gianna."

Rolling her eyes like my words are empty threats, she starts leisurely walking up the stairs, so I start after her.

"Where do you think you're going?"

Her pace picks up when she notices that I'm hot on her heels.

"Don't be scared, Carson. I'm only going to do to you what you planned on doing to Gianna." My voice is dripping with condescension. She pauses to see my face. Now she gets it. I hope she sees every ounce of hate, venom, and depravity I have for her.

"You wanted me like this, Carson. Well, now you got me." I give her a second to take in my words and watch as fear seeps into her eyes before I say, "Run."

I may have been locked in the basement and starved for the past six days, but the adrenaline pumping through my veins now would give any grown man pause if he saw me coming. Hurtling up the stairs like a bull in a china shop after Carson, I suddenly halt when I hear her let out a blood-curdling scream just as she crests the top of the open staircase. That's when I notice Mason rounding the corner. He must have taken her by surprise. She takes a frightened step back, forgetting the staircase behind her, and falls back down the steps. I move out of the way of her body and watch as it hits each step on its descent with a crack. These steps are made of hard pine, not a scrap of padding in sight.

When I look up at Mason, his eyes widen with the realization of what happened. "August, what the fuck?" He throws his hands into his hair, and I shake my head.

"I didn't ask you to follow me in. I said I'd be out in ten minutes."

His face goes pale with shock.

"Come on, we need to get out of here."

He remains frozen as I start to head down the stairs. I clap my hands in his direction, trying to snap him out of his mortified trance.

"Let's go. We have to go."

Once I reach the bottom of the stairs, I can see that Carson's body has landed at an unnatural angle. Her neck is clearly broken. I wouldn't consider myself a heartless person, but I can't say I'm proud of myself at the moment. Maybe it's because she gave me countless reasons to hate her over the past week. Reasoning aside, I can't find it within me to care that she's dead, and I know that's incredibly fucked up. I also know we need to get the hell out of here before someone finds us.

When Mason finally decides to join me at the bottom of the staircase, he looks at her body and curses, clearly distraught by everything that has taken place. Then we both walk out.

* * *

After we left the estate, Mason drove straight to his place. We didn't speak a word. When we entered the condo, he went straight into his office and slammed the door shut. Since I haven't seen a shower in over a week, I go down the hall and help myself to it. My desire to get clean outweighed my need to eat. Standing underneath the scalding hot spray of the shower helped release a lot of the tension that had built up in my body over the last six days. Recalling the events of this past week and how I thought Mason left, how I thought Gianna chose him, and how the two people in my life that I considered friends unfathomably betrayed me, I can't help but feel beaten.

I was never under the misconception that Ethan and I were

anything more than fake friends, but I didn't realize the depth of his treachery. The man hates me something fierce, which makes today's events that much easier to swallow. Ethan didn't care for Carson. In fact, I'd bet good money on it that he was using her all these years just to spite me. There was never going to be a happily ever after for us. I always knew she was messing around on the side—I just never knew with whom. Maybe if I'd cared enough, I would have noticed it was him. I had my reasons for keeping her around. It kept my parents happy, and the sex wasn't bad. Who gets rid of a girl who brings other girls to the party? But I never knew how genuinely vile she was. In hindsight, I would have parted ways sooner had I known how deep her hatred ran.

I couldn't tell you what I had planned when I followed Carson up the steps. Killing her would not have been premeditated. I've never given much thought to killing anyone. All I knew was that I wouldn't allow her to walk out of the house and get her hands on Gianna. Mason showing up out of nowhere and scaring the shit out of her was a freak accident that I couldn't have planned better if I tried.

In the end, she got what was coming to her. You can't screw people over figuratively and literally repeatedly and not expect that shit to catch up with you. Clearly, Mason has been watching the house all week, and I need to find out what he knows. Begrudgingly, I exit the shower and find his room to look for something to wear. Helping myself to a pair of joggers and a soccer hoodie, I make my way out of his bedroom to the office. I'm about to open the door when I notice a pizza box on the counter. Fuck, I'm starving.

Heading over to the kitchen, I help myself to the remaining pizza. I'm just about to go to the refrigerator for a drink when Mason walks out of the office. When Mason looks up at me, it's as if he's surprised to see me sitting at his counter eating his pizza. Maybe he is. I think everything feels too surreal for him right now. It's as if he's just going through the motions on autopilot. I continue eating, waiting to see if he'll speak first. He makes his way toward the refrigerator, opens it, and grabs a beer before pulling out another and sliding it down to me. We both stay silent as we crack open the tops and take a few long swigs.

He breaks the silence. "We have a lot to talk about."

Turning, he grabs another beer from the fridge and walks back to the office, calling, "Let's go."

I pick up another slice of pizza, grab my beer, and follow him. When I get into the office, I take a seat in the only other spare chair in the room.

"I scrubbed the security footage at Carson's house and looped in old footage to make it look like nothing was out of the norm. There isn't a camera with a direct shot of the stairs, so her fall should look exactly like an accident." His eyes hold mine for a beat before he goes on.

"I know from what little interaction Ethan has had with Carson that he is actively looking for Gigi with plans of staging an accident once he finds her. There's a man named Ed apparently watching her parents, and I don't think Ethan had any part in tampering with my brakes."

I nod in acknowledgment of everything he said. It was a stretch that Ethan was involved in his accident from the start. The probability of someone being after his dad was more likely. But now, I wouldn't put it past him. "We know that Gianna is somehow a threat to a future windfall. Have you gotten any closer to figuring out how Gianna is a part of that?"

Steepling his fingers and leaning back in his chair, he shakes his head. "No, that's why I broke into the estate to speak to you. The recurring theme of this entire charade seems to be keeping you and Gigi apart. Apparently, if you don't know about her past, then you can't unravel their plans. I'm hoping that if I tell you her story, you can make sense of how they play into it."

As much as I wish it were my girl sitting here telling me her story, I know it needs to be Mason right now. "Mason, I want to help, but we don't have much time. Once Carson's body is found, Ethan will know I escaped, and he'll make a play. Everyone has a backup plan. Can you give me the CliffsNotes version? I can tell you if anything stands out."

Taking a deep breath, he collects his thoughts and leans back in his chair to look at the ceiling before he begins. "Let's see, CliffsNotes version of her life. The family is originally from California. Her mom decided to move back to Missouri to be with her side of the family when she couldn't put up with Marco's bullshit anymore. Marco was the epitome of the stereotypical entitled, spoiled rich kid who did whatever he wanted, bought whatever he wanted, and had Mom and Dad's money to back him when he fucked up."

Well, now I know why she wanted to steer clear of me. Her dad let her down, and she expected me to do the same, cut from the same cloth and all. I listen as Mason continues.

"Marco bounced from career to career for years, never really staying put. He ended up following Maria and Gigi to Missouri. Coming here was a fresh start, and he seemed to stay clean for a few years until he lost both his parents within six months. They left him over two million dollars, which was a lot of money fifteen years ago. When he returned to Missouri, he decided to retire since he had his parents' money. Eventually, with all the free time on his hands, he got bored and started running with the wrong people, who, strangely enough, he met at the golf course, but addiction doesn't care about race, gender, or social status. He started using again with his new friends and invested money with them to start a business venture. Unfortunately, the company never got legs, and he lost his investment, and the remaining funds fed his new addiction and—"

I stop him before he can continue. "Ethan said she stood in the way of him getting his payout. Did she ever mention any of her dad's friends' names or the company that didn't make it?" As much as listening to him recount her upbringing explains a lot about her character today, we are in a time crunch.

Immediately, he sits forward and pinches the bridge of his nose, deep in thought. "I want to say Suncom or Sun—"

I jump out of my seat so fast the chair knocks back. "You've got to be fucking kidding me! Suncast Media? He invested in Suncast Media?" I say it like a question, but it's more of a statement because I already know the answer. Now everything is coming together. My uncle Eduard's involvement, Ethan's, and I'm sure his dad's. If Gianna's dad was a golfer, it only makes sense that he ran into Robert and Eduard back in the day. They have always been avid golfers and thick as thieves. "Grand Media started out as Suncast Media. They went through a rebranding process a few years after they started to target new markets and become more of a global brand. If her dad was an initial investor and bought stock in the company—it's worth millions."

Mason curses under his breath before pounding on the keyboard. "When I was digging through Ethan's financials the other day, nothing seemed amiss, but I learned that Grand Media plans to go public at the end of the month. That must be why they're so adamant about keeping you apart and getting rid of Gigi."

The mention of them hurting her makes me want to rage. I want to find Ethan myself and kill him for even thinking about laying a finger on her. The thing is, I never pegged him as this type of guy. Someone who would go to such lengths to ensure his own financial gain. Grand Media is already a multimillion-dollar company. Killing someone for more money when you already have more than enough is just heinous. I can almost guarantee that Robert asked Ethan to help him with this, and Ethan has always wanted to earn his dad's approval. Robert was an absent father, prioritizing work, money, women, and fame over being a dad. If this earns Ethan points with his father, he'll stop at nothing to accomplish his wishes.

"We need more information. Can you do some digging and verify that our theory is correct, that Marco did, in fact, buy shares and still technically owns them? We need to know who the players are to take them out." I'm pacing the room, wondering if my dad ever made any investments with Robert early on. I need to figure out if there's any possible way he has a horse in this race. After all, my grandfather hired Maria, and my father brought her on at Reds after he died to ensure she still had a job. I'm hoping that was out of the kindness of his heart and not to keep Maria under his thumb. I don't voice those concerns out loud because I know Mason will have our answers soon enough. Right now, I don't want to give him any more reasons to doubt me or my intent. I'm worried about my dad's involvement and my family. That's when a thought hits me. I know what their next move is. "He's going to use her family to draw her out."

Mason's eye immediately finds mine, and he slams his fist down on the desk. "Damn it!"

"I need your phone. We need to get security on Gianna's family, and you need to tell me where she is."

He closes his eyes. "Yeah, okay."

Surprisingly, he tosses me my phone. "How do you have my phone?"

Shrugging his shoulders like it's no big deal, he says, "You left it in my car last Saturday in your rush for answers." That means he has had access to all my shit this entire week. He knows I'm clean. Immediately, I call up my friend who I box with at the gym. He's an ex-SEAL who runs his own security company.

"Max, it's August. I was wondering how fast you can get me a guy tonight? I need your best. Money isn't an issue." I place the call on speaker so that Mason can hear the conversation.

"August! I missed you in the ring yesterday, brother. It's not like you to miss a session, and now this call. You know I have your back. I can have a guy ready within an hour. Send me the details of the job."

"Thanks, Max. I'll send over the specifics now."

Mason blows out a breath. "Someone's home."

I hurriedly make my way around the desk to look at the screen and watch as Ethan comes through the front door and makes his way to the kitchen. The stairs that Carson fell down are opposite the kitchen and not directly visible from the front door.

"Mason, I need to get my girl. You need to tell me where she is."

Putting his head in his hands, he lets out a string of curses. I know he's torn. Mason wants to go get Gianna, he wants to protect her, he wants to save her, and I can't fault him for wanting those things, but I'm hoping that he trusts me to do the same.

"She's in Florida. First, you'll need to fly into Destin. Once there, you'll need to rent a car and drive to Emerald Beach. I'll text you the address of the house she's staying at."

I'm fucking relieved that he's not putting up an argument and that, apparently, I've earned his trust, but I'm nervous to ask my next question. "Who is Gianna staying with?"

He rights himself and smirks as if something is funny. "She's staying with an old friend. I think you've seen him a time or two."

I clench my fists as my blood pressure rises. "She's staying with the biker fuck? Out of all the people in her life, you send her off with one who wants in her pants?"

"As much as you might not like it, August, there aren't many people in her life that she can just disappear with. He's been around for years, and Gigi is not interested in him. If you love her, maybe you should try trusting her."

I shake my head and start heading toward the door. "I need to borrow your car to get to my plane. She's coming home, and we're staying at my house with personal security placed on the perimeter. You said the company goes public by the end of the month, which gives us a week to unravel everything. I think I know how to bring them down without anyone else getting physically hurt, but I need you to dig up the paper trail that incriminates them."

He shakes his head and leans back in the chair. "I'm not your personal hacker, August."

I shrug. "Okay, go get Gianna, and I'll hack the records."

He knows damn well I can't hack shit. I would have to hire someone. It's sinking in that I'm leaving to get Gianna, not him, and I can tell it's eating him alive.

Standing up, he reaches into his pocket and throws me the keys. "I want to know the minute you have her."

I nod and walk out.

* * *

When I got to the beach house, Gianna wasn't there, but the biker boy was. Apparently, he was on his way out to meet up with the girls and his roommate. I explained to him that I was there to take her home. Of course he didn't trust my word without calling Mason to verify, which he did. The guy doesn't like me, and that's fine. I'm not here to make friends.

Following Bryce to the beach in my rental car, all I can think about is whether she will be happy to see me. When she walked out of the room at the hospital, we had been official for maybe an hour. What I don't know is if any of this changes things. Does she think I can't keep her safe? Does she know I've been fighting for her? Does she blame me? I'm torn out of my thoughts once we reach his store. Climbing out of the car, Bryce comes over.

"They should be down at the bonfire over there." He flicks his head toward the raging fire by the water's edge. "I need to run into the shop, and then I'll head over." He starts walking toward the shop before I have time to respond, which is perfectly fine with me. I have no desire to make small talk with the guy.

Every molecule in my body wants to rush to the bonfire, find Gianna, scoop her up in my arms, and never let her go. Just being this close to her makes my heart race. I stop at the boardwalk and take a minute to calm my nerves. While I may have spent the last week tied up in a basement obsessing over her, it doesn't mean she has spent any time worrying about me. A big part of me can't help but wonder if I'm not the guy she wants to see tonight.

The sun just went down, it's dark, and tons of people are down by the fire. Spotting her from back here on the boardwalk would be nearly impossible. I'm about to start heading down when movement from the perimeter of the fire catches my eye. Blond hair, tan skin, and curves I'd recognize anywhere stand up from a beach towel. My stomach is in knots as I watch her pull down her jean skirt that had ridden up, giving me a quick peek at that perfect ass. She's talking to her friend, who I now know is Vivian, and gesturing toward the food trucks. Before I can put one foot in front of the other, I see her throw her head back, laughing. The sight has me rooted where I stand.

Watching her, knowing she doesn't know I'm here, is a special treat. Here she is, with her friends, in her element, and as I look on, I get a glimpse of the man I want to be. I want to make her laugh, I want to put that smile on her face, I want to be her everything. Gianna makes her way toward the food trucks, kicking up sand as she walks, and I stay frozen in my spot. She's wearing a black bikini top and a jean skirt, her hair is unkempt from being blown around in the wind, and her skin is sun-kissed. There's no doubt that she has been down here all day. She looks fantastic, relaxed, and better than I remember, if possible.

As she gets closer in her approach, a thought passes my mind. I wonder if she can feel my eyes on her, feel me watching her every move. The idea hasn't even left my mind when her big green eyes snap up to meet mine. Gianna stops dead in her tracks, and I swear my heart stops. One look from her is all it takes to break me. For a split second, the look that crosses her face is like one of disappointment, but it's gone just as fast as it came because in the next breath, she's running toward me with a massive smile on her face. Stepping into the sand, I only make it a few paces off the boardwalk before she jumps into my arms, wrapping her arms around my neck and her legs around my waist.

God, I forgot how good she smells, how soft her body is against mine, how incredibly perfect she is. Since the moment I met her, this woman has consumed me. I know it's madness and foolish to be so utterly devoted to someone I barely know, but life is inherently risky, and you can't win if you don't take the chance. She is a bet I'll make every time because betting on her is choosing me. With her, I'm the person I've always wanted to be.

I hold her tighter and breathe her in deeper before murmuring against her neck, "Say it's me."

Her entire body tightens around mine as if she's trying to forge a deeper connection while she mindlessly runs her fingers through the hair at the nape of my neck. "It's always been you," she whispers into my ear.

Those four simple words almost bring me to my knees and instantly become my new favorites. I try to pull her back to look at her face, but she doesn't let me go, so I bury my face into her neck and place an open-mouthed kiss on the spot below her ear. Her skin instantly pebbles beneath my mouth, and I feel her smile against my neck.

"Gianna, please release me so I can kiss you, baby. You have—"

She cuts me off before I can finish my sentence, sealing her lips over mine in an all-consuming kiss. The minute her lips touched mine, I was a goner, breathless, wrecked. All the hell I went through this past week was worth it for this moment. We've never been great with words, but right now, she's kissing me with a passion that matches my own, and I know without words that she is mine. When her tongue parts my lips, seeking entrance, I let her take it. I'll give her anything. Everything I have is all hers if she wants it. Her legs are still wrapped tightly around me, and her sexy little whimpers mixed with her soft body molded against mine have me rock hard. I pull back, breathless from our kiss as she unhooks her legs and slides down my front until her feet are flat on the ground.

"August, I'm so sorry."

*What the hell is she sorry for? Sorry for kissing me?* I still have her tight against my body as I peer down at her with a questioning gaze. I'm about to start probing her when she begins to speak.

"When I left Mason's room, I had no idea I'd be kidnapped and taken to Florida. They put sleeping pills in my drink, and the next thing I knew, I was here and told that I couldn't have any contact with anyone back home. I wouldn't have left you, August."

I'm pissed and relieved all at the same time. Mason didn't mention the part about drugging her, but the only part I can focus on is that she didn't leave me. Many questions ran on a constant loop in my mind while I was tied up. *Did she willingly leave me? Did she think I couldn't keep her safe?*

"Baby, I didn't know I needed to hear those words until you said them. You have no idea how much that means to me."

She reaches up and runs her fingers through my facial hair,

which is almost a beard since I haven't shaved in six days. "This is new." The way she's smiling at me tells me she likes it. Then, placing her hands on my chest, she pushes me back to take in the rest of my ensemble. Her eyes rove over my body from head to toe. "What are you wearing, and where are your shoes?"

I'm wearing gray joggers and a navy blue soccer hoodie that belong to Mason. There was no way I was wearing his underwear, and our feet aren't the same size. As soon as I knew where Gianna was, I made zero detours. I needed to get to my girl. There was no way I would waste another minute without her by my side.

"I like this look on you. I've never seen you so casual." She gives me a sexy smile before lowering her hands from my chest to the waistband of my sweats. The next thing I know, she's dipping her hand inside and grabbing my cock. "I really, really like this look." She strokes it once, twice, and I can't help but groan before I grab her wrist and still her hand. As much as I want to let her continue, we are standing out in the open on the beach, and this seems very out of character for her.

"Gianna, what are you doing? How much have you had to drink?"

She steals her arm back like a child that's just been scolded. "I didn't realize you were the only one who got to take what they wanted."

I stare back at her, amused by the fact she believes I don't want her to touch me. "Baby, you can touch me whenever you want. I fucking love it, but the girl I was with a week ago wouldn't have made that move."

Her face heats with embarrassment before she turns to walk away. Grabbing her wrist to keep her from leaving, I spin her back around.

"Gianna, you don't get to do that. You don't get to walk away because you think you understand something you don't. A lot has happened over the past week, and we need to talk but know this: I have never been more sure that you are my forever, my happily ever after, my whole world, so don't ever walk away from me thinking you're not my everything."

Her lower lip trembles, and she drops her gaze to the sand, no doubt hiding unshed tears. Putting my hand under her chin to bring her face back to mine, I'm met with glassy eyes.

"Don't cry for me. Not here, not now, not ever. I can't bear it."

Then, wrapping her arms around my middle, she buries her face into my chest and hugs me tight. That's when I notice Vivian approaching with the asshole I punched from the club in tow, and just like that, I'm pissed again.

"Gianna, what is that shitbag doing here?"

Raising her head from my chest, she looks over her shoulder before releasing me from her bear hug, only to tuck herself into my side and fuck if that action doesn't make me melt. My girl doesn't want to stop touching me, and I'm basking in that awareness.

"Oh, that's Aiden. He is Bryce's roommate."

Grinding my teeth and clenching my fists, I try to rein in my fury. "Mason and I are going to have words. He really sent you to live with biker boy and this fucker?"

She swats my chest and then playfully says, "Someone's jealous."

I grab her ass hard, and she gasps before I say, "No, baby, I'm greedy and selfish. I don't share what's mine." Her lips are parted, and I see she's turned on. All I want to do is suck that bottom lip into my mouth, but we have company.

"Gigi, I thought you were bringing back drinks. When you didn't come back, we decided to come to see what was taking so long. Now I know." Vivian quirks her eyebrow mischievously while openly checking me out.

"Vivian, this is August. August, this is Vivian and Aiden. I don't think you've all formally met."

Aiden gives me a nod before heading back toward the fire, which is ideal. I have nothing to say to him, and I don't care to have him around Gianna.

"Well, August, it's nice to put a face and a body to the man I've heard so much about." Again, she's openly checking me out from head to toe, and I know Gianna must notice, but she doesn't seem fazed in the least. I've been so drunk on reuniting with Gianna that I forgot we need to get going. The plane is waiting for us. I told the pilots I'd only be an hour or so, and now that Carson's body has been discovered, we really need to get back.

Clearing my throat to snap Vivian out of her obvious gawking, I say, "We'll have to catch up once everything calms down, but unfortunately, Gianna and I have to get going."

Gianna looks up at me with a furrowed brow. "Wait, we're leaving right now? I don't even have my things. What about Vivi? She came with me."

"Don't worry about anything, Gigi. I'll get all our stuff and bring it back with me. I'm going to stay down here a little longer. I'll come back when everything settles back home."

A smile takes over my face when the girls hug and do some secret handshake. That's what a true friendship looks like, not the ones I've grown up having. A friendship forged out of true love and affection rather than necessity or coercion. Vivian may have been checking me out, but she wasn't trying to hide it from Gianna, and I think Gianna shrugged it off because she knows the true colors of her friend. Just because she's looking doesn't mean she'll try to touch. Vivian is a true friend who has her back through thick and thin, and it's evident Gianna trusts her immensely.

Once they've finished their goodbye, I take Gianna's hand, and we head back to the car, both wearing goofy smiles. There could be any number of reasons for our relentless smiles. Maybe it's because this is the first time we've walked together holding hands, or perhaps it's because we're officially a couple in the eyes of the people who matter. But whatever the reason, I'm fucking hooked.

## TWENTY-SIX
### Gianna

This afternoon, lying on the beach with my best friend, I did a lot of soul-searching. For years I've put myself and my needs on the back burner. I buried the person I wanted to be because I feared she'd be rejected. I'm not shy, but I knew people wouldn't see me for who I was. Instead, they'd just see where I came from and dismiss me based on my circumstances alone rather than my merit. Drug addicts who couldn't get their shit together couldn't possibly raise a child who would rise above. No, I would lie, cheat, and steal just like my parents.

Being here, away from my family and the stigma that has followed me around my entire life, I've been able to breathe for the first time in years. Yes, the people I'm with still know my past, but my past doesn't have to define me. I can still be the free spirit I've always hoped to be. I can still make mistakes. I don't have to fit into any specific box because there's a vast world out there, and I am but one tiny little speck, barely making a ripple. We get one life to live, and I don't want to live mine with any regrets. In ten years, when I look back on this moment in my life, I don't want to say *I wish I had let him in. I wish I had let him see all of me. I wish I had let him love me.*

Mason has had my heart for the past nine years. For nine

years, I buried my feelings for him because I didn't want to lose what we had. On some level, I knew he cared deeply for me, and that was enough. Today, while I stared out over the ocean for hours and reflected on my own heart, I realized why it's not Mason. While I may have loved Mason first, it couldn't have been the right kind of love because I would have never fallen for August if it had been.

So now, as I take the hand of the most beautiful man I've ever laid eyes on, I can't help but smile with the knowledge that he is mine. He came here for me. While brief and heavily shrouded with drama, the stolen moments we shared meant something to him. I was important to him. It's easy to tell someone what they want to hear but showing them can be much more complicated.

Mason was always my hero, saving me from broken promises, pain, and sorrow, ensuring my world was intact. Then August showed up and rocked it. He was willing to play the role of the villain and burn everything I ever built down if it meant I was his in the end. So when a man enters your life threatening to tear it all down, you let him and don't look back. After all, were the walls really protecting your heart if you built them because you were already broken?

We finally reach his car, and where I expected him to open my door, he doesn't. Instead, he pulls me into him, stealing my breath away with his thirsty gaze. My God, this man unravels me. He places his right hand on the curve of my neck before sliding it up to the back of my head, where he wraps his fingers around my hair and pulls my head back before slowly bringing his lips down to mine. I can't help the moan that escapes me the second his lips graze mine, and he smiles against them before teasing me with the slowest open-mouthed, intense kiss I've ever had. My legs feel like they will give out at any second, but then he pulls back. The move has my eyes snapping open, only to find him smiling at me.

"I need to get you into this car and return to the airport. If I stand here kissing you a minute longer, that won't happen." He kisses my forehead and opens my door before jogging around to his side. As he gets in the car, I can't help but notice the massive bulge in his pants, and I smile. I like knowing I affect him as much as he does me. Looking over to grab my hand, he notices where my eyes have zeroed in. Biting his lip to stifle his smile, he says, "It missed you, too, but we don't have time for that look."

I want him so bad it physically hurts, and then I get an idea. Moments ago, he said I could touch him anytime I wanted, and that's just what I'm going to do. For my plan to work, I decide to wait until he pulls out onto the highway. It's getting late, and there aren't many cars on the road. Unfastening my seat belt, I release his hand and smile inwardly at the frown that momentarily takes over his face from the fact we are no longer touching until that same hand reaches down and grips his thigh. Glancing over at me, he raises an eyebrow in question. That's when I get on my knees in my seat and lean over the center console to place a kiss on his neck before seductively saying, "You said I could touch it whenever I wanted. Can I use my mouth?"

He lets out a slow, "Fuck..." as he pushes his head back against the seat. Before he can object, I slowly slide my hand up his thigh until I reach his crotch, where I trace my finger over the outline of his erection. Leisurely, I move my hand up to his waistband, seeking entrance, but before I can free him, he covers my hand with his own, halting me. "Baby." His breathy plea sounds more like a request for mercy than an argument to stop. When I look up, I can tell his breaths have quickened. He wants this, but there's trepidation. He wants to make sure I know what I'm getting myself into.

I give him a coy smile, then bend down to where he's laid his hand over mine and kiss the back of it before slowly peeling it off. With his hand no longer stopping me, I pull his sweatpants down, freeing his cock. My God, it's enormous. Why don't I remember it being so big? That's when it hits me I've never really had the chance to explore him intimately. While he's been inside me, and sure, I've seen it penetrating me, as it sits before me standing at attention, I'm fucking awestruck. There's no way I can possibly take all of him. However, I'm not backing down. I need him to know how much I want him, so I place a kiss on the tip before running my tongue along the vein that runs to the base. His thighs tighten, and I can tell he likes my mouth on him. I trace my tongue back up his length, and when I reach the top, I take him into my mouth as far as I can go.

"Damn, your mouth feels so good." His praise makes me clench. I'm so turned on. I suck him harder, take him deeper, but he's still not all the way in. Moving my hand to the base of his cock to make up for what I can't fit, he says, "No, baby, you wanted it, so you're going to take all of it."

*Why do I want to please him so much?* The next thing I know, he has moved his hand to the back of my head, where he slowly adds pressure, pushing me down a little more with each bob of my head.

"Relax that pretty throat for me."

I do as he says, and the next thing I know, his cock is all the way in, hitting the back of my throat.

"Fuck, you're such a good girl. I love knowing you missed my cock as much as it missed you."

My swimsuit bottoms are now thoroughly soaked, and I want nothing more than to reach between my legs and find my own release. However, hearing August's words of praise and his dark moans of pure ecstasy is addictive. I want this to be about him because he's right, I fucking missed him. I need to show him how much in ways words can't express. For now, fucking seems to be the way we convey how much we crave the other person. It's when I feel the most connected to him. When we are intimate, there's no question I'm his. I see it in his eyes and hear it in his voice whenever we're together. He thrusts into my mouth two more times, and my eyes start to water.

"Baby, I'm going to come in your mouth, and you're going to take every drop."

I nod greedily as best I can from this position. I want to taste him. I want his taste in my mouth until I can have him inside of me.

The next thing I know, hot ropes of cum hit the back of my throat, and he's grunting. Swallowing as best as I can, I don't release him until his cock stops jerking. Then, pulling off, I lick my lips and pull his pants back over his crotch. When I meet his gaze, it's ablaze with passion and fury. He grabs me by the back of my neck and quickly pulls my mouth to his, swiping his tongue through my lips before releasing me to put his eyes back on the road. Now I'm the one who's breathing heavily as I sit back in my seat and start to refasten my seat belt. I can see him stealing glances at me out of my peripheral.

"Tasting myself on your lips is the hottest fucking thing I've ever done."

I shift in my seat, trying to alleviate the ache that has built up in my core. If he says one more sexy line to me, I swear I'll come on the spot. Picking up my hand, he interlaces our fingers and kisses the back of mine.

"The minute we get on that plane, you're in trouble."

I don't respond, just look out the window. I don't want him to know how excited I am about boarding the plane, but I can't help but feel like a desperate ho. Shooting my shot and grabbing him on the beach, coupled with giving him road head, has me feeling dirty. I'm not a slut but fuck me if he doesn't make me want to be one. I need to try to rein in my carnal desires for this man and maintain some level of self-respect. August must take my silence for something it's not.

"Baby, talk to me. You have no idea how good that was for me if that's what you're worried about." He squeezes my hand to pull my eyes to his before returning his attention to the road. I can see the honest concern on his face, so I give him a half-smile.

"I'm glad you liked it because I've never done that before."

That must make him happy because he flashes me a huge smile right before squeezing my hand, which consequently only makes me self-conscious. It almost feels condescending, like a pat on the back. I know he's more experienced than me, and I'm not his first blowjob, but I want it to be special, as lame as that sounds. For a moment, I thought it was. Releasing his hand, I turn my focus out the window.

"What's that smile for? Are you saying you could tell it was my first time? You just said it was good."

He's quiet for a beat too long, so I risk stealing a glance. His face is serious, and he reaches across the seat to take my hand back. "What? Gianna, no, I smiled because I can't help how happy it makes me knowing that I'm the only one who has had you in the most intimate of ways." Then, still unsatisfied that his words hit home as intended, he adds, "You might be surprised, but I can count on one hand the number of times that I've received a blowjob, and yours was by far the best. Not even in the same league as the others."

There's no point in trying to mask the smile that takes over my face. I pleased my man, and he's happy. He's right, though. I am surprised he hasn't had more blowjobs. I know he's had a girlfriend since high school. Isn't oral something all couples do when they're intimate? How could she not want to please him in that way? I'm about to start asking him about his past, finding out all there is to know about this man I'm obsessed with, but he's parking the car before I get a chance, and we're not at an airport.

"I thought you said we had to catch a plane home tonight?"

My comment must have caught him off guard because he gives me a perplexed expression. "We are at the airport." He looks forward at the building in front of us, and my confusion must dawn on him. "This is a private airport. I have my own plane."

My eyebrows shoot up in surprise, and before I know it, he's exiting the car and coming around to my side. Opening the door, he holds out his hand for me to take. As I look down, I realize he's still barefoot, which makes me smile. The man was so rushed to get to me that he didn't bother to waste time getting shoes. This man is everything. With his hand in mine, we walk straight through the small building and onto the airstrip. Pilots are stationed outside the plane, waiting at the steps to greet us.

"Good evening, Mr. Branson. The plane has been refueled, and food has been delivered per your request. Are we still flying straight through to St. Louis?"

"Yes, Jasper, straight through. Thank you for accommodating me with such short notice."

The pilot tips his hat. "No problem, sir. Enjoy your flight."

Right now, I can't help but feel like Julia Roberts in *Pretty Woman* when some exuberantly rich man whisked her away on his private plane. Of course I knew August had money, but not this kind of money. It is intimidating. I could never give him anything that he doesn't already have. He can have anything or anyone he wants, and apparently, that's me.

Checking my insecurities at the door, I tell myself I'm not going to hold back anymore. I'm going to open up and stop pushing him away. That means I can't let my self-doubt creep in and steal my happiness. He must feel my unease because he squeezes my hand and gives me a supportive smile before pulling me up the stairs.

Once we board the plane, I'm rendered speechless. The interior is so luxurious. Big, creamy white captain's chairs line the sides of the cabin, contrasting with dark mahogany wood tables and trim. There's clearly a bedroom toward the back as the door is ajar, and I can see a bed. This is so much more than I ever thought I'd experience. I was homeless a few short months ago, and now I'm riding on a private plane with my boyfriend. I give myself a minute to let that last part sink in. *August is my boyfriend. Oh my God, August is my boyfriend!*

I slip my hand from his and take a seat on one of the plush cream-colored leather captain seats. This is all so overwhelming, and my heart rate increases as a wave of nausea takes over. *Oh no, I'm going to pass out.* I drop my head between my legs, which is the last thing I should do, but it's all I can manage. I need to lie flat, but it's too late. The last thing I hear is August curse, and then I'm out.

\* \* \*

When I wake up, I'm lying on a bed with a cold towel on my head in a private cabin. August has his back to me, grabbing something from the counter. When he turns around, he notices that my eyes are open and rushes over.

"Gianna, seriously, we need to get you to a doctor or something. It can't be normal to have these episodes." He sits on the bed beside me, pulling my hand to his lips and kissing my fingers. I can tell he's been beside himself.

"I'm sorry. I haven't eaten since the afternoon, and everything was so overwhelming. Do you have orange juice?"

Reaching the nightstand beside me, he hands me an orange juice with a straw. The fact that he remembered what I would need when I woke up makes my stomach flutter. Mason was there to tell him what to do the last time I passed out, but this time was all him. He listened, and now he's taking care of me. I drink all my juice before he hands me a cookie.

I give him a shy smile. "Thanks."

"What exactly triggers these spells? You said it's blood-sugar-related, but just now, you said you were overwhelmed."

*Damn it.*

I hadn't meant to say those words out loud. Then, taking a breath, I remind myself, *no running*. "It's always the blood sugar that's the main cause. The rest is on me. If I don't let my blood sugar get too low, I can handle normal highs and lows associated with stress, but when I forget to eat, my body can't adapt. I'm sorry."

He leans in and kisses my cheek. "You have nothing to be sorry for. I'm just trying to understand."

*Why does he have to be so sweet, so perfect?*

"August, you live a very different life than anything I've ever experienced. I was literally homeless a few months ago. Apart from today's outfit, you're always so refined, polished, and cultivated, and I forgot about that other side of you for a moment. Let's just say, stepping on this plane reminded me quickly how unsophisticated I am."

His eyes frantically search mine before he takes my face in his hands. "I don't see you as unsophisticated at all. You fit perfectly into my world because you're not from it. I want real, genuine, and authentic. You are all the things that can't be bought. Every man at that fundraiser wanted you on their arm and not just because you're gorgeous on the outside. You are beautiful from the inside out, not tainted by greed, materialism, or envy. I don't plan on giving up my money. I rather enjoy having it, but if wearing sweatpants every day makes you feel comfortable and happy, I'll gladly do it. I won't let anything keep me from having all I ever wanted."

I swear my ovaries are weeping right now. August is searching my face for a reaction, but all I can do is stare at every flawless feature on his. His hair is messy and unkempt, yet sexy as hell, which is absurdly frustrating. The facial hair that I'm sure isn't being purposefully grown only makes him more handsome, if possible. Then to top it off, his hopeful hazel eyes are locked on mine, patiently waiting to see how his confession affects me.

Reaching up, I grab the neck of his hoodie and pull him in to kiss me because there are no words that can express how I feel. When our lips collide and my tongue swipes up against his, I'm falling, and I don't care if I ever get back up. I've never had someone want me with as much passion and desire as August.

Breaking our kiss, I grab his chin to keep him from pulling away. "Let me show you how much you mean to me."

He closes his eyes, our lips centimeters apart. "Baby, I want that so much. You have no idea, but I need to let the pilots know we're ready to take off."

"Oh, I didn't realize we hadn't taken off." I flush with embarrassment at the fact everyone is waiting on me.

"Hey, don't be embarrassed. When you passed out, I told the crew we couldn't leave until I knew you were okay. I wasn't going to be stuck in the air with a medical emergency."

I nod and let him leave. Once he's gone, I take a minute to look around, and that's when I spot a charcuterie board on the table by the window. I quickly walk over and start shoveling the delicious meats and cheeses into my mouth before looking for a bathroom. I need to freshen up. I'm sure I look like hell after being on the beach all day and then passing out.

Looking over my shoulder, I notice a small door on the other side of the bed and figure that must be it. When I open it, I'm shocked to find an actual full-sized bathroom. I was totally expecting the standard closet-sized bathroom that commercial planes have. Looking in the mirror, I notice my hair is an absolute disaster from blowing in the wind all day, my skin is heated from the sun, and my mascara is smudged. I grab a towel and quickly wash my face. As much as I want makeup on while trying to seduce my man, there's no salvaging what's left. The cool water on my face feels so refreshing. It's been a long day, and I didn't realize how drained I was. Once I finish with my face, I re-dampen the towel and start running it over my arms, stomach, and down my legs to wake me up.

My whole body breaks out in goose bumps from the chill, but before I can stand back up, August clutches me by my hips and thrusts his erection against my ass. When I stand up, his hands caress my stomach before sliding up my abdomen and seizing my tits in his greedy hands. When I look in the mirror and catch sight of him behind me, squeezing my breasts, kissing my neck, and worshipping my body like I'm a fucking goddess, I almost come on the spot from the visual.

His eyes meet mine in the mirror, and he whispers into my neck, "See how good we look together, baby?"

I nod in agreement, and he smiles.

"Do you like watching me touch you?"

I swallow what little saliva I have left in my mouth and nod again. That's when he releases one of my breasts to pull the swimsuit ties at my neck and back. My breasts are now entirely bared to him, my nipples fully erect and begging for his touch.

Placing a kiss on my shoulder, he drags his fingers down my back before coming around to my front and dropping to his knees. My eyes are glued to the mirror as I watch him trail kisses down my stomach before unbuttoning my jean skirt and pulling it down my legs. I'm now standing in nothing but my bikini bottoms. My breasts are heavy, my core is throbbing, and I'm aching for release. I've practically been begging for it since I touched him on the beach earlier. If I'm honest, I've been craving it all week. I've missed the way he makes me feel, how he looks at me, and the tenderness in his touch. That's when it hits me—he's stopped touching me. Dragging my eyes away from the mirror, I look down and find him sitting on his haunches, smiling up at me with amusement.

Then I'm mad. He's supposed to be touching me. "What could possibly be funny at this moment?" I stomp my foot, and he laughs. That's it. "August, I'm not in the mood for this right now." I turn and walk out of the bathroom, throw myself onto the bed, and pull a pillow over my exposed breasts.

He's out there in a second flat, wearing a scowl. "Gianna, you know I don't like it when you run from me."

Shooting him a dirty look, I reach for another pillow and throw it over my face. I don't want to look at him. In the next breath, he's straddling me and throwing the pillows off me. I know he wants an explanation. Closing my eyes, I say, "I thought you wanted me, but you were just teasing me. You knew that was a new experience for me, and you had to make fun of me. It's frustrating how none of this is new for you."

That's when I feel him get off me, which again wasn't what I was expecting. I thought maybe he'd kiss me and apologize for laughing at me while I was ready to let him ravish me.

"Gianna, open your eyes," he orders, leaving no room for argument.

When I do, I see he has removed his hoodie and is now pulling down his sweatpants. His massive erection almost reaches his belly button, and damn it, I want it so bad.

"Does this look like I didn't want you as much as you wanted me?"

I close my eyes again. It still doesn't explain why he laughed. Now he's on top of me again, sweetly cradling my head between his forearms, holding himself above me, kissing my forehead, cheeks, and nose.

"I was smiling because you were standing in front of me, wanton with lust over the way I was touching you. I had the hottest girl I've ever seen before me, wearing nothing but bikini bottoms, looking like a fucking present for me to unwrap. All I had to do was pull a string, and I'd be in heaven."

When I open my eyes, his lips are a hairsbreadth away from mine, and I crash my mouth to his, plunging my tongue deep, wanting to get as close to him as possible. My body is ablaze with the desire to have this man inside me. Finally, I push him off me, and his eyes widen in surprise. For a second, he probably thinks he fucked up again—but he didn't. That's when I stand up, untie my bikini bottoms, and watch as his expression softens. He doesn't take his eyes off me as I climb up his body and align my soaked core with his cock. As much as I want to take him inside of me, I also want to tease him as he did me.

Lowering myself down on top of him, I let my wet lips glide over his length, stroking him without taking him in. Ever so slowly, I start rocking against him, creating a delicious rhythm that hits my clit at just the right angle. Looking down, I find his hooded gaze on me, his plump lips parted in ecstasy, and I need a taste. Leaning down to take his mouth, my nipples brush against his chest, causing me to let out a deep moan. When my lips meet his, I'm too lost in the delicious sensations taking over my body to move my mouth.

"Christ, this is how you want me? You don't want my cock buried deep inside that warm pussy, stretching you, filling you?"

That dirty talk is all it takes to send me over the edge. I shamelessly continue riding out the throes of my orgasm until he flips me onto my back, lifts one leg around his waist, and slides home in one thrust. We both let out an audible gasp, and he stills, letting my body adjust to his size. Bringing his lips down to mine, he slowly kisses me before gradually pumping into me. Everything feels so good. I don't want this moment to ever end. His cock hits that spot deep inside of me repeatedly as his lips leave mine to trail kisses down my jaw. When he starts to suck on the spot below my ear that drives me crazy, I begin to spiral. One of his hands slowly starts kneading my breast and tweaking my nipple, sending delicious tendrils of pleasure straight to my pussy, making me clench.

I'm about to come, but I want him to come with me, so I say, "Baby, I'm so close."

Suddenly, he pauses and pulls his face away from my neck to look at me. I notice his expression is cautious.

"You just called me baby."

Furrowing my brow, not understanding this sudden line of questioning in the middle of sex, I'm left speechless.

"You've never called me anything but August."

I hadn't realized this, but I haven't. August means so much to me now that it is hard to contemplate that there was a time when he didn't, and maybe that's because there never truly was. "I can pick a different name if you don't like it." I rock my hips into him to remind him to keep moving.

He half-smiles and thrusts in deep. "You know I more than like it. You are the only one I've ever gone bare with. This is everything to me, Gigi. You are everything."

I wrap my legs around his waist to hold him deep and kiss him with all I have, using my body to show him what my heart feels. I love August, but I can't say that out loud. It's too soon, and I don't want to scare him away. But knowing I'm the only one who has ever had him bare feels intimate. It's like he's giving me a part of himself that he never trusted anyone else with. I love knowing I'm the first to have him this way. Bringing his forehead to mine, he keeps his eyes on me as he strokes that delicious spot deep inside me over and over. As his eyes stay pinned on mine, I can't help but feel like maybe we share the same truth. It's not long before I feel myself squeezing him and contracting around his length, and we both find our release.

Falling on top of me, he buries his face in my neck as I lightly trail my fingers up and down his back before wrapping my legs around him. I'm not ready for him to pull out. I don't want to lose the feel of his body pressed against mine, the warmth from his touch, or the completeness I feel with him inside me. My fingers continue their lazy exploration of his back as his breathing steadies and my eyes become heavy. It's only seconds before sleep takes us both.

\*\*\*

The sound of a phone ringing wakes me. Out of habit, I roll toward the nightstand to silence the noise. When my palm hits the cold surface of the side table, my eyes shoot open, and I remember I don't have a phone and I'm not in my own bed. I'm still on the plane, sleeping butt-naked with August.

He must be extremely exhausted because he doesn't even stir. The phone is on the table across the room, so I get up, hoping to silence it before it wakes August. I want him to get some rest, but when I see it's Mason, I can't help but answer.

*Why is Mason calling August?*

"Mason?" I answer with an unnatural pitch to my voice.

"Hey, Gigi." His voice sounds exasperated.

"Why are you calling August?"

He lets out a long sigh. "What do you mean? Have the two of you not talked about anything that has happened while you were away?"

*Shit,* I should have seen that coming. I really don't know what to say. I'm sure as hell not going to say I've been a little occupied sucking his dick and riding it to ask what the hell has been going on. God, I'm such a bitch. Instead, I opt for a clipped, "No."

"Well, are you guys going to deplane anytime soon? I've been out here for ten minutes."

*Oh my gosh, we've landed. We're home.*

"You're here on the tarmac?"

"Yes, Gigi, I'm here. Now hurry up and get out here."

"Okay, see you in a minute."

Running around the cabin, I search for my discarded clothes. I really should have been more responsible and asked the important questions. Getting kidnapped and told you can't have contact with anyone back home is a big deal. This entire situation is serious. Every time I'm around August, this happens. My judgment gets clouded, and I do things completely out of character. Maybe things will change now that we are officially a couple. I had no idea Mason would be here when I got off the plane. In fact, now that I'm thinking about it, why didn't he come to get me in the first place? Now that I'm dressed, I lean over, run my fingers through August's silky hair, and kiss his cheek.

"Wake up, baby. We've landed."

He starts to stir, and I place a kiss on his lips.

"We've landed. Get dressed." When I go to pull away, he clasps my wrist.

"Where are you running off to? I want more of those."

I smile down at him. He's so damn sexy, especially when lying naked in a bed that he just thoroughly fucked me in. I place a quick kiss on his lips before slipping my hand out of his grip.

"Mason just called. He's outside waiting. Get dressed, and I'll meet you outside."

His eyes go wide. "What do you mean he's outside?"

Turning, I start walking toward the door. "I mean, he's outside on the tarmac. I'm going to go say hi."

I'm already through the main cabin when he calls out, "Gianna, wait."

I hear what sounds like him rolling off the bed, no doubt hastily fumbling around, looking for his clothes to catch up with me, but I want a second alone when I see Mason, so I don't wait. The last time I saw Mason, he was lying in a hospital bed, telling me he still wanted everything. I know I don't have time to tell him how I feel, but I at least want to walk off this plane alone and not rub it in his face that I'm with August.

When I reach the stairs to exit the plane, he's leaning against the side of a blacked-out Tahoe. My heart stumbles the moment his eyes meet mine. *Why does he have to be so fine?* Those damn blue eyes get me every time. Not to mention his swagger. The man is always dressed in joggers and tight-fitted T-shirts that show off every toned muscle of his fit physique. These thoughts will get me nowhere. I made my choice, and it's not him. I close my eyes to tear myself out of my lustful haze before descending the stairs. I've made my bed, now I must lie in it.

"Hey, Gigi, I'm so sorry about everything. I hope you can forgive me for sending you away like that. I asked you if you trusted me before you left my room, and a part of me feels like I may have betrayed that with the actions that followed."

I can see in his eyes that he genuinely regrets how he handled things, but when it's all said and done, he was trying to look out for me. Throwing my arms around his neck, I hug him tight. He's hesitant but eventually loops his arms around my waist and hugs me back. *Why did he hesitate?*

"Thank you," I mumble into his neck. His breath catches, but before he can respond, we're interrupted.

"Croft, I'm going to have to ask you to stop touching my girl. She made her choice."

Mason takes a deep breath before he releases me, and I swing around to face August. I swear I'm going to punch him in the throat. Did he really have to say that now, of all the times? Before I can react, he's by my side with his arm wrapped around my waist, squeezing my bare hip and pulling me into his side.

"What's so important that you needed to meet us at the airstrip?"

Mason's gaze is focused on the hand August has on my hip, and I see him set his jaw. He's mad and hurt, but there's something else there that I can't quite place. I try to pull out of August's grip, but he only tightens his hold. Mason pulls his gaze from my hip up to my eyes, and I swear I see actual pain. Something is very wrong.

"Mason, what's going on? You know I can see it. What aren't you telling me?"

He searches my face, for what, I don't know, before dropping his eyes to the ground. "There's been an accident."

August tightens his grip on me and protectively pulls me to his front, wrapping his arms around me.

"Mason, what do you mean? Who's been in an accident?" I ask.

"Gigi, I'm so sorry, but your dad is dead."

It takes a moment for those words to register and truly sink in. A normal person would be consumed with pain and grief, but I don't feel anything. *Why don't I feel anything? What is wrong with me? I'm just staring back at him, watching his lips move but hearing no words.* That's when August ushers us into the SUV.

"Let's go. We need to get out of here." He puts his hand on my lower back and guides me toward the car. Once I'm in, he fastens my seat belt before entering the driver's seat. Mason climbs in the back, and we take off.

"Why the fuck didn't you tell her what happened over the past week?"

When I glance at August, he tightens his grip on the steering wheel and rolls his lips. He's mad, but I don't think he's mad at Mason. He's angry at himself for the same reason I'm annoyed with myself. We both chose to prioritize each other over the circumstances. He's not holding his tongue for Mason's sake. He's doing it because he blames himself. I know this because I feel the same guilt for not asking questions. As much as I want to reach across the armrest, hold his hand, and comfort him, I can't bring myself to move. I feel completely numb. *What was the point of the past week? All the stress, worry, and pain were for nothing.*

"Mason, can you tell me?"

August shakes his head before turning toward me, his eyes filled with sadness and regret.

"Just tell me, please." I look out the passenger side window, not wanting to see anyone or feel anything.

"God, Gigi, I don't even know where to start."

August reaches over to take my hand, and I let him. Mason must see the gesture because there's a pregnant pause before he clears his throat and continues.

"August has been held hostage for the past week at the Bradbury Estate by Ethan and Carson."

My head snaps to August in shock, but he doesn't meet my gaze. Instead, he keeps his eyes fixed on the road. I know he can feel my stare, but he doesn't acknowledge it, so I return my focus to the window. Being held hostage seems like a big deal to me, so the fact that he didn't tell me means he doesn't want to talk about it.

"He escaped this afternoon. There was an accident, and Carson died."

My head swings back around to look at him, and still, he gives me nothing, eyes forward, glued to the road. I can't believe what I'm hearing.

August was held hostage up until this afternoon, by his girlfriend since high school, who is now dead. I want details, but I'll wait until he's ready to tell me. "August, you came straight to Florida to get me?"

Still, he doesn't give me his eyes. My question only earns me a brush of his thumb over mine before he squeezes my hand tighter. The car stays silent for a beat before Mason clears his throat and picks up where he left off.

"I had been surveilling the place all week, trying to figure out how you were tied into all this, and all I could come up with is that they were trying to keep you and August apart for a reason. That's when I knew I needed to get to August and figure out how your past might be tied to what's happening now. When I showed up, he had already been working on escaping."

Mason takes a noticeable deep breath, and August flicks his eyes up to the rearview mirror. I can tell they're communicating something they don't want me to know. I'm so done with the secrets and half-truths I could scream. August has always been honest with me, even to his own detriment. Sure, he has been crude and demanding, but that's how I knew he wasn't walking on eggshells to protect my feelings. That told me he thought I was strong, that he knew I could handle it, and tough shit if I couldn't. *So what's changed?* Fuck this. I'm not playing games. My dad is dead. I drop his hand right before he glares at me.

"Don't give me that look. I saw what just happened between the two of you. I thought we were done keeping secrets from each other. You can't ask me not to hide, only for you to go and do it."

He shakes his head and sets his jaw. "Gianna, that look had nothing to do with me keeping anything from you. We told you Carson died today. I also escaped today. Do you think those two things are not related?"

Keeping my eyes pinned on him, I let his words sink in. Carson is dead, and he and Mason were there when it happened. When I glance back at Mason, his eyes are pinned to the back of August's head with a blank stare. The details I thought I wanted suddenly don't interest me. Whatever happened at Carson's house is undoubtedly still raw, and I'm not sure they have had time to process it. This is something I don't need to know, at least not right now anyway. I nod in understanding and return my gaze out the window. After a few minutes, Mason continues.

"We returned to my place, where I gave August a CliffsNotes version of your past. That's when we found the connection. Your dad used to play golf with Eduard Haas and Robert Grand back in the day. Remember how you told me your grandparents left him money after they died, but he squandered it? Well, it turns out he bought stock in Suncast Media, which originally returned no profits, but over the years, Robert rebranded it and grew it into a multimillion-dollar company now known as Grand Media. Your father owned forty percent stock in Suncast Media. The shares he owned are now worth nearly five hundred million dollars. Clearly, your dad had no idea that he still held stock. Robert and Eduard were the only other investors, and it's obvious that they intentionally kept him in the dark. After some more digging, I discovered their plan to forge a transfer of ownership from your dad to themselves and claim all the capital gains when the company goes public."

I hear Mason take a deep breath, and I know he's rubbing his forehead without even looking at him. He does it whenever he is nervous, stressed, or deep in thought. It's his tic, but it's also his tell. That head rub means he cares that he's focused on what you're saying, you have his attention, and he's trying to fix it, and God, if that doesn't pull at my heartstrings. The man I've been infatuated with for the past nine years, my best friend and confidant, just spent the past week going to bat for me once again. I want to crawl into the back seat and curl into him as I've always done. To rest my head on his chest and breathe him in. In choosing August, I am losing my best friend. Mason and I will never be what we were, and it fucking hurts, but I also can't imagine walking away from the man sitting next to me.

Bringing my hands to my temples, I start rubbing slow, methodical circles, trying to stave off the headache I'm getting from all this never-ending drama that is my life. I can never catch a fucking break. Blowing out a breath, I refocus my thoughts before asking, "You believe they killed my dad?" The car was already silent, but now it seemed everyone was holding their breath. Neither one of them wants to acknowledge my question, either because they don't know the answer or they don't know how I'm going to react. Finally, turning around, I look Mason dead in the eye. "Tell me."

If his eyes could speak for him, I know what they'd say. He feels sorry for me, and he wants to fix it, but you can't bring someone back from the grave.

"He was found in his car, unresponsive from an apparent drug overdose, outside the Grand Media development." That's where Dad was working.

"Why did you call it an accident?"

He looks out the window as if choosing his following words wisely. "I think we both know why I called it an accident."

That's when it hits me. Ethan threatened my dad's job if I didn't go to the fundraiser with him, and he specifically told me not to mention anything to August. I said all this to Mason before I left for the fundraiser. It wasn't an accident at all. It was murder. He was set up.

"I should have never left Ethan's side the night of the fundraiser. I should have just sucked it up until he was ready to leave, but I was so mad. I just needed to breathe."

"Why would you say that? There was no way I was letting you leave with him," August chimes in.

"He's right, Gigi. Leaving with him wouldn't have been a better choice."

"You guys don't know that. He specifically told me not to tell August about our date, or he would basically make sure my dad would be unemployed. Since August was pounding his face in by the night's end, I guess he thought death was a more fitting punishment." Putting my head in my hands, I take deep breaths, trying to calm the anxiety threatening to swallow me whole. While I'm still not sad, I'm upset that I'm the reason for his death.

August hits the steering wheel. "Gianna, if this is anyone's fault, it's mine. I pursued you, not the other way around. You can't blame yourself for your dad's death. Ethan is not going to get away with this."

The car suddenly comes to a stop. When I sit up, I notice we're at August's cabin. I turn to him in utter disbelief. This is the last place I need to be right now.

"August, why are we here? I need to be with my mom and Elio. I haven't spoken to them for a week, and now my dad is dead. What do they think happened to me?" Reaching across the center console, August attempts to hold my hand, but I jerk it back. I'm tired of these men pushing me into doing what they think is best and filling me in on the details after the fact. His eyes frustratedly hold mine for a beat before he answers my question.

"You know this is my safe house. Ethan has been looking for you since you disappeared last week. Armed security is on its way to watch the perimeter. You can't leave."

"But what about my mom and Elio? They're not safe either."

Before he can respond, Mason breaks in. "Your mom doesn't know that your dad is dead. I only heard it through the police scanners, which I monitored due to the Carson incident. She is also unaware that I woke up from my coma. I stole your phone before you left and have been texting her with false updates. She thinks you've been by my side this entire time. As soon as I heard the news about your dad, I knew they were making their move, so I texted her on your phone, asking if she could come to help prepare the apartment for my arrival. August hired a guy to watch them before he took off for Florida. Once I get back home, I'm going to fill them in."

I can't help but be somewhat shocked at Mason's well-thought-out plan. I might be a little creeped out if I didn't know Mason's true character and intent. However, he should know better than to rely on my mother for anything. That's the one plot hole in his plan.

"Did you offer to pay her for her help?" The words are out of my mouth before I can filter them. My mom doesn't do anything for me out of the kindness of her heart. She always expects something from me in return. August turns to look at me, dumbfounded by my response.

Mason squeezes my shoulder from the back seat. "I didn't, but she agreed to come anyway."

This can't be happening. I hurriedly jump out of the car and start pacing, unsure what to do next. August and Mason are quick to follow, but they hang back, giving me the space I need to process. But I don't need any more time to process it. This is all my mess, not theirs. My family is beyond fucked up, but I don't need saving from them. I've handled them for the past eighteen years. What are a few more?

"Mason, I'm going with you. If there's an armed guard there anyway, what's the harm?"

"Gigi, they think you and I ran off together over a week ago. I can't hide anymore because I need to keep hacking, but you need to stay out of sight. Babe, you were left as the sole beneficiary. The target on your back is huge. It's not worth the risk."

I'm so mad I could cry. "I don't care about the money, Mason. I've never had money. I can't miss what I've never had. They can have it all. I don't want it."

August comes over and wraps his arms around me. "Gianna, we know it's not about the money, but it's too late to just give it up. They've already taken things past the point of no return. I was held hostage, and there's reason to believe your dad didn't overdose. You can't just walk away now. They will come for you no matter what. Now we must play the game."

That's where he is wrong. *We* don't have to play the game. I need to play the game. I'm done with having men feel like they need to fight my battles. I don't know what happened today or how Carson met her end, but I hate that it could have been at the hands of a man I love. My family has been fighting demons my whole life, and that's one thing I'm good at.

Pushing out of August's arms, I run around to the driver's side of the Tahoe, climb in, and lock the doors. This is something I need to do on my own. I'm looking for the keys when I spot them in the center console. When I turn the key in the ignition, I'll be damned if The Verve Pipe's "Freshman" isn't playing on the radio. *What kind of serendipitous hell have I gotten myself into?*

I'm about to put the car in drive when August starts banging on the window.

"Baby, please don't do this. We already know we're stronger together. They win when we're apart. I lose you every time, and they get the upper hand. Stay with me. You can make the calls. I promise, no secrets."

When I look up, his forehead is against the window, fists clenched on either side, his eyes are downcast, and his chest is heaving. I can see his pain. His words hit me then, "they win when we're apart" because our love makes us weak. They've wanted to keep us apart from day one, and if I leave right now, whatever they've got planned just got that much easier. While being deeply loved by someone can give you strength, it can also be your greatest weakness, especially when you're apart and people use that love against you. While August and I haven't expressed that we love each other, there's no denying the deep, soul-penetrating connection we share.

Mason is a few feet behind August, standing with his hands in his pockets, eyes locked on me, almost like he knows what my next move will be. It's as if he's already seen this play out, and maybe he has before. Mason is expecting me to run. That's why he's not trying to stop me. The lyrics of the song ring out, and I hear the parts of the song Mason omitted. While he may have likened the lyrics to us being young and needing time to grow, the more relatable lyric may have been my inability to take advice. I did things my way and for good reason.

Looking back, that's what I did. I didn't physically run, but I built up my walls and shut people out. I thought I was broken back then, but now I know that was never really true. Was I fractured? Maybe. Damaged? Sure...but I was always whole. Even in my darkest despair, I never gave up hope that I could make things different for myself. If I persevered, I could rise above my circumstances and live the life I wanted. I ran to Mason for comfort, not because I needed him to fix me. There was no advice that he could ever give me that I would have listened to. I was with him because I'd found someone like me in him. Someone who was lost, alone, and searching for more.

As more lyrics ring out, my heart breaks all at once because I realize all this is my fault. I fell in love with Mason first. He never wanted this moment right here to happen. But I was always there chasing his love. All this time, I thought I had to earn his love to prove to him that loving me would be worth it, but he was there loving me all along. Maybe it was the right love, but now it's the wrong time—either way, it was love all the same, and I didn't treat it right.

It may be too late for Mason and me, but I won't make the same mistakes with August. If I want him, I need to let him try. I need to let him in, even though it scares me, even though I might get hurt. Looking back at August, I see his eyes are on mine, but he's not mad. It's like he fully understands why I want to run, and right now, I don't think he'd blame me if I did, but his eyes are begging me not to. That's when I hit the unlock button on the doors. His eyes dart to the lock before he bolts to my side of the car, flings my door open, and pulls me into his arms.

"Don't ever do that to me again, baby. Please don't ever run from me."

As he holds me tighter than I think anyone ever has, I can feel his heart pounding, and I know I made the right choice. August would fight regardless of whether I ran or wanted his help because that's what he's always done. Since the first day we met, he's fought for me. He fought for me even when he wasn't sure he wanted to, and now it's my turn to fight for him. That must start with me letting him in. If I want to keep him, I can't push him away.

Mason comes around the car. "I need to get back to my place to meet up with your mom and brother." His tone is short and clipped.

"August, can you give me a minute alone with Mason? I promise I won't run." I can tell by the tension in the arm he still has around my waist that he's not happy with my request, but he kisses the top of my forehead and lets me go. That's why I couldn't help but fall in love with him. August is possessive and demanding when he wants to be, but for me, he yields. While he wants to consume me, he also wants me to choose him and desire him because it's what I want and not what he's demanded.

When Mason got in his accident, August walked away simply because I asked it of him. At the time, I assumed he had given up, that what I thought we shared wasn't as potent for him as it was for me, but I couldn't have been more wrong. He was taking my lead, giving me what I needed, and trusting that I would return to him. August is so much more than I ever expected him to be. He surprises me at every turn. August doesn't fit into any of the boxes I've constructed over the years, and maybe that's because I'm not used to people proving me wrong, but I think more than anything, it's because I've never had anyone want to be my everything.

## TWENTY-SEVEN
### Mason

I'm sitting in the driver's seat, one leg in the car and one out. Gigi wants to talk. The thing is, we don't have anything to talk about. She made her choice, and it's not me. I won't grovel at her feet and beg her to choose me. I've kind of already done that more than once. What I am done with is playing nice. She wants truths. Well, I have plenty.

"Mace, look, I'm sorry. I never meant for any of this to happen. Everything has happened so fast, and you're the last person I want to get hurt because of my shit life." She drops her head down and fiddles with her fingers.

"Gigi, that's a bunch of crap, and you know it. None of this would be happening if you had just chosen me. You would be going home with me to see your family right now. Your dad would still be alive."

Her head snaps up, and her bottom lip trembles as she fights to contain the tears welling up in her eyes. I know that was a low blow, but it's the truth, and I'm not leaving anything unsaid. "They've been after my family all along, Mason. How is that fair to say?"

That's the thing about truths. We don't always like hearing them; sometimes they hurt like hell. I shake my head and look out the window. I don't want to tear her down like this. I fucking hate this, but I want her to see what she's done. Ever since I've known Gigi, I've always wanted to rescue her, protect her, and make everything better. Somewhere along the line, I got lost in that desire. It consumed me. We were both broken in different ways, both searching for something, so when we felt like we had nothing, together we had everything. We could have had everything, but she chose wrong.

"You chose wrong, Gigi. Bottom line. The reason they came after you was because August took notice of you. They knew they had to keep the two of you apart so their scheme would go undetected. Clearly, they've been watching you for years, making sure your parents were high enough that they never realized their money was there all along. If you had chosen me, your dad would still be alive. Do you know why? Because there would have been no chance of anyone unveiling their plan, but you just couldn't stay away from him. You could have been blissfully unaware that your dad was ever robbed, that those men were ever after you, and that you had money."

The more I talk, the angrier I get. I slam my fists on the steering wheel. "Why can't you get it right just this once!"

I catch her startle out of my peripheral from my outburst. Clearing her throat, I know she's about to speak, so I turn my attention to her. She steels her spine when she notices I'm now looking at her. The tears she was holding back have now been released, and I can see she's mad, but I know it's more than that. She's hurt that I'd say those things to her because I never spoke to her that way growing up.

Gianna would lay her problems at my feet, but I was nonconfrontational. I didn't want her to hurt, so I made her feel good. I'd hold her until she stopped crying and kiss her until she stopped thinking. Now that I'm looking at her, knowing I'm the one who caused the pain, I want to take it all back, but I won't. She tries to sound unaffected when she speaks, but her words are meek at best.

"Mason, this right now is bullshit. Yes, I've made a mess of things, but you haven't been completely innocent in all this yourself. You know I always loved you, and you took your sweet time coming around, didn't you? It's interesting how you never wanted anything more from me until you felt like someone else might actually get what you thought belonged to you. What you thought would always be waiting. If you thought I didn't notice your odd timing of professing your love for me, you're wrong. You and I both know that wasn't fair."

She's not wrong. All along, I've known what I was doing. I was trying to keep her from August and win her back. I knew he meant more, and I didn't like that I was losing her, but that didn't mean I didn't love or want her. I've already started this tangent, so I will finish it. May as well get all the breaking done at once. I don't care to ever have this conversation again.

"You want to talk about fair, Gigi? Was it fair when you kissed me for the first time, hoping for it to change our relationship? Was it fair that we never got serious about anyone else because, in the end, we always came back to each other? Was it fair that you claimed to be mine all this time, but I never really had you?" That last line was a knife to the heart because it's the fucking gut-wrenching truth.

"The thing about me and you is that you always liked to play the innocent card, Gigi. You liked to think I was this pillar of strength for you, but you know in your heart that's not true. You just didn't want to see it. Our story worked best when you were chasing me, believing I was pushing you away, but if you truly looked, I never once pushed you away. You knew I was just as broken as you, and that's why we fit so well. You let me inside, you let me get close, and together, we got lost."

"I can't believe you'd say that. You're right. You may never have pushed me away, Mace, but I didn't see you pulling me closer either."

Her words cut deep because they're true, and I know they'll fester inside of me and rot a hole in my chest where my heart used to be. When I glance over at her standing in the driveway in her swimsuit and jean skirt, shivering with a tear-soaked face, I hate myself. We did this to ourselves.

"This is the last time, Gianna. I'm seeing this through, and then I'm out."

I don't give her time to respond before closing the door and driving off. Finding the words in my heart and saying them out loud made me realize I couldn't blame everything on her. None of our stories are fair, but that's love. It's messy; sometimes, we're not meant to be with the people we love. Now I have to find a way to make peace with losing the only happiness I ever had and move forward now that she's gone. I let her slip through my fingertips, and I only have myself to blame for that.

## TWENTY-EIGHT
### *August*

As much as I wanted to give them privacy, I couldn't. The minute I got in the house, I headed straight to my office and pulled up the security footage to listen. They have history, a past, and as much as I hate it, I know she cares for him, and that's precisely why I'm listening. *Does he still have her heart?* I watch Mason slam the door on the SUV and pull off, and I'm about to go outside and get my girl and comfort her, but I don't. Instead, I watch as she stands glued to her spot, frozen in place. Her only movement comes from the tilt of her head when she looks toward the sky to gaze at the stars. Watching her stand there in the dark, I can't help but wonder if her thoughts are of him. *Does she believe Mason was right when he said she chose wrong? Does she want to go after him?* I'm not insecure, but the thought of her leaving me strikes a chord, one I was unaware existed, and now I need a drink.

Standing in the kitchen, I'm pouring myself a glass of wine when I hear the front door open. We've had an incredibly long day, it's just past midnight, and she's still in her swimsuit. There's still much to discuss before we go to bed, but she needs a shower. Fuck, I need a shower, but I want to take care of her. I may have been through a lot this week, but she just found out she lost a parent and maybe something more. Taking a sip of my wine, I watch as she enters the front door and aimlessly walks over to the kitchen island, looking dejected and tired. I want nothing more than to pull her into my arms and hold her, but that never ends well for us. No words are ever had.

"Baby, I know we have so much to talk about, but why don't you go take a shower and unwind for a minute? I'll put something on the bed for you to wear when you get out."

Surprisingly, she doesn't argue. She just nods. She turns around and pauses. That's when I remember the last time we were here, she only saw this room. Gianna has no idea where the master is.

"It's the hallway off the office, straight back on your right."

Again, no words. Instead, she starts heading the way I instructed. I still can't tell where her head is. I'm sure most of it is shock, but Gianna has never ceased to amaze me. There's a reason I was stunned when I found out her age. She doesn't carry herself the way a typical eighteen-year-old would. Gianna's life experiences from her youth have matured her years beyond her age. The roles are suddenly flipped again, and this woman has made me feel less than sufficient simply by being strong. I'm struggling not to be insensitive and tactless, but I can't help but feel insecure because, while she may not see it in herself, it's written all over her identity. She doesn't need a man; any man who's in her life will be there because she wants him to be and not the other way around. I want to be that man.

Once I hear the shower turn on, I head down the hall and into the master bedroom. In the closet, I grab one of my T-shirts and a pair of boxers for her to change into. After laying them on the bed, I send a quick text to my personal shopper to have clothes brought over first thing in the morning for her. Exiting the master, I decide to call Mason before Gigi gets out of the shower. The fucker didn't have to talk to her like that tonight of all nights.

When I return to the great room, I head over to my bar to grab something more potent than wine and pour myself three fingers of bourbon. Before putting the cap on, I take a pull straight from the bottle for good measure. Then, picking up my glass, I grab my phone off the kitchen island and head over to the wall of windows. The view of the Ozark Mountains never gets old. It has a way of grounding you and putting everything in perspective, which I need before making this call. The phone rings once before Mason answers.

"What do you want, August?"

Is this guy serious right now? I'm not even going to bite because I know he's been through hell and back tonight. He's had a decade to love Gianna, I've had a month, and I couldn't imagine the torture he must be enduring at this moment. That being said, he didn't have to be an ass.

"You know tonight wasn't the night to unload on her."

"Is that what you called me about, August? To lecture me on how I should handle Gigi?"

"No, Mason, it's not. However, it took a great deal of restraint for me not to come out there and kick your ass. You will not speak to her like that ever again. I'm giving you a pass tonight. It's been a long week and an even longer day. I know you're going through some shit, but you will show her some respect."

I can hear him take a deep breath. He's clearly biting his tongue, but as long as we are clear, that's all I care about. I'm about to ask about Gianna's family when I decide he needs to hear one last piece of my mind.

"Mason, today was not your fault. You can't blame yourself for Carson's death. I saw the look on your face when you watched her fall to her death. If you need someone to blame, let it be me. I chased her. I put the fear in her. She was trying to escape me. You were simply in the wrong place at the wrong time."

Again, silence. I check the phone to make sure he didn't hang up on me. He didn't. That's when I realize it's quiet, too quiet. The shower is no longer running, and a reflection in the window catches my eye.

Gianna is standing at the entrance to the great room, and I'm pretty sure she just heard everything. I would have told her eventually, but it's not something I would have shared tonight. She has been through enough today. This conversation didn't need to happen, but I'm glad she knows. There's more I want to say to Mason, so I don't acknowledge that I know she's there. I promised her no secrets when I asked her not to run, and I plan on keeping my word. She's worth whatever fallout I must live through as long as she's by my side.

"I think I have a plan to take down Ethan, but I need to know if you have all the evidence backed up and verified on Robert and Eduard? We need a paper trail, and we need it by morning. Do you think you can have all that squared away?"

"Yeah, that's not going to be a problem." He's clipped and terse. This conversation has gone as far as it's going to go. That's when I feel Gianna's hand on my shoulder. She gestures for me to hand her the phone, and my heart sinks. I reluctantly hand it over and walk away to give her some space.

Walking over to the living area, I sit on the couch before I hear her ask, "Mason, have you told my mom?"

God, I'm such a selfish dick. I thought she wanted to talk to Mason because she already regretted choosing me. No, she wants to ask about her family. Of course that's what this is about. Fuck, I need to get my shit together. I have never been so insecure, and I hate it. This isn't me. I get what I want, and if I don't, I take it. That's how things started with us. She pushed, and I pulled because she'd be mine no matter what, but now I find myself conceding to her every request.

I've just sat down on my leather sectional facing the main window wall, bourbon in hand, when I hear her ask, "Can you put my mom on the phone?"

I study her body language. She's tense, and her body is clearly riddled with stress and anxiety. If the conversation I overheard her have with Mason is anything to go on, I imagine she's also feeling pretty lonely since the one person she used to run to isn't here.

"Okay, thanks, Mace. Thanks for everything." Her voice sounds weak and defeated, but I can tell she's trying to force warmth and gratitude into it all the same.

She stands there looking out the window after hanging up, lost in thought. I'm about to ask why Mason didn't let her talk to her mom, but then she turns around, and when her eyes meet mine, I can't help but take a moment to admire her.

In front of me stands a strong woman who has pushed aside her insecurities, which have undoubtedly formed her into who she is today. I know choosing me meant burying the fears that held her back from putting herself first. I'm not the safe route. Unlike Mason, I'm new and untested, representing everything she swore would be her ruin.

Gianna thinks she hides it well, but it's clear her basic physiological needs were always inadequately met. The woman is beyond beautiful, but I know she struggles with eating. The few times I've seen her eat, it's always a snack, never a meal. Whether that's due to a lack of availability or self-induced due to stress, I'm not sure, but now that she's with me, that will change. Her episodes are not normal. In training, it was a granola bar for breakfast, lunches were scones, and she mostly pushed the food around her plate in the few dinners we'd shared. Since she didn't speak to her mom just now, I know her emotional needs are just as deficient. The woman is barely holding herself together.

Standing before me, wearing my T-shirt with her long hair framing her tear-soaked face, I can't help but notice how vulnerable, how bare, how exposed she is to me right now, and I'm in awe. She's choosing to give me her trust and let me take care of her when she has nothing left to offer, and I want nothing more than to be that man for her.

When she starts to walk my way, I brace myself for the hit my senses are about to take. When she's near, I can't help but smell her, feel her, taste her, but right now, I want to be the man she can confide in, the man she trusts, the man she leans on.

I set my glass down on the coffee table before settling back into a comfortable lounge position. My goal is to look approachable and open to listening. Talking hasn't been our strong suit, but I want her to feel safe and cared for. I've just outstretched my arms over the back of the couch when she throws her leg over my lap, straddling me. Before I have time to process that move, she's pressing open-mouth kisses down my neck. *Fuck.*

"Gianna, don't take this wrong, but maybe we should talk." I keep my hands on the couch because I know all hope of talking will be lost if I touch her. Any chance I had at being a better man will go to shit.

"I don't want to talk right now. I want to forget. I want the pain to stop. Please make it stop." She buries her face into my neck and then whispers in a shaky, sad voice, "Please touch me."

Bringing my arms up, I wrap them around her back and hold her. I'll keep her forever if she lets me. Every moment with her has been nothing short of genuine. I've never had a woman with whom I've felt such a soul-deep connection. She's the one real thing in my world full of fake.

"Baby, if you don't want to talk right now, that's fine, but let me take you to bed. We need to get some sleep."

She nods in agreement, and I wait for her to stand, but she doesn't. A few more seconds pass before I realize she's not going to let me go, and that thought makes me happier than it should. I should be thinking about all the other things threatening to fuck up her life, all the things I already have, but my selfish ass can only focus on how she wants me right now.

Bringing my arms down her back, I sit forward with her on my lap, readying myself to stand while holding her. When I slide my hands under her ass to lift, I discover she's not wearing my boxers. Now I'm gripping her bare ass. I take a deep breath and try to calm my racing heart. This woman unravels me. She's everything I could have asked for, and because of that, I'm taking her to bed to sleep, nothing more.

Walking down the hallway toward the master with her wrapped around me, my hands still gripping her perfectly plump, bare ass, I try to ignore my arousal. The problem is that she's making that nearly impossible, especially when she nuzzles into my neck and kisses my throat. As soon as we enter the bedroom, I quickly place her on the bed and pull the covers back for her to get under, but she stops my hand.

"August, you're already what I want. Can you please be what I need?"

Without hesitation, I answer, "Always."

The word leaves my mouth before I have time to process it because nothing has ever been truer. I would do anything for her. Releasing my hand, she says, "Please," before she slowly starts to lift her shirt off. With that, the last of my resolve is shattered. Tearing my hoodie off over my head, I throw it behind me before making my way to her on the bed. I gently push her down and settle on her before kissing her long and slow. This is a moment I want to savor because she turned to me. At this moment, she trusted me with her heart. I've never seen Gianna as anything but beautiful inside and out. I would have never known how deep her scars ran were it not for the fact I wanted her to be mine.

If kissing away the pain also kisses away the self-doubt, uncertainty, and years of mistrust, I'll gladly do it. I want her to see what I see. The strongest steel is forged by fire, and the hellfire she has endured has made her nothing short of a warrior. Trailing kisses down her neck, I make my way toward her breasts, where I take a nipple into my mouth before she arches into me, forcing more of her into my mouth. Looking up, I notice she has thrown her head back on the bed, and her eyes are closed. That just won't do.

Releasing her nipple, I say, "Baby, if you want me to keep going, I'm going to need your eyes on me. I want my girl to watch me take care of her."

What I said is only partly true. The main reason I want her eyes on me is so that she can watch me love her. Once her eyes are back on me, I swirl my tongue around her other nipple in slow, methodical circles until I feel her hips buck against me, seeking friction. Smiling against her breast, I take the bud into my mouth and suck hard. She gasps, and I release her breast with a pop before kissing my way down her stomach until I reach my desired destination. I slowly spread her thighs and place a kiss on the inside of each one before looking up and meeting her heated gaze. With my eyes locked on hers, I run my tongue right up her center.

Her eyes roll back, and she lets out a raspy, "God, yes."

Her legs tremble as I work my tongue in and out of her tight hole, and I know she's close. I add a finger and she immediately clenches around it. Sucking her clit into my mouth, I gently bite down, pushing her over the edge, screaming my name through the throes of her orgasm. I continue to pump my finger into her as she rides out the waves while I lick up her sweet juices.

When I feel her start to come down from her release, I fully intend to look up and find her lying on the bed with her eyes closed, but she's not. Her eyes are still locked on me, hooded with desire. Fuck me if that's not hot. Gianna didn't just want me to make her feel good. This beautiful woman wants me, all of me. I get to my knees, shove my sweats down, and line up my throbbing cock with her soaked pussy. When I look down, I can't help but tease her and watch as I rub my tip through her wet folds before dipping into her warm heat.

"Baby, please," she begs, and my eyes snap to hers. That term of endearment from her lips directed toward me is all it takes to make me move. I'll always give her what she asks for. Immediately, I begin to sink into her, one delicious inch at a time. Slowly pushing in and pulling out to gain more depth as she acclimates to my size. My lips hover right above hers, and our eyes are locked on each other when I fully seat myself. We both moan out our shared ecstasy at the feeling of me being buried so deep. I swear every time with her is like the first, and I have to do everything in my power to stave off my impending orgasm.

"You feel so good." The words spill from my mouth in an adulation unlike any I've ever known. This woman is my world. I've never been more sure of anything in my entire life. I lean down to kiss her, but she turns her mouth away before I can make contact. I forcefully push into her to bring her eyes back to mine, and she smiles.

"Kiss me."

She shakes her head. Searching her eyes, I try to get a read on her emotions.

*Why doesn't she want to kiss me?*

I push in hard again, and she gasps before putting her hand

on my cheek and saying, "Thank you for loving me so I could find the strength to love myself."

I pause for a second at the word love. I haven't said the words I love you, but in so many other ways, I've basically told her as much. There's no question that I do, in fact, love this woman. Age and circumstance be damned. I'm lost in her eyes when she wiggles her hips to remind me to keep moving. I pump into her in long, slow, tantalizing strokes before laying my forehead against hers. Her eyes are locked on mine, and I'm lost in an emerald abyss where I feel like I can sense her soul and all her heart. But even that feeling couldn't prepare me for the words that would come out of those pouty lips with a gasp.

"August, I love you."

Momentarily stunned, I continue slowly rocking into her as I pull my head back to refocus my eyes on hers. The way hearing those words makes my chest tighten, I can't be sure that I was genuinely living before hearing them. It's as if those words from her mouth give my life purpose. I have no words because love doesn't even begin to cover how I feel about this woman. Holding her gaze, all I can manage is, "Yeah?" It's a question, but I need confirmation that the words I heard were real. That they weren't a figment of my imagination. She nods, and I pump into her one, two, three more times as her words sink in and free me. I know she's right there with me because I feel her clench around me. Slamming in deep with one last thrust, I fill her up. With our release, I crash my lips to hers in surrender. If there was any doubt before that she was mine, there isn't now. I reluctantly pull my lips from hers and make sure her eyes are on me when I say, "I'm so in love with you, Gianna Moretti." No more words are spoken before we let sleep take us.

\* \* \*

My alarm goes off at 6:00 a.m., and I feel even more exhausted than if I had stayed awake. Sometimes it's better to stay up and push through the fatigue rather than catch a few hours of rest. To my right, Gianna is still asleep. The alarm didn't even faze her. We had a significant breakthrough in our relationship last night, and I can't help but feel that things from here on out will be different.

My ego has definitely taken a hit since I met Gianna. I've found myself questioning everything, which is truly out of character. However, you can't help but be somewhat self-conscious when you put your heart on the line, hoping the other person reciprocates. Now that we both know where we stand, I think there will be less tension outside of the fucking.

Crawling out of bed, I'm careful not to wake her. She doesn't need to get up quite yet, so I'm going to grab a quick shower and check in with Mason. When I walk into my master bath, I'm reminded of one of the reasons I love this house: it has a natural stone steam shower. I waste no time getting in. Letting the scalding hot water fall over my back, I steal a few minutes of peace before I let my mind go over the plan for the day.

During my flight to Florida, I spent most of my time planning and setting our trap. When I learned how Eduard and the Grands were tied to Gianna, I knew I needed to contact my dad's lawyer. Years ago, we had a board member embezzle money from the company and coerce other faculty and a few board members to stay quiet using fear tactics. Ultimately, he was caught and charged with embezzlement and criminal coercion, for which he did seven years.

Robert Grand and Eduard are trying to commit securities fraud, which is punishable under federal laws. If I can get the lawyer all the proof, there's no doubt in my mind that I can have an arrest made by lunch. You must act fast with this type of fraud because people like Grand will run. They have the kind of money that can make them disappear. I know that while he may run, he won't hide for long. He likes the spotlight and fame too much and always has. Money, women, and fame are too high up on his priorities list to stay in hiding. We must strike today before they have time to follow suit with their plan B.

Ethan knows Carson is dead and that I escaped. The video Mason scrubbed was flawless. He sent it to me on the plane. I'm literally seen leaving the basement and then leaving the property with no lapse in time. I have no reason to be in hiding, so I don't plan to. Over the years, we've pulled some pretty shitty pranks on each other. One time we left Grant tied up to a tree for an entire day for no other reason than we were high on Molly. Over the years, I've experimented with the typical drugs most college students frequent to have a good time. Outside of the occasional party, I don't care to use them. As a med student, Grant never took drugs, so he didn't find it funny. He didn't talk to us for weeks.

What's going on between Ethan and me runs deeper than that, but I'm hoping he buys my bluff and makes a surprise visit. I plan to call Grant for an early morning tee time like nothing is amiss. One thing I can count on is Grant sending Ethan an invite to join us without fail. Countless times I've called Grant when I'm avoiding Ethan, and he plays big brother, not wanting to break up the trifecta, so he calls Ethan and invites him anyway to patch things up.

I'm just getting out of the shower when Gianna walks in wearing my shirt. *Why is it so hot when chicks wear guys' shirts?* I quickly grab a towel and wrap it around my waist to distract myself from the direction my thoughts were going. When I look up, I don't miss the sexy smirk she's now sporting. I know exactly what she's thinking. Crossing the room, I place a chaste kiss on her cheek before slapping her plump ass hard.

"Get in the shower. We don't have time for that look."

I promptly exit the bathroom before I lose my willpower to tell her no. Getting dressed in my own clothes somehow feels like a reward. I spent the past week tied up in the same outfit, only to change into another man's sweatpants. While I wasn't lying when I told Gianna I'd wear sweats for her, I would be if I said I didn't like to look good, and for me, that's a good pair of chinos and a polo. Once dressed, I head to the kitchen and start a cup of coffee while dialing Mason. He answers on the first ring.

"Yeah."

*Who answers the phone that way?* "Were you able to get all the evidence?"

"Yes, I sent it over to the lawyer an hour ago."

"Great, I'll call him when I hang up with you. I'm going to drop Gianna off at your place in an hour. Will that be a problem?"

He's quiet for a moment. "Does she want to come to my place?"

Well, shit, that's a good question. I hadn't thought about the fact these two probably don't want to see each other after last night.

"Honestly, I haven't asked her. She's in the shower. I assumed she'd be safe with you and would want to see her mom and brother."

Again silence. "What's your plan, August?"

"If all the evidence is lined out and showing that Robert Grand and Eduard were planning to commit securities fraud, the plan is to have the feds come in right away before they have time to run. I doubt you have anything linking Ethan to that fraud, so I plan to confront him and get his confession in person."

"Recording someone without their knowledge wouldn't be admissible in court."

"Yeah, I know that. I plan on being on camera. So if Gianna says yes, can I drop her off at your place?"

I hear him heavily exhale before he reluctantly says, "Sure." And the line goes dead.

Normally, I'd be pissed with someone just hanging up on me, but I get it. I thought I lost Gianna when I was tied up in the basement, and I've only known her for a couple of weeks. I can't imagine losing her after a decade. But that's on him. He had his time, and he squandered it. Someone who has known her for so long should have known that his timing wouldn't go unnoticed. Gianna hasn't had an easy life. But, like me, she learned to read between the lines early. Everyone wears multiple masks. The true talent lies in identifying their intent for deception, and she did with him.

When the doorbell rings, I'm momentarily caught off guard before I remember that I ordered clothes to be delivered for Gianna. Heading toward the door, I hear the shower shut off. I was instantly enraged when I saw her in that gown Ethan had bought her. I wanted to be the one to spoil her and buy her nice things, and now I have my moment. While it will be short-lived, at least I have it. If everything goes as it should, Gianna is about to be a wealthy woman in her own right.

I'm just bringing all the clothes into the room when Gianna exits the bathroom wearing a towel on her head and one wrapped around her body. I swear I've never seen a prettier woman than the one right here without a trace of makeup on. "What's all of this?"

"Well, you're more than welcome to wear my clothes all day, but I thought you might want some of your own items to keep here."

She walks toward the bed where I've laid out the bags. "August, these aren't my things. These are the things you bought me. I don't need a handout. I don't expect you to buy me things just because we're together."

Okay, when I saw this play out in my head, I didn't see anger as an emotion that would come forward. "Gianna, I bought all this so you'd have things here when you stayed. I want to buy you things. I want to spoil you. Please don't make this into anything more because it's not."

Walking over to her, I pull her into my arms and place a kiss on her lips. She hugs me back before placing her head on my chest.

"Can I ask you something?"

That makes me smile because now I know I've got her. "I'll let you ask me something if you accept these gifts I bought you."

She pulls out of my arms and walks over to the bed to take a seat. She nervously fiddles with her fingers. "Does it make me a bad person if I'm relieved that my father is dead?"

That was not the question I was expecting. Making my way over to the bed, I sit and take her hand in mine. Rubbing my thumb over the back of her hand, I choose my next words carefully. On the plane, I had time to reflect on the events surrounding Carson's death and how her death ultimately made me feel, and I can't help but think maybe her grief toward her dad is similar to mine.

"I think sometimes the people we care about have a way of hurting us deeply. In the beginning, we make excuses for their behavior. Then we blame ourselves for how they treat us or how we let them treat us, but eventually, we become numb to the pain. Once the pain disappears, we're left with anger and resentment, which eats us alive. So to answer your question, no, I think relief is a perfectly natural response to your grief. You know you'll no longer be tormented with anger and resentment."

She fiddles with our hands, lacing our fingers together only to unlace them again. My heart can't help but feel bewitched by this simple action. It makes me smile on the inside that I get to be this guy for her. I get to be her confidant. "Thank you." Her eyes meet mine, and I can see that my words made her feel better. A long minute passes, and I'm still sitting there, stuck in a trance that is all things her. Finally, dropping our hands, she pulls me out of my daze. "You're the one who said we don't have time for extracurriculars this morning, so I'm not sure why you're still staring at me."

That makes me laugh out loud. Getting off the bed, I head toward the door just as she starts looking through the bags. I'm closing the door when I catch sight of her dropping her towel. I can't help but groan in protest. Throwing the door wide open, I say, "How the hell do you expect me to walk away when you're standing there looking like a fucking goddess?" Running back over, I tackle her to the bed and suck her perky tit into my mouth. She's laughing and trying to push me off when my phone rings. Reaching into my back pocket, I grab my phone and answer, keeping her firmly pressed beneath me. "August speaking." I swirl my tongue around her other nipple, teasing her until I hear the lawyer's voice ring out.

"August, are you by a computer?"

Jumping up, I release her and hurriedly walk to my office.

"Yes, John, what's up?"

"Is Gianna with you?"

"Yes, she's with me, John. What's this about?"

"I need her to sign the contract I'm sending over. Technically, I will represent her, but the second the news of their arrest breaks, her face will be scattered across the news. I need to be able to speak on her behalf."

I run my hands through my hair. Of course this is all necessary, but I hadn't thought about how this could or would thrust her into the spotlight. "John, is there any way we can keep her anonymity?"

"Son, my job is to protect her, but we need to be prepared for a worst-case scenario. Get the contract to me ASAP and expect arrests to be made by ten a.m. A close friend of mine is expediting the warrants."

"Thanks, John. I'll send these over as soon as we finish the call."

He hangs up just as Gianna walks into my office, fully clothed in jeans that look like they were painted on and a long-sleeved white tee. "Who was that?"

"That was the lawyer I contacted last night to help you. Gianna, your dad left you as the sole beneficiary on his stock portfolio when it was set up. Robert Grand and my uncle will go to federal prison for securities fraud. You will need someone to settle his estate and represent your claims in court. Gianna, I can't make any promises. He will try to keep all this private, but sometimes anonymity can't be maintained."

The expression on her face is pensive, so I give her a minute to process while I press print on the documents she needs to sign. The sound of the printer firing up breaks her out of her daze. Grabbing the papers off the printer, I bring them back over to my desk. "You need to sign these papers so that John can represent you. Arrests will happen at ten a.m."

"Do you trust this John guy?" she questions, her face full of concern.

"Yes, Gianna, I trust John. He represented my family back when Alaric embezzled money from Reds."

"Will you review the paperwork and make sure everything looks okay before I sign it?"

Now her hesitance and look of concern make sense. Giving her a soft smile, I gesture for her to come over and sit. Rather than take the chair across from mine, she comes around my desk to sit on my lap and fuck if my heart doesn't skip a beat from the tenderness of the action. I bite my lip to stifle the ridiculous smile I'm trying to hold back from the thought of her finding comfort in me, but when she subtly pushes her hair behind her ear and peers over her shoulder at me, I lose it.

"Gianna, you have no idea what you do to me." I pull her against my chest and pepper kisses down her neck.

It's not long before her hand finds the bulge in my pants. "Oh, I think I do because you do the same thing to me every time I look at you."

I know I have to stop this before it gets out of hand. We honestly don't have time for this. I could get lost in this woman for hours, but we need to focus right now. Placing one last chaste kiss on her shoulder, I release her before stilling her palm that's currently rubbing against my erection. When she groans in protest as I go to stop her, I have to lean my head against her back and dig deep to ignore every desire that's screaming at me to bend her over my desk right now.

Once I've regained my self-control, I say, "Gianna, I can promise you that you're going to be sore tomorrow, but right now, we need to get this paperwork to John."

She lets out a shaky breath before placing her hands flat on the desk. "Okay, then let's get to it."

Because nothing is ever that easy with Gianna, I'm skeptical about the sincerity of her willingness to commit to the task at hand. But in true form, she surprises me. I start reading the document aloud, pausing to explain things when she asks. Once we're done, she signs the paperwork and loads it back through the scanner sitting on my desk. I immediately send it over to John, not wanting there to be any reason for delay with everything that's happening today.

"Thanks for that. I've never had reason to have a lawyer, but I know I shouldn't sign anything I don't understand." Her timid confession tells me that asking for my help made her feel vulnerable.

"Baby, don't do that. Stop overthinking this. I'll help you however you need, but you can do this, Gianna."

Turning, she leans into me and rests her forehead against mine before placing her hand on my cheek. "I can, but it doesn't mean I'm not grateful for you."

I close the mere centimeters between our mouths and take her lips in mine. I'm not sure what today will bring, but as long as she's mine, that's all that matters. When I part her lips, she eagerly dips her tongue into my mouth, and I can feel her beginning to shift in my lap. My girl is greedy, and I fucking love that she can't get enough of me.

I'm just about to stop her once more when she says, "August, please. We can be quick, I promise." Her eyes frantically search mine, and I can see the blush rising in her cheeks. It makes her nervous to ask what she wants from me. *But why?*

"Answer something for me. You know you have me. So why does it make you nervous asking me for something you want?"

She rolls her eyes before moving to get off my lap, but I quickly grab hold of her to keep her in place.

"You don't get to run from me, Gianna. Not anymore."

"August, forget it. You said we need to go, so let's go."

Now I'm pissed. I don't want her to hold back on me. "We'll go after you answer my question and not a second sooner."

She releases an exasperated sigh before pinning her eyes on something behind me.

"You're the only man I've ever been with sexually, but you're also the only man who's ever rejected me."

Her admission dumbfounds me. "What the fuck are you talking about? I rejected you? When the hell have I ever rejected you?"

She bites her lip once again before averting her gaze.

So, I grab her chin, pull her face to mine, and grit out, "Explain."

"Well, for starters, there was the night at the club in the closet, and then when you came to pick me up on the beach in Fl—"

I cut her off before she can finish. "You can't be serious right now. I'm pretty sure both times I had a raging boner that I'm sure you didn't miss."

She shrugs her shoulders. "Yeah, well, you also didn't do anything about it, kind of like right now."

"You're trying to get me to bend you over and smack that ass, aren't you?"

Her expression gives nothing away. I can't tell if she's trying to incite me or if she genuinely thinks I didn't want her just as much as she wanted me. Either way, I'm rectifying that now.

Moving my hands to her hips, I lift her off my lap and place her on the desk in front of me. My quick movement was unexpected because she yelps in surprise.

"August, what are you doing?"

"Making sure my girl doesn't forget how much I fucking want her." I push her back to lie on the desk before quickly unbuttoning her jeans and pulling them off. She wanted quick, so I don't waste time undressing. Instead, I stay entirely clothed, only freeing my cock. Spreading her legs, I rest one on each shoulder. "You wanted this, baby. Just fucking remember that when you can't breathe." That's all the warning I give her before I slam into her in one quick stroke.

Her breath catches in her throat before her eyes roll back in her head. I haven't given it to her rough yet, but when I see her hands slide down the desktop to grip the edge, I know she wants it that way. Pulling out, I repeat the action two more times, earning me deep, throaty moans of intoxication. She loves it. I just wish she were fully naked so I could watch her tits bounce every time I slam in deep.

"You're such a fucking good girl. You take my cock however you can get it." I could watch how her face contorts in sheer ecstasy from how I make her feel all day, but I swear she has the prettiest pussy I've ever seen. I can't get enough of watching myself disappear inside her. I start pumping into her at a piston pace when she cries out, "Fuck yes, don't stop."

My eyes snap up to her face, and I find her watching me, which makes me go even harder. I want her to be sore. I want her thinking about me wringing out every last drop of pleasure from her body until I get to do it again. The problem is, I'm a sucker for those eyes, and when I see they're dilated from pleasure and filled with love like they are right now, I'm a goner. I know it's the same for her because her pussy starts to choke my cock. Bringing my thumb to her clit, she immediately starts to climax, and I hold myself in deep, finding my own release. My stamina has gone to shit with this woman. Falling on top of her, I rest my head in the crook of her neck.

"Later, I want a do-over. You're too fucking perfect, and I can't last."

Her chest vibrates as a laugh escapes her lips. Her hand strokes up my back as she brings it to rest at the base of my neck, slowly running her fingers through my hair. I don't know what it is about that simple action she does, but it melts me every time. It's her way of comforting and loving me, and I can't help but get drunk off it. As much as I want to stay like this forever, we must go. Pushing off her, I kiss her quickly.

"Baby, we really do need to get going."

Standing, I tuck myself back in and grab her jeans for her. Crossing the room, I pretend to busy myself with something in my file cabinet for two reasons. One, I want to give her privacy to straighten herself out, but two, I need to mentally prepare myself for the next tidbit of information I need to share. She clears her throat and I assume that must mean she's done righting herself. When I turn around, she's perfectly flushed with that just fucked glow, and she starts to nervously fidget under my gaze as I've noticed she always does.

Walking over, I pull her into my arms, kiss her forehead, and prepare myself for her reaction to my next words. "Gianna, I don't want you to get upset, but I need to take you to Mason's place."

Her body tenses as she slowly pulls back and peers up at me like I'm crazy.

"Hear me out. I'm sure you want to see your mom and Elio, and I need to handle Ethan. I need to know you're safe while I'm out. If you don't want to go, I understand. I can make arrangements to bring them here. Guards already surround the house. I didn't think you'd want to be locked up inside with one while I'm gone."

Pulling out of my embrace, she starts pacing the room. "I want to make sure I understand my options clearly. I can either leave and be subjected to the torture of seeing Mason or stay and suffer in silence with some stranger. Thanks for the stellar choices."

I close the distance between us and take her hand in mine. I lazily draw circles on her palm in hopes of calming her nerves. Touching instantly calms both of us. "I know this isn't ideal, but I have to leave. I need to try to corner Ethan before the feds arrest his dad. You can't be alone right now, so this is me trying to compromise. I know I'm making you pick between two shitty choices, but it's all I've got right now, and we need to leave."

Closing her eyes, she gives her consent. "I'll go to Mason's."

I can tell it's the last thing she wants to do, but today I'm strong enough to know it's because she doesn't want to hurt him, not because she thinks she made the wrong choice. I kiss her lips quickly before pulling her with me toward the door. We need to hurry up and get to Mason's so I can get to the golf course.

## TWENTY-NINE
### *Gianna*

On the way over to Mason's, August filled me in on everything expected to go down today and how he plans to trap Ethan into confessing his plans for premeditated murder on tape. August seems to think he'll admit to everything if he can get him riled up enough. It all sounds good in theory, but I'm not sure I believe that Ethan harbored enough hate to commit a murder or even set one up. I understand the adage of keeping your friends close and your enemies closer, but August's account of his transgressions sounds more like jealousy than anything genuinely scandalous. While I know drugging someone and holding them against their will is technically a crime, he didn't hurt August. Hell, my own friends drugged me and took me out of the state. If anything, his theory proves we have questionable taste in friends.

I'm so caught up in my thoughts that I don't realize August has pulled up outside a condominium complex. "Where are we?"

He gives me a surprised look and narrows his eyes in confusion. "We're at Mason's."

I don't get a chance to respond before he exits the car and comes around to open my door.

"There isn't much here. Mason moved in right before the accident."

That makes sense. Mace mentioned moving out a while back, but I didn't realize he had a place already picked out. Staring up at the building, I'm reluctant to go in. Once I do, I have to face my mom, Elio, and him. I'll have to own all my feelings instead of burying them down deep as I've always done. When I was in Florida, I decided I was turning a new leaf. I'm going to live for myself instead of bottling everything up and shutting people out. Letting people in doesn't mean they'll hurt me. They can only hurt me if I give them the power to do so.

August must sense my hesitance because he pulls me into a hug, which calms my inner dialogue. He holds me for a few long moments until I break the silence.

"Can we just run away?"

I feel his chest vibrate with laughter before he places a hand on either side of my face and pulls me back. Searching my face for signs of actuality, his hopeful gaze lands on my mouth.

"Kiss me, August." The request leaves my mouth on a breathy plea. I genuinely love this man and don't want him to go.

Leaning down, he takes my lips in his in a slow, sensual embrace. His tongue tenderly strokes mine, and I can't help but wonder if this man's touch will forever make me weak in the knees. I just want to stay in this moment. Unfortunately, I know I need to face my reality. Reluctantly, I pull back, and as I do, he catches my chin and peers down into my eyes.

"Gianna, I'll follow you anywhere. When this is over, let's go away for a while, you and me."

I nod in agreement, pushing up on my tippytoes to place one more kiss on his lips before we walk hand in hand up to Mason's door. "I'll be back as soon as I can, baby. I'm sorry I can't be here for you right now."

I know what he's saying. He wishes he could be there when I speak to my family, but it's probably better that he's not. Sharing parts of my life with August doesn't bother me, but everything is still raw. It's probably better that I have this conversation on my own.

"I'll be here when you get back." It's on the tip of my tongue to ask him to stay, but not for reasons he'll like. However, if I've learned anything, it's that you never know what cards you're going to be dealt, so I do say one last thing. "August, you could stay. I don't think we need to go after Ethan."

I can tell my words have caught him off guard as his eyebrows shoot up in surprise, and he rolls his lips, no doubt contemplating his next words.

"Gianna, I've told you everything that happened over the past week. The conversations Mason overheard, the plotting and planning that went into trying to keep us apart, not to mention my drugged capture. I don't understand why you feel this way, and as much as I want to discuss this with you and hear you out, now is not the time. I really have to go." He leans in and gently kisses my lips before catching my eye. "I love you. Let me take care of this. Let me take care of us."

My heart stumbles over those three little words. Last night when he told me that he loved me, not only were we in the middle of sex, but we were extremely exhausted. I didn't say it expecting him to return the sentiment, and a small part of me considered that he might have said it out of obligation. This is why I'm at a loss for words because I know now that this man loves me without a doubt. My tongue feels heavy in my mouth, while my heart feels like it might beat out of my chest. Before I can respond, he's taking off down the stairs. Once he's out of sight, I muster up the strength to knock on the door. When Mason answers, the look on his face seems remorseful, but that can't be it because how could he feel sorry for me after all I've done to him?

"Hey, Mace," I squeak out, my voice way too high-pitched to hide my nerves. I'm anxiously wringing my hands when he throws the door wide open to let me in. Walking inside, I notice the place is bare bones, which makes sense given everything that has happened. I expected to see my mom and Elio immediately, but they are nowhere in sight.

"Where is everyone?" When I turn to Mason, I notice he's still standing by the door, blankly staring at me. *Great*.

Pointedly raising my eyebrows at him in question seems to

snap him out of his trance. He runs his fingers through his hair and nervously approaches the refrigerator. "Your mom is taking a nap. She didn't sleep much last night, and Elio is in my office playing video games."

Taking a seat on one of the barstools at the island, I watch him shuffle through the fridge before pulling out what looks like Chinese and Diet Dr Pepper, my favorites. It's as if he can't resist twisting the knife deeper into my heart.

"Mace, why are you doing this? Why are you making this harder?"

His jaw sets, and he thins his lips before returning to the fridge to grab a beer. "Look, Gigi, I know last night was shit timing to lay everything on you, but it didn't make any of what I said less true. This right now is me being what I've always been: comforting."

He pops the top on his beer and takes a long swig. Once his eyes return to mine, I give him a sympathetic smile. I love Mason, I genuinely do, but I love August more. I hate that it has come to this. The last thing I want is to lose Mason, especially now.

"Mason, you know what we were was so much more. I'm sorry for the role I've played recently, but I think you knew what you were doing."

Setting down his beer, he leans on the island, and his ripped arms flex as he grips the edges. "Gigi, you're right. I waited too long, and that's on me. It wasn't until the night I picked you up at Reds and saw the possessive scowl on August's face that I realized I might lose you. In less than one day, he saw what I've known for the past nine years: that you are a rare treasure. I'm not perfect. I'm far from it, and you know it. But none of it matters now. You made your choice, and now I have to live with it."

When he's done speaking, our eyes stay locked, both of us frozen in the finality of his words. As harsh as that might sound, there's nothing more to say on the matter. I wish he'd own his own ugly, but he won't. He's only ever shown me the side of him that he wanted me to see. I only wish he knew that I loved him anyway. A loud pounding on the door breaks the silence.

"Gigi, go to my office," he clips out before heading to the door. He peers through the peephole and reaches behind his back to clutch a gun tucked in on his lower back.

"Mason, what the fuck is that? Why do you have a gun?"

He turns, giving me an aggravated glare. "Why do you think I have a gun, Gigi? Protection."

As if that's explanation enough, he peers through the hole as if the gun is no big deal. "You've got to be fucking kidding me."

"Who is it, Mace?"

He turns to look at me, wholly outraged. "It's fucking Ethan Grand."

"Oh my God, are you serious? How the hell did he find us?"

Before Mason can answer, Ethan calls out, "Let me in, Mason. I know you're in there, and I'm here to see Gianna."

Mason mumbles, "This guy can't be for real right now," before he opens the door.

"Ethan, you have some real nerve showing up here after everything. You're lucky I don't fucking shoot you on the spot."

Ethan throws his arms out wide. "Go ahead. I'm not here to hurt her."

"Why the hell should I believe a word that comes out of your mouth?" Mason chides.

Letting his arms fall to his sides, Ethan runs one hand through his perfectly unkempt blond hair. "I guess you shouldn't, but I'm asking that you do." Ethan's wearing light blue ripped-up jeans, a gray Henley, and white sneakers, looking hot as fuck as per usual, but he also seems a little worse for wear around the edges, like he hasn't slept. He catches sight of me and nods in my direction. "Why don't you ask Gianna if I can come in?"

My interest is piqued; I'll admit that much. Not to mention Ethan had me the night of the fundraiser, and he didn't commit any heinous acts. In fact, he was somewhat thoughtful. Don't get me wrong, he was still a pretentious prick, but at least he was cordial.

"Let him in, Mace."

Mason throws his hands into his hair, clearly pissed that I'm agreeing to Ethan's demands. "Gigi, are you serious right now? He wanted to kill you."

Ethan scoffs. "When did I say I wanted to kill her?"

Mason looks like he's about to lose his mind in frustration. "Just let him in, Mace. You have a gun if he tries to pull anything."

He shakes his head and releases an exasperated breath of defeat before throwing the door wide for Ethan to enter. "Make one wrong move, and I swear I won't hesitate to pull the trigger," Mason adds as Ethan steps around him to enter.

Ethan throws his hands up defensively and strolls into the condo, casually taking in the space before coming to the island to stand opposite me. I study his mannerisms, searching for a crack in his armor and finding none. He wears his cocky, arrogant playboy mask well, but today there's something else. He's looking at me differently, and I can't place it.

"Princess, you'll have to stop looking at me like you want to jump my bones. It's inappropriate."

I scowl at him before walking around the island to grab the beer Mason didn't finish. The nerve of this guy. "Ethan, why don't you stop with the antics and get to the real reason you're here? I'm sure it's not to flirt with me."

Mason has taken up residence at one of the vacant barstools, where he's openly glowering at Ethan. He's biting back words I'm sure will start flying at any moment if Ethan doesn't stop his bullshit.

"Why did you let me in, Gianna?"

I'm unsure where he's going with this line of questioning, but I take the bait. "I'm not scared of you, Ethan. You had your chance to hurt me, and you didn't. In fact, you were pretty decent, all things considered."

Turning his stare to Mason, he asks, "Do you have anything stronger than beer?"

Mason lets out an irritated huff before shuffling over to a cabinet and pulling out a bottle of whiskey. Ethan and I watch him open one empty cabinet after another before finding a coffee mug and placing it on the island in front of Ethan.

"All right, Ethan, you have your drink. Now start talking." Mason all but barks out before posting up on a barstool to my right.

He's getting impatient, and I can't blame him. After everything that's happened, Ethan isn't the person I want to be giving my time to right now.

"I'm not sure where to start, Gianna, but I'll start with: I never planned on physically hurting you. If anything, I wanted you for myself." Pausing, he throws back a shot of warm whiskey and winces as it goes down. His expression is a mix of shame and regret, which doesn't make sense. I realize I'm not the catch of the day, but I can't be that bad.

"Yes, the disgust on your face right now is really selling your claim that you found me attractive and had no plans to hurt me. Why have the tracker installed on my car if you had no plans of harming me?"

He winces and rubs his hand over his chest, probably from a mix of my words and the alcohol. "I used Mason because my goal was to fuck up your relationship with August. The night he showed up to take you home, I knew using him would kill two birds with one stone. The two of you clearly had feelings for each other, so rubbing that in August's face helped. Keeping you both in the dark was necessary, so I took advantage of your relationship with Mason to accomplish that goal. Plus, I needed to keep tabs on you. As far as the rest goes, I'm trying to get to that."

"Well, you should probably hurry up and get there before Mason's hospitality runs out." I know the last thing Mason wants to hear are accounts of how other people used our relationship against us. A relationship that no longer exists.

Ethan leans back against the counter, crossing his arms over his chest before sizing up Mason. For a second, it almost feels suspiciously protective, but that can't be it. Before I have any more time to analyze his body language, he starts talking.

"I admit that I was out to sabotage your relationship with August, but not just for my own selfish reasons. I was there and prepared to make you mine the weekend you ran into August at the club until August stepped in and laid his claim. I was so fucking livid when I found out who you were that night. He had literally just finished explaining to Grant and me that you were a mistake."

I'm not going to lie. That confession still stings. It's the one and only time that August wavered in his decision to pursue me. Ethan pours himself yet another shot and throws it back. At this rate, he'll be passed out drunk before he ever gets to the reason he is here.

"August and I have always had a frenemies bond. I don't think either of us was ever under any illusions that we were true friends, but it worked until it didn't. The day after we went to the club, I went golfing with my dad. It wasn't a surprise that he wanted to talk about August. After all, I spent most of my teen years being compared to him. The interesting part was when your name rolled off his tongue without pause. It was as if he was well acquainted with everything regarding you, and I was immediately intrigued. Why would a man like my dad know anything about a girl like you? Why would my dad give two shits about who August is fucking?"

I would be shocked if I didn't already know that Robert was after my dad, but Ethan seems genuinely shaken. Again, he pours himself another shot but doesn't take it.

"I'm not as shallow as you may think, Gianna. While I've always wanted to please my father, I won't follow him blindly. However, in so many words, he told me I needed to keep you and August apart if I wanted my inheritance. I'll admit, I like being rich. I like what this lifestyle affords me, but my curiosity was piqued. My father doesn't ask much of me. In fact, I've always felt like I'm this major disappointment for him, so when he asked this of me, I knew I wouldn't fail him—that is until I did my own digging."

I walk across the room toward the fridge and grab another mug and ice before snatching the bottle of whiskey away from Ethan. His mouth curls up on one side in a half-smile when he watches me pour myself a shot over ice before stepping around me to grab some ice for himself. This entire scene is a little too comfortable, and my stomach churns at the thought I'm betraying August by not immediately alerting him that Ethan is here. Mason must notice the direction of my thoughts because he gives me a nod and picks up his phone to text August. Ethan must notice our silent conversation because he quickly makes a plea.

"Please don't text August. I need to get this out first."

"Ethan, August deserves to know you are here. He's spent the last week locked up in a basement because of you, and I've been on the run."

"Yeah, I get that. But you need to know my intent was never to kill anyone. Carson wanted to play with August. She got some kind of sick pleasure out of messing with him, and I needed him distracted while I tried to figure out my father's plan. You already know about your dad's investments, but the rest will rock your world."

"Well, then, let's hear it! I haven't had the best week, and my life wasn't exactly easy, so do your best."

He slowly nods in understanding before throwing back another shot. "Well, I'm your brother."

His words don't immediately sink in because there's no way in hell Ethan *fucking* Grand is my brother. This must be another one of his many schemes, and my dad is dead because of him. That's it. I'm done playing games. I can't believe I thought giving him a chance to speak was worth it.

"Ethan, it's time for you to leave. My dad is dead because of you, and you have the audacity to come here and fuck with me after everything you put me through? I hope there's a special place in hell for selfish pricks like you."

Mason walks over to Ethan and clasps him by the shoulder to gladly escort him out, but he slams his hands down on the counter in protest; his eyes are haunted, and his body is shaking.

"I'm not fucking lying about being your brother. I can prove it. I've already sent off samples for testing to be one hundred percent sure there was no mistake. But what do you mean your dad is dead?"

When his eyes meet mine, I can tell he's sincere, and now it's me who's a wreck. Now it's me facing hard truths. "He was found last night outside the new Grand Office Suites site, unresponsive in his car from an apparent drug overdose."

His shoulders slump as he drops his head. Part of me wants to go over and comfort him, but I don't know him well enough to know if that's what he needs right now, so I stay put.

"Can you tell me how this is possible?"

He slowly lifts his head, and his eyes say what I'm sure his mouth won't: *I'm sorry.* "My dad is a wealthy man, so it struck me as odd that he was going out of his way to rob your father of what was his. Even without your dad's stock, he would still be on his way to billionaire status. So I hired a private investigator to look into my dad's business dealings with your father. At first, nothing stuck out on paper, but that's when I realized it was never about the money. It was a personal vendetta.

"The year your dad invested in his company was six months before my dad filed for divorce. I always assumed the divorce was because my dad had a wandering eye and didn't want to share his success with my mother. He was a cold fucker in that way. The divorce files were sealed, but I had them hacked and found out he served my mom with an NDA and offered her payment for her silence in keeping my paternity a secret. The documents didn't disclose who my father was. It took a lot of coercion, but eventually, my mom agreed to tell me everything. Apparently, she had a one-night stand with your dad on a business trip when she and Robert were only dating. My mother says that my true paternity was only discovered once they tried to have more kids. However, Robert is an intelligent, calculating man. I don't think it's a coincidence that your father happened upon him at a golf course and invested with him. I believe Robert suspected I wasn't his long before the test confirmed it. He was only biding his time until the moment was right to strike.

"When they tried to have more children after me, the doctors told Robert he was sterile, and there was no way I could be his. In hindsight, how I grew up and that he isn't my biological father makes sense. He was never there for me and missed every big event, every milestone. I came last to his work and women, and now I know it's because I was never really his."

My eyes are locked on Ethan's, and I can't help but feel sorry for him. I've judged him from the moment I laid eyes on him. Just because he's rich doesn't mean he is immune to emotional abuse or neglect; it doesn't mean he isn't a person with feelings. Growing up, I hated the feeling of being judged. We didn't have money, my parents were addicts, and we moved around so much that I had no real friendships. Now I'm sitting here realizing I've done just that to Ethan. I've unfairly labeled him. Before I notice what I've done, my legs have carried me to the other side of the island, and I've wrapped my arms around Ethan in a side hug. Initially, his body is rigid and cold, but he turns slightly and hugs me back when he realizes I'm not letting go.

"Gianna, there is one last thing I need to tell you, and it's going to hurt like hell. I know you have no reason to put any faith in me or trust me whatsoever, but now that I've found you, I'm not letting you go."

I pull my face away from his chest and release my hold on him to look at him. "You realize I'm your half-sister, and I'm dating August, right? There's never going to be an us. That's fucking sick."

He furrows his eyebrows before pinching the bridge of his nose. "Shit, that came out wrong. I meant that I've always wanted a sibling, and now that I have you, I'm not going anywhere. I want to be a part of your life. I want to help you. This is why I need to know where your mom is. I don't think she's innocent in all this."

Tearing my gaze from Ethan's, I look over at Mason, wondering if he sees any validity in Ethan's assessment. He's standing against the countertop, arms crossed, deep in thought, when suddenly his eyes dart to mine, and he shakes his head.

"Gigi, we need to get you and Elio out of here."

"Mace, tell me what you're thinking?"

Ethan doesn't waste any time ushering me toward the front

door while Mason jogs across the living room. I assume the door he's about to open leads to his office, where he said Elio was playing video games.

"Mason, please just tell me."

Before he can respond, the door down the hallway opens up, and my mother walks out, gun in hand, pointed directly at me.

"Ethan, I'm going to need you to step away from my daughter now."

What surprises me is how Ethan steps in front of me rather than step away before saying, "That's not going to happen, Maria. She is all I have left since you took Mario from me."

Now my head really is spinning. I've never thought my mom was a malevolent woman. Sure, she mistreated me, but I saw her as a woman who couldn't escape her addiction, and I paid the price. This right here is downright diabolical. Who points a gun at their own child? She must be on drugs; that's the only thing that would explain this mayhem.

Stepping out from behind my new human shield, I say, "Ethan, she won't hurt me. She's my mom." Now that Ethan is no longer blocking my view, I can see that Mason is still standing in front of the office door, but now his gun is drawn.

"Mason, please put the gun down. Why do we have guns drawn anyway? Mom, what's going on?"

"Well, now that we're at this point, you can cut the mom crap. I'm not your mom. Of course you might have discovered that sooner if you weren't so busy whoring it up with Mason, August, and apparently your half-brother from the looks of it."

This can't be real. That was a loaded sentence that my brain isn't letting me compute. "What do you mean you are not my mom? Who's my mom then?"

"Don't know. That bitch died giving birth, or at least that was the story I've always been told. Who knows, maybe she ran for the hills and left you with your dad when she realized what a piece of shit he was."

None of this makes any fucking sense. Why did she stick around all those years when I was young, taking me from place to place? I always thought she was trying to leave my dad, but why bother taking me if I was never her child?

"I don't understand. If you're not my mom, why did you take me all those times?"

Shaking her head, she lets out an annoyed sigh as if my line of questioning is such an inconvenience.

"Insurance, of course. I had to play the devoted fill-in mom card and act like I was the better parent. You already know I was your dad's third wife. I knew one day he would inherit his parents' money, and I would be there for it. You, my dear, were my golden ticket. Whenever he would consider divorce, I would play the loyal mom card. The only problem was, he left you everything."

Maybe Dad was onto her all along. I found it strange that he left me as the sole beneficiary, but seeing as Maria isn't my real mom, things are adding up. It's possible he never really loved Maria but thought I needed a mother figure around. Maybe he left me everything because I was the only thing that was a part of him. Well, besides Elio—however, Elio wasn't born when this deal was made. Elio came years later, and since he thought he lost his investment, it makes sense that it was never amended. Which leaves the question?

"Is Elio my brother?"

Maria's eyes dart to Ethan before she responds. My heart immediately drops because I know whatever answer she's about to give me will be complete bullshit. That's her tell. When she lies, she can never look you in the eye.

"Unfortunately, yes, Elio is Mario's son. A drunken mistake that I tried to abort, only to fail multiple times."

Before I had time to swallow those harsh words, many things happened simultaneously, and I wish like hell the next thirty seconds could have played out differently. But what's life if not a series of imperfect moments scattered throughout our short lives, set as reminders of the things we endured that either broke us or built us. That day, I lost my first love, let go of my hate, and embraced my new reality—I just wish I could have been there for it. No sooner Ethan lets his guard down for me than the front door swings open with August barging in. His eyes widen when he sees Maria pointing a gun in my direction. He immediately tackles me to the floor right as a gunshot goes off. On cue, my body gets clammy, my chest tightens, and I feel lightheaded. I hear myself murmur August's name before everything goes black.

## THIRTY
### *August*

On the drive to the golf course, all I could think about was how I hated leaving Gianna. Something about leaving her felt off, and when she mentioned her reservations about Ethan, I couldn't deal, so I left. Before I ever reached Mason's, texts from my father started blowing up my phone. He wanted me to call him immediately. It was the last thing I wanted to do, but I also needed answers only he could provide.

The phone only rings once before he answers, "August, what the hell is going on? Why are you working with John? Does this have anything to do with Carson? What have you gotten yourself into, son?"

Fuck, that's a lot to unpack. First, I could have sworn there was something called client confidentiality. I know he and John are good friends, but damn. I'm not surprised he knows about Carson. Our families are close. After all, our parents are the reason we ever dated.

"Dad, God, no, I had nothing to do with Carson's unfortunate death, and I'm not the one in need of John's services. Is that all you called me for? To make sure I wasn't bringing shame to the family name?" I grit my teeth to bite back my annoyance so that I don't say something I'll regret.

"August, why would you ever say something like that? You need to understand how this looks from my perspective. John sends me a heads-up text that he's helping you with something on the same morning that Carson's mom calls to tell me that there was an accident and Carson has passed. Then, to top it off, I found out you weren't in the office this week."

I can't blame him. That all does seem very suspect.

"Dad, Carson and I hadn't been dating for the past six months. She only attended your fundraiser with me because you and the Bradburys orchestrated it. I wasn't going to rock the boat for you on your big night."

I don't answer his question regarding work because this isn't the time to tell him that I won't be returning or that I was tied up in Carson's basement for the past week. I'm praying he's too occupied with the other events to notice.

"Well, I'm disappointed to hear that, but it doesn't matter anyway, seeing as she is no longer with us. You know we always liked Carson for you, but I didn't know you weren't happy with her. How about we get lunch together on Monday when I'm in the office?"

I'm unsure what he's playing at with the Carson card, so I stay silent while trying to figure out his angle. Maybe the fact that she's dead has him biting his tongue because there's nothing he can do to salvage the relationship, but I know damn well what I've said very much displeases him.

For a split second, I think maybe I've read him wrong all these years and put unnecessary stress on myself, but then he says, "Well, I guess since the two of you haven't been seeing each other for a while now, it's not too soon to set you up with the Carmichaels' daughter." And there it is. This is why I never second-guess myself.

My gut instinct is never wrong. I knew my father was trying to find a way to slip in his agenda, and now I know what my follow-up words must be. I'm not embarrassed by Gianna by any means. In choosing her, I'm choosing myself, so I know when I tell my dad I have a girlfriend and it's her, I'm also done with everything else. From here on out, it's my life. I won't be running the family business, I won't be living on the right side of the highway, and I sure as hell am done with all the pretentious keeping up with the Joneses shit my parents make me attend at their beck and call.

"Dad, thanks, but no, thanks. Not only am I capable of finding my own girlfriend, but I also have one. Look, I really need to get off the phone."

I don't immediately say who it is because I need to catch him off guard. Deep down, I don't think my dad had anything to do with this mess the Morettis are in, but since Maria worked for my family for so long, I can't just turn my head. If there was evidence, I have no doubt Mason would have found it. While I never voiced my concern out loud, I know his interest is protecting Gianna. I'm confident he's explored every secret he thinks I might have to find something to hold above my head and bring her back to him. But I need to hear this from my dad myself, nonetheless. I know I hooked him with that last line. He wants to know who it is, but because he feels rushed that I'll hang up, I'll know by the tone of his voice if he has any reservations about Gianna Moretti.

"Well, who is it, and when do we get to meet her?"

I can tell he's taken aback and surprised. He would never say I couldn't date someone, but I know the type of woman he wants me with, and it's not someone with Gianna's background.

"Actually, you know her. I've been seeing Gianna Moretti for a few weeks now."

"Gianna? I thought she was dating Ethan Grand since she was on his arm at the fundraiser."

There was no pause between my last breath and my dad's response. He didn't stumble over his words, there was no audible gasp, and his questioning of her involvement with Ethan sounded genuine. This leads me to believe he has nothing to do with the mess Gianna is in with Robert and Eduard.

So I lie to save face. "Since I was previously committed to bringing Carson, Ethan brought Gianna as a friend." My dad doesn't need to know about any of this drama, and I don't want to give him any more reasons not to like her.

"As long as you're happy, son, that's all that matters. Gianna is a beautiful woman, which makes you a lucky man. Your mother is going to want to meet her. Maybe you guys can come by for dinner next weekend?"

I am completely shocked by the outcome of this conversation. It makes me think I've misread my parents all these years, but I know that's not the case. Either way, I don't have time to dwell on it because just as I'm about to hang up the phone, he says, "Oh, and, August, don't think I haven't noticed how you avoided my questions about work. I expect to see you for lunch on Monday."

I don't even have a chance to reply before he hangs up on me. *Damn it.*

I pull up alongside Grant's car just as he steps out.

He comes in for a pound hug. "You must have really fucked up with Ethan because I couldn't persuade him to meet up. What's with you guys lately? It can't really be over that girl." Before he finishes the sentence, I'm rounding my car to get back in.

"Sorry, G, but I have to go. I'll make it up to you, I swear." I get in my car and floor it back to Mason's. Regardless of where Ethan might be, I need to be with Gianna. I never should have left her to begin with. But if this knot in my gut is anything to go off, then I know precisely where Ethan is. He found her.

* * *

I feel like it took me an hour to drive ten minutes, and my nerves are shot. As I pull down Mason's street, movement from the side of the building catches my eye, and I notice a boy climbing out of a third-story window. He is literally walking along the window ledge over to the gutter. *Fuck.*

Of all the times to stop and help a pedestrian, it would be right now when I desperately need to get to my girl. I quickly text my security detail, asking him to meet me on the side of the building. There's no way I would ever be able to forgive myself if something terrible happened to this kid and I didn't at least try to help.

When I park my car and cross the street, the kid has already started scaling down the gutter. I have no clue how I'm supposed to help him, so I quickly scan the area, trying to figure out a plan of action. There's a big trash can on wheels a few feet away. I sprint over to the bin and start pushing it toward the kid so that if he slips, he'll have something to break his fall. Or at least jump to when he gets close.

Sure enough, right when I have the can in position, the kid's hand slips, and he falls. *Shit.* Climbing up the side of the bin, I look in and see the expression of utter shock on the kid's face. He pats his hands up his arms and legs before looking at me with an expression of relief and horror.

I extend my hand for him to grab to pull him out. "You're lucky I was here, kid. What the fuck was worth sneaking out and almost dying?"

He takes my hand, and I pull him up.

"My sister, she's in trouble. My mom has a gun, and I think she's going to kill her. She tied me up, but I got loose and climbed out to find help."

*Fuck.*

My heart suddenly drops into my stomach when the realization sets in. He just climbed out of a third-story window. Mason lives on the third floor, where Gianna's younger brother and mom are currently staying.

"Is your sister Gianna?"

Surprise crosses his face. "Yeah, you know her?"

I don't respond. Instead, I take off toward the front of the building. Marc rounds the corner just as I do. "We have to get upstairs. Gianna is in trouble. Her mom has a gun."

The three of us head up the steps two at a time.

Once we reach the top, I say, "Hey, kid, what's your name?"

"My name is Elio."

"Why don't you hang back here?"

He nods and heads over to the staircase, where he perches himself on the top step before nervously putting his hands in his hair. He's on the verge of tears. The kid can't be any older than ten, and I feel like an ass for not knowing his name. I'm in love with his sister, and I don't even know her brother's name.

I'm about to reach for the door handle and throw it open, but Marc stops my hand.

"August, we don't know what we're walking into. I should go in first. I'm armed, and I'm your security."

"Marc, I hired you to protect Gianna. When I open this door, she is your priority, not me. If she's in trouble, shoot first, ask questions later."

He nods, and I throw the door wide.

Scanning the room, I see Mason has a gun pointed at Maria, and Maria has one pointed at Gianna, and fuck me if Ethan isn't standing right beside Gianna. Knowing I must capitalize on my unexpected interruption, I charge Gianna and take her down right as a single shot rings out. I'm lying on top of her, cocooning her with my body when another shot fires.

After the second shot is fired, Marc calls out, "Call nine-one-one."

A hand lands on my shoulder, and Ethan says, "You can get up. She's down."

I have so many questions, but they'll have to wait.

Immediately, I look down to make sure Gianna is okay. Her face is pale, her lips are blue, and she whispers my name right before her eyes close.

"Fuck, she's been shot."

As Mason runs over, Ethan drops to his knees beside me, phone in hand. I'm scanning her body, trying to figure out where the bullet hit her. When I see red on her side right below her heart, I lose it. Without hesitation, I rip her shirt and find no point of entry.

"August, it's not Gianna who's been shot. It's you." Ethan points out.

"What? That's not possible. I don't even feel anything." When I look down, I see blood spilling from the wound. He starts to take off his shirt, but I stop him.

"Ethan, I am not taking anything from you. I'm fine," I spit out, each word laced with venom and hate. Before I have a moment to think of what to do next, Mason has come back from the kitchen with a towel.

"Put pressure on it to help stop the bleeding."

"I don't give a fuck about my wound. Help Gianna!" I can't help but yell at this point. Mason looks across the room at Marc, who is now kneeling beside Maria's body. From the looks of it, she's dead.

"August, she's most likely having another stress-induced sugar episode. She should wake up here shortly."

*Is he serious right now?* I look over at Ethan, who has the same perplexed look on his face as I do.

"What the fuck, Mason? Are you in shock or something? You can't just assume that is what's happening now." He reacted similarly at Carson's. I'm just pulling Gianna into my arms when the paramedics rush in. Immediately, they see my blood and start trying to tend to me. "No, help her. I'm fine. Please help her."

Ethan clasps me on the shoulder. "August, you're losing too much blood. You need to let them help you."

When I look down, my pants are now soaked.

"Fine, but only after she's taken."

The paramedics have already started strapping her up to a stretcher when another one comes through the door. I'm about to direct that one to Gianna's mom, but a man standing beside her points at me and says, "Take him. She's gone."

This can't be happening right now. Fuck, how did this day go so sideways? That is when I remember Elio. "Mason, Elio is in the hallway."

His eyes practically bug out of his head. "Shit, I can't believe I forgot about him. Wait, how did he get in the hallway?"

I'm just about to start explaining when Ethan holds up a hand to stop Mason before saying, "I got this. We'll meet you at the hospital."

"Ethan, the fuck if you will. I'm not letting you take Gianna's brother." Mason and Ethan exchange a look I don't have time to decipher because the paramedics are now rolling me out of the condo.

"Mason, you better not let that fucker take Elio." When we enter the hallway, I spot Elio, and he's asking one of the paramedics if he can ride with his sister. That's when I demand, "The kid rides with her or me, or I'll have you fired."

Once we've made it outside, I watch from my stretcher as Gianna is loaded up. She's still unconscious, and they're giving her oxygen. I know from experience this isn't a regular spell. I may have only witnessed two, but I know she should have started waking up by now. Elio climbs into the ambulance with her, and my chest starts to tighten. My body feels clammy, and it's a struggle to hold my head up. Laying my head against the gurney, I struggle to pull air into my lungs. Shit, I can't be fucking dying.

Suddenly, Marc and Mason are by my side. Good, I need Marc. "Marc, follow Gianna to the hospital or send a guy. She can't be alone right now."

"August, don't worry about Gianna. I already have someone en route. I can't leave the crime scene. Take care of yourself, and I'll see you when you get back." That's the last thing I remember before everything fades to black.

## THIRTY-ONE
### *Gianna*

The steady beep of an ECG machine finally stirs me awake. Two things immediately stand out when I open my eyes and take in my surroundings. Elio is cozied up next to me on my cot asleep, and an armed guard is at my door. Company aside, my mouth is parched, and my body feels like it got hit by a Mack Truck.

*What the hell did I do now that landed me in this hell?*

The day's events slam into me all at once as I try to piece together what happened. The last thing I remember is August tackling me to the ground as a shot was fired. *Oh shit, was I shot?* I look down to examine myself for any injuries and come up short. The rustling on the bed must have alerted my security detail of my wakened state because he turns around. His eyes soften before he speaks when he catches me patting my body down.

"You are not injured. From what I gather, you passed out from your hypoglycemia. The doctors are now monitoring your heart for any signs of bradycardia. Apparently, you've neglected your health issues for far too long, and now they're catching up with you."

His tone is curt as if my being laid up is inconvenient for him, which doesn't work for me. "Look, I'm not sure who hired you, but I am by no means anyone special, and I sure as hell don't need a bodyguard, especially one who clearly doesn't want to be here. So please, feel free to leave."

The man's eyebrows shoot up in surprise at my remarks. "No, ma'am, you've misunderstood. Your condition hits a little too close to home for me, and it's unsettling." He seems genuine in his rebuttal, but there's sadness in his eyes. I'd like to ask him more about what condition he thinks I have, but in doing so, I might be bringing up a sensitive topic for the man. Instead, I change the subject.

"What is your name, and who hired you?"

"My name is Ben. I'm an ex-SEAL who contracts out security detail for high-profile people. I box with your fiancé at the gym."

Now I'm the one caught off guard. *My fiancé?* I'm just about to question him when a commotion in the hallway earns our attention.

"If you assholes don't want to lose your jobs, you'll let me back there. She is my fucking sister." Ethan sounds exceptionally pissed.

"Ben, it's okay if we let Ethan back. I don't feel like he's a threat to me."

Ben shakes his head. "I'm sorry, Gianna, but I have strict orders to keep him away. There are two police officers stationed outside your door as well."

"Ben—"

I'm cut off as Ethan starts yelling again.

"I'm not a fucking threat to her. You assholes should be going after the fucker who is." Now I really want to see him. What the hell is he talking about? I move to get out of bed, and the door swings open as Vivi comes rushing in.

"Gigi, you're awake. How are you feeling?"

What the hell? How did Vivian get here so quickly? I only left Florida yesterday. I'm about to respond and start asking questions, but Elio sits up and wraps his arms around me. I immediately hug him back. He's holding on to me as if his life depends on it. Vivi sits on the edge of the bed, and her eyes look glassy like she's about to cry.

"What's wrong, Vivi? What's going on?"

She averts her gaze and swallows hard.

"Gigi, I got here as soon as I could. Mason booked me a red-eye ticket on the first plane home."

"Wait, what do you mean a red-eye ticket?" I quickly look over at the window, and it's clearly still daytime.

"Gigi, you passed out. You've been in here for twenty-four hours. When I got in this morning, you still hadn't woken up. When Mason told me about your dad and then your mom, I knew I had to return as soon as possible."

"What the hell? I've been out for twenty-four hours? What do you mean what happened with my mom?"

My comment must have affected Elio because he pulls back to look at me before saying, "Mom's dead, Gigi. You're all I have left." His eyes immediately fill with tears, and he puts his head back on my chest. I realize my parents were shitty, but losing them is traumatic through the eyes of a nine-year-old who doesn't know any different. I'm sure he's sitting here thinking of all the worst-case scenarios of what might happen to him now that he doesn't have a mom or a dad.

"Don't worry, Lo. I'm never going to leave you. I promise we're going to have the best life. Do you hear me? We're going to get through this. I'll figure it out. I'm going to take care of you. No one will take you away from me."

I gently rub my hand up and down his back, letting him cry on my chest when the door to the room slams open. Immediately, Ben tackles Ethan to the floor as two officers follow suit into the room. I can't take any more fighting or gun violence. I've lost two parents in the past forty-eight hours, and I'm not about to subject Elio to any more savagery.

"I swear to God, if you assholes don't get your shit together this instant, Ethan will be the least of your worries." Surprisingly, that got everyone's attention.

"Ben, you are an armed security detail assigned to protect me. Do you not feel you can still do that job with Ethan in the room?"

His eyebrows pinch together in question like my comment doesn't make sense.

"Ethan wants to see me. I want to see him. If he tries to harm me, you are armed."

Ben nods and climbs off Ethan's back so he can stand.

Ethan chimes in, "Thanks, sis!"

"Ethan, just because I'm letting you in doesn't mean I trust you. Ben is not leaving the room, and if you piss me off, I will not hesitate to have you thrown out."

His posture slightly deflates. "I thought we hugged it out back at the apartment before the shit hit the fan."

I know his comment isn't meant to be funny, but I can't help it. I burst out into a fit of laughter. It's the most absurd thing I've heard. "Yes, I'm sure when August gets back, he'll see it that way."

Ethan's body goes rigid as everyone else in the room goes eerily silent, and panic sets in. I assumed, like Vivian, he must have stepped out, but I should've known better. August would never do that. He would never leave my side. My heart immediately drops into my stomach as I climb out of bed and cry out.

"Where is he?"

Vivian is immediately at my side to steady me and close the back of my hospital gown. "Gigi, he just got out of surgery. He took a bullet to his abdomen and—" She doesn't get to finish the sentence before I start heading toward the door and down the hallway, destination unknown.

Everyone is hot on my heels when I turn around and point at Vivian.

"Take me to him now, Vi."

Her eyes search mine, pleading with me to stop my crusade, and that's when I see it. Her eyes focus on something over my shoulder, and I anxiously follow her gaze. When I turn around, I see Augustus Branson charging down the hallway.

"You little slut, if my son dies because he got mixed up with some low-life piece of trash looking to trap him—" He doesn't finish the sentence before Ethan steps out from behind me and punches him square in the jaw. Augustus stumbles back in shock before saying, "You're no better than her. You'll end up like your father, broke and in jail, mark my words. Stay away from my family or—"

Ethan cuts him off again, "Or what, Augustus? That piece of trash you're referencing has more money than both of us combined, so you better choose your next words carefully."

I couldn't care less about this entire confrontation. While Augustus's words sting, I learned long ago that words mean nothing. His words are vile, but I've heard worse, and I'm not giving him the power to hurt me. I quickly step around both of them while they're distracted and take off down the hall in the direction that Augustus came from. When I reach the end of the hall, I briefly catch a woman resembling August's mom entering a room. While I've never met her in person, there are family portraits from every generation displayed in the front lobby of Reds. Miranda has an unmistakable silver birthmark that runs through her long brown hair. Without pause, I follow her in.

"Gianna, you can't be in here. Please leave. Can't you see you've already done enough? Do you really think this is what he wanted? That this is what he signed up for when he met you? God willing, he'll see his mistake as soon as he wakes."

Now those words, those words cut deep because she's right. August is here because of me, but I'll be damned if I leave his side. "If anyone gets to tell me those words, it's the man lying in that bed, not you. He took a bullet for me because I mean something to him, so you'll have to excuse me for not buying into the bullshit you're spewing."

I'm done letting people interfere with our relationship and spark doubt. After this weekend, I know without question that August loves me, and now it's my turn to carry the torch and be there for him. Ethan and Ben come rushing into the room, drawing Miranda's and my attention. Ben's expression softens when he sees whose room I've entered, but his following words take me by surprise.

"Gianna, you can't run off. The feds are still looking for Eduard."

Before I have time to process his words, Miranda chimes in, "Sara's Eduard? Why are the feds after Eduard?"

Now Augustus has entered the room, and Ethan quickly steps in front of him before answering. "Easy. While you guys have been standing here casting stones at a woman who has more class in her pinky finger than both of you combined, Eduard has emptied Sara's accounts and went into hiding to escape going to federal prison for securities fraud. However, upon searching his residence, they also found evidence that he hired a hitman to plant lethal amounts of fentanyl in our father's car, which caused his death. Your son was one of the people who discovered the plot to take down the Moretti family and uncovered Eduard's involvement."

Wow, that was information overload, for sure. Ethan not only said "our" father, but he also defended my name. It would appear that he genuinely is trying to step up, make amends, and be someone worthy of keeping around. I can't believe I'm saying this, but at the moment, I'm glad he's here. Still, I can't help but feel guilty about his presence when I know August hired men to keep him away from me. I'm just about to ask everyone to give me a moment with August when his father speaks up.

"I don't give a damn about any of this shit. At the end of the day, that girl put my son's life in danger." The anger in his voice is palpable, and spittle is flying from his mouth as he addresses the room.

"Everyone who is not related to my son will exit this room at once unless they plan on spending the evening in jail, seeing as they have no right to be here."

The entire room is silent, and nobody moves an inch until he yells, "Now!"

Ethan starts to cross the room to come to my side and escort me out, but the heavens must have finally decided to show me some grace because August opens his eyes at that exact moment. When his eyes land on mine, I know I'm not going anywhere.

I rush over to his side, attempting to keep my tears at bay, when he says one word, "Baby," before lifting his hand to cup my cheek. Tears instantly spring up from my eyes and I'm unable to stop them. This man has been through hell and back for me over the past two weeks, and I'm still worth it for him.

I cover his hand with my own and lean into his embrace, but it's not enough. Leaning down, I put my forehead to his. "If you ever take a bullet for me again, I'll kill you myself."

He smirks. "Deal, now kiss me before I really do die."

I can't help but smile at his playful tone. Clearly, he can't stand my lag in response to his demand because he winces as he leans in to capture my mouth. When my lips brush against him, my heart feels like it's about to gallop out of my chest. I love this man so much. Don't get me wrong, I'm not rushing down the aisle to marry him or have his babies, but I know without a doubt that he's my person. I was meant to find him.

His lips part, and his tongue gently skims over mine before he pulls back with a groan and says, "Baby, I fucking love you, but I need to know how it's possible that Ethan Grand is in the room right now because I paid good money for him not to be."

Because I wasn't done with our kiss, I lean in and give him a sensual peck, eliciting another groan. I swear this man is insatiable. He's just been shot, yet all he can think about is his desire for me. I'd be lying if I said I wasn't just as greedy.

Taking a deep breath, I pull away and give him a sad smile. "Well, he's kind of my brother."

He pushes his head back into the pillow, closes his eyes, and says, "You've got to be fucking kidding me." To which Ethan just chuckles. I shoot him a glare that clearly says now is not the time, and he casually shrugs before taking a seat across the room, making himself all too comfortable.

Regardless of our relationship, I know I still have reservations about Ethan, and so does August. I don't want August assuming that we've suddenly become thick as thieves while he was out, so I add, "If it makes you feel better, he only just got past security because I allowed it. You haven't missed much. But I was done with the violence after Ben tackled him. Elio has been through enough. He didn't need to see that. Ben knows he can resort to violence if need be, but so far, Ethan's behaved."

Truthfully, Ethan has been more than all right, but I'm sure that's the last thing August wants to hear. When Miranda speaks up, I'm reminded that we still have a room full of prying eyes. "August, as your mother, I think we deserve some answers, don't you?"

August reaches for my hand and grips it tightly before loosening his hold. Slowly, he starts to rub his thumb across the tops of my knuckles in a soothing motion that puts me at ease. I hadn't realized how strung out I was until that simple act. "Mom, I'm unsure what you want to hear from me. Gianna is my girlfriend, and it's clear from the disappointment written across your faces that you don't approve. The thing is, I'm no longer living my life to please you. I'm done with the act."

"Son, the press is already having a field day with this. You can't expect us to believe this is your choice. When you told me you were dating Gianna, I wasn't surprised. Any man with eyes can see she is beautiful, but she is not marriage material. You've just been shot, you nearly lost enough blood to warrant a transfusion, and you are in no condition to be making these type—"

"Dad, that's enough!" August shouts so loud that it startles me. He gently squeezes my hand again, and I can't help but melt. My entire life, no one has put me first or thought about my feelings, and I've gotten used to being overlooked. This right now is between August and his father, but August is acknowledging that I'm getting caught in the crossfire, and he's got my back.

"I am with Gianna, and that's not changing anytime in the foreseeable future. I don't need your money, I don't want to take over Reds, and I'm done wearing a mask. I've never wanted Reds. Not once have either of you ever asked me what I wanted. Because I was born male, you assumed this would be my legacy. The two of you have had every detail of my life planned out from the second I was born. It was clear that I needed to fall in line, and for a long time, I accepted it. It's not like I had a terrible life or knew another way, but that all changed when I met Gianna. I found something real, something worth living for. I can be my true self with her. She sees me for who I am, not for what I can offer her, which now isn't much, considering she has more money than anyone in this room. This is my life, the person I choose, and if you don't like it, you don't have to be a part of it."

Now it's my turn to squeeze his hand. If I could make this entire room full of people disappear, I most certainly would because all I want to do is be with my person. I want to snuggle up to him in his bed, hold his hand, and finally talk about all the things we've never said, but I know that will have to wait. Movement from the hallway catches my eye, and that's when I see Vivian hugging Elio while rocking him back and forth in her arms. While I love August and want nothing more than to be with him right now. I have to be there for my younger brother. He just lost his parents, and this situation got way out of hand. I wanted to see August and make sure he was okay. I've done that. Now, I need to be a mom.

I squeeze August's hand one more time before dropping it. I give him my best we're okay smile before I move to step away. He grabs my gown, concern written all over his face.

"Baby, where are you going?"

Hastily, I step back toward his side before my gown reveals my backside to the room. When he sees me closing the back, he grinds his teeth, clearly annoyed that I almost flashed the room.

"August, I have to take care of Elio." I nod toward the hallway, and he follows my line of sight. Realization and empathy flash across his expression.

"I don't need to be here for this. None of this is important right now. My brother just lost his parents, and while they may have been crap, it's all he's known. Seeing me laid up in a hospital bed probably more than traumatized him. I have to go."

"You're still in a gown. You clearly haven't been discharged. We'll have them move you to my room."

"August, I'm fine. I'm not staying here a second longer than I need to. Elio clearly hasn't changed or showered in two days. He needs to go home."

When I say the word "home," it hits me that there's nothing left for us at home. Sure, we have clothes there, but now it's just an empty house. It was never truly a happy place, but it was all we've ever known. August and Ethan have said I have money, but I'm sure that's not something I'll see for a while. I'm sure things will be held up in court for some time before I can touch it.

"Where are you planning on going?" August is now attempting to sit up, and while it's clearly painful, he does so anyway, throwing his legs over the side. Were it not for the gown and machines hooked up to him, you'd be none the wiser that the man nearly died.

"August, I'll be fine. Ben can escort me."

But of course Ethan can't stay quiet. "They can stay with me. She is my sister, after all."

I know that's going to piss August off, and normally I would step in to defuse the tension. But as I stand here glaring at Ethan for his ignorance, something else dawns on me. Ethan has made no attempt to comfort Elio. I am his sole focus. That can only mean one of two things: I'm being played, and Ethan isn't my brother, or Elio isn't his brother... which could mean he's not biologically mine either. Back at the apartment, he mentioned that he sent samples off for genetic testing, but he's also acted as if he is absolutely certain I am his sister.

"Damn it! I just need to get out of here. I need answers. I'm not doing this in front of your parents, who fucking hate me anyway. This is my fucked-up life, August. They're right. You're better off without me." I know I don't mean those words, but I'm furious, and I'm done with all this crap.

I storm off toward the door as August calls out, "Gianna, I swear to God, you better not walk out that door."

He can't see that I'm putting us first by walking out this door right now. August needs to address things with his family, and I need to take care of mine. So before I enter the hall, I turn back and say, "August, it will always be you."

\* \* \*

Once I'm back in my room with Elio and Vivian, I call the doctor to start my discharge paperwork. I know what my health issues are, and hopefully, now that I don't have toxic parents calling the shots, I can focus on getting better. I'm not starving myself because I think I'm fat or have some sort of death wish. Most of the time, I simply forget to eat because I'm busy or my mind is focused on other things. The same thing happens when I start to put food in my mouth. My mind wanders, and then I get stressed about timelines, money, work, and stability.

"Gigi, what's your plan? Are you and Elio going to go back to your parents' house? If it's too hard to go back, you know my mom will let you guys stay with us. There's plenty of room in the basement."

"Vivi, I know we could stay with you, but I don't want to put anyone out. I don't know what we're going to do. I have some money I had put away for moving out that will help us get by, and I'll figure something out for work. Clearly, I won't be going back to Reds. I still have that chunk of money Mason loaned me for Florida. Oh my God, Mason. Where's Mason?"

I don't miss how Vivian's eyes immediately shoot to the floor, and I know what she'll say before she even says it.

"He's gone, Gigi."

*I knew it.*

"When he called me, he explained everything that had happened and said that I needed to come home immediately because you would need someone you could trust and count on, and it wouldn't be him. It couldn't be him. I know you've made your choice and are happy, but Mace needs time. He's been through a lot too."

I know she's right. Mason put everything out there for me, and I shut him down. While I know he is crushed now, once he's had time to sit with my choice, he'll see what I felt in my heart the second he asked me for more. I'm not really his first choice. We already said what needed to be said, there's no closure needed, but it still hurts losing someone you've always been able to count on for a good laugh, a hard cry, or an ear to bend. I hope it's true that time really does heal all wounds because I can't imagine not having his friendship back."

"I'm not surprised, but it does suck."

"Hey, I have a great idea. What if I come with you guys back to the house? It could be like good ole times, and we have a slumber party."

I can't help but watch Elio's reaction to her suggestions. He's just sitting on the end of my cot, legs crossed, fiddling with his shoestring, deep in thought. Leaning forward, I put my hand on his shoulder and gently squeezed before asking, "Elio, what do you want to do, buddy? Anything you want, we'll figure it out, I promise."

What he says next surprises me. "Is Ethan my brother?" I don't know where he's going with this line of questioning. When I think back to the night Ethan showed up at the house to pick me up for the fundraiser, Elio seemed so stoked that Ethan Grand was at our door, but his body language now seems unsure.

"Well, he says he's my brother, so that would make him your brother too."

His eyes search mine, and he nods, seemingly pacified by my response, but I can tell he has more questions.

"Elio, what are you thinking?"

"I'm thinking that you're not really my sister."

Ethan chooses that moment to come strolling into my room like it's his. Ben, my silent bodyguard, moves forward to stop him until I hold up my hand to signal he's okay. I don't address him because I need to finish this conversation with Lo.

"Lo, what gave you that idea?" Maria did say that Elio was, in her words, 'unfortunately Mario's.'

"When Mom was tying me up back at Mason's to use me and get you to sign all those papers, she called me her bastard son and said, 'I guess you're going to come in handy after all.' I know what a bastard is, Gigi."

"What the hell, you were tied up? Mason said you were playing video games." This is news to me, and what paperwork?

"She had a stack of papers with her that she was going to

threaten you to sign by using me as bait to force your hand. Lucky for me, she's not very good at tying knots, and I was able to escape out the bedroom window. I was climbing down the gutter when your boyfriend showed up and saved me. He pushed a trash can under me, breaking my fall."

"Oh my God, Lo." I pull him into my arms. "I'm so sorry. I had no idea that she would ever do something like this." I really am stunned. Maria was a terrible mother, but I never thought she had such malice running through her veins.

"I'm just glad I was able to save you, Gigi. She planned on killing you regardless."

Vivian and Ethan are watching me hold Elio with shock written all over their faces. We are all reeling from the last few weeks' events. The scandals that have come to light and how deep they ran are staggering.

"Even if you're not my real sister, will you keep me?"

My eyes shoot up to Ethan's because I know he knows something, but he just shakes his head. If he knows something, now is not the time to share, or maybe he's waiting to get the results back. But the results don't matter. Elio will always be mine.

"Lo, blood doesn't make us siblings. Love does, and I will always love you."

"Can we stay at Ethan's place?" His voice has the tiniest bit of excitement at the potential prospect.

When I look at Ethan, he's wearing a shit-eating grin like he just won the battle he's been fighting this entire time. Then he strolls over to the bed and says, "I had a feeling I was going to like you," right before he rubs Elio's head.

"There's no way in hell you're staying at Ethan's place," August announces as he walks in wearing what appear to be hospital scrubs while gripping a cane. While his walk is slow, his stature is still as commanding and powerful as it's always been. "You'll be coming home with me tonight."

"August, you are in no condition to leave the hospital. You can't be serious," I frustratedly chime in. He needs to stay in here.

"Gianna, if you think for one minute I went through all this bullshit just to let you walk out of this hospital without me, then you really have no idea how I feel about you. I said all I needed to say to my parents. You matter to me, you're important to me, and wherever you are is where I want to be."

I'm off the cot before the last word leaves his mouth, throwing my arms around him and kissing his perfect lips.

Ethan coughs right before Vivian says, "Gigi, your gown."

August curses before closing my robe behind me. "Gianna, if you don't have clothes, I'll have a nurse grab scrubs."

I don't miss the irritation in his voice.

Ethan moves toward the door. "I'll go track some down. As nice as that ass is, I definitely don't need to keep seeing it." Luckily, he ducks out before August has a chance to respond.

August raises his hand to cup my face before tucking a strand of hair behind my ear. "You're coming home with me, where you belong. Elio can have whatever room he wants, and we'll figure the rest out later."

I nod in agreement and place another chaste kiss on his mouth. With his body pressed against mine, a quiver runs down his torso. "August, come on, you need to sit. Stop trying to save me and be some macho badass. I'm not some damsel in distress. Believe it or not, I can take care of myself. I've managed the past eighteen years without you." I start walking him over to the cot to sit.

"First of all, I am a macho badass, and I wouldn't be down here shaking with weakness if I wasn't chasing my hard-headed girlfriend who refused to stay by my side."

"Wow, I never pegged you as the gaslighting type," I tease.

"I'm not above begging at this point if that's what it takes." He grabs me by my waist and pulls me between his legs before laying his head on my stomach. I'm rubbing my hands through his hair, wondering how I got so lucky in finding him. His devotion has never wavered. Time and time again, he has proven my past doesn't matter.

Looking up, I make eye contact with Vivian, who has been sitting across the room, texting away on her phone for the past few minutes. Which, come to think of it, is very peculiar. She's not one to keep her head buried in her phone. In fact, most of the time, she can't remember where she left it. I raise a brow at her in question. I'm about to ask what she is so consumed with, but Ethan returns.

"Got the scrubs. Now, if you could go put these bad boys on, we can hit the road."

"Ethan, Elio and I are staying with August. As much as I appreciate your generosity—"

"Gianna, let me stop you right there. While I understand that you guys have seen me as a threat for the past few weeks, that is no longer true. Technically, it never really was. I already explained all that to you, but Eduard is on the run, and his vendetta with you might be personal now."

In my gut, I know what he is saying without actually speaking the words. He believes Elio might be Eduard's.

"Gigi, what if I tag along tonight? Elio, would you like that if I went with you to August's place?" Vivian takes a break from texting to throw her hat in for a sleepover. Now I know something is going on for her to invite herself over.

Ethan rocks back on his heels like he just got an idea. Then, taking a cue from Vivian, he adds, "Well, then I'll come too! Just like the old days, right, August?"

I can tell August isn't happy about everyone inviting themselves to his place. This means it's the perfect time for me to duck out. I snatch the scrubs from Ethan's hand before walking toward the bathroom and throwing them over my shoulder, "You guys work it out while I change."

Pulling on the scrubs, I hear August and Ethan yelling. The bathroom door mutes their voices enough that I can't make out what they're saying. No doubt, Ethan is insisting on coming with us, and August is telling him hell no. All I know is that if Ethan is indeed my brother, which for some reason, I believe deep down in my gut that he is, the two of them will need to bury the hatchet.

When I open the door, the room falls silent before August says, "It looks like everyone's coming home with us."

## THIRTY-TWO

### *August*

From the moment I met Gianna, I knew things would never be the same. All it took was one touch, and I was hooked. I wouldn't say it was love at first sight, but I knew she was different. I knew she was not only something I wanted but something I needed. But I couldn't have guessed that choosing her would take me on this ride. It's raw, uncharted, insane, and currently completely unhinged, yet somehow, she's managing it all with grace. Apart from her slight freak-out in my hospital room earlier today, she has remained composed, no doubt for Elio's sake, but that type of strength and resolve shows maturity beyond her years.

So I'm not surprised she wastes no time focusing all her energy on Elio when we get home. She has reason to believe he is not her biological brother, yet she loves him anyway. I'm not saying I wouldn't feel the same way if the roles were reversed. However, knowing that she's choosing to stay by Elio's side, regardless of how hard it might be for her to become a mom at such a young age, is powerful. Gianna's age initially shocked me, not because of the age gap but her maturity. Of course the older we get, the less of an issue it will be for society, but on a personal level, I didn't know if a relationship with her was even a possibility. Most girls her age don't have the emotional stability or growth that she has to be ready for the things I want. Walking away from Gianna would have been one of my biggest mistakes, and while staying almost cost me my life, I have no regrets. I'd do it again if it led me to this moment. Her in my house, making it feel like home.

"August, can you point me toward the guest bedrooms so Elio can pick one out?"

Usually, I'd show them myself, but I'd be lying if I said I wasn't fatigued. Making my way to the sofa, I call out, "They're all in the opposite wing from the master." I point toward the hallway off my office. "There are three rooms down that corridor. If the two of you want, take a walk with Gianna to see where you'll be sleeping."

When everyone leaves the room, I pull out my phone and text the LPN I lined up before leaving the hospital to let her know that I'm home and she can stop by. I'm not an idiot. I know I should have stayed at the hospital, but I couldn't have stayed there without Gianna. I'm settling on the couch when Ethan and Vivian walk back in. They are both taking in the place and appear to be impressed. I know the house is impressive. What's not to love about a sprawling cabin on the side of a mountain overlooking ridge upon ridge of trees with no other home in sight? But Ethan grew up in my world, and this is not what we are used to. Our houses were traditional, in well-established, old-money neighborhoods with furniture meant to be looked at, unused, and staff meant to be seen, not heard.

This is not something someone with my pedigree would typically buy, and he's surprised. I have no clue what Vivian thinks. I don't know her, and I most certainly haven't discussed her with Gianna. If her childhood was as sordid as Gianna's, it doesn't show, but then again, I never would have guessed Gianna's was as rough as I now know it was.

"August, do you want me to get you something from the kitchen? A drink, maybe?" Vivian's voice has a nervous energy. While she hasn't had to endure the same trauma that Gianna has just gone through, I can tell it has her feeling unsettled.

"That would be great. There should be some water bottles in

the refrigerator. I had the place stocked Saturday before everything hit the fan. Please feel free to make yourself at home."

As she makes her way to the kitchen, Ethan heads toward the wet bar in the corner of the living room.

"I didn't say you could make yourself at home, asshole."

Ethan turns to me with a smirk that has checkmate written all over it. He's had this self-important swagger since I woke up, which I assume is because he believes being Gianna's half-brother wipes the slate clean. Too bad it doesn't fucking work like that. Gianna has yet to return from the guest wing, which means she's taking her time getting Elio settled in. Ethan saunters back to the couch with two tumblers of whiskey. He hands me one before taking a seat opposite me. I accept the drink even though I have no plans on drinking it. I'm sure whiskey is the last thing I need to consume right now.

"August, look, I know shit between us recently has been ugly. I'm not going to bullshit you and try to make excuses about how I didn't want to fuck with you because I did. You were always the perfect son, the one Robert constantly compared me to, and I apparently could never measure up. Your family never missed a sporting event, a Sunday church service, or an award ceremony. Seriously, your mom volunteered every chance she got to be present at school, even in college. While you saw it as annoying, I was envious. My family was never like that. Robert never came to anything. I was his puppet, only brought out when he had reason to show me off. Now I know that's because he wasn't ever my dad. So when you lost your mind over Gianna that night at the club, I was done playing nice and—"

I cut him off. He's not going to try to pass this off like he hasn't been backstabbing me for years. "Ethan, Carson told me the two of you have been fucking for years, so don't give me some bullshit lie that this is a recent development and you haven't had your claws in my back since high school."

His eyebrows shoot up like he wasn't expecting me to know that. "I never fucked Carson. That was bullshit to get under your skin. I did let her suck my cock a few times over the past month, but I never fucked her. Carson has wanted to fuck for years, but she wasn't my type, and fucking her wasn't worth it. Not to mention I think we both knew she swung for the other team. I'm aware that I don't have the best moral compass regarding women, but I wasn't going to fuck my friend's girlfriend. Like I was trying to say, she has been after me for years and hit me up when she got back in town. I turned her down. That's how I knew she was back before you because she called me for a booty call. The night she showed up at the club was all me. I was trying to fuck up your shot at landing Gianna. I didn't start taking blow jobs until after that night, and I had a reason for allowing it. After you left the club that night, we got a drink at the bar, and she started mouthing off how she couldn't wait to be done with you and how soon it would all pay off."

Ethan pauses to take a long pull from his whiskey, and as he does, I continue dissecting his body language. I've known Ethan for years and can tell when he's bending the truth or outright lying. When he stalls like he is now, I know he's not bullshitting. Ethan is smooth as hell when it comes to lying. Hell, part of being a media mogul's son is personifying what sells, whether that's who you are or not. Therein lies the problem. Eventually, you start believing your own lies, and they become your reality. Right now, he's uncomfortable, but if everything he says is true, he has every right to be. My focus is and will be Gianna, but I'm not blind to the fact that Ethan, too, just found out his biological dad was murdered.

Leaning forward, he rests his elbows on his knees, drink in hand, before continuing. "I'm not going to lie. I wanted in on whatever scheme she was hatching. I was tired of seeing you get everything, so I used her. The more I flirted, the more information she spilled, and that night after she blew me in the Uber on the way home, she said, 'If you help me take down August, I'll let you in on a little secret.' Of course my interest was piqued and—" He stops talking when he sees Gianna enter the room. When he looks at her, I see empathy in his expression. Even though I hate it, I know it means he cares about her.

"Is Elio asleep?" Vivian questions. I almost forgot she was even here. She's been so quiet.

"Yes, I rubbed his head for about ten minutes until he passed out. This is all so overwhelming. I don't know what to believe, how to feel, or what to do. I feel so utterly lost."

She takes a seat on a barstool at the kitchen island, and it makes me wish I weren't injured and weak because I want to walk over there and comfort her, but I also don't want to get up.

"Why don't you go take a shower? Try to unwind and refresh." Ethan's idea is not bad.

"Nope, the first thing she needs to do is eat so we don't have another episode. I swear, Gigi, I'll be moving in here to ensure you eat if you're not careful."

Vivian then walks to the fridge and pulls out meats and cheeses. I take a deep breath and try to settle my frustration with not being the one to make that vital suggestion. When Gianna glances my way, I'm unsure what she sees, but it has her crossing the room to me in no time flat.

"August, you're fucking pale. What's wrong? What hurts?"

"Honestly, I'm not in any pain. I'm fine. Everything is fine. The LPN should be here any minute."

Her brows furrow, and her eyes narrow on me. "You don't look fine. Here, put your feet up. Maybe you should be lying down instead of sitting." She starts scooting the giant ottoman over for me to put my feet up before heading to the kitchen and running a washcloth under the water.

When she returns, she straddles my lap, pushes my head back, and says, "Now don't move. You need to sit here with this towel on your head. This should help your blood flow." After the towel is positioned precisely how she wants it, she attempts to move, but I hold her in place.

"If I have to sit like this, then you have to stay right here, and while you're at it, tell everyone to leave the room."

She swats my arm. "August, the last thing you need right now is me sitting on your lap, constricting any more blood flow."

Ethan doesn't miss the opportunity to make a crude

comment. "You're definitely not going to be restricting the blood flow in that position. It just might not be flowing where you want it."

She climbs off my lap before storming back into the kitchen.

"Thanks, dick!" Fucking cockblock.

"August, I really don't care to watch you fondle my little sister."

"You didn't have to come back here! In fact, I made it abundantly clear that not only did you not need to, but I also didn't want you to."

Vivian cuts in, "Both of you need to give it a rest. None of us want to be in this situation, yet here we are. You guys need to finish your conversation regarding Carson so we can bury that hatchet. I'm not sure where Ethan's comments were going, but it doesn't sound good, and we need all the details so we can put this to rest."

Ethan grabs his whiskey and throws it back in one go before picking up where he left off. "Like I was saying, you pissed me off. Carson wanted to take you down. I was jealous and all in. When I went golfing the next day with my dad, he mentioned that I needed to keep you and Gianna apart. Again, my interest was thoroughly piqued. How the hell did Robert know who Gianna was? But more importantly, why did he care who she was fucking? That afternoon, I returned to Carson's as a surprise, hoping she'd feel special and spill more details. The housekeeper let me in and informed me that Carson was in her room. When I got to her door, it was abundantly obvious she had someone in the room with her, and it was a male, which caught me by surprise. If she was fucking a man, it was because he had something she wanted. When I cracked the door, I found Eduard pounding into her from behind. I was about to shut the door and head out when he started talking. He said, 'If you want your piece, you need to do your job a little bit longer. We didn't come this far to fuck it up now. You'll need your payout if you want to be done with dick.' I left the door cracked and paced the hallway, seeing if anything else worth hearing would be discussed, and as they were cleaning up, he said, 'If any accidents come from this, you don't get paid.' At the time, I didn't think anything of it, but as things started to unfold, I now believe it could mean—"

"That Elio could be his," Gianna chimes in from the kitchen with a mouth full of crackers.

Ethan turns around and nods before adding, "I started keeping tabs on Eduard after that day, and while I never caught him with Maria, per se, I did see them standing by his car talking rather intimately the day I came to see you for the fundraiser. Sitting in my car, I watched them for some time. You could tell they were being cautious about being seen together, which struck me as odd because they work together. Talking shouldn't be awkward. When I saw him brush his hand over the top of hers while handing her a huge manilla envelope, my suspicions were confirmed. Looking back, I think he handed her the paperwork she brought to Mason's for you to sign."

Gianna drops her food to her plate. She clearly can't stomach the details of this conversation. I would imagine knowing the woman you thought to be your mom plotting your death isn't easy to hear.

"Gigi, if this is too much, we can change the subject, but you need to eat." Vivian really is a good friend. I can't believe I doubted her loyalty.

Gianna's head snaps toward Vivian, sitting on the countertop, phone in one hand and prosciutto in the other. Gianna narrows her eyes before saying, "How about you tell me who you've been texting all night?"

Vivian slows her chewing and takes a hard swallow before thinning her lips and releasing them with a pop. "Gigi, you already know the answer to that question."

Gianna holds her eyes for a moment, clearly silently communicating something between them. I don't even have to guess what they're not saying aloud. I'm positive it has everything to do with Mason. He bolted after the shit hit the fan at his place, and while I haven't talked to Gianna about it, I think it's safe to assume he hasn't spoken to her since.

"Okay, fine, here's a better question. How about we skip to the part where you tell me when we can expect the blood tests back?" Gianna turns to look Ethan square in the eye. He furrows his brow before looking down at his phone.

"What's today, Tuesday? I should have them back tomorrow, but does it change anything?"

"No, it doesn't change my relationship with Elio."

I don't miss how she looks up at me when she says that before looking back at her plate. We haven't had a chance to discuss how this affects us and our relationship, and I can tell that's weighing on her.

"What about us?" Ethan asks, a hint of doubt in his tone. He's concerned she may not care to have a relationship with him.

"Ethan, it's safe to say we currently don't have any type of bond. That said, if you truly are my brother, I want to get to know you, but you'll have to give me some time to wrap my head around all this. While you never hurt me, you did threaten and use me, which, brother or not, are shitty things to do to a person. I'm sure there's much to love about you, but you have to let me get there in my own time."

I could have done without the love comment, but I get it. I love my siblings. We would do anything for each other. If my sisters didn't live out of state, I'm confident they would have been at the hospital. One is on holiday in Europe, while the other just had her first baby. My phone was inundated with texts after I left the hospital, and I assured them I was okay and there was no need to rush home on my account. However, I know that won't stop them. I expect them to be here within the next week, assurances or not. I'm their brother.

That's how I know if Ethan is indeed Gianna's brother, any relationship they form could ultimately garner feelings of love. That doesn't mean I'm not somewhat jealous. I've worked my ass off for this woman, and overnight, Ethan gets the type of lifelong, binding, insta-love attention I'm yearning for from her. I know we are a couple. She says she loves me, but I haven't had her long enough to feel secure in those words.

"I can respect that. But know that I've always wanted a sibling. I hated being the only child, so I'll warn you now that I want everything. Birthdays, holidays, family vacations, and—"

I cut him off right there. "Ethan, I'm sorry to break it to you, but I call dibs on everything on that list."

Gianna laughs out loud, and I swear it's the best sound in the world, and I can't wait to hear more of it. For her to be able to find any humor considering everything we've just been through is a miracle. I know I shouldn't be, but I'm waiting for the other shoe to drop, and I want to be the one to help her pick up the pieces should she need it. I'm aware she's more than strong enough to do it on her own, but I'm hoping that in helping her, I can stitch in pieces of me.

There's a knock at the door, and Ethan flies out of his seat. Now it's my turn to laugh. I already know who it is. I have security around the entire premises, and I gave them the all-clear for my LPN when she arrived. Before I can say anything, he's heading toward the door, trying to act casual like he didn't just get freaked out by a knock. When he opens the door, an old woman comes in and immediately gasps when she sees me.

"Oh dear, you can't sit up like that with a wound to your abdomen. You must lie flat on your back for the next twenty-four hours minimum, with your legs elevated. We need to keep the pressure off your stomach muscles and give them time to heal. Where's the bedroom? We need to get you situated."

Gianna jumps off her stool to come over and assist in helping me back to the master.

"Gianna, I can walk. I'm not an invalid."

"I know you're not, but I'd like to take care of you the same way you like to take care of me."

I let her win this one because I win anyway if she genuinely feels that way about me.

After the nurse leaves and I've been comfortably situated in bed with meds administered, Gianna excuses herself to ensure Vivian and Ethan are good for the night. I'm not in any pain, which is good. Discomforted, yes, but the main issue is I feel weak overall, which I hate. I hate feeling vulnerable, and that's precisely what I am. The nurse said she would bring some vitamin IV therapy for me to take first thing in the morning. It will speed up the replenishment of minerals and vital nutrients in my bloodstream that were depleted from the trauma my body sustained.

When Gianna returns, she comes over to the bed. "Can I get you anything before I hop in the shower?"

I can't help but groan in jealousy over her taking a shower. Not only do I want to join her, I desperately want to take a shower myself.

"No, baby, I'm good. Go take a shower. I had your clothes moved to the closet while we were gone."

She smiles. "I guess dating a possessive control freak has perks. If you hadn't bought me those clothes, I'd be resigned to these scrubs and your T-shirts."

"Hey, my T-shirts look damn good on you." I pull her to me and gently squeeze her hip. "In fact, it would make me extremely happy if you wore one to bed tonight."

The last time she was here and wore one of my T-shirts was the hottest I've ever seen her. Seeing her dressed down with no makeup on almost brought me to my knees. I've never been around a woman who wasn't always fixing her makeup or clothes to ensure she looked runway ready. She doesn't ever try to be anything but herself, and that's something I crave. I've never had something so real, and I want every moment she'll let me have.

Leaning down, she kisses my forehead. "Since you made such a convincing argument, I'll see what I can do, but no funny business tonight." She shakes her finger at me before walking off. I don't argue because I know I can't win with words, but we'll see how much of a fight she puts up once I get my hands on her.

\* \* \*

Gianna's been in the shower for a small eternity. I feel like I've been waiting to have her since the moment I met her. Lying here staring at the ceiling, I've thought of everything I want to say, gone over all my concerns, and thought of a response to every possible question she might ask me regarding everything that's happened over the past few days. It hasn't gone unnoticed that she hasn't once asked about her newfound windfall. Gianna's never had money, so having it probably hasn't sunk in.

Technically, she doesn't have it yet, but that's only until the paperwork is changed to her name. Not only did Mario buy stock in the company, but it also turns out he was forty percent owner, which means she doesn't have to sell shares to draw money. Gianna can make an owner's draw on the equity of her dad's investments at any time. Those investments would grant her a multimillion-dollar salary yearly. I know her focus right now is Elio, or it seems that way. Regardless, I know I'll follow her lead. Whatever she wants to discuss or not discuss is what will happen.

The bathroom door finally opens, and she walks out wearing my high school lacrosse practice T-shirt. Her hair is wet, her face is bare, and her long legs are on display. "Gianna, get in this bed right now. I swear if I have to wait another second to touch you, I might die."

She laughs before shutting off the bathroom light and heading to bed. She pulls back the covers on the opposite side before climbing under them and tucking herself into my side. With her head on my chest, I wrap my arm securely around her back and breathe her in as contentment settles over me. We lie there for long moments in silence, just breathing.

When I start trailing my fingers up and down her back in a calming motion, she finally breaks the silence and says, "If you keep that up, I'll be asleep in two minutes," which makes me chuckle.

"Baby, if you want to go to sleep, we can. If you want to talk, we can do that, or we can do other things." I reach around and cup her breast through her shirt to ensure she doesn't miss my innuendo.

"August, no way. You are in no shape for that. Besides, we

should take this time to actually talk. There's a lot that needs to be said." Her voice at the end sounded unsure, and I fucking hate that.

"Gianna, look at me." When her eyes meet mine, I see the uncertainty and insecurity all over her face.

"You're fucking crazy if you think anything that has happened changes how I feel about you. If anything, I'm more committed. I know you're dedicated to Elio, which is a lot, but we'll figure it out. We'll make it work together."

Closing her eyes, she takes a deep breath before resting her head on my chest. "I don't expect you to take this on. August, we're dating. We're not married. I'm not moving in here and putting this obligation on you. Your parents weren't murdered. Mine were. This is my mess. I want you to be a part of my life, but I don't expect you to take on the depth of responsibility that has now fallen into my lap. You are young. I realize that you care about me and want to help me, but burdening you with this isn't fair, and—"

I cut her off right there. "Gianna, this is my decision, not yours. This is my life, and I get to choose, and I choose you. I don't know how else to make it clear that I'm all in. I thought maybe taking the bullet for you made that fact abundantly clear. But since it didn't, let me make it crystal clear. I am all in for as long as you'll have me and maybe even after that. You're so fucking stubborn that I think I'd chase you even after you told me to go to hell if only to convince you of what I already know. You are mine. You are my person. You are my Gigi. If you push me away, it's only because you're scared of letting me in, scared that I'll hurt you because everyone who should have loved you right never did. Baby, I'll never hurt you. I only want to be the man you lean on, the man you see before you close your eyes at night, and the one with his arms wrapped around you every morning. I want to be the man you trust with your heart because you have all of mine."

Looking up at me with those big green eyes, glassy with

unshed tears, she says, "August, I want that so bad, you have no idea but—"

I put my finger to her lips. "Then trust me, trust me to have your back no matter what, trust me to be what you need, and trust me when I say I love you because I have never said those words to anyone else. I've never felt them in the depths of my soul like I do for you."

Leaning up, she covers my mouth with hers in a sweet, gentle kiss, giving me a little taste of her tongue before pulling back to look at me while running her fingers through my hair. "It will always be you, August. I know I'm hard to love, but I'm so glad you're doing it anyway because there's no one else I want by my side."

I reach up and put my hand behind her neck to pull her mouth to mine in a searing kiss that has me instantly hard. I've been craving her since the moment I woke up. Not a second goes by that I don't want her, and not just sexually. Everything about her calls to me, her smell, her feel, her taste. I've been hooked since the first time I touched her. Her hand slides down my stomach before dipping into my boxers to grip my hard length. When she feels how ready I am for her, a moan of appreciation escapes her throat, and I swallow it, answering with my own euphoric sigh.

Breaking our kiss, she slowly leaves a trail of open-mouth sensual kisses down my jaw to my neck, where she finds my ear and gently nibbles and flicks her tongue against the shell before making her way down my torso. I'm so incredibly turned on right now that I can barely breathe, but I know I must stop her. If she gets too far down and sees my bandages, she'll instantly feel terrible, and the mood will be dead.

Grabbing a fistful of her hair, I gently tug. "Baby, I want to try something new with you."

Her curious eyes search mine, and she kisses my chest. "Okay, what do you want me to do?"

For someone with no sexual experience outside of me, I'm always shocked at how eager and willing she is to let me have my way. This is the one area of our relationship where she has always seemed to trust me explicitly for some reason.

"I want you to take that shirt off so I can watch those perfect tits bounce while you ride my face."

The only light in the room comes from the moonlight streaming through the top peak of the A-frame windows. Nevertheless, just enough is being reflected that I don't miss how her face heats with discomfort.

"August, you can't be serious."

I don't miss the unease in her voice, but it's not because she doesn't want to.

"Do I look like I'm joking? I'll sit up and put you there myself, or you can come willingly. Your choice." I know she'll give in. She doesn't want me moving more than necessary. Blowing out a breath, she reaches for the hem of her shirt and slowly pulls it off. She's stark naked underneath. My hands grip her thighs in appreciation before I flatten them and run them up her toned stomach to her petite breasts. When I palm one in each hand and squeeze, she lets out a moan of ecstasy before gently grazing her clit against my erection. I can tell she's worried about putting pressure on my pelvis, and I need to distract her before she gets too caught up in her head.

"Gianna, get up here."

She stills her hips before slowly crawling up my torso. Once she's above my face, she looks down, wide-eyed and flushed with embarrassment. No doubt, in this position, she feels exposed.

"I want you to grip the headboard and lower yourself."

She does as asked without hesitation, but she only lowers herself an inch, not nearly enough for me to have my way with her, and she knows it. But I know exactly how to get her to close the distance. I slowly drag my index finger from her knee up her thigh, blazing a trail of goose bumps as I go. When I reach the apex of her thighs, I know she's expecting me to touch her, but I don't. Instead, I methodically knead the inner muscles of her thighs, slowly getting her to spread for me. Once I feel her slightly relax into my touch, I tease her slit with the tip of my finger.

Initially, she lifts slightly from the unexpected contact, but when my hands don't chase her, she comes back down, this time closer than the last.

While she's close, she's still not where I want her. Sure, I could pull her down and force my mouth on her, but I want her to come to me because she wants it, because she's comfortable, and because it's on her terms. The one thing that's been in front of me all this time, but I've failed to trust, is that she wants me. She says it herself, 'It's always you, August.' The part I haven't been good at, and that doesn't come easy, is trusting those words and finding the patience to wait for her to come to me. Now that I know the depths of her struggle growing up, I understand why. Gianna does trust me, but it doesn't come easy to her. When I look up, I see her looking down at me with a mix of lust and trepidation.

I take one hand and run it up her stomach until I reach her breast. Gently, I squeeze her breast before taking her nipple between my thumb and forefinger, lightly twisting it. One thing I've learned about my girl is that her small breasts are sensitive. She throws her head back with a moan and slightly lowers as she does. I use my other hand to rub slow circles over her bundle of nerves, eliciting yet another heady moan while another inch is gained. Finally, her hips slowly start to rock as she releases her inhibitions. I want to shower her with praise for trusting me with something clearly outside her comfort zone, but I also don't want to take her out of this moment. While I know a part of her loves how vulgar I can be, it also makes her tense up, and right now, that's not what she needs.

When I remove my thumb from her clit, I make sure to tweak her nipple, ensuring she doesn't miss a moment of pleasure as I drag my middle finger through her soaked lips before teasing her tight hole. The sensation of me at her entrance spurs her on because she closes the distance, grinding her pussy onto my hand. When I add a second finger, I bring my hand closer to my face. She's close enough now that I can suck her into my mouth, but I let her ride out her pleasure for a few seconds longer before I remove my hand entirely and stick my tongue into her tight pussy.

"Fuck yes," she cries out.

My cock is literally weeping, I'm so turned on. I've never taken a woman in this position and had her fall apart from my touch in this way. I'm driving my tongue in and out of her, and she's now fully riding my face with no insecurities holding her back. I reach around and spread her cheeks to tease her puckered hole right before I suck her clit into my mouth, and she screams my name before exploding from the sensory overload. I lap up every drop, nipping and sucking while she rides out the aftershocks of her orgasm.

When she stops rocking, I look up to find her watching me, arms slack from exertion, eyes hooded with lust as she holds the headboard. I squeeze her ass, still perched in my hands.

"I want this pussy wrapped around my cock now."

She slightly sobers from her ecstasy-induced haze. "August, I'll take care of you, but not like that. I don't want to hurt you."

I slap her ass hard. "Let me make you feel good. I know this greedy pussy wants more. Do you trust me?"

She nods emphatically.

"Good, now take my cock out and straddle it." I watch every move as she dismounts my face and crawls along my side. Her breasts are swaying while her plump ass is in the air. When she reaches my briefs, and my dick springs free, she licks her lips in appreciation.

"See something you want to ride?"

She gives me a cocky smile. "You better stop teasing me. I think I'm the one in control here."

That makes me laugh. "You think I wouldn't pounce on you and have my way if you weren't following instructions like a good girl right now?"

"Ha-ha... Very funny, but I think you're enjoying this a little too much to stop me."

She's now straddling me. My cock is in her tiny hands as she takes the tip and runs it through her swollen lips. I slide my hands through my hair to regain control of my pending orgasm.

"Baby, I want you to get off your knees and get into a squatting position." I fully expect her to question my direction, but she doesn't. Instead, once she's in position, she grabs my cock and rubs it up and down through her wet slit. "Stop teasing me and put it in."

Her eyes snap to mine and lock before I feel her line me up and slowly take me in. My eyes never leave hers. I don't have to tell her what to do next. She slowly starts to bounce, finding the angle that feels best. Her eyes never leave mine, and I'm a goner.

"You're so fucking sexy. If you want to have a chance of coming again, you'll have to stop giving me that look."

Her eyes tell me what her heart is screaming, but her head is too stubborn to let the words come out of that pretty mouth. She trusts me, she loves me, and she is irrevocably mine. When her eyes leave mine, it's to look down and watch herself taking me in. Watching my cock disappear inside her while that pretty pussy is spread wide for me on full display in this squatting position is the hottest thing I've ever seen.

"Shit, Gigi, you need to get there. Rub your clit."

She starts rubbing herself without question as she picks up the pace of her bouncing. Her tits are swaying, her lips are parted, and I can feel her pussy starting to squeeze my dick. I know I said I'd let her lead, but I'm so fucking turned on. When I know she's on the precipice of her orgasm, I grab her hips and slam her down hard as I thrust in deep and shoot ropes of seed deep inside her womb. We both scream out our climax before she falls forward on top of me, careful not to put her weight on my abdomen.

"August, I love you so much." Her mouth finds mine, and our kiss is rough, raw, stripped-down, and exposed. I know with each pass of her tongue over mine, each nip at my lip, and every suck that she is giving herself to me. When she finally pulls back, it's to roll off me and lie beside me. "Sorry, I'm too tired to stay like that, baby."

Unable to take it, I roll onto my side and pull her into me.

When she calls me baby, it unravels me. That term of endearment coming from her mouth is like a drug, and I can't get enough. It makes me feel like I mean something to her as if I've finally breached her walls. I know she tells me she loves me, and I believe her, but a nickname that comes from her subconscious without thought means that, without question, I've engraved myself on her heart. Her mind might want to convince her to take it slow, be leery, and be on guard, but her heart already knows it belongs to me. A slight groan escapes me from the movement. I'm not in pain. More or less, it feels like I've pulled a muscle in my entire abdomen.

"August, come on, you need to lie flat. The nurse said as much before she left." She's gently trying to nudge me to my back, but I don't budge.

"Gianna, I just want to hold you. Let me hold you, and I promise I'll roll back over in a little while."

She relaxes back into the pillows, and I can't help but pepper her face with kisses. When her smile fades, I pull back, assuming the reality of the past few days must be coming back to the surface.

"Tell me. Let me help you."

"August, I don't believe the direction of my thoughts is where you think they are."

"I want to know regardless. I want to know everything about you, Gigi."

She fidgets with the sheets. "I don't know. It's not something I want to say out loud because it makes me sound insecure, and that's not exactly how I feel."

Now I need to know. "Gianna, what the hell is it? Tell me." Her eyes look straight up at the ceiling, avoiding my penetrating glare, and I can tell whatever it might be, it's uncomfortable for her. Bringing my thumb to her chin, I lightly tilt her head back toward me before kissing the side of her mouth, along her jawline to her ear, where I whisper, "Please." I lift my head to meet her eyes when I hear her exasperated sigh.

"Sometimes, after we finish, I just wish that those moments

could be your firsts like they are mine because, for me, they feel like so much more than just sex. I'm not jealous of the fact that you've been with other women before me. It's just that, I don't know..." she trails off, blowing out a frustrated breath before gently adding, "I don't even have words."

"Baby, are you kidding me? Just because I've had other partners doesn't mean they made me feel anything. I've never experienced sex with anyone else the way I experience it with you. You ruined me for anyone else the first time I had you." I pick up her hand and lace our fingers together. "I knew then you were it for me. Gianna, I don't want to talk about this lying in bed naked with you, but there's never a good time to bring up another woman..."

I relax back onto my pillow with her hand firmly clasped in mine. "I was with Carson since I was sixteen. At that age, all that's on a guy's brain is getting off. We honestly didn't have much sex in the beginning. It wasn't until our senior year of high school that we started fucking. One night at a party, we took mushrooms, and Carson ended up finding a third to join us. After that party, I never had one-on-one sex with her again. At the time, I thought it was her kink, but now I know it's because she liked women, and I was her cover. Before that, when we'd hook up, it was just that: fucking, no kissing, no lying together afterward. Just a quick fuck before putting our clothes back on. I tried to go down on her once to return the favor when we were young. It lasted maybe ten seconds before she would say, 'Just fuck me.' For me, that doesn't even count. You are the only woman I have pleasured that way, and I fucking love how you respond to it. Every time I've had you like that is uniquely yours. I've never wanted to do that for anyone else. The way you rode my cock just now was another move that is only yours. I love knowing that sex with me is much more for you because it is for me, too. Now that I know how you feel about sharing firsts with me, I'll ensure you have them."

She turns onto her side, leaning in. Her plump lips find mine and coax them apart so she can dip her sweet tongue inside and rub it against mine. I swear I'll never tire of kissing her.

"August, I know we should talk about what's happened and what's pending, but if you meant any of the things you've told me, I feel like none of it matters. The results of the blood test don't matter. Elio will stay with me. My mom's results are pointless. Biological mom or not, the woman tried to kill me. Robert's in jail, and Eduard is on the run, but I don't think he's after me the way Ethan assumes. Maybe he has a vendetta because I messed up his plan, but you're just as much to blame. If anything, we're both targets in that regard. I don't believe Elio being his really changes anything for him. He has already up and abandoned the two kids that he does have with your aunt. I don't think Elio, a kid he never raised, would be a prized possession for him. As far as money goes, I'm not going to lie and tell you that I'm not beyond happy to have it, but I think it will take time for that to sink in. I guess I'm saying that, if none of what we've been through has changed your feelings about me, and you're truly all in, I'd like to stop talking about everything and move forward. I don't want to wake up tomorrow and discuss it anymore. I just want to be done."

"I meant every word, Gianna. Tomorrow, we'll just move forward. No more looking back." I kiss her forehead and lazily run my fingers up and down her shoulder before slowly drifting off to sleep—content that I get to be a part of her tomorrow.

## THIRTY-THREE
## *Mason*

**6 MONTHS LATER**

The minute I saw Gigi standing at the top of the steps deboarding August's plane, I knew she was his. The truth is, I knew from the moment I laid eyes on August that he would be the one to take Gigi away from me. That fact rocked me. It shook me to my core because I knew I'd lose my only constant. The only thing that made me want to be a better man was her. I don't care what Gigi believes. I fucking loved her. I still love her, and that's why I have to stay away.

Before I left, I told Gigi I was done. I was going to help her get through that one last mess. At the time, I didn't realize how messy that last problem would be. I don't think any of us could have predicted the absolute hell that would come next. What mother plans to extort their daughter by holding their son hostage as leverage? I wouldn't have anticipated that Maria could be so callous and cold-hearted. Maria was the most significant source of Gigi's pain growing up. She was the one who tormented her physically and emotionally while she was young, but I would never have suspected she'd attempt murder. However, the minute Ethan asked where she was, I knew in my gut that she had her hand in all this. I wanted to get Gigi out of there, not just because of Maria, but because I wasn't sold on Ethan's claim that he was her brother. I didn't go to the hospital with her after she passed out because I knew August had her guarded. Ethan wasn't going to get away with anything, and I needed to keep my word. I told Gigi I'd help her with this one last thing—and it wasn't done.

Not only did I want to make sure the arrests were made as August planned, but I wanted to look into Ethan's and Maria's claims about their relation to Gigi. The girl has had a shit life as it is. She didn't need any more drama added to her plate. So when Ethan mentioned there was an NDA, I knew that meant there was a file I could hack. Sure enough, there was a file containing the details of Ethan's true paternity, and it was not Robert Grand. I still can't believe how that panned out. I fully expected I'd get to beat his ass for lying, but he is now Gigi's problem.

On the other hand, Maria was a bit harder to research. Unfortunately, I didn't have DNA to run a test, so I went off her word and looked into hospital records. Maria said she didn't know what happened to Gigi's bio mom, but I found it peculiar that she specifically mentioned dying while giving birth. I thought maybe it was just a coincidence that she used those words, but as it turns out, that's precisely what happened.

While the cops were at my place going over the events that led to Maria's death with Marc and me, I monitored police scanners and news leaks to see if Robert and Eduard were arrested as planned. The feds took Robert into custody immediately. Being the media mogul that he is, his girlfriend at the time posted on Instagram the spot they were eating brunch. Needless to say, she led them right to him. As hours passed and there was still no word on Eduard, I knew he ran, and I suspected he'd run the minute he found out Carson was dead.

The week August was held up in Carson's basement, I found footage of Eduard screwing Carson multiple times. It turns out he promised her a cut of the money he was planning to steal from Gigi if she cooperated by keeping August out of the picture and distracted. He offered Carson enough money to set her up for life so she wouldn't need a rich man to care for her. I never got the chance to share all this with August because of how quickly everything escalated after I went to the Bradbury Estate to sneak in and talk to him. In the end, Carson falling to her death sort of made the point moot.

Carson's family had been losing money for years, and her parents were trying to marry her off. Eduard capitalized on that by offering her enough money that she wouldn't need to marry a man for his wealth. However, Carson was smart. She was not the kind of person who wouldn't have a backup plan for her backup plan, and that's exactly what all three men were. Carson was clearly into women. I'm almost positive the brunette whose face she was riding the day August escaped was her girlfriend. I saw her coming and going multiple times on security footage.

Initially, I assumed she only liked women, but ultimately, I believe she was bisexual and favored them. She was too inherently jealous over August's and Ethan's enthrallment with Gigi for it not to be more. Ethan was a playboy who could give her the cover of a committed relationship while she had her girlfriend on the side—or at least, that's why I assume she wanted him over August. However, the more convincing theory is that over the years, their open relationship made Carson resentful of August. Ultimately, I know that the type of relationship Carson had to offer August was not one he would have liked, but I think he would have settled for it if he hadn't met Gigi. Carson was emotionally invested in both men, whether she wanted to see it or not. The truth lies somewhere in the middle; now, we'll never know.

Draining his wife's accounts, Eduard fled with her money, every last penny. He owned stock in Grand Media but not ownership like Mario. After digging, I found the paper trail between Eduard and Robert. Robert was using Eduard to do his dirty work and eliminate Mario. Robert never planned on taking any of the money for himself. He'd intended to give it all to Eduard as payment for getting Mario out of the picture. Gigi getting hired on at Reds and meeting August was not in his original plans, so he had to enlist the help of Carson and Maria to get him what he needed.

Eduard bribed Carson with money and Maria with a relationship. It was easy to conclude that Maria had been in on the scheme for years, but she wasn't. Her involvement was recent. Maria was a lying, cheating addict herself. She could concoct a story to fit what narrative she wanted without batting an eye. I understand why Gigi questioned her relation to Elio. Given how everything played out, it was easy to assume he was Eduard's.

He was a man whore who fucked anything with two legs. When Gigi was young, she mentioned Maria would run away with her but that her dad would always find them. Those times that Gigi recalls being taken are how a child's brain compartmentalized what was happening. She remembers going to unfamiliar places that weren't home like her mom was running away to escape, but the reality was very different. Maria was having affairs while on benders, which is why Elio's paternity was questioned. Ethan jumped the gun and assumed that because Maria and Eduard were fucking at the time everything went down, they had been together for years. I think Maria believed that Eduard wanted to run away with her so that they could be together. He was her meal ticket out of the shit life she'd made for herself.

It took me the past six months to finally track him down. Yes, I never stopped looking. I'm not one to brag, but I'm damn good at IT, and hacking is my specialty. The fucker was good. Eduard was prepared for the moment he might have to flee, but he finally fucked up, and I got him. I'd been using facial recognition software from day one, so I knew he had changed his appearance. Clearly, he was using a new alias as well. His mistake was hiring a new security company to manage his compound in New Mexico.

My number one goal in moving to Silicon Valley was to expand our company, and I've done that and then some. This place is a tech dream. Anyone and everyone looking to break onto the tech scene comes here to do it. I convinced my dad to take another investment risk on a promising securities start-up, which paid off. Not only has the company proven to be highly profitable in the right hands, but it gave me the break I had been looking for in Gigi's case. By chance, Eduard hired that same company a month prior to install fingerprint scanners in his safe rooms, and when his prints hit my system, I felt like I had just won the lottery. Finally, I'd caught him, and now I could keep my word to Gigi and maybe move on.

The day I found him, I wanted nothing more than to pick up the phone and tell Gigi I finally got him, that she was safe and no longer needed to look over her shoulder, but that was the last thing I could do. I've thought about calling her every day for the past six months. I played out all the potential outcomes in my head, and none were good. I am the last thing she needs. She chose August because she believed he was what was good for her, and I need to accept it.

I would have changed for Gigi. We would have been perfect together. I could have made her happy. The problem is, I didn't believe that until it was too late. I didn't believe I could be the man she needed, and I thought I still had time to try to be what she deserved. The first time I saw August glaring after her the day she got in my car, I knew my time had run out. He was all in. *Hell, who wouldn't be?* She's fucking perfect, baggage and all.

The problem was never her. It was always me. I'm not an idiot. Vivian and Gigi were the epitome of what best friends should be. They love each other to the core, and the two have no secrets that the other doesn't know. Because of that, I knew Gigi was aware that there was another side to me. I chose to believe it didn't matter, that she believed in the man I showed her, but now I think she felt she could fix me, and I'll be damned if that's not exactly what I'd hoped would happen. With her, I didn't care about drowning my sorrows in a bottle, going on benders, or hooking up to numb the pain. I didn't have half of the real problems Gigi had. I was a preppy boy with divorced parents, big deal. The problem was deep inside my core. I was painfully disturbed, alone, and lost. Gigi was the only thing outside of my regrettable proclivities that ever calmed the raging storm inside.

I'm sure she hates me and possibly resents me. Hell, by now, she might even regret me because I walked away. Maybe that's for the better because I don't know that I could handle knowing she still harbored any love for me. No good could come from that. I walked away to be the better man. I let her go because I loved her, and I'll stay away for the same reason. Now I'm just waiting for the day I don't think about her, so maybe I can find me.

## THIRTY-FOUR
### *Gianna*

**1 YEAR LATER**

The sun is setting over the Ozark Mountains, and the leaves of the black gums, bittersweets, and dogwoods have just started turning brilliant hues of yellow, orange, and red. Sipping on my wine, I can't help but feel like one of the beautiful trees standing tall before me. The past year of my life has been unhinged, unscripted, and unpredictable. Just like a tree goes barren in the winter, appearing ugly, cold, and dead, at its roots, it is solid and sturdy, weathering the storm, only to come back stronger, more fruitful, and more beautiful than before. Reflecting on the past year's events, I can't help but feel like I had to go through a season of drought to embark on this new season of growth.

"Baby, can you grab me a plate for the steaks? They're ready to come off the grill," August calls over from where he is posted up at the BBQ, drinking a highball.

"Yeah, I'll grab one now. Are we going to eat outside tonight?"

"I think so. It's too nice tonight to miss out on this view or this weather."

Watching him stand at the grill in sweatpants and a long-sleeved Henley is the hottest thing I have ever seen. The man still takes my breath away. I keep waiting for the day when I won't find him so swoon-worthy, but that day has yet to come.

I get up from my Adirondack chair and call out, "I'll grab everything to set the table while I'm inside." He simply waves his spatula at me while taking a swig of his drink.

August and I moved in together right after I got back from Florida. Initially, Eduard was still on the run, and they had yet to find the man hired to stage the drugs in my dad's car. August was convinced that until the man was found, I wasn't safe anywhere but with him. However, the longer I stayed and said threats disappeared, it became apparent I was there because neither of us wanted it any other way. Living in the cabin has been a fresh start for all of us. When we met, it felt like the universe was somehow conspiring against us. Every time we were together, we were interrupted or put in impossible situations, making genuinely getting to know each other nearly impossible. I believe we both relied on some intrinsic instinct that told us the other person was worth the risk regardless of circumstance.

Elio and I never went back to the house in St. Albans. Losing a parent is never easy, even if that parent felt like the source of your pain. The week after my father died, the DNA tests Ethan ordered came back. They confirmed that Maria was not my mother. That fact should have brought me comfort. At least my biological mother hadn't tried to kill me, but it did nothing to numb the hurt and deep sadness. Mother or not, Maria basically raised me, and the fact that, after eighteen years, she felt no attachment to me whatsoever hurt. The hardest part about all of it was that at some point, I became numb to the pain, the offenses started to blur together into one, and after I picked up the pieces enough times, it became my normal.

"What's taking you so long?"

I was so lost in my thoughts I didn't even hear him approach. August now has his arms wrapped around my waist from behind as he kisses me softly in the places that only he knows best. All the places that melt me, eternally making me weak in the knees. I let him trail delicious open-mouth kisses down the side of my neck a little longer than I should because heat starts to coil low in my belly.

"Hmm, Gigi, you know we can have dessert before dinner tonight, baby, but I need to pull these steaks off the grill, or they'll burn."

Turning in his arms, I take his lips in mine, slowly coaxing his mouth open with my tongue before dipping it inside and tasting the notes of spiced plum that remain from the whiskey he's been sipping all evening. When my tongue brushes over his and I pull the hairs at the base of his neck, he lets out a heady groan. I do really need to eat dinner. It's been hours since we had lunch, and I've already had half a bottle of wine. Reluctantly, I break our kiss, earning a dispirited sigh. Then, playfully swatting his chest, I ask, "Do you think this will ever wear off?"

He squeezes my ass. "You teasing me? Or..."

Wiggling out of his embrace, I face back toward the counter and gather up the dishes I had been collecting to eat outside before he distracted me. "No, you know exactly what I'm talk—"

Grabbing my chin, he looks me square in the eyes. "I was only teasing, and no, I don't think it wears off when it's right." He kisses my forehead before helping me collect the sides I made to go with the steaks. Once we make it back outside on the deck, he says, "You never did answer my question back there."

I give him what I'm sure is a perplexed expression because I honestly don't recall him asking me a question. Once his mouth was on me, anything that came before blew away with the wind.

He gives me a knowing smile. "You were clearly deep in thought when I came in. What's going on in that head of yours? Are you worried about the trip tomorrow?"

"No, I'm excited about taking a vacation. We should've done it sooner. I've never been to Cayman, and Elio has never been to the beach. I was a hot mess when I dropped him off at Ethan's this afternoon, but Ethan calmed me down. I'm unsure how he can get away with using that playboy charm on me when I'm his sister. While I was having a freak-out session about ensuring Elio was packed and ready for tomorrow, he literally winked at me and said, 'I'll buy him whatever we forget.' I know he means well, but I don't want Elio to grow up using money as a crutch and—"

August cuts me off. "Baby, you're freaking out right now. Elio will not grow up to be some entitled prick. Specifically because of you, but also because neither Ethan nor I will let him. I've learned a lot about myself going through all of this with you, and I think Ethan has as well. Neither one of us liked how we grew up, nor did we care for the role models we had around us. He'll learn respect, decency, and manners. It's okay to indulge once in a while, and that's what we're doing. We are going on vacation for two weeks. People take trips every day, and you've never had one. One vacation will not turn Elio into a spoiled brat. I promise."

He pauses to take a drink of whiskey. "You know I support you in whatever you choose to do, but have you put any more thought into going back to school? Maybe finding something outside of Elio will help."

August thinks I worry too much about Elio, but everything we experienced was incredibly traumatic. I haven't returned to work or looked into school because I needed to put myself and Elio first. About a month after the arrests were made, I gained access to my father's investments, which are now technically mine. My father wasn't only an investor. He was part owner. Mario owned forty percent of the company as a silent partner. Now that is all mine.

"My stress has nothing to do with the fact that I don't have a job, hobby, or school to focus on. We've discussed this, and I thought we agreed that being a stay-at-home mom was a job. I like how you focus on my lack of extracurriculars, yet you don't seem to have any yourself."

Dishing out the salad and placing a baked potato on each of our plates, I understand his perspective, but I'm not sure he fully grasps mine. My goals are not the same as they were before meeting August. School is important, but I don't think I'll regret putting my family first. Getting out of my head is my biggest hurdle. Elio is going to be fine. However, I'm lucky I have Ethan to help. Don't get me wrong, August has been amazing, but Ethan being in the picture allows August and me alone time.

Ethan and I share custody of Elio. Technically, I'm Elio's legal guardian, but Ethan has him just as much as I do. The same week we discovered that Maria wasn't my biological mother, we also discovered that Elio was Mario's son. Initially, we suspected there was a good chance that he was Eduard's due to how everything went down in the end. When they got the news, Elio and Ethan were over the moon with excitement about being legit brothers. Elio maybe a little more. When he found out Ethan was his real brother, he said, "I can't believe I have a brother, and he's Ethan Grand."

In the press, Ethan is portrayed as a wealthy playboy. He drives expensive cars and lives lavishly. While those things are true, they don't paint an authentic portrait of who he really is. After getting to know him, I discovered that the playboy attitude is his "brand." It's not who he is in private. He told me in so many words that he tries to emulate what sells because it's what's good for the bottom line. We rotate who Elio stays with every other week, but we all see each other most weekends for family dinners regardless of whose week it is. August and Ethan were able to bury the hatchet for the most part. It took some time for August to fully come around, but knowing he was my brother and not going anywhere anytime soon helped speed up the process.

"Are you kidding me? I don't care if you ever work another day in your life. I love having you home all the time. I wasn't trying to infer that you weren't doing enough. I was only trying to say doing something for you that is only yours would be good for you. It would be an outlet for you. As far as my extracurriculars, the one sitting in front of me seems to take up a lot of my time."

I don't miss the sexy wink he throws my way.

He's not wrong; we spend an unhealthy amount of time attached at the hip. Ever since I moved in, I swear we've spent most of our days decorating and going from store to store, trying to find the perfect pieces. Sure, we could afford an interior designer to execute our plans with precision and ease, but doing it myself brings me immense joy, and he feeds off it. August doesn't need to work—technically, neither of us does. He invested the trust fund his grandfather left him at a young age, and it has made him more money than he could ever spend. Regardless, I know what he's trying to say, and he's coming from a good place, but because I've had a hard time expressing my feelings, I don't think he truly grasps my happiness.

"August, I know you mean well, but caring for Elio makes me happy. Being a homemaker, cooking, organizing, scheduling, running him to all his sporting events, and being here with you brings me deep contentment. It sounds ridiculous that those mundane tasks make me incredibly happy, but it's because I grew up longing for those things. I always wanted structure, security, and a loving home. Providing that for Elio is everything, but I'll try to rein in my excessiveness so I don't stress everyone out."

He's out of his seat the second the last word leaves my lips, coming around to my side of the table. Bending down on one knee beside my chair, he renders me speechless with those dazzling hazel eyes. "You're perfect. I don't want you to ever change. Don't for one second believe anything different." Bringing his hand to my cheek, he rubs his thumb across my bottom lip. "Everything we have is all I want." Standing, he leans in to leave a closed-mouth kiss on my lips that lingers long after he heads back to his seat.

"Gigi, seriously, though, enough with the heavy. I want you to be excited about tomorrow. I'll spread you out right now on this table if that's what it will take to get you to shut that pretty brain off."

I can't help but roll my eyes at his empty threat. "August, we both know there's no way in hell you'd delay me eating any meals."

Putting his fork down, he quirks a brow at me. "Was that a dare? You think I can't give you pleasure and feed you simultaneously?"

I nearly choke on the water I'm drinking at his reply. "As tempting as that sounds, I think I like my steak on my plate."

This time, he laughs a deep belly laugh. "Where did you think I was going to put it?"

I don't even respond because I've got nothing. Anything and everything August does is sexy as hell. He knows he more than pleases me. So I change the subject. "Have you heard back from John regarding if I will be called to testify during Eduard's appeal?"

"Actually, John called right before you got back from dropping Elio off. I planned on bringing it up before you distracted me. John said the appeal would be denied as he doesn't have a leg to stand on. Eduard was caught red-handed. The files Maria brought to Mason's the night everything went down had Eduard's fingerprints all over them, not to mention the paper trail we were able to link to him on attempted murder as it relates to you and murder for hire on your dad. The securities fraud was nothing compared to the murder charges. He's not getting out of prison anytime soon. I still can't believe that Maria would use her son as bait to lure you into signing over your inheritance. Regardless of whether it would work, putting her son through that was heinous."

Maria was many things, but a good mom was not one of them. Knowing my biological mom died giving birth to me brought me some peace in that I knew she hadn't abandoned me. But I can't help but wonder if my dad truly loved her. It's possible that if he had the right woman by his side, his addictions might not have taken over his life. As for Eduard, he can rot in hell. The few interactions I had with him only solidified how pompous and vain he was. The man thought he was God's gift to the world and acted like it. I can't help but wonder what a man like him must feel like being locked up.

"Do you think that's why Robert committed suicide? Because he didn't want to spend life in prison?"

August takes a swig of his whiskey, deep in thought. We've discussed everything related to the events that brought us here at length, but Robert's end was a shock. "Honestly, I believe a man as prideful as Robert Grand couldn't stand the thought of having his name dragged through the mud. Since he left everything to Ethan, I don't think he ever had plans to divulge the truth about his paternity. Robert worked his ass off to get where he was. He built his company from the ground up, and it became his identity. The scandal coming out was more than he could handle. He couldn't bear to witness his labor of love die. In the end, his work was all he had."

After Robert committed suicide, Ethan became the face of Grand Media. Being in the spotlight doesn't bother him, and unlike August, he wanted to take over his father's company. When Robert was arrested, Ethan struggled emotionally with many things. Finding out the person you thought was your dad never was was one thing, but then finding out he attempted to kill your biological father and sister was another. Ethan was so mad for so long. It was too late when he finally worked up the spirit to speak to Robert and try to get answers. Literally, the day Ethan was planning to visit, he received the news of Robert's suicide. He was upset. While Robert was absent for most of his upbringing, he was still the family patriarch, someone Ethan spent years trying to please. For his efforts, Ethan was only ever the shiny toy that Robert would bring out when it suited him. The part Ethan doesn't understand to this day is why Robert left everything to him when he was never his heir.

"I just hate that Ethan feels unsettled with everything. We both want answers that we'll never get. I suppose only time will bring acceptance." Taking a sip of my wine, I look over the horizon to watch the last few seconds of daylight disappear behind the trees.

"I don't think he feels unsettled at all. I'm sure he'll always speculate on Robert's true feelings toward him, but when everything was said and done, Ethan got what he always wanted. He wanted to take over Grand Media, and now he gets to do it on his terms instead of in his father's shadow."

"You're probably right, and I'm just projecting."

I start stacking my plates to walk dishes back into the house, but August stops me. "Gigi, talk to me. What's that supposed to mean? I thought we had moved passed everything. Did the news of a possible appeal dredge up old skeletons?"

Eduard's appeal brought to light a few things we'd been kept in the dark about, and I haven't wanted to discuss them because I honestly don't know how I feel about the discoveries.

"What was it you said earlier? Oh yeah, that was it: 'Enough with the heavy.' I don't want to keep looking back because it keeps me from moving forward. I just want to let it go and find peace."

He subtly narrows his eyes at me, and I know he doesn't buy the bullshit I'm spewing, but I don't want to talk about the elephant in the room. So instead, I push my chair out and once again start clearing the table.

"Let me clear the table tonight. I was hoping we could use the new hot tub. You go get ready, and I'll clean up." August comes over and quickly kisses me before picking up the plates and heading toward the kitchen. August didn't come with me to Ethan's this afternoon because the contractors were putting the finishing touches on the hot tub we had custom-made.

A few months ago, sitting on the deck, taking in the sunset, I casually said, "The only thing we're missing out here is a hot tub." After that, he ran with it. The following day, we were meeting with contractors to install a custom in-ground hot tub right off the deck's side. To say it turned out amazing is an understatement. It looks like a natural hot spring that you would find in Colorado and blends effortlessly into the cabin's foothills.

We've learned a lot living together. Even the added stress of raising a preteen hasn't been an obstacle that would keep us apart. August knew I wasn't leaving Elio, regardless of our genetic ties. We're still unsure why Maria told Elio he was a bastard child. She could have just said it flippantly without regard for the true meaning, or she was indeed sleeping around and believed Elio was the product of that affair. In the end, the point is moot because he is mine.

\* \* \*

Sitting on the floor in the walk-in closet I share with August, I'm debating on my choice of swimsuit for the evening. A few months back, I made an impulse buy online after seeing my social media page flooded with sexy swimsuits from a new trendy women's boutique. It's a cheeky number for sure, one that August has yet to see.

Mostly, I would say my style tends to be more conservative. Growing up, I never wanted to draw attention to myself, and that has stayed with me. This suit is definitely out of character for me, but I want to impress my man. It's a black string bikini. The top is V-cut with crisscross ties that wrap around my front and tie in the back, while the string bottoms sit high on my waist, leaving little to the imagination in the back. Glancing in the mirror, I have to admit I look good. I've gained a few pounds over the past year, but they were needed. August likes to take credit for the fact that since we've lived together, I haven't had one fainting episode. He makes sure I never miss a meal. It doesn't hurt that he lavishes every inch of my body with his lips every chance he gets, making me feel secure and beautiful with my new curves.

Making my way to the kitchen, I catch a glimpse outside and notice that the landscape lighting has yet to come on. August is nowhere to be found. That must mean he went to check the breaker, so I head over to the wine fridge to grab a bottle and two glasses before heading out.

When I make my way out onto the deck, my heart drops. There's a pathway of candles for me to follow all the way to the hot tub where August awaits. Currently, he has his back to me while he looks out over the infinity edge on the far side of the tub. I do my best to keep quiet and commit this entire scene to memory. I wouldn't have believed it if you had told me that August had this side to him when we first met. Don't get me wrong, he is still very confident and demanding as hell, but for me, he bends; for me, he is soft, and this right here is one of those moments.

Of course my endeavors to be inconspicuous fail. Once I've made it halfway to the hot tub, August turns around. We've always had this sixth sense where the other is concerned. I can feel him in a room before I ever lay eyes on him and vice versa. Immediately, I can tell he likes what he sees. His gaze darkens, and he flashes me that panty-dropping smile while crossing the tub to meet me.

When I reach the hot tub, I set the wine and glasses down on the side deck before descending. I could have held the glasses and bottle as I entered, but I needed a reason to turn around. August may like the front, but he'll love the back. The warm water lapping at my calves feels divine, and I must resist the urge to walk all the way in. I don't even attempt to look at August because turning around would be a lost cause. Taking a deep breath, I pull in a lungful of confidence and spin around to bend and grab the glasses.

Hands instantly squeeze my ass and spread my cheeks, only to roam their way up to my hips in a slow, tantalizing gesture meant to inflict sweet torture before wrapping around my waist and pulling me flat against his front. His teeth graze the shell of my ear, where he murmurs, "This better not be something you were planning to wear on vacation."

I don't even get a chance to respond before he turns me around and covers my lips with his. He plunges his tongue into my mouth, plundering every inch, taking what he knows belongs to him without abandon before reaching down to grab my ass. He squeezes hard enough to cause a whimper to escape my throat. The sting only stokes the fire that started building in my core when I looked at him. I can feel his hard length pressed against my belly, making my insides clench in anticipation. Reaching down, I try to stroke him but barely graze the tip before he breaks our kiss and stills my hand. He's panting as he rests his forehead against mine.

"Baby, I want you so bad, you have no idea. I was not expecting you to come out wearing lingerie. You may think this is a swimsuit, but this is a fucking thong meant for my eyes only." He's moving his fingers up and down under the band that rests between my cheeks as he tries to stave off his arousal and stabilize his breathing.

"August, what's wrong? What's so important that it can't wait until after?" I grind myself against his length, and he lets out an agonizing groan of discontent before breaking away. Which leaves me feeling a tad insecure. I mean, I just came out wearing a hot-ass swimsuit with fuck me written all over it, and he's basically turning me down.

"I wanted to talk to you about something, and it's kind of important."

Shit, I thought I was escaping this conversation earlier when we stopped talking about the heavy, but when it comes to Mason, August can't help himself. It turns out that Mason was the tipster who alerted the feds to Eduard's whereabouts. We only learned that this past week when court documents from Eduard's arrest were unsealed. Unfortunately, Eduard wasn't arrested until six months after Mason moved to Silicon Valley to expand his dad's IT company. This means for all that time, he was still watching out for me.

To this day, Mason and I have yet to talk. It hurts and doesn't, all at once, if that's even possible. I reached out to Vivian when we got the news about Mason's involvement because she still occasionally talks to Mace. She said he threatened to hang up the phone when she asked him about it. Vivian told me that he constantly contacted her the first week after he left, asking for updates about me. But then, one day, it was like a flip was switched, and he stopped. I haven't tried to reach out to him, and in the beginning, that pained me deeply, but now it's turned into resentment.

"What's wrong? Talk to me." August is always so in tune with me, so how he is dumbfounded by my sulky mood now is baffling.

"Oh, I don't know, my boyfriend just got me all hot and bothered, only to turn me down. You know I don't wear stuff like this, and I wanted you to like it, but—"

He crosses the hot tub and pulls me to him. "Baby, I more than like it. I fucking love it—"

"Apparently not enough." It's my turn to cut him off. "If it were enough, we wouldn't be talking right now, not to mention you cut me off to talk about another man."

Releasing me, he jerks back like I've just slapped him. "What are you talking about, or better yet, who are you talking about?"

"Oh, you mean to tell me you didn't want to talk about Mason and pick my brain about how I feel regarding his involvement in the arrest? August, I do not have feelings for Mason. Yes, he was a big part of my life, and I have regrets, but not the type of regrets you think."

Before I finish my tantrum, he throws his hands up in defeat. "Okay, I guess we're talking about this."

I'm unsure why he's acting like this isn't what he wanted to discuss, so I get to it. This is the last thing I want to discuss, but it must be said. "August, Mason held me back. For as much as he helped me, he hurt me, and it kills me that you think for one second that I have regrets about choosing you. I don't talk about him with you because I don't want to bring up an ex—if you can even call him that. He is a sore subject for me. The what-ifs have festered like a sickness threatening to choke out any love I may have once held for him. But I know that I'm looking to place blame. He's an easy target because he left. It's easy to say because of him, I lost a week with my dad, and because of him, people died that maybe wouldn't have if you and I had been given a chance to figure things out organically. The problem is that I only bury myself under my own mountain of regret for all the blame I place on him. I need you to know finding out that Mason was still involved in everything long after he cut off communication with me doesn't change anything."

"Gigi, I know that you believe Mason didn't love you the right way, and I'm not trying to say that he did or infer that I know anything about what you guys had outside of what you've told me. But I know Mason cared about you deeply. I worked with him to get you back and watched him selflessly put aside his desires to keep you. He told you back then that this was the last thing he would help you with, and I think he was simply seeing it through. Mason couldn't stand that Eduard got away any more than the rest of us could."

August is probably right, and the chances of Mason indeed still carrying a torch for me are slim, but it doesn't mean I don't hurt inside. Losing someone who had a starring role in your developmental years is hard. Nine years of friendship just up and walked away. I understood his need not to see me daily, to keep his distance, but it's been a year.

Standing up, I start making my way over to the bottle of wine I brought out, wishing like hell I would have had the foresight to pour my glass before ever entering the hot tub. "August, when I told you I wanted to wake up and look forward, not back, I meant it, but I still feel guilty as hell about how I handled everything with Mason. If I had done things differently, I could have spared him—"

"Stop," he cuts me off with one word. "Don't do that to yourself. Mason chose to do everything he did. You can't keep beating yourself up about the choices he made. They were his mistakes to make just as much as they were yours. You were upfront with him from the beginning, and he stayed. He knew the risks."

When I reach the wine, I glance over at August, who has his eyes keenly glued to my every move. That's when I decide to twist the knife. He's the one who wanted to have this god-awful, pointless conversation in the first place. I don't need to pop out of the water to reach the glasses, but I take a step up anyway so that my ass is out of the water just enough to tease him.

After pouring my glass, I sweetly ask, "Would you like a drink?"

When I turn back to face him, he bites his lip and shakes his head. "I know what you're playing at, Gigi, but I didn't want to talk about Mason."

I purse my lips as I consider his words, making sure to give him an incredulous glare as I return to my seat opposite him. When I get settled, I hold his eyes across the hot tub for a few long moments, both of us unmoving. I'm trying hard to get a read on his emotions, but I keep coming up blank. I have no idea what he wants to talk about. Then I remember he mentioned us staying at his parents' house for a few days while we were in Cayman to have alone time. The problem is, he knows I'm not comfortable staying there.

"Is this about staying at your parents' house? Because if I'm being honest, I'd rather not. Your dad said terrible things to me that day at the hospital. I don't expect an apology by any means. Hell, part of me doesn't blame him. If Elio got caught up in that same type of mess because of some girl, I'm not sure I could grant any grace either. But add in the fact that they blame me for you leaving the company. It all makes me really uncomfortable."

He rolls his eyes and lays his head back on the concrete surround, clearly perturbed. "Are you serious? I knew you didn't want to stay there, and you've been biting your tongue for the past week. Baby, if you don't want to stay there, we don't have to. I did want to show you the property, though. It was my grandfather's place, and I grew up going there. I have lots of good memories in that house. Out of all the people in my life, surprisingly, I think my grandfather understood my desire to strike out on my own path. We were close, and I think he knew the family legacy wasn't mine to uphold." He splashes water on his face and runs his hands through his hair. Whenever his parents are brought up, it instantly makes him anxious.

His relationship with his parents has always been strained, but now that he's with me, it's worse. They are cordial at best when I see them, but I know they blame me for August leaving the company. It doesn't matter how much he has told them his departure had nothing to do with me; they don't buy it. But I hate being the reason he doesn't see his family regularly. I wouldn't wish that on anyone. I stay silent, regretting my decision to broach this topic. I'm obviously striking out tonight. Both subjects I brought up were not what August had in mind, and I'm starting to feel like I've put a damper on the evening in a significant way. August must see the apology in my expression because his eyes soften before he comes over to pull me into his arms.

"Don't do that. I'm sorry that the topic of my parents always gets me so riled up, but I need you to understand that I was like this before you. Stop blaming yourself for this mess. You live in the house I bought and kept secret for years because I knew I would one day stop being their trophy son and start living for myself. You may have been the catalyst that brought that change on, but it was inevitable. Things are going to change, and they're going to come around sooner rather than later."

Releasing me from his hold, he brings my arms up and places them around his neck before kissing my forehead. When I look up to meet his gaze, he quickly averts his eyes. He is acting so strange, and for the life of me, I can't figure it out. I casually start raking my fingers through the hairs at the base of his neck, a move I know he loves, which earns me a half-smile before he pulls me with him to a seated position that has me straddling his lap, making me all too happy to oblige. When his eyes find mine, I can tell he has more to say, but the words aren't coming easily to him, which is new, even for August.

"Gigi, I spent the better part of my life trying to be someone I wasn't, but I never lost hope that one day I would be able to lead the life I wanted to live. That's what drew me to you. I saw that same fire in your eyes the day I met you. You knew what you wanted, but you wore a mask. The same mask I wore. You didn't want the world to see the real you because there was no way they'd understand. I know this because it's the same way I've always felt. How could anyone relate to a rich boy not wanting money and a legacy handed to him? For you, it was how could anyone see past your circumstance and not believe you to be a product of your environment. You only let people see what you want them to see, and I saw myself reflected in that. I knew then that I had to have you." His words resonate deep within my heart because I've always felt that my soul recognized him before I did. He knew me best before he ever met me.

"Since you decided to throw in the last few words about how

you had to have me, I suppose I can suffer in silence and go to your parents' house if it makes you happy." I place a kiss on his forehead, his nose, and finally his mouth. He briefly lets me tease apart his lips and dip my tongue in to taunt his before he places a hand on my chest and pulls away. I'm starting to feel self-conscious here. No amount of seduction is working on him tonight. I mean, I'm straddling the man's lap in a thong bikini, for crying out loud.

"Gianna, as much as I love playing happy family with Ethan, this is our first trip together, and I'd rather have you all to myself. We don't have to stay at my parents' house if it bothers you that much. We can stay wherever you want." Now his hands are lazily playing with the band of my bikini bottoms, and I know I need to get this next part out before I lose my ability to think.

"August, I have never given you any reason to believe I enjoy being around your parents. In fact, anytime we meet with them, someone goes out of their way to please me beforehand, but I'll do it if you think it will make things better."

He knows I have mixed feelings about his parents or anyone from his world. They're all a bunch of impostors. There's usually some sort of disagreement involving me ignoring him, only to end up writhing beneath him in complete ecstasy for long hours after that.

"Baby, if you want me to fuck you, all you need to do is say so. I realize you have an insatiable appetite, where falling asleep with my cock deep inside you and waking up with my mouth on your pussy could be considered less than sufficient, but we don't need to make up reasons to fight just to get laid. I'm more than happy to put in extra hours during the day."

I can't help but roll my eyes. He knows he's being facetious.

I can't help but shake my head at his antics, but when he starts playing with my bottoms again and brings his lips to my shoulder, my focus quickly reverts. Wrapping my arms around his head, I hold him against my chest. Holding him brings me a type of comfort I've never felt, and because I know it does the same for him, he lets me.

For long moments, we stay immersed in a tender embrace. Wrapped in his arms, all noise fades away, and it feels like only he and I exist. I could let him hold me for hours, and when we're not doing other things between the sheets, that's precisely what he does.

"Gianna, look at me, baby."

When I finally let go and pull back to meet his gaze, his eyes are soft, but there's something else there that I can't quite place.

"This night has gone in the opposite direction of what I had planned. First, you came out wearing the sexiest fucking swimsuit I've ever seen, pissing me off and turning me on all at once, then you started talking about another man and my parents. All topics I didn't care to discuss, but I listened anyway because I'll always listen to you. I want to know what's on your mind and in your soul so that I can know your heart. You're everything to me, Gigi, and—"

I cut him off before he can get another word in. There's nothing more this man needs to say. I love him with all that I am. I rob him of his voice and breath as I steal his mouth. This time when my lips meet his, he lets me in without reserve, and I aim to show him with my kiss what my heart has known all along. He is mine. August thinks he doesn't know my heart, but that couldn't be further from the truth because all along, he's trusted it without knowing. He did as I requested whenever I asked anything of him, even when it pained him. He gave me what I demanded because he knew what I needed and trusted that my word was enough. The words of others were weightless until him. With him, I find myself hanging on to every word and trusting wholeheartedly that each one is true.

Running one hand through his hair, I pull him closer as I try to deepen our kiss. My tongue sweeps against his in slow, tantalizing strokes, and it doesn't take long before I feel him harden beneath me. I show him how pleased I am with his response by grinding my clit against his length. A groan of pleasure rumbles from deep within his chest as he finally grabs my ass hard in appreciation. Finally, my man is going to have his way with me, but right when I think I've got him where I want him, he pulls back.

"Gigi, please just..." He's really struggling now, and I feel bad for not understanding what's happening. This nervous side is new to me. Fiddling with the crisscross of my top, his eyes finally find mine. "I love you so much. I've been trying to tell you all night that I want to spend the rest of my life making you the happiest woman in the world. I want to go to bed with you in my arms every night so that you're the first face I see every morning. I want you to promise to be my forever. I need you to be my forever, Gigi."

His eyes are searching mine for what feels like an answer. Suddenly, the setup, his behavior, and his confession all make sense. My eyes go wide, and I'm rendered speechless.

## THIRTY-FIVE
## *August*

A year ago, I felt like my life would forever be endless obligations, unrelenting fake relationships, and infinite misery, living a life that wasn't mine. Then she walked into my life. The day I met Gianna was when I suddenly had a purpose outside the life I was predestined to live. I wouldn't call what we had love at first sight, but a part of her soul called to mine, and I knew I couldn't stay away. Being near, touching, and having her became as necessary as breathing air.

My entire life has been filled with expectations, the role I needed to fill, the people I needed to please, and the woman I should marry. I didn't want any of it, and I became resentful and jaded. I didn't appreciate what I had because I was forced to be someone I wasn't. Ethan told me the root of his issue with me was that I was always ungrateful for everything I had. My answer was that the grass always looks greener on the other side. I envied him for his apparently carefree lifestyle while he envied my seemingly traditional established one. Ultimately, we both agreed our feud was ridiculous and had nothing to do with our actual character.

Yes, he hooked up with Carson to spite me, and if Carson had been the girl of my dreams, I might have been upset, but I was using her just as she was using me. We both got what we wanted from our relationship. I showed up to her funeral with Gigi on my arm. I told her everything about the night Carson died, the circumstances leading up to it, and our history. I held nothing back. I wanted Gigi to know everything. A part of me needed her to know everything.

A few days later, I decided it was time to talk with my father. I needed to sit down and tell him about the life I wanted. The things that would make me happy. I was intent on manning up and owning my shit. The events of the last year showed me that life is too short to spend it doing anything less than what you love. The week after I got shot, I returned to Reds to pack up my desk and have lunch with my father. I held nothing back and confessed everything I had buried deep over the years. Every instance where I almost confronted them, the purchase of the cabin, and how, with every ounce of my being, I knew one day, with or without Gigi, I would have eventually ended up in the same place. Letting him down and not filling his shoes the way he'd planned for the last twenty-six years of my life was hard.

When I was through getting everything off my chest and laying all my cards on the table, I couldn't bear to look at him. I didn't want to see the disappointment in his eyes. My dad was a great father, a fantastic husband, and an astute businessman, and for these reasons, I always stayed the course and did what was expected of me because I didn't want to let him down.

> *That day, he finally broke the silence and said, "Son, look at me."*
>
> *I'll never forget the look in his eye when I did. It was filled with sadness, remorse, and anger.*
>
> *"August, you know I think you're making the wrong decision with this, and your mother and I can't help but believe this is due to Gianna's influence. You met some girl from the wrong side of town with no family values or moral compass, and now, suddenly, you want to leave behind a legacy that's been yours since the day you were born. This is why your mother and I pushed you to date girls who came from the same—"*
>
> *I didn't let him finish his sentence. There was no way I'd sit*

*around and let him bad-mouth the woman I love. She was my future, and if he wanted to be a part of it, he'd need to show some respect.* "Dad, let me stop you right there. This decision was in the making long before Gianna came into the picture. I just finished explaining that, but you always choose to hear what you want. What I wanted never mattered. Reds isn't my legacy. It's yours. I stayed for you, but now I'm choosing me. You don't need to understand my decisions. You just need to accept that they're mine to make, not yours. If you want to be part of my life, you must accept that she is part of it. If you took the time to learn anything about her or us, you'd know she fought my advances at every turn. Everything I endured was of my own doing and not because I was under the influence of a piece of hot-ass pussy."

A few weeks prior, I wouldn't have used that type of vulgar language around my father, but after hearing the words he used on Gigi at the hospital, I had zero qualms about parroting them. From the scowl on his face, I knew he hated that he had lost his cool that day in the hospital.

As he sat across the table from me, rubbing his jaw and contemplating his following words, he couldn't keep the look of utter disdain off his face. The man is savvy as hell when it comes to business. Of course any other man sitting across the table from him would assume he was deep in thought, but I had no doubt he was spinning his following words, so when he finally chose them, I got up and left.

"August, I won't stand in your way if this is what you want."

That day, it would have appeared that he was swallowing his hate, but because he's my dad, I knew they were a dismissal. I hadn't gone to that lunch seeking his approval, so the fact that I didn't get it hadn't fazed me at all. By the end of lunch, I felt like a new man. I finally left Reds and got out from under my dad's thumb. The love of an incredible woman awaited me at home, and I finally felt the freedom to do as I pleased. But ever since then, I've had one thing on my mind: making Gigi irrevocably mine.

Sitting here in the hot tub with Gigi on my lap, I've confessed my deepest desire I've carried with me since the first time I had her. I was going to make her mine. She would be my last; she just didn't know it. Society would say we're too young to get married or we haven't been dating long enough, but I've never been one to embrace social norms, and I'm so done with waiting. However, now that the words are out of my mouth, I feel like I'm going to be sick.

Gigi looks completely caught off guard and maybe even uncomfortable, and the thought that she might say no is suffocating. "August, what are you saying? Are you asking me to marry you?" She twists on my lap like she's trying to get free, but I don't budge. I can't let her go.

*Wait, what did she just say?*

"What? Yes, I'm asking you to marry me. Isn't that what I just said?" I'm so nervous I can't even think straight. *Shit, the ring.* Reaching for the ice bucket, I grab the engagement ring—probably should have led with that. I flip the lid open and ask, "Gigi, will you please make me the happiest man on earth and marry me?"

Her hands fly up to her mouth as she stares at the ring, and I can't help but feel like I need to throw disclaimers her way to make sure I haven't scared her off.

"I know you're young, and maybe this is too much too soon, but we can have a long engagement, years if you want."

She shakes her head, and my heart drops.

"August, I don't need a long engagement, and I don't need more time to know that you're the man I want to grow old with. So my answer is yes, I want to be your wife."

Immediately, I stand up and spin her around in my arms before setting her on the edge of the hot tub and putting the three-carat cushion cut solitaire on her finger. "I just have one question."

I look up at her, overwhelmed with bliss. "Anything, ask me anything."

"Why the hot tub?"

It takes me a second to follow her line of thought. "Why did I propose in the hot tub?"

She nods, and I smirk. "When we officially moved in together, this was the first thing we discussed buying. We researched it together, chose it together, and bought it together. I thought about making some grand gesture in front of our family and friends, but ultimately it wasn't us. Maybe it seems juvenile to propose in a hot tub, but it felt right when I thought about how this was our first big purchase and project as a couple. After this, we went on to decorate the formal dining room, guest bedrooms, and design a garden. It only made sense to me to propose in the spot where it all began. Where we started to build our world together."

Her eyes are glassy with unshed tears, and her silence is killing me. "August, you have no idea how happy you make me. All you said about my age and our short courtship is true, but I don't need more time to tell me what my heart has always known. You are my twin flame. We are two parts of the same whole, you are the yin to my yang, and I believe I was always meant to find you. The intensity I felt for you from day one was intimidating and terrifying, but I was drawn to you like a moth to a flame. I couldn't stay away because you were always meant to be my home. I love you with everything I am."

I don't waste another second pulling her into me. Covering her mouth with my own, I relish how her soft lips feel pressed against mine, the way her body's luscious curves mold against my own hard planes. Her body beckons me, and I'll be damned if I don't give her what she needs. Pulling back, our breaths mingle as we pant. Her hand slides up to the nape of my neck, where she combs her fingers around the hairs at the base.

"It's always been you."

"I'm taking you to bed, wife." I playfully bite her bottom lip, hoist her into my arms, and step out of the hot tub.

"I'm not your wife yet. You better keep playing your cards right."

I can't help but laugh. That smart mouth gets her in trouble weekly. "That mouth just earned you a good pounding." When I finally reach the master, I throw her down on the bed, and her eyes widen with anticipation. I swear, I think she mouths off just to get fucked hard.

"Take off your top and spread those pretty thighs for me. I want to see my pussy."

Sitting up, she unties her top in one swift movement, revealing hard nipples and perfectly round tits. I want to pop one in my mouth and suck hard, but that can wait. I need to make her squirm first.

"Lie back down and keep your eyes on me, or I'll stop."

She promptly does as I say, and I can't help the overwhelming feeling of devotion that consumes me. This woman saved me when I didn't know I needed saving. She has trusted me with her body from the start, letting me take it without reservation, knowing I'll give her what she needs. Now she's giving me her heart, trusting that I'll do the same, and I can't help but be in awe of the loyalty she's granted me. Catching my thumbs in the waistband of my trunks, I pull them down and step out toward the bed. A bead of pre-cum glistens on the top of my dick, and she notices. Clenching her thighs together, searching for friction, I quickly shake my head and tsk.

"Spread those legs, baby. You'll get release when I say."

Groaning in frustration, she reluctantly lets her legs fall open. I take my dick in my hand and rub my thumb over the crown, spreading pre-cum around my engorged head before pumping myself from base to tip, keeping my eyes locked on hers. Her hand starts to trail down her center toward her clit, and I can't help but grip my dick harder when the rock I placed on her finger catches my eye. She's mine, all mine. No other man will ever have her. I'm her first, and I'll be her last. The thought alone is enough to make me lose it right there.

"On your stomach. Let me see that ass you thought to tease me with tonight."

Again, she moves without hesitation. She looks heavenly, lying flat on her stomach with her head turned to the side and her dark-blond hair sprawled out down her back. Her skin is perfectly sun-kissed and soft, the kind you can't help but lick. She still has her thong swim bottoms on, and her ass looks fucking edible. Climbing on top of her, I straddle her ass and let my dick graze the valley between her cheeks. She doesn't flinch or shudder from the action. Instead, she pops her ass up in invitation.

*Fucking hell.*

"You want me to take this virgin ass, just like I did this sweet pussy?"

She nods as I dip my finger under the crotch of her swimsuit and drag a knuckle through her soaked folds.

"Fuck, Gigi, you're always so wet for me." Removing my finger, I let her swimsuit snap back into place and her lips pop open from the sensation. Leaning down, I run my tongue up the center of her back, watching her skin prickle with need as I make my way to her neck. I suck the skin at the base, leaving a mark before giving her a truth. "The day I take this perfect ass, baby, it will be my first."

When she reaches her hand up over her shoulder to pull my mouth to hers, I let her. I know she has insecurities about not being experienced, and even though I assure her at every turn that she's the sexiest woman I've ever been with, I still think a part of her doesn't believe it. I knew giving her this would mean something. Her tongue gently caresses mine in an unspoken dance of love. She wants to give me everything as much as I want to give it to her, and in this, she gets something no one else has, and I know that feeling is intoxicating because I feel it every time I'm with her, knowing I'm all she's ever had. Breaking our kiss, I hold her chin between my thumb and forefinger, ensuring her eyes are on me before I say, "I'm going to give it to you, but not tonight. You're not ready."

Nodding in agreement, she says, "Okay, but I want you to have it."

"Now that I know you want it, you better believe I will have it." *Fuck.* The thought of taking her perfect ass makes my dick so hard it hurts, but I need to prepare her. Releasing her, I stand up and smack her ass. "Ass up." Once her ass is in the air, I slowly trail my fingers up her thighs to the base of her cheeks, where I palm each one and squeeze, leaving my prints before grabbing her bottoms and pulling them down to reveal her soaked center. "You're so fucking wet it's dripping down your thighs. You want this cock bad, don't you?"

"I always want you, August." Her voice is husky and full of lust. My girl has an insatiable appetite for my cock, and I love every minute I spend keeping her satisfied.

Dropping to my knees, I blow on the heated flesh of her pussy before saying, "Reach down and spread these lips for me."

When she reaches down with her left hand to spread her pussy lips, that ring on her finger catches my eye. Fuck, I don't think I can take much more of torturing her. I'm tormenting myself in the process. Placing my hands on her hips, I pull her back onto my face, running my tongue up her center like a starved man.

"Fuck, August, don't stop. You're so fucking good at that." My girl loves it when I eat her pussy, and I do it every chance I get. I spear my tongue into her tight hole, fucking it good as she rocks against me. I'm so turned on by this new position with her that I'm rutting against the bed. *Shit.* "Baby, I'm going to come."

Her orgasm hits, and I quickly stand up, rubbing my dick through her lips and spreading her juices all over my cock before pushing into the hilt in one swift move. She gasps from the intrusion, and I give her a second to acclimate before I pull out to the tip and slam back in. Each time I pull out and slam my dick back in, my balls hit her pussy, and I can feel her arousal drip down them. Fuck, I love how her body responds to me. This time when I pull out, I keep one hand on her hip to steady her while I run the other through her wetness, pulling it up her center to her tight, puckered hole. I rub my finger around her pink hole, and she stills momentarily.

"Can I touch you here?" I'll never do anything she doesn't want me to, and if she wants to wait, we will wait.

"August, I want everything with you."

Her words slice through my chest, and I swear it feels like they squeeze my heart. They're so loaded, raw, and unfiltered. Fuck, I need her. I line my dick up with her entrance and slide in at the same time I push my thumb into her ass. As I pump her with my dick, I'm not sure she's noticed my thumb until she says, "More."

"You like my thumb in your ass?" I hadn't realized I had stopped moving until I felt her press her hips back against me.

"Yes, it feels so full, so good." I can't help but notice how her pussy is clenching me tighter, and I'm not ready to come yet.

"Fuck, baby, you're so hot. You know I've never put my finger in someone's ass either."

My name leaves her lips on a breathy plea, and I know what she wants because I want it too. I pump into her like this two, three more times before flipping her onto her back, spreading her thighs, and settling on top of her. I cage her in my arms and slowly pump into her before kissing her lips softly.

"You want everything?"

Her eyes search mine, and I can tell she's studying my face and the intent behind my words. I brush a stray hair out of her face before kissing her forehead. Her pussy is really starting to strangle my cock, and I know she's close.

So I ask, "Are you going to have my babies?" I'm not going to lie. Since the first time I fucked her bareback, that's all I've thought about. Maybe it's a guy thing because, with no barrier, it's like there's this innate need to fill her up with my seed and claim her, mark her, mate her. I want that so bad.

Her arm wraps around my neck as she pulls my lips to hers, slowly swiping her tongue against mine, answering my question without words, and that's all it takes for me to lose it. The woman I love is under me, giving me everything and accepting everything I am. I collapse on her, and we lie there completely spent, wholly sated, and perfectly content. I've never been more at peace than I am with her. She is everything I never knew I needed. When you find the one your heart beats for, hold on tight and never let them go. When I finally find it in me to pull out and roll off her, I pull her to my side and let my hands mindlessly roam her body. She's giving me forever, and I couldn't be more grateful.

"You have no idea how happy you just made me."

She playfully swats my chest. "August, you realize I'm still on the pill, right? We didn't just make a baby."

I can't help but chuckle at her comment. "Yeah, I know."

Lifting her head, she looks at me quizzically. Wondering what I'm getting at. Taking her free hand in mine, I lace our fingers together. "Thank you for trusting me when it was hard. When I know it reminds you of all that was lost. I know my background was a trigger for you because it was the same way your dad was raised, and he lost everything. Choosing me wasn't easy, but you need to know I'm so glad you did."

She leans up to softly kiss my lips before straddling me. The move isn't meant to be seductive. It's meant to grab my attention. I can't take my eyes off her, and she knows it. "August, I unfairly judged you when we met, but once I saw you, I couldn't unsee you. I'd rather risk it all and lose everything than go a day without you. You are worth it every time, and I can't wait to show you how much—every day for the rest of our lives."

My world starts and stops with her. Without her, I am but a shell of a man. Without her, I would forever be missing out on half of my life. All I ever needed was for her to say it was me, and she did.

**THE END**

# Also by C.A. Ferro

**Want Mason's story?**

Read it now in Wicked Beautiful Lies.

Wicked Beautiful Lies: A Taboo Romance

Trope list: Taboo/forbidden, Mistaken Identity, Enemies to Lovers, Dark Secrets.

Sweet Venom: A Why Choose Romance

Trope List: Taboo, Enemies to Lovers, Friends to Lovers, Dark Secrets, Different Worlds, Unrequited Love.

\* \* \*

**Copper Falls**

Rewriting Grey: Romantic Thriller

Trope List: Reclusive Author, Siblings Ex, Forced Proximity, Secret Identity, Small Town.

Rewriting Grey: A Small Town Romance

Trope list: Reclusive Author, Small Town, Siblings Ex, Secret Identity, He Falls First.

\* \* \*

**Summer Nights**

DIG: A Second Chance Romance

Trope list: Sports Romance, College Romance, Dark Secrets, Emotional Scars, Second Chance, Redemption.

Fade Into You

Trope list: Arranged Marriage, Sports Romance, Small Town, Single Dad, Mistaken Identity, Unrequited Love

# SALT

Trope list: Age Gap, Best Friend's Daughter, Protector, Angsty, Secret Romance, Forbidden.

## Hating the Book Boyfriend

Tropes: Best Friend's Sister, All Grown Up, Snowed In, One Bed, Holiday Romance.

# About the Author

L.A. Ferro has had a love for storytelling her entire life. For as long as she can remember, she put herself to sleep, plotting stories in her head. That thirst for a good tale led her to books, where she became an avid reader.

The unapologetically dramatic characters, steamy scenes, and happily ever afters found inside the pages of romance novels irrevocably transformed her. The world of romance ran away with her heart, and she knew her passion for love would be her craft.

When she's not trailing after one of her three crazy kids, she loves to construct messy 'happily ever afters' that take her readers on a journey full of angst, lust, and obsession with page-turning enchantment.

For extended epilogues, ARC Team opportunities and to ensure you never miss a launch, please subscribe to her newsletter:
https://www.authorlaferro.com/contact

Made in United States
Orlando, FL
17 April 2025